# of BLOOD and HONEY

A BOOK OF THE FEY AND THE FALLEN

of BLOOD *and* HONEY

A BOOK OF THE FEY AND THE FALLEN

STINA LEICHT

Night Shade Books
San Francisco

First Edition

ISBN: 978-1-59780-213-0

Printed in Canada

Night Shade Books
Please visit us on the web at
http://www.nightshadebooks.com

To Dane Caruthers
Always remember these three words: as you wish.

Callaghan [in frustration] remarked, "You know, Mr. Paisley, we are all the children of God."

Quick as a flash came the implacable answer. "No, we are not, Mr. Callaghan. We are all the children of wrath."

—from *Ireland* by Paul Johnson

Chapter 1

"Got one of the yabbos, sir!"

Liam lay on the cracked pavement with a British soldier's boot planted in the center of his back, struggling against the pain to breathe. Thoughts galloped through his head in one long stream. *Oh-God-please-don't-shoot-Wasn't-throwing-stones-I-don't-want-to-die-I'll-never-sleep-with-Mary-Kate-if-I-do-Shite-Jesus-I'm-sorry-I-swear-I'll-never-touch-her-again-I-know-it's-a-mortal-sin-no-venial-no-mortal-oh-for-fuck's-sake-what's-the-difference?*

The BA soldier leaned closer. Liam could feel his breath on his neck and itched with the need to escape the cold gun barrel pressed to the back of his skull. As if to illustrate the point, the thud-thud of riot guns went off somewhere. Peppery CS gas drifted by in a wispy clump. Among the crowd, those caught without vinegar-soaked handkerchiefs gagged and coughed. Someone shouted in the chaos. Liam guessed it was one of the Frontliners—the boys who regularly rioted on Aggro Corner—because the words weren't complementary of BAs, nor, apparently, the farm animals that might accompany them on cold lonely nights.

"Don't you fucking move. Bullet may be rubber, but at this range it *will* fuck with your day. You got me?"

"Y-Yes, sir," Liam said, desperately trying to remember the Act of Contrition, but the pressure on the back of his head won out over Sister Margaret's ruler as far as his memory was concerned. He began to shiver—whether from cold or fear he wasn't certain. He'd seen what happened to Annette McGavigan last September. She'd been standing with a group of girls watching the Frontliners at their work—hoping to collect a rubber bullet souvenir. Everyone did. In the course of the riot, a BA fired into the crowd. Liam had happened to glance her direction when the top of her head had come off. It'd given him nightmares for weeks.

1

A pair of boots appeared inches from his nose. Afraid he'd be kicked in the face, Liam flinched. The BA whose foot rested on his back brought down his full weight. Liam went from struggling to breathe to not breathing at all and for an instant the gun dropped one level of importance beneath the ache of his ribs.

"I said, don't move, Irish scum."

Part of the prayer finally surfaced. *I am heartily sorry for having offended Thee.* It repeated over and over like a cracked record. He *was* heartily sorry—very fucking heartily sorry for not having gone straight home to his stepfather's flat in Bogside. *I am heartily sorry*—

Something smacked the corrugated iron covering a gutted building not far away, and an explosion went off. It was difficult not to throw his arms over his head. When his ears recovered he heard the sharp crack of live rounds.

"Is this one of them?" the new BA asked. His accent was crisp and very English while the other was more nasal and clipped. Both sounded foreign.

"Yes, sir. Saw him throwing rocks over there," the nasal voice said.

Liam gasped in an attempt to explain that he was only watching, that he hadn't even cheered—well, not much—but the only word to escape his lips was, "Didn't."

"Shut it, you."

"Get off him, Private," the BA officer said. "He's choking."

The weight lifted, and the world went from black and dark gray to black and dingy concrete. Liam gulped air. *Oh, Jesus, please. I just want to go home.*

As if he had read Liam's thoughts, the BA officer said, "Give the names of the other rioters, and we'll let you go."

No. Can't. Frontliners are Bogside, he thought. *Won't be a coward. I won't. What'll Mary Kate think, I go and give them over?* Liam shut his eyes.

"I see," the BA officer said. "Take him away."

The gun barrel vanished, and there was an instant of relief before Liam's hands were yanked behind his back. Pain shot up both arms, and cold steel trapped his wrists. The clock-tick of the cuffs locking into place crystallized the realization that he wasn't going to see home or Mary Kate or his mother for what might be a long time.

Two BAs pulled him up from the pavement, and his knees gave out almost at once. They yanked him up again, more roughly the second time. There were no more explosions or insults or thrown rocks. A few feet away, a young boy snatched a rubber bullet from the ground. The Frontliners were long gone. The Royal Ulster Constabulary advised people to go about their business—whatever that might be—provided it did not include watching people being arrested for standing on the street. The RUC weren't popular, and one brave soul told them what they could do with themselves. The crowd began to break up nonetheless.

The open doors at the back of the Saracen Armoured Personnel Carrier threatened to swallow him up.

"Liam!" It was Mary Kate.

He searched the street but didn't see her. For an instant, what he did see gave him pause. A grizzled man with wispy white hair and a blood-red cap gave him a toothy smile. His eyes glinted red, and his teeth had been filed to sharp points.

The soldier gave Liam a shove, and he stumbled. They threw him against the door of the Saracen. He crumpled and for a few moments wished like hell he'd been born a eunuch.

"Let him go, you bastards!" she shouted. "He wasn't doing anything!"

He wanted to warn her off, but he didn't have the breath. The soldiers didn't wait for him to recover; they tossed him into the gaping maw. Others stumbled up behind him. With his arms trapped behind his back he couldn't get up even if he could manage it. So, he lay as he was, curled up in a tight ball, his eyes watering from the pain. The doors slammed closed, shutting out the light. Someone screamed.

"Shhh. Easy there, son. Easy. You'll be all right," one of the men sitting on the bench in front of him said.

Liam looked up. He had good night vision—better than anyone he knew. As his eyes adjusted to the darkness he got the impression of an elderly man with curly grey hair. He was leaning forward to make room for the handcuffs at the small of his back. Liam matched the shadowy face with the voice. *It's Mr. O'Keefe,* he thought. Mr. O'Keefe lived in the Creggan, a block of council houses near St. Mary's.

"Roll onto your back as much as you can. Then sit up," Mr. O'Keefe said, "Take your time."

The doors at the front of the Saracen thumped closed. By the time the engine roared Liam was able to sit up. The transmission snarled into gear, and the Saracen rolled forward with a jerk. With nothing to hold on to, he slid across the floor.

"Don't you worry," Mr. O'Keefe said. Liam wasn't sure who the reassurance was for—himself or Mr. O'Keefe. "You've not been in trouble before. Like as not they'll let you go after a chat on Bligh's Lane."

One of the others snorted. Liam thought he recognized him as a regular from the Bogside Inn. Rumor had it the man was a volunteer for the Provisional IRA.

"Don't lie to the boy," the Provo said. "We're proper fucked. Bound for Long Kesh, we are. You wait and see."

Liam's heart stopped.

Mr. O'Keefe's voice was so sincere that it almost hid the sound of his panic. "Don't worry, son. I'll look after you."

It was the last white lie Liam allowed himself to believe for nearly three months.

Chapter 2

Londonderry/Derry, County Londonderry, Northern Ireland
15 November 1971

Kathleen Kelly knelt in St. Brendan's church vestibule, slid a coin into the offering slot and touched a lit match to one of the few candles available. It took two tries, and her hand visibly shook as she blew out the match. Fear for her eldest son mixed with anger, tightening her jaw. Hadn't she told Liam to stay away from the ones who were causing trouble? Had she not told him to be careful? She'd been down to Bligh's Lane three times in the past twenty-four hours but still the RUC—the Royal Ulster Constabulary—refused to tell her anything. She had no idea where Liam was, if he were hurt, or what could be done to get him free. In spite of everything she'd done to keep the lad safe he seemed determined to get into the worst of it. None of her other children were as much a problem. Quiet and obedient, they were for the most part, but not her Liam. She supposed it was his father in him.

Why have I not heard from him?

She struggled with old feelings of abandonment and guilt and whispered a Hail Mary, imploring the Mother of God to intercede. Kathleen breathed in the church's perfume of old incense, furniture polish and hot beeswax to slow her heart and ease the tension in her shoulders. She knew there wasn't much hope. After all the sins she'd committed—sins for which she'd paid dearly and yet, still didn't regret—she couldn't bring herself to ask the Lord directly for help, but surely He wouldn't punish her boy for what she'd done for love.

The sins of the father shall be visited upon the sons.

Once more she thought of Liam's father and resisted an urge to light another candle, pulling her coat tight instead. She had fought with him the last time they'd spoken and six months had passed since then. She knew because she'd counted every day. It'd been her own fault, of course. Much as she loved the man, all she ever seemed to do was drive him away. She added a quick prayer in spite of herself. *Mother of God, I know he isn't one of ours, but would there be any harm to look out for him, nonetheless?*

She got up and exited the church, almost walking into her neighbor, Geraldine McKenna. The McKennas lived in the same apartment block, the same floor but three doors down. Geraldine was a small woman in a faded wool coat. Her head was down, and her shoulders were up.

"Is something wrong?" Kathleen asked.

Geraldine looked up, and Kathleen saw her eyes were brimming with tears. She was only a few years older than Kathleen but looked twice that.

The worry does that to you, Kathleen thought. "Have you had word?"

Geraldine's son and husband had both been arrested in August. It had been awful, and Kathleen remembered it well. The soldiers had come in the middle of the night and kicked in the McKennas' door. The banging and shouting had terrified the children. Both men had been sent to Long Kesh internment camp. With more being rounded up every day, it was a common enough story—one Kathleen wanted no part of. She had troubles enough of her own, and all those years ago when it was rumored that she had run off with a Protestant only to have the man die before the babe was born—wasn't it the very same Geraldine who'd turned her back? It was right that those who stirred up trouble drew the attention of the BAs. Perhaps breaking into homes was a bit harsh, but terrorism had to be fought. The IRA went too far. Kathleen believed it. Only now it was her Liam the BAs had lifted, wasn't it?

"Our Michael is sick. A fever. Got the letter this morning." Geraldine sniffed. "They won't let me in to see him. I called."

"I'm sure he'll be fine," Kathleen said and upon seeing Geraldine's distress, regretted her previous uncharitable thoughts. "Probably nothing. A wee cold."

"My Barney isn't political, you know. Never has been. So, why is he in prison? All our men. Without so much as a trial. And whatever for? They told us the soldiers were to protect us from the Loyalists. I wish the BAs had never come."

Hoping to stem the stream of animosity, Kathleen said, "Come by the flat later. We'll have some tea. It'll soothe your nerves."

"Mrs. Foyle told me about your Liam. I'm so sorry."

The meddling old baggage, Kathleen thought. *Why couldn't that woman keep her gob shut for once?* Her Liam wasn't like the ones that rioted on Aggro Corner. He was a good boy. He didn't cause trouble—at least, she didn't think he did.

The sins of the father.

She shut her eyes against the thought and swallowed.

"They'll see he's innocent. They'll let him go," Geraldine said. It was a lie, that was easy to see, but it was comforting to hear nonetheless. Geraldine pulled the damp white scarf from her head, shook rain water from it and then replaced it. "I'll light a candle for him as well."

"That's very kind." The words that passed over the lump in Kathleen's throat were just above a whisper. "Thank you." Unwilling to continue the conversation, she gave her excuses and made to leave. Before she did, Geraldine cast off a sympathetic look that made Kathleen want to scream.

She took a steadying breath and blew it out her cheeks as Geraldine vanished inside the church. It was Wednesday. There was much to do before school let out and the little ones came home. There was the mending to do. Her husband seemed to put more holes in trouser pockets than any man alive. It had started to rain while she was inside the church, a soft mist, and she opened the umbrella she'd brought with her. The street in front of the church was empty. Rubble formed a hill opposite and not far away from that was the Army check point she'd have to pass through before reaching her flat. As she walked she focused hard on the list of things she needed to do to keep from thinking of Geraldine's face, and as a result it wasn't until she'd passed the churchyard gate that she noticed she was being followed. Screwing up her courage, she whirled and was struck dumb by the sight of the very person she'd been thinking of earlier.

"Is it really you?" She blurted it out before thinking. There never seemed to be a pattern in his arrivals. She'd spent years searching for one.

Tall with black hair and pale blue eyes, Bran looked every bit as handsome and wild as he had the first time she'd met him. *That's not entirely true,* she thought. *Is that grey in his hair?* He stood on the other side of the churchyard wall, rainwater dripping from his hair and shirt. As always his clothes were outdated—all but the pegged jeans she'd given him long ago. *Pegged jeans, ancient linen shirt and bare feet. It's a wonder no one notices him, a man like him.* It was then she saw the bloody gash in his shoulder. He hadn't even bothered to bandage it yet. "I need to speak with you, Kathleen." His voice was grave. "It's important."

"You're hurt."

"It's nothing. Please. I don't have much time."

"You never do."

"Oh, now. Don't start in at me already."

"Was you that left before it was done," she said.

"And was you that won't leave with me at all."

"I married Patrick and stay with him I must."

"I'll fight him for you. I am of the Fianna. He won't have a chance of winning. But he'll release you before it came to that, surely. He doesn't love you as I do."

"I don't want to hear anymore." She passed a hand over her face to hide from the knowledge that he was right.

"Ah, sweet Kathleen. I'm begging you."

"Don't!" Recovering herself, she looked around to see if anyone was listening. "And where were you sixteen years ago? Why were you not begging then?"

"I was in a *Sídhe* gaol. We talked about this before."

"And we'll talk about it again. But it won't make a difference, will it? It changes nothing. It's married I am and married I'll stay."

He sighed and nodded. "As you wish it."

"It isn't what I wish at all. But it's how it has to be." She hated it when he blamed her for the very thing that made her so unhappy. He should've come to her when she needed him. She'd waited for six years, and her with his illegitimate child. The hurts she'd suffered from her own mother were enough to kill her. At the last she'd agreed to marry Patrick. It'd been clear her mother was right after all. Bran wasn't coming back, and Liam needed a father. Except Bran had returned, but it was too late. It was always too late. Sometimes she found herself hating him. No matter his war. No matter his honor and his oaths. To be fair, she knew the situation was her responsibility too. She should never have let herself love him, but she'd been young and stupid.

Well, she wasn't young and stupid any longer.

"Kathleen, please," he said. "It's important. For you and the babe."

"He's not a babe anymore." She found herself walking toward the churchyard gate. "You'd know that if you'd but seen him." The gate squealed when she pushed it open. It was a sound distilled with years of loneliness, pain and grief.

"Was you who won't tell me of him. Was you told me to stay away. Was you who said he was too young to understand."

"Oh, shut up."

Bran smiled that charming smile of his, and it melted her anger all over again. "Tell me. Something. Anything of him at all. Is he big and strong like his father?"

She sighed and blinked the blurriness from her vision. *He's grown into the very spirit and image of you. My heart aches every time I see him.* "I don't want to talk about it."

They walked together between tombstones and Celtic crosses to the back of the churchyard. When she was sure they were far enough from the street she stopped beneath an ancient oak tree. "What is it that's so important?"

Bran's face clouded. "You may be in danger. I'll shield you both as much as I can, but the war with the Fallen has taken a bad turn, and I'm needed elsewhere."

"You're always needed elsewhere." *And if you wanted the truth of it, that's the very reason why I'll not leave this life for you. I can't count on you,* she thought. *I can't trust you'll stay and be a father to my children. I can't even trust you'll appear in regular intervals.* She stood a little straighter in spite of the emotions ripping her apart. "Well, what is it?"

"Do you know of a creature called a Redcap?"

"You've come from the Other Side to warn me of a bogey man?"

"He's real, Kathleen, and he's sworn to destroy my men, me and mine. One by one."

"Why?"

Bran looked away. "It's lovely here. So peaceful."

"Don't you shy away from my question. You'll tell me straight, or I'm walking out of this churchyard and never speaking to you again."

"Oh, Kathleen."

"I mean it." To emphasize the point she took three steps toward the gate.

"Wait!"

She slowly turned to face him but otherwise didn't move or speak.

"Please! It's important!"

The urgency in his voice frightened her, but she wasn't about to let him know he'd gotten to her, or how much she needed him. "Out with it, then."

"It's only that I wished to speak of more pleasant things first. Rest in the shade of the oak together a while. Talk. Like we used to. When we first loved each other."

"I've no time for your pretty words. I should not have had it then. So, say what it is you've come to say. Or I'll make you swear to speak only truth—"

"You would put such a thing upon me? You would bind me so?"

She didn't understand why it was he felt so bound by the promises she forced out of him, but it had always been so; and because his word-bond was the only hold she had on him, she had always been careful of it. Bran was a proud man. She knew there was a limit to how far she could push without breaking him. And break him, she could. She'd seen it. Extracting that promise regarding Liam had come close enough. *So many years. So much pain.*

Why do I torture him so? She narrowed her eyes and set her jaw, waiting with a shuddering heart.

"I told you of the war with the Fallen. The ones the new religion brought with it."

She nodded. She didn't know what to think of the things he'd told her over the years—that the old myths were every bit as real as the Church. Such thoughts were enough to shake the foundations of her faith. *The Good Folk warring with fallen angels.* She wasn't sure if she should believe him. In truth, she couldn't even be sure what or who Bran really was.

Bran said, "There have been setbacks."

"Go on."

"The Fallen have summoned allies from over the sea. The Redcap is among the worst," Bran said. "Very powerful. He established a *rath* not far from the coast. Me and my men broke it and burned it to the ground."

"That's all?"

"It's been a long war even by our terms. Lies mixed with truth goad the fires of hate. Some of our own have died the final death. Emotions run hot, and there are those who thirst for revenge," Bran said, staring at a tombstone. "Things were done at that *rath* that shouldn't have been done. Things that went beyond the normal terms of war. It doesn't matter that I wasn't the one who perpetrated the acts, or that the ones that did have been punished. They were my men, and they stepped over the line. I'm responsible."

"Oh." A cold gust blew from the north, tearing at the scarf on her head and stinging her cheeks.

"Please, Kathleen. For my sake. For the boy's. Be careful of strangers." He closed his eyes. "The iron will do no good against the likes of him. Uncle Fionn says you'll have to use your bitty cross. Keep it with you at all times. Tie red thread around it. Good Irish linen will do the trick."

"I will."

"Make sure the boy does the same."

It was her turn to flinch. "He's gone. They've lifted him."

"Who?"

"The BAs. The British Army. Who else? He's gone, and I don't know where they've taken him." It felt good to tell someone who wasn't merely interested in gossip—someone who could help. "Will you get him home?"

"I'll do what I can. I swear it."

"Thank you." Her breath hitched and suddenly the tears were pouring down her cheeks enough to compete with the rain. Bran opened his arms to her, and she dropped her umbrella and went to him, grabbing his waist as if she were drowning. Maybe she was. She certainly didn't care who might see. Most of her life was spent being strong for other people. For once she would have something for herself. She needed him. She needed this. It didn't matter that it was against everything she'd been taught to believe and everything she taught her own children.

She felt him tug away her scarf. His hand smoothed her wet hair and slid down her back. "Shhhh. There now," he said. "My beautiful Kathleen."

A derisive sound worked its way up her throat.

"You doubt me? It's the truth, I'm telling."

She felt him kiss the top of her head, and she gloried in his tenderness. After a while she reached into her coat pocket, fishing out her handkerchief. She pulled back and wiped her face. Her nose and cheeks felt half-frozen. Her hair was sticking to her skin. She was shivering now. It was so cold in the churchyard.

"Better?" he asked.

"Yes. Thank you."

He lifted her chin and before she could speak a word against it, he kissed her. She didn't fight it. Worse, against her better judgment, she kissed him back. The strength of her passion made her forget all but the fire that ran through her body. His hands crept beneath her coat and inside her blouse. His fingers were cold at first but grew warmer by the time he plunged into her bra. Her pulse quickened in response. When she was sure someone was going to notice she released him and stepped back. "I have to go."

"Stay. Give me a little something to keep warm." He winked.

"I thought you had to be somewhere?"

"Uncle Fionn can wait."

"And your son? What of him?"

He combed the fingers of his right hand through his hair, a gesture she'd seen her eldest son replicate in every way since he was a boy. She shivered again and this time it wasn't the fault of the chill.

The sins of the father.

Bran said, "You're right. I'll go to him."

"He knows nothing of you, or your kind," she said, buttoning her blouse. "Bear that in mind when you find him."

"You've never told him anything?"

"Nothing at all," she said. "I'm still not sure he'd understand. He... he looks like you. You'll know him by that at least."

A flash of pride and surprise shot across his expression.

"Let me tell him in my own way," she said. "It has to be done gently."

"Don't worry. He'll never even know 'twas me."

"Good." She tucked in her blouse and smoothed her skirt. "How do I look?"

"Like a beautiful woman in dire need of a good bedding."

"Hush now!" A laugh burst out of her before she could stop it. She covered her mouth to catch it but was too late. "I'll have you know, I'm a respectable woman."

He arched an eyebrow at her. "Ah, more's the pity. For I love you, Kathleen O'Byrne, and I always will."

Kelly, she thought. *I'm Kathleen Kelly, but not at this moment.* She allowed herself an indulgent smile in spite of herself. "I love you too."

"Are you sure you'll not come with me?"

Retrieving her umbrella, she decided the rain had already done its work and closed it. Let them think her mad for walking in the rain. It was the same rain that ran over her lover's body and the only intimacy she'd ever share with him again. "Ask me another time." Before her resolve could break, she turned and ran out of the churchyard like a school girl.

As she went, his voice floated after her. "I'll love you forever, Kathleen."

She couldn't help thinking that forever was a long time for one of the Good Folk.

Chapter 3

Long Kesh Internment Camp
Lisburn, County Down, Northern Ireland
December 1971

Trailing behind Kevin O'Donohue, Tom Finney and Hugh Conner, Liam paced the perimeter of the chain link fence in the cold and battled intense homesickness. He used to believe men didn't weep for their mothers no matter how frightened they were, but a few days in the Kesh had taught him otherwise. Men cried in the night when others couldn't see. It didn't matter that with forty prisoners packed into a space designed to hold half that many that there was every chance of being heard. The hearing wasn't the issue. It was the being seen. So it was that the first lesson he'd learned from Long Kesh was that men didn't acknowledge what happened in the dark no matter what.

Each night their cots were shoved edge touching edge in order to fit inside the old tin Quonset hut. Of course, about all that did was keep the rain off since the space heater didn't work past the first row of cots. Built in the 1940s and intended for use as an airplane hanger, the barrack was bloody freezing and the air seemed crowded with the hacking cough of the sick.

Being the youngest in his "cage"—the term the prisoners used for the fenced compounds inside the Kesh—meant that at best he was tolerated or at worst, bullied, which wasn't much different than the outside when he thought about it. It didn't hurt that Liam was taller than average. He had a good three inches on Kevin and a whole foot over Tom and Hugh. Some of the older prisoners liked to joke and call him the "big man." Although, what the others didn't have in height they made up for in brawn, unlike Liam.

"You want a smoke, Liam, my lad?" Kevin was eighteen and as luck would have it, from Derry. He had sandy-colored hair that brushed his shoulders, and he walked with a limp, the result of a confrontation with a BA.

A blond guard in the tower above them looked down at them. Something about the way he was staring spooked Liam.

"Sure." He accepted the cigarette, uncertain what to do with it. His mother didn't approve of smoking—not that he'd had the money for it, anyway. As a result, he'd never smoked in his life and didn't carry matches or a lighter. His stomach tightened in a jittery knot. He was afraid of shaming himself. He didn't know Kevin well, having only seen him in the streets around Derry. The other two were from other parts of the country, and he didn't know them at all, but it was easy to see that Tom and Hugh didn't approve of Kevin's sympathies.

"Aren't you going to light it?" Tom squinted at him.

Hugh sneered. "Maybe he don't got a light."

Stuck, Liam looked to Kevin, who pantomimed placing the cigarette behind an ear. "Oh," he said, taking Kevin's hint. "Ah. I think I'll save it. For later."

Hugh laughed. "Look at him. A right cool one, he is."

"To be sure," Tom said. "Until someone knocks the piss out of him. Then we'll see him crying for his mammy like a babby."

Kevin said, "Maybe Liam is saving it for trade."

The chain-link fences between the cages were where one went to barter with the other prisoners. News, books, food—all flowed through the fences from one cage to the next. The entire make-shift prison was connected like one big organism in this way. Some Loyalists were known to barter with Catholics upon occasion. Cigarettes made good trade because no matter the brand they crossed the divides.

Hugh asked, "Saving it for trade? What you got in mind must be special. What might that be?"

"Don't know, yet," Liam said. "But I'm sure I'll think of something."

"He's sure to think of something," Tom said in a sing-song falsetto. "Oh, pull me other one."

"Knock it off yous," Kevin said. "Let's talk to the boys in the next cage. Maybe one of them got the paper." Kevin played football and was among the best in spite of the leg. He liked to keep up with the Derry City team as well as Celtic—not that there would be any football news. The season was well over, but there was always the speculation about next year's season.

The moment Kevin's back was turned Tom's expression changed into something that said Liam was no better than a dog's leavings and whispered, "Going to pound the shite out of you, mammy's boy."

Liam was confused as to why Tom insisted on calling him that. There'd been no word from home yet, and he hadn't had a visit either. He was starting to wonder if his mother had forgotten all about him.

Hugh gave him the two fingers and then trotted to catch up with Kevin.

Deciding it'd be best to stay behind, Liam paused and considered his options, but Kevin turned and shouted for him to stop lagging. He glanced up at the blond guard who was still watching with an intent expression. A chill ran down Liam's back for no reason he could name and that settled it. He ran after Kevin.

Dinner consisted of a thin stew which Kevin warned him not to eat with a shake of the head. Liam put his spoon back down and reached for the slice of bread balanced on the corner of the bowl. Tom kicked him hard under the table, and when Liam reached down to massage the hurt out of his shin Hugh snatched the bread slice and glared. Taking a big bite, he paused to give Liam a toothy grin. It was easy enough to get the message: *Don't say a word, or you'll regret it.*

Liam drank his tea in silence. A strange prickling sensation started in his fingers, shot up both arms and slammed into his chest. Breathing became difficult. The tingling grew painful. He tried rubbing his palms on his jeans to make it go away, but it didn't work. Increasingly uncomfortable, he reached down and shifted his chair. The instant his hand gripped metal, the feeling stopped.

"Sit still, you wee shite," Hugh hissed.

Fuck you and your fucking friend, Liam thought and went back to his tea. He imagined giving Hugh a good kicking and the prickling returned. Experimentally, he touched the edge of his chair. Again, the sensation receded. *Interesting.*

Guards strolled along the edge of the canteen, the blond man from the tower among them. Liam looked away before anyone could notice and caught the stench of bad cologne with an undercurrent of stale beer as the man moved closer. Something brushed the back of Liam's neck when the blond guard went past. Instinctively, Liam jerked away.

"What's with you?" Tom asked.

"Sod off," Liam whispered.

"I heard that," Hugh said.

After dinner Liam decided to take a walk. The others were off practicing football to keep warm and while a good runner, Liam was shite at football. The older ones were off playing cards or writing letters in the study hut. Each cage had four or five huts which included living quarters, the recreation hut with the washroom, the study hut and the drying hut where wet clothes were hung when the weather was bad. In Liam's short experience, the weather was almost always bad. He'd heard the drying hut was where you went when you wanted to be alone. However, he was new and wasn't sure it'd be safe. So, he pulled up his collar against the north wind and buttoned his coat. He considered what Mary Kate might be doing. It would be Christmas soon, and if they didn't release him, it'd be his first away from home. Christmas was his favorite holiday. His mother did the baking every year, filling up the flat with the smells of fresh bread, biscuits and tea.

His stomach rumbled.

It was no good torturing himself. He changed the image in his head from the kitchen to the sitting room. His Aunt Sheila would make a huge paper chain out of yellow construction paper with the help of the little ones. The tree would go up next week, and if he were home, the thing would annoy him something fierce—not the smell. He loved the smell of fresh Christmas tree, but no matter how small it was it would take up half the room. Now, he wished for nothing more than to be tripping over it in the dark on his way to bed. His chest ached, and he blinked back tears, taking a deep breath of cold air.

Furtive whispers to his left stopped him. Too late, he saw it was Tom and one of the other young internees. A glimpse of ragged magazine pages and a photo of a bare breast told Liam that Tom was negotiating the use of his most recent and most valuable commodity—three pages ripped from a copy of *Mayfair*. Liam had heard that Tom and Hugh were charging for five minutes alone behind the shed with the photo of your choice.

Blushing, Liam brought his shoulders up and continued walking in the hope that he'd not been noticed.

"Liam!"

Dread knotted Liam's stomach in an instant.

"I'm feeling generous today. You can have a go at Eleanor for that cigarette you been holding."

Liam shook his head no. The heat in his face spread out to his ears. He turned his face away.

"What's the matter, mammy's boy? Never seen a snap of a naked bird before?" Tom asked, retrieving the wrinkled pages. His latest customer vanished down the path in hurry.

"I have," Liam said. "My stepfather has whole magazines. Not only a page." At age twelve he'd stumbled upon a copy of *Mayfair* hidden in a cupboard and was found out before he'd had a chance to peek inside the cover. Patrick had nearly beaten the life out of him and had threatened worse if Liam said a word to his mother. The next day the magazine was gone, and he'd never had another chance since.

Tom said, "All right, then. One cig."

"Smoked it," Liam said and shrugged in an attempt to look worldly. It was a lie, of course. He'd given it away to another prisoner who'd asked for it.

"Oh. That's a pity, that is," Tom said. A rueful smile flitted across his face. "You know, maybe I feel a bit bad about you going hungry tonight. Tell you what, I'll make it up to you. I'll let you have a go at Eleanor for nothing."

Liam blinked.

Holding the photo out, Tom said, "Well? Go on. What are you waiting for? You queer or something?"

While Liam didn't trust Tom, he didn't want to miss the opportunity either. He moved closer and reached for the torn magazine page. The blonde woman in the photograph rested against a mound of white fur pillows and was wearing a pale blouse so sheer that it might as well not have been there at all. Lips parted and eyes half-closed, she cupped the underside of each breast with delicate hands. Her nipples showed through the cloth as small knots of dark pink. The blouse was unbuttoned from just below her breasts down to the hem—spread to display an expanse of smooth belly and rounded hips. She wasn't wearing any pants, and her bare thighs were parted wide enough for him to spot a dark cleft nestled in soft, sparse curls.

The image felt slick against his fingertips. His breath caught as a memory of an afternoon with Mary Kate popped to mind—the time they'd been snogging, and he'd grown bold enough to slip his hand up under her skirt. His fingertips had brushed warm yielding wetness an instant before she'd slapped his hand away. He hadn't seen, but—

"Fuck you, mammy's boy," Tom said, laughing and snatching back the photo.

Liam was grabbed and pulled behind the shed. Turning to see who had accosted him, he was then shoved in the back. Icy gravel bit into his palms as he hit the ground. Rolling over, Liam spotted Hugh looming over him.

"Me and Tom," Hugh said. "We got something to tell you."

The ground was wet, and Liam tried to get up to prevent soaking his trousers, but Tom put a boot in his chest and pushed him back down.

"Right," Liam said. "So, yous don't like me. I get it."

"Wouldn't say that. You got your uses," Tom said. "Hugh here gets hungry."

"That I do."

"Here on out, you're to give him your bread at dinner," Tom said. "Don't worry, you'll still have the stew or whatever's on offer. It's fine if you get hungry enough. And sometimes the screws don't even piss in it."

Hugh laughed.

Culchie cow fuckers, the pair of them, Liam thought. He wanted to break Hugh's nose for him but knew he didn't have the strength. Best he could do was run, but here he was, flat on his back. The wet had soaked through his trousers now and the frigid ground was getting to him. His stinging palms tingled with the cold. He could feel blood oozing from the cuts. The prickling sensation flowed through his veins, up both his arms and legs and nestled in his chest fast as an electric shock. He thought of what happened at dinner and wondered what it might mean.

Tom said, "Look at me when I'm talking to you, you wee fuck."

Left with little choice, Liam glared up at the bastard. When he did, Tom's confidence faltered. Liam blinked. *He sees something. But what?* Startled, he didn't notice Hugh until it was too late and took the kick full in the side. For a moment he forgot all about Tom and the tingling under his skin. Curling around the pain, Liam prepared himself for a beating.

"Get him up and hold him," Tom said. "I want to get a few good ones in."

When the blows stopped, Liam was left gasping on his knees—one hand on the metal shed to keep from falling face first. His bruised sides throbbed with agony which slowly faded into a dull but constant ache. The pain was bad but would pass soon enough.

"Tell Kevin we gave you a hiding," Hugh said, "and we'll really lay into you next time."

The pair of them walked off, laughing.

There wasn't much Liam could do about Tom and Hugh, but there was plenty he wanted to do. He decided to bide his time, though. There was bound to be an opportunity eventually, and when it came he'd bloody well take it.

"Kelly! William Ronan Munroe Kelly!"

The two guards calling his name stood in the center of the yard. Thinking it might be a message from home, Liam got up from the ground. Everyone seemed to be watching as he crossed the yard.

"Come with us," said the first guard, "like a good little taig."

Liam kept himself from reacting to the insult, but his jaw tightened nonetheless. "I've not done anything."

"You will soon enough." The first guard laughed and there was a nervous edge to it that sent a jolt of adrenaline through Liam's veins.

"Stop it, Bert," the second guard whispered.

Something's not right, Liam thought.

Each put a hand to an arm as if they were afraid Liam would rabbit, and he was escorted from the yard and the cage. He endured a search and then went through a wire tunnel and into the next cage. When they reached the infirmary the stench of death was overpowering. They took him up the stairs to an office, but the surgeon wasn't anywhere in sight. The room was small and painted white with a barred cell to one side. No one was in it. Liam's heart thudded in his chest like a Prod's bass drum. He tried to think of what he'd done to be singled out. Had he committed an infraction? Nothing came to mind. "What's this, then?" he asked.

Neither guard answered. They shoved him in front of a desk positioned at one end of the room and waited until the door slammed open. The blond guard entered and sat down in the surgeon's chair behind the desk. He didn't so much as gaze in Liam's direction.

"Get him ready," the blond man said.

"Right," the second guard said. "Clothes off. Now."

Liam's heart staggered. "What?"

"Strip search. Stop your gawking."

Shaking, he stripped down to his kacks. The room was warmer than the barracks but not by much. Cold air prickled against his skin. He was visibly trembling now.

"Shed the rest."

"What? No!"

One of the guards slammed a night stick into Liam's back, and he went down. Unlike Tom and Hugh, the guards knew their business. The pain was terrific, and Liam couldn't breathe for what seemed a full fifteen minutes.

The blond man's chair squeaked. "You seem to be operating under the misconception that you have a choice. Do as you were told."

"On your feet, taig."

Liam got up from the floor, shed his underpants and covered himself as best he could with his hands. Shame burned his cheeks, and he stared down at the ground.

"Will you look at that," one of the guards said. "Catholics. No wonder there's so many of them."

The burning in his face worsened.

"Get him over to the cell," the blond guard said, licking his lips. His tone was bored, but there was tension in it that spoke of extreme interest.

Pushed to the right, Liam was next positioned a short distance in front of a cell door and shoved. Liam caught himself before he fell into the steel bars face first. He was up on his toes now. His legs were kicked apart, and he kept himself from tumbling by hanging onto the cell door. The trembling got worse, and it was hard to keep himself from falling. He tried to get into a more stable position but was slapped on the ear.

"Did anyone say you could move?"

A drawer on the desk slammed and there was a metallic clink. A chair scraped the floor. "That's enough. You can leave now, gentlemen."

Liam felt the blond man press next to him as he heard the other guards leave. Keys rattled in the lock. The blond guard grabbed Liam's wrist and snapped a cuff around it. The cuffed wrist was then yanked up above his head and shoved against a bar closer to his face. He lost his balance. Left cheek and shoulder slammed into iron. The second cuff was looped through the cell door. His cheekbone throbbed.

The blond man spoke in Liam's ear. "Grasp the bar next to your left hand."

Terrified and humiliated, Liam did as he was told. The second cuff went around his right wrist. *It's only a search,* he thought. *Nothing more. Perfectly normal. It'll be over with soon.* He'd heard about body cavity searches from one of the other prisoners. By the description it sounded horrible, but it could be lived through. A lot could be lived through, he'd come to understand. He tried to slow his breathing. He was sweating in spite of the chill. The stench of cologne and stale beer filling Liam's nose was enough to make him sick. The painted white iron bars pressed into his palms. The cuffs burned cold on his wrists, and his legs ached. His whole body prickled. The blond man pressed closer. Rough uniform fabric brushed against Liam's skin. A hand slid down his back, cupped one butt cheek and squeezed.

Liam's heart stopped.

"My name is Philip Sanders. You may call me Phil." Sanders reached up to smooth hair from Liam's face. "Tell me something," Sanders said, lowering his voice to a whisper. "Have you fucked before?"

The hand slipped between Liam's legs, and he stopped breathing.

"Tell me." *Squeeze.*

Liam screamed. A hand clamped hard over his mouth.

"Not a sound," Sanders said. "Do you want the others to know you for a fairy?"

After that, Liam shut his eyes and prayed, but there was no God in Hell.

It was dark when he was dumped back in the cage. He was glad of that. No one could see his shame. He should've died fighting, but he hadn't. He'd let that man do what he would. Worse, he'd— *Don't think about that.* He staggered back to the barracks, keeping his mind as blank as possible. *Nothing happened.* He wanted to be sick, but he didn't want the others to notice. They'd see it in him if he wasn't careful—see it in him as Sanders had. They'd see Sanders had— *A shower.* That's what Liam wanted. The other prisoners were off playing at football by the sound. They were always playing at football or betting on any random thing because there wasn't much else to do in the cage. He went around the backs of the buildings until he reached the Quonset hut that contained the washroom.

The pain had been horrific. The memory of Sanders's voice sent a shard of ice through his chest. *I'm to be your first. Isn't that sweet?* Liam closed his eyes and shuddered. *The shower,* he thought. *Have to make it to the shower.* He checked to see if anyone was inside. There was no one. He didn't bother to strip—just turned the water to the coldest setting possible and stood in the stream. When he was sure he could move again without getting sick he then took off his wet clothes, picked up the soap and started scrubbing at the blood and shite. It took ten washings to get the feeling of Sanders off him. Then he sat on the frigid concrete floor and curled himself into a tight ball. He waited for the icy water to numb his skin and then cried in silence, hiding his tears in the shower's stream. He wept until he felt as blank as the cinderblock wall. Then he dressed in his wet things, avoided the mirror above the washbasin and went to bed early. He didn't sleep. He merely lay in his cot and stared at the tin wall, huddling under his blanket in his damp clothes and wishing himself dead.

Sometime before lights out a jar of what the others jokingly called "Murphy's Poteen" made the rounds. Usually Liam didn't bother to sample the contents. The smell of it made his eyes water. However, this time he accepted the jar and drank as much of the foul brew as he could stand. Maybe it would kill him, or maybe he'd go blind. He deserved it. He hadn't fought, not hard enough. He wasn't natural. He'd—

Kevin frowned at him. "What did you do to your face?"

Memories surfaced of having his head slammed into the bars for struggling. Liam shoved the images down and away into the dark. He didn't have the energy to speak. So, he didn't. Unable to get an answer, Kevin let him be.

A storm rolled in during the night, and the wind fairly screeched with the force of it. He listened to the corrugated tin rattle and the water drip from the ceiling, thoughts alternating between emptiness and memories of stark terror. The weather let up after a few hours, but the wind continued to howl. Dreams flitted past his eyes like shredded phantoms as he half-dozed—images of a huge black wolfhound. The creature was searching for him. The knowledge was strangely reassuring. He couldn't have said why. His next recollection was of being shaken. He choked back a scream and forced open his eyes. There were grey patches showing through the bars on the window. Everyone appeared to be gone. One of the older prisoners stooped over him. He'd never learned the man's name.

"Come on, lad," he said. "You'll miss the morning line up."

Liam didn't move. He didn't care if the guards came and shot him.

"You look a fright," the older prisoner said. "Do you need to go to the infirmary?"

"No!" Liam shot up off the cot before the old man could call for the surgeon. He stuck his feet in his shoes and stumbled outside. A headache smacked into his brain with the brightness of the light. It was a slammer—the worst he'd ever had. He wanted to throw up but did his best not to show it. His body was a mass of bruises, and his arse was sore. He purposely didn't think of why. Taking a place at the back of the group and as far away from Kevin, Tom and Hugh as he could manage, he waited while the guards called out the names.

Christmas came and went. He didn't care. He didn't join in the stories and the singing of the songs. He didn't even attend the Mass. He couldn't, not with such a great sin on his soul. There was no chance he'd go to confession. He didn't shave either—because shaving meant looking in the mirror, and he didn't want to see what Sanders saw. As luck would have it, Sanders seemed to be away on holiday. Liam kept a watchful eye nonetheless and was careful not to be alone with any of the guards if it could be helped. It was weeks before he stopped jumping at shadows, or ceased shuddering each time his name was called. A few days after Christmas he got a package from home containing a card from his mother, two letters from Mary Kate, biscuits, tea, a brown neck scarf and a pair of thick socks. The biscuits and tea never made it past the guards. The only reason he knew they'd been in the box was because they'd kindly left him the crumbs and crumpled wax paper. As for the scarf, Tom took it off him two days later, giving him a black eye in exchange. At least he had the socks, for which he was grateful, and the letters, which he hid where Hugh wouldn't think to look. He desperately wanted to know what Mary Kate had written but couldn't read them. So, Liam carried both letters with him close to his skin, the paper growing dog-eared with each passing day.

One day, he was making his usual route around the cage when he spotted a huge black wolfhound on the other side of the chain link fence topped with razor wire—the area between the fences that everyone called "No Man's Land." The cage was surrounded by other cages on three sides. This was the fourth, and it provided a view of yet another fence, a guard tower and brick wall. How or why the great beast had gotten inside No Man's Land was beyond Liam. The creature had no collar and looked nothing like a guard dog—the BAs used Alsatians. The strange wolfhound pressed against the fence and whined. Thinking of the dreams, Liam moved closer and saw the beast's fur was caked with mud. *Dug under the wall, then.*

"Hello," Liam said. "What's your name, boy?"

The wolfhound pushed his muzzle through the chain link and whined again. Liam put his hand up so the dog could sniff him. The hound licked his fingers and something in Liam's chest loosened.

"You're a friendly one, aren't you?" Liam asked. "Bit mad too. No one breaks *into* this place." He checked the area before sitting down in the gravel, but he needn't have worried. Everyone, except for Tom and Hugh, left him alone now. Although it was never mentioned, Liam knew why. It was because of what had been done to him. On some level the others knew without being told and were afraid that they'd be next.

"You can't stay, you know," Liam said. "You'll have to scarper before the screws come." That was the most Liam had spoken in weeks. His voice felt rusty, but it was nice to have someone to talk to—even if the poor thing didn't understand a word he was saying.

The beast moved its muzzle to a diamond-shaped space close to Liam's face and licked him on the cheek. Liam laughed. It felt wonderful to laugh. He hadn't laughed since before—*your first*—hadn't laughed in forever.

"There's no telling what the screws will do if they find you here. Probably shoot you," Liam said, forcing his hand through the links to stroke the dog's fur. He suddenly felt better than he had in a long time. "Thank you for the visit. If you see my Ma—"

The hound growled.

"Where did that monster come from?" It was Hugh.

Liam brought his hand back through the links. He wasn't afraid the wolfhound would bite. Somehow, he knew the dog wasn't snarling at him.

"Why were you talking to it?" Hugh asked, picked up a stone and threw it at the dog. It hit the fence and bounced off. He selected another, smaller. Sharper.

"What's it matter to you?" Liam asked, getting up from the ground. Hugh could beat the shite out of him, but Liam didn't care. He wouldn't have the poor lost thing tortured. Liam shivered with electric energy and narrowed his gaze, willing Hugh to forget the dog, to go the fuck away. Liam focused with all his hate.

Hugh blinked. The fear was plain on his face as he took a step back. The dog barked.

"Put down the rock, Hugh."

In a daze, Hugh dropped the stone.

Stunned, Liam stared in disbelief. The wolfhound barked again.

A thought occurred to Liam, and he decided to take the chance. "I'll have my neck scarf back, you fuck."

Hugh pulled the brown scarf from around his neck and held it out for Liam to take. Liam wrapped himself in its warmth and felt more comfortable at once. "Now, get the fuck away from us."

"It's fucking mad, you are."

"Aye. Sure. The dangerous sort of mad," Liam said, "and you've made me all the madder." He smiled in satisfaction as Hugh panicked and ran.

"Thanks," Liam said, but when he turned he found the wolfhound was gone.

Chapter 4

The wolfhound didn't reappear, but Sanders did, and Liam returned to his former dread. The nightmares came back and several times he woke up screaming in the middle of the night, which didn't endear him to the rest of the barracks. So, he stopped sleeping as much as he could, starting in fear at furtive movements in the dark. The others began to avoid him outright—Hugh having told them of the wolfhound and of being bespelled. Liam was cast from his food clique which meant he couldn't share food parcels and was once more left to eat whatever the guards served. Rumors were whispered just out of his hearing and sometimes within it. His eyes glowed red when angered, and he growled in his sleep, the others said—proof he was possessed by a demon. That was why he didn't go to Mass when it was offered or look in mirrors. They said he'd grown the beard only to hide the devil's sign. In addition, a ghost was said to haunt Cage Five at night, and its howls could be heard in the wind on the other side of the hut's tin walls. Several men moved out and into whatever accommodations could be arranged in the other huts. Hugh and Tom remained. Soon, Hugh stopped eating, fell sick with a fever and then died in the infirmary. Shortly after that, Tom was mauled by an Alsatian during a barracks inspection. The wounds quickly became infected, and he lost an eye and three fingers. About the only positive effect was that word got around that bad things happened to people who crossed Liam. When two guards were reported missing, those outside blamed the 'Ra, but those inside Cage Five suspected otherwise. A rumor surfaced that a shredded uniform sleeve was all that had been found of either man. Both were said to have beaten Liam, and soon the suspicions spread to the guards. A few prisoners knew the rumors for rubbish, Kevin being one of them, but even those who didn't believe began to keep their distance after the story of the uniform sleeve. It didn't help that as the guards grew more and more nervous, they increased the frequency of their late night raids, and thus, the entire hut was short on sleep as well as temper.

In the end, Liam was left with no company but Mary Kate's letters. He was painfully slow at the reading, but after a few weeks he'd made it through the first and was rewarded with the knowledge that she missed him and would be waiting for him when he got out. She wrote about her family and his, filling him in on various small events and reassuring him that he'd not been forgotten. With newfound motivation, Liam got through the second letter within a few days. He wanted to answer her and made several attempts to do so but couldn't bring himself to send them. His little sister Moira had better handwriting, and she was five.

When he wasn't reading and re-reading Mary Kate's letters he spent his time hiding from Sanders, but being ostracized made it difficult. The time would come, much as he dreaded it. He could see it in Sanders's eye. So, Liam prayed for the strength to fight, muttering every prayer he knew in the hope that God hadn't abandoned him as well. The day finally came when his name was called in the yard. Two different guards waited for him, and it gave him a moment's hope that the inevitable hadn't arrived, but once again he was led out of the cage, through the wire tunnels and gates to the infirmary, and once again the surgeon's office was empty of anyone but Sanders.

"Strip."

When Liam didn't obey, the guards beat him down and yanked the clothes off him. Again, he was shoved against the cell door at that awkward angle. Again came the burst of cold against his naked skin as the other guards left. He shut his eyes and tried to breathe using bruised ribs. A hand circled his wrist. He listened to the metallic click of handcuffs being opened. Sanders's hot breath tickled his ear, and Liam couldn't keep himself from trembling. *Fight, damn you! Move!* But he was frozen. The tingling sensation—the one he had come to associate with intense emotion—had gathered enough force now that his skin itched with it. Terror spiked his heart at the feel of a rough hand on his bare back.

"Not a sound, or they'll—"

know you for a fairy.

"Our little secret. There's my sweet—"

Quick fire rage cramped his jaw. *Never fucking touch me again,* he thought. *I'll kill you. I'll fucking—* He struggled against the sluggish weight of time to shove an elbow backward and into Sanders's face before the cuff locked into place. *—kill you. I'll—* The prickling grew worse, far worse than it had ever been. A swarm of electric insects crowded underneath Liam's skin. The sensation engulfed him and then devolved into agony and the horrible feeling of bones and muscles stretching into foreign shapes. The cuffs dropped to the concrete floor with a clatter. An overwhelming hatred wrenched control from him. —*kill you. Kill YOU. KILL*— His vision blurred, and a snarl escaped his clenched teeth. Sanders stumbled, his face lengthening into a soundless shriek. Liam pulled air into his lungs, and an inhuman howl filled the infirmary from floor to ceiling. Sanders clawed at his holster. —*YOU. FUCKING KILL YOU.* Liam swung. The hand that connected with Sanders's jaw was coated in black fur and tipped with long obsidian nails. Four long lines of blood appeared just before the wounds gaped, revealing the stark white of bones and teeth. Watching from a numb and distant place behind the rage, Liam felt queasy.

Sanders stumbled in a panicked retreat, his left cheek in tatters and his eyes bulging. He collided into the desk, tripped over a chair and upended it. Landing with a crash, he scrabbled on the floor from the broken chair like a crab, the ruin of his face soaking his shirt in gore, his jaw moving in odd jerks as if the scream born in his throat was too gigantic, too tangled to get out.

The scene faded into black and white, and then Liam was watching an old horror film through holes in a mask with a long black nose. The room was smaller somehow, and he wasn't himself anymore. Someone or something was acting for him—a great black beast whose rage propelled him across the room to Sanders—the guard who had raped and tortured him. The guard who had to be taught that some things, some people, were best left alone. A cloud reeking of ammonia, terror and sour sweat blurred Sanders's features, blunting its humanity. Two steps. Liam watched the beast shred Sanders's shirt and then kneel—no squat—one furry knee in Sanders's solar plexus.

Trembling and weeping, Sanders finally found his voice. "No. Don't. Please stop."

A savage pant—almost a laugh—puffed foul breath that blew hair from Sanders's forehead. Sanders raised a fist, but the beast caught his arm with ease and slammed it on the concrete floor. Liam felt bones give way with a sickening snap and was pinned between satisfaction and revulsion. Sanders howled. A talon plunged into the flesh beneath the man's nipple, the screams changing timbre as flesh blossomed gory gashes. Hurried blows thundered against the other side of the locked infirmary door, announcing the arrival of the other guards. Shouts.

Sanders let out a high-pitched shriek. "Get it off me! Get it off me! It's a monster! Get it off! Oh, God! I didn't know! I'm sorry!" His eyes were no longer focused but round with madness.

The black beast straightened, standing on its—*paws, haunches*—the crawling electric pain returned, intensified and then vanished. Liam looked down in shock, reading against his will the crooked letters that had been etched into bleeding flesh. They spelled one word: *F—A—I—R—Y.*

I didn't do that, he thought, backing away from the terrorized guard. *I didn't. It was a—*

"Monster!"

Wishing he could shut up Sanders, Liam wiped a hand slick with blood against the outside of his bare thigh. Gobs of skin compressed into hard lumps were jammed under his fingernails. Adrenaline jolted through his veins in violent tremors.

The door slammed open, and the guards swarmed in. Naked, Liam slipped to the floor and cowered against the far wall. A group clustered around the now gibbering, pointing Sanders.

"Kill it! Mah-mah-monster!"

Three of the men turned to see where Sanders pointed. Upon spotting Liam covered in gore, they descended upon him.

And the kicking began.

Chapter 5

"Kathleen." Bran's whisper rode upon a breeze that sent trash dancing in circles on the crowded street. Broken bottles tinkled, and people held up their hands to keep the grit from their eyes. Then both Bran's voice and the wind were gone.

Scanning the area, Kathleen hefted her shopping bags. The folk of Derry went about their business—not having heard the voice or noticed anything strange. Stopped as she was in the middle of the walk, she thought surely someone must've noticed something. The flow of humanity merely made its way around the obstruction. One man bumped her and then apologized. Not far away, a group of young people clustered around the front of a business. They held signs that read "End Internment," "British Troops Out" and "Special Powers Out." An Army checkpoint at the end of the block bunched traffic on either side of the barricade as soldiers patted down young men and checked papers. She didn't see Bran anywhere, but as crowded as the street was it didn't surprise her. On the other hand, the voice could've been the result of wishful thinking. It'd happened before. She shrugged to herself and continued on.

"Kathleen, please." His voice was more urgent.

She stopped again and looked around more carefully this time. It was then she spied the abandoned shop across the street. A shadow flitted behind the boarded up windows and broken glass. She waited for a cluster of British soldiers to pass the store front before she made her way across the street between idling cars and military vehicles. It had been a sunny morning in spite of the cold, and the pavement was dry, although it wouldn't be long before a mist would coat all in icy damp. Grey clouds ruled the afternoon sky. It'd be dark soon.

She reached the store front and peered between the boards nailed across it. "Where are you?" she asked in a whisper.

"I'm right here, love."

She couldn't prevent herself from starting at the sound of his voice. Turning, she saw him leaning against the edge of the doorway. "I really wish you wouldn't do that," she said.

"Can't help it. To see the look on your face."

"I don't know why I bother talking to you at all."

"Because you love me. You know you do."

"Ah, go on."

"Have you been well?"

"I have."

Although his outward display of good humor hadn't changed, the tension in his jaw relaxed somewhat. "It is good, then," he said.

She joined him in the shadows and breathed in the scent of him—earth and leather. There was something about that smell that never failed to make her tremble with need. Why couldn't she feel the same about Patrick? He was her husband, was he not? "Why have you come? Have you found our Liam? He's in the Kesh, you know."

Bran nodded, his face growing serious. "I saw him. He's yours and mine, true enough. A fine lad, he is, and brave. You can be proud of him, Kathleen. But it's a terrible place. The stench of it stretches for a mile into the Other Side. I couldn't reach him. Too much iron. But I did what I could, not that it matters. He'll be out soon, I'm thinking."

"And what did you do?"

"I merely reminded a few mortals that there are consequences for crossing certain people." He gave her one of his cagey smiles—the one that all but said, *Do you really want to know more? Because it's sure I am that you don't.* "Anyway, it isn't as much what I've done."

She swallowed her anxiety, sure he was right that she didn't want to know more. "All right then. Tell me of Liam. Is he well? He doesn't write." She didn't want to mention Liam couldn't write very well and therefore, wouldn't. It was too comforting to see the swell of pride as Bran spoke of their son, and she didn't want to risk bruising that connection, tenuous as it was.

"He'll be fine enough, whatever happens. He can protect himself. He's not mortal. He has the Glamour. I saw him use it."

She frowned. "What is it you're going on about?"

"No real harm will come to him from mortal folk. Any who does him a bad turn will not have a good end. And those that do him good, will profit by it. It's in his blood. I've seen it."

The sins of the father, she thought and shuddered. "I don't want to hear any more."

Bran raised an eyebrow. "Did I say something wrong?"

Once again old questions surfaced in Kathleen's mind. *Is Bran the reason Patrick's business ventures have never flourished? Has Bran broken his promise? Does Patrick suffer because I chose him?* She sighed, knowing she couldn't go on thinking like that, or she'd go mad. Her lips pressed together. "I have to get the dinner on the table."

"There's something I must ask of you."

"What is it?"

Reaching inside the pocket of his pegged jeans, he produced a small silver coin. "Have you a way to discover what this is?"

Two heads graced the front—a bearded king and a queen. A crown was depicted above and between them both. She couldn't make out the words stamped into the edge in the dim light. She set down her shopping and leaned closer. "I think it's English, but it could be Spanish or French or Italian for all I know."

"Anything more?"

"It's very old," she said. "I've never seen the like. May I hold it?"

He gave it to her, shuffled his feet and gazed down at the street. He was wearing boots this time, she thought perhaps because of the pavement. She knew him enough to know he was uncomfortable in this place of broken glass and steel. It suddenly occurred to her that it was a powerful sign that he'd risked venturing this far into the city.

Tilting the coin into the light, she thought she could make out "Philip et Mari," however, the edges were too worn, and she couldn't read the rest. The stamp on the back was impossible to make out—all but the cross that bisected the entire piece. "I don't know anything about old coins," Kathleen said, "but it feels real enough."

"Of course it's real," he said. "That isn't the question. Where did it come from? There's no date upon it that I can find. I must know more."

"Why is it so important?"

He sighed. "The Redcap left it, and I must know the answer to its question."

"Why?"

"I'm to guess his name. If I don't, everyone—my men, you and Liam—will pay the price."

She stared at him. "This is a game?"

"Not one of my devising, I assure you." He sighed. "I'm a warrior, Kathleen. Give me a sword and an enemy to fight. A ford to guard. A hunt. I can track boar or stag across anything. Tactics, yes. Give me a battle. It is what I'm made for. Not this. It's useless, I am."

Studying his features, she could see the pent-up frustration in the set of his jaw. He looked poised to hit something. She understood his helplessness and anger. Had she not felt it herself for most of her life? Looking at the coin in her hand, she began to see she had some small power again. *At last.* "Is this everything—the whole clue?"

"Yes," Bran said.

"May I keep it? I must show it to someone."

He nodded. "You're clever in these things where I am not. Do you think you might discover something?"

She opened her handbag and fished for her handkerchief. When she found it she tied the coin inside the cloth and dropped it into her bag. "I'll do my best."

"We must find the answer soon."

"If I do find something, how do I reach you?"

"Go to the churchyard. Call out my name. I'll hear you and come if I can."

It was the first time he'd given her a means of reaching him in all the years she'd known him. A ball of gratitude and anger lodged in her throat. She didn't want to think about what it might mean. "Thank you."

He reached out and touched her cheek. "Have you been safe?"

"I have."

"You've your bitty cross?"

"With the red linen thread." She nodded. "I've done the same for the children. I've asked Father Murray if he could get a crucifix to Liam, but we're having trouble arranging a visit."

Bran moved closer. His warm breath caressed the side of her face. "Come with me, Kathleen. As the Fallen gain more power this place will only become more dangerous. Let me take you away."

"I must get home," she said, fearful that a neighbor might spy her. "I'll see you in the churchyard." She fled the doorway before he could stop her.

"This is very old," Father Murray said. "How did you come by it?"

Kathleen bit her lip. It wouldn't do to lie. He needed to know all there was to know if he were to help her. She'd confided in Father Murray before, and not only had he treated her as if she were perfectly sane as she'd spoken to him of spooks and fairies, he'd been a great help with her Liam. He'd been understanding of her Liam's circumstances—more so than she'd ever expected or hoped. If there was someone who could help, Father Murray was the one. It was safe enough. There wasn't a chance in the world of Patrick overhearing anything she said in the parochial house kitchen. She breathed in the scents of comfort and spiritual home but restricted her gaze to the inside of her teacup. "I got it from *him*, Father."

Father Murray reacted as if the coin were red hot, dropping it onto the table and spilling his tea. He hopped up from his chair. "What is it?"

"Only a wee coin, Father," she said, attempting to hide her amusement.

He looked down at the shilling. "Oh. Yes. I see."

She went to the sink for a towel in order to clean up the mess. "I must know where it came from. You went to University. I thought maybe you'd know."

"Didn't you say that *he* brought it to you? Doesn't he know?"

Although she'd once told him Bran's name, it seemed neither of them were willing to bring themselves to speak it. "He needs its origins and history, if that's possible. It's important."

Father Murray frowned and then got up, checking the hallway before shutting the kitchen door. "I've never asked this before." He paused. "But how often do you see... him?"

It was her turn to be uncomfortable. "Before Liam was born, I saw him every day. But now? Sometimes I don't see him for years. We've met twice in the past three months. And he keeps pressing me to leave with him. Something is wrong, Father. I'm frightened."

Father Murray's expression grew more distressed.

"Don't worry, Father. It's married I am and married I'll stay. I may not be a good woman, but I'll not break my vow." She sipped her tea.

"Don't be so hard upon yourself. You were young. Such beings can be very persuasive." He stared out the window, thoughtful. "You must be careful. They have great power to do harm."

"Not my Bran," she said, but doubt lurked in the back of her mind. She'd seen Bran angry only the once, and that was after she had married. She had been angry too, telling him to leave her forever. He'd said he never would and that he'd kill Patrick. The fierceness of Bran's rage had been terrifying, and that, more than any other reason, had been why she'd kept Liam from him. Patrick could be cruel, she knew, but it was a mundane cruelty—a cruelty that had boundaries and could be reasoned with. "Bran has good in him. I told you so before, Father. If he didn't, would my Liam be such as he is?"

"The Bible says that fallen angels can give a fair appearance."

"He's no angel, fallen or otherwise," she said. "He's a púca. Didn't I tell you so? And sure, all the stories of them are dark and foreboding, but that's not my Bran. He's a good man. I trust him. He's looked after us even after I married another. He always has." She didn't look Father Murray in the eye. Even she could hear the self-deceit in her words.

Father Murray sighed. "I hope you're right."

"I am." She said it with more confidence than she felt, and knowing that he was only humoring her made the silence that followed stretch raw across her nerves. "I've something I wish to ask you, Father. It's about my Liam."

He looked up from his tea. "What is it?"

"You told me to watch for… unnatural things around him."

"Has something happened?"

"I don't know. But Bran said he'd seen him at the Kesh and that he'd used 'the Glamour.'"

"How?"

"I was too afraid to ask."

Again, the silence pulled at the tension in the bright hominess of the kitchen. Father Murray shifted in his chair and then took a sip of tea.

"I can have someone check on him," Father Murray said.

"But we've tried to get a visit. No one will let us in."

Father Murray nodded. "I've made arrangements to meet with a member of the Advisory Committee next week. It's worked before. Liam has no political connections. They'll have to release him."

He sounded so certain that she breathed a sigh of relief. "Thank you, Father."

"Now, about this coin," Father Murray said. "What makes it so important?"

"Bran says we must discover the name of a monster before the creature harms my family." She didn't mention that it was actually Bran's safety and not her own that was the worry. As good a man as Father Murray was, his understanding did have its limits, and it seemed those limits began at Bran.

As if to illustrate the point, a skeptical look flitted across Father Murray's expression. "What sort of monster?"

"A Redcap." She whispered it and put her hand to the crucifix at her neck lest the creature hear its alias spoken and come calling.

"All right, Mrs. Kelly," Father Murray said. "I'll check my sources at Queen's University and Dublin. We'll see what they have to say." He reached into a pocket and produced a clear vial. "In the meantime, keep this with you. It's holy water."

The tension in her neck loosened at once. "Thank you, Father. I don't know what I'd do without you."

Father Murray escorted Mrs. Kelly to the door and then watched her until she vanished down the street. He didn't look forward to the call he was about to make, and he wanted to give the situation full consideration before he did so. From the day he'd first seen Liam he'd known there was something different about the boy. Dangerous—even at the age of thirteen. All Father Murray's training and experience said as much, but after he had spoken to the lad—a mistake, so certain members of the church leadership had claimed—it had been difficult to believe Liam anything but an innocent. Even so, it had been quite a struggle keeping him in school and out of trouble for as long as he had, but it had been done to positive result. Father Murray had previously maintained a distance from his subject lest others view his observations as muddled with an overabundance of sentiment. Nonetheless, it was easy to see that Liam had grown into a good lad with a good heart. And if that were so, was it possible Mrs. Kelly was right about the boy's father?

Careful, Joe, he thought. *That is an argument you won't win.*

The thing that worried him was the report of Liam using "the Glamour." If that were the case then the situation was far worse than Father Murray had thought possible, and his experiment had failed. He didn't want to believe it.

St. Francis, give me guidance, he prayed. *What am I to do?*

Returning to the kitchen, he cleared away the tea and washed the dishes. When he was done he went to the table and picked up the coin. It was a shilling piece, he was fairly certain, and based upon the woman depicted on the front it appeared to be from the Tudor era. If that were the case, it was quite valuable. He decided to give his friend at the University in Dublin a call first. See what could be discovered.

As for the disturbing report about the Glamour, well, that was second hand, was it not? He would do some checking before he made that call. If he weren't allowed to visit Liam directly for whatever reason the British were concocting this month, there were other internees in the Kesh. The first to come to mind was Mrs. McKenna's son, Michael—although, it was said the lad had taken a turn for the worse. Father Murray had heard rumors that conditions in the Kesh were appalling. Illness was common. Michael McKenna was but one name among the many recited each Sunday at Mass. With both husband and son interned and eight children still in school, poor Mrs. McKenna was beside herself. Were it not for the community pulling together to help, the McKennas would've been hard pressed to make ends meet.

Mrs. McKenna has enough concerns, Father Murray thought. *Perhaps it would be best to start with Kevin O'Donohue.* He'd been released a day ago. The two lads had attended the same school. They knew of one another. Surely, it was possible Kevin might have news of Liam Kelly?

Father Murray pocketed the coin, putting off his report to Bishop Avery, certain in the knowledge that the right decision would come to him. He did, however, go to the phone and request to be connected to his friend, Paul, in Dublin.

Chapter 6

Londonderry/Derry, County Londonderry, Northern Ireland
16 January 1972

"Blessed be the Lord God of Israel, for he hath visited and redeemed his people."

Kathleen bowed her head while Father Michael began the graveside ceremony. Father Murray handed off the thurible to one of the altar boys—the eight-year-old McGowan boy whose name Kathleen couldn't remember at the moment — and the heavy scent of burning frankincense faded away. The second altar boy, another of the McGowans, stood straight as a soldier, holding the parish's brass cross like a banner. His fingers were white, and when he shivered the big cross at the top trembled with him. A cold wind saturated with mist blasted the mourning huddled shoulder to shoulder around the open grave. Father Murray quickly moved to assist Father Michael with the open Bible, saving his place in the reading. Black umbrellas dotting the crowd recklessly propelled their owners against one another like sailboats anchored in a harbor during a brutal storm. Kathleen kept one hand on her scarf to keep it from flying off her head. Seemingly untroubled, Father Michael droned on.

"That we should be saved from our enemies and from the hand of all that hate us—"

Geraldine McKenna sobbed into a sodden white handkerchief. Kathleen stood tense at Geraldine's right, watchful of those around her. Old Mrs. McKenna scowled from the opposite side of the grave, claws at the ready like a harpy. Kathleen damned well knew who that look was for, and it wasn't Geraldine or Barney McKenna, but there was nothing to be done. As always, she must endure.

Barney sniffed and put a supportive hand under Geraldine's left elbow. The remaining McKenna children, ages four to thirteen years, had lined up next to their father who'd been temporarily released from Long Kesh for the funeral. In spite of the news reports, the make-shift prison had a frightful reputation among nationalists. The Kesh had certainly left its mark on Barney. His back was stooped, and his face was grey with grief. The damp hair sticking out from under his flat cap was now mostly white. Kathleen could've sworn he'd aged twenty years.

And Michael lasted less than five months in that place, she thought. Michael McKenna had been a strong lad when he was arrested—just like her Liam. *Young. Healthy.* Nonetheless, it'd been the pneumonia that had killed Michael. The corpse they'd returned to his mother had been thin and bruised. Kathleen tried not to consider what that might mean in relation to her own son.

She'd been in the hallway when she heard Geraldine's scream through the open door and had rushed into the McKenna's flat. Shoving past the stone-faced constable, she'd wrapped her arms around the hysterical Geraldine. Years of unacknowledged resentment had vanished in that instant of terror and sorrow. Alone, Geraldine had collapsed under the weight of her grief. So it was that in those first hours, there'd been no one but Kathleen to answer the phone or to meet the children on their walk from school or to see to the baby or to make the dinner. And there she'd remained until Geraldine's in-laws had returned from Belfast late in the evening. She had tried not to take old Mrs. McKenna's cold thanks personally, but it hadn't been easy.

Some sins are never forgotten, no matter the penance, Kathleen thought.

Unfortunately, Geraldine didn't seem to be dealing with the shock of losing her eldest son. She'd done little more than stare at the walls and weep. Dull-eyed, she wouldn't eat, wouldn't dress. Were it not for the Valium prescription Kathleen didn't think Geraldine would've slept either.

And how is it I would be, were it my Liam lying in that hole and not young Michael? And him only seventeen, she thought, blinking back a fresh bout of tears. *Liam will be seventeen soon.*

Mary, Mother of God, please, she prayed. *Don't let them give him back to me in a box.*

Liam was healthy and safe for now. Father Murray had whispered the news to her in Geraldine's kitchen during Michael's wake. Recently released from Long Kesh, Kevin O'Donohue had seen Liam three days ago. It'd been all Kathleen could do to keep from sobbing her relief into Katie Molloy's pickled cabbage. Later, her joy turned to shame when old Mrs. Cunningham asked her what it was she had to be happy about.

All were reasons why Kathleen would have preferred to be safe among her own, but Geraldine had asked if she would stand by her during Michael's funeral, and Kathleen had found it impossible to refuse.

"Glory to the Father, and to the Son, and to the Holy Spirit as it was in the Beginning, is now and will be forever. Amen."

"Amen."

Father Michael circled the coffin, sprinkling the holy water and muttering a blessing in Latin. Kathleen scanned the crowd for Patrick. Most of those attending the funeral were women and children. The news headlines, television and radio were dominated by crowing Unionist MPs proclaiming that all those arrested were IRA or terrorists. Kathleen considered herself a moderate. She held no animosity for the British. Her own father had lived and worked in London, but even she was finding the reporters more and more difficult to believe.

Shifting in order to view the back of the cemetery better, she spied Patrick standing by the gate. He hadn't taken a place with her sister, Sheila, and the children. Kathleen felt her mouth pinch into a flat line. Bleary-eyed, he hunched inside what passed for his best jacket, shirt and tie. He'd been at the wake most of the night and had been sound asleep when she and the children had left for the funeral Mass.

Two British soldiers and a constable were stationed outside the cemetery gate. The soldiers stared at the mourners, rifles at the ready. She gritted her teeth against a sudden stab of fear and looked away. *They must be here for Barney.*

Father Michael traced the sign of the cross over the coffin. "*Réquiem æternam dona ei, Dómine.*"

Nervous and restless, she attempted to focus on the funeral, but movement under the huge oak at the back of the churchyard drew her attention from Father Michael's Galway-laced Latin. She squinted at the edge of a shadow running the length of the trunk. Suddenly frozen, her heart stumbled. Was it the IRA, come to honor one of their own? While Michael had been known for a regular at Aggro Corner, if Geraldine were to be believed he hadn't been political. On the other hand, it wouldn't be the first time such a thing had been kept secret from the family. Kathleen glanced to the soldiers and then back to Barney. No one seemed to have noticed.

Mother Mary, please don't let it be a sniper.

"*Et lux perpétua lúceat ei. Requiéscat in pace. Amen.*"

"Amen." She repeated the word along with the other mourners, unaware she'd done it. *If it is, will the children be able to get away safe?*

"*Anima ejus, et ánimæ ómnium fidélium defunctórum, per misericórdiam Dei requiéscant in pace. Amen.*"

"Amen."

The shadow shifted again. This time she recognized him and gasped.

Bran.

He seemed vigilant as if standing guard. When he saw her he gave her a businesslike nod and a wink—acknowledging her presence but not indicating he had any need to meet or speak with her.

Still, no one seemed to register he was there.

What is he doing here?

The funeral ended, and Freddie McGowan led the procession out of the graveyard. The littlest McGowan boy followed, carrying the Bible in front of him. Then Father Michael and Father Murray joined the procession. The crowd made a path for them, and Freddie's brown curly head vanished in the sea of adults. The cross seemingly floated over their heads of its own accord, stopping at the cemetery gate and the soldiers. The air filled with the sounds of mourners preparing to leave. Two elderly ladies walked past the oak. One of them brushed Bran's sleeve. She apologized without noting who it was she'd bumped and joined the others politely waiting for the grieving family to exit first.

"What is it? Is something wrong?" Barney asked her, frightened.

Kathleen paused before answering. "No. Everything is fine."

"We should get back to the flat," Barney said. "They'll be coming for me after the dinner."

Geraldine's dull eyes grew sharp, and she clutched Barney's arm in a panic. "No! I need you home! They can't take you from me! Not now!"

He curled a protective arm around Geraldine and made soothing noises. "There. There. Calm yourself now. It's going to be all right."

"No it won't! They'll kill you too. Like they did our Michael. He didn't do anything!"

Kathleen forgot about Bran and turned to help Barney quiet Geraldine. Slowly the hysterical cries faded into sobs. Kathleen and Barney were able to half carry her as far as the gate. Then Geraldine tore herself free from Kathleen's grasp.

"Go away home, yous! Murderers!" Geraldine pointed a finger through the iron gate bars at a young private.

The private brought his rifle to bear. All at once, someone screamed, the mourners scattered, and the constable dropped to a defensive crouch. Kathleen tensed up in anticipation of gunfire. She scanned the churchyard for Sheila and the children, but didn't see them. Father Murray stepped next to Geraldine. Barney rushed in to pull his wife from danger. Kathleen moved to follow but felt a cold hand on her wrist.

"Stay back," Bran whispered in her ear and tugged her toward the shelter of a tombstone.

"They let my boy die! He was sick! And they let him die!" Geraldine turned away from the soldier, throwing herself into Barney's arms.

Father Murray held his hands up, and at the sudden movement the end of the rifle changed targets, digging into his chest. It made a dent in his vestment robes. "She doesn't know what she's saying." His tone became steady and quiet. "Please, Private. Put down the gun. This is a funeral. These people are grieving. No one here means you any harm."

The young Private's face was pale, and his grey eyes were wide. He blinked and swallowed. Kathleen thought she saw him shudder as the rifle was lowered.

"Thank you, Private," Father Murray said.

Crouched behind a large tombstone with Bran, Kathleen let go of the breath she was holding.

"That could have been a mess," Bran whispered.

Kathleen nodded, afraid to speak. Glancing up and to her left, she saw Barney comforting his wife less than six feet away.

"And you almost walked right into the middle of it," Bran said, keeping his voice low.

"What are you doing here?" she asked in a fierce whisper, still searching for her children.

"Protecting you from your own foolishness, it seems."

"What about your war? I thought you had more important things to do?"

Bran smiled in an obvious attempt at charm. "What could be more important than keeping my sweet Kathleen safe from harm?" He brushed her cheek with his knuckles.

The gesture was so tender that she winced and checked to see if anyone was looking. "You have to leave," she said. "Now. Before someone sees you."

"Let them. What does it matter?" He edged closer.

Unable to stop herself, she closed her eyes and breathed in the scent of him as she always did and remembered a time when she'd been truly happy. "There'll be talk."

"It's only words, love. Mortals have short memories."

"Not all do," she said. "It's a married woman, I am. That may not mean much to you. But it means a great deal to me. I swore an oath when I married Patrick—"

"You keep your oath, but does he do the same? And where is he?" Bran gazed across the churchyard at the thinning crowd.

She stood up and dusted off her dress. "He's gone to the pub, I imagine."

"And the coward left you and the children to the danger?"

And how is it what you've done is any better? "I'm serious. You must go. Now."

"Ma!" Little Moira ran to her from across the churchyard.

Sheila had the rest of the children with her and was tracing her own path through the tombstones. Moira wrapped her arms around Kathleen's legs, almost toppling her over. Kathleen reached down and straightened the scarf covering Moira's brown curls. "Were you good for your Aunt Sheila?"

"Yes, Ma. Who was that man?"

As it turned out, Moira wasn't the only one who'd seen.

Chapter 7

Londonderry/Derry, County Londonderry, Northern Ireland
29 January 1972

The concrete walls of the tenement flat reverberated with the sounds of warring children and clanging pans, the sounds of seven people packed in a cramped space. Four-year-old Jamie and five-year-old Moira sat on the floor, fighting over a rag doll—their matching brown curls the same shade as their mother's. Little Eileen was unsuccessfully negotiating a truce. In between the screaming Liam heard his Aunt Sheila gossiping with his mother in the kitchen.

The cacophony and the scent of boiling chicken meant home, but Liam couldn't have felt more alien. He surveyed his half siblings and noticed—not for the first time—that he resembled none of them. The months he had been gone only intensified the feeling of separation. He was weary and wanted nothing more than to sleep; anything to stop the thinking and remembering, but sleep wasn't an option. The crowded sitting room doubled as his bedroom. In any case, when he did sleep he only dreamed, and he didn't want to dream either.

He got up from the lumpy couch that served as his bed. When he did his mother appeared, blocking the hall. It was always like that now, as if she were tuned to his every movement. The room became quiet.

"Will you be home for supper?" she asked, her voice fragile. The heat was out again, and she was wearing two sweaters to keep off the chill. She folded her arms across her chest, and then she seemed to reconsider lest he take it as a threat, and instead dropped her arms to her sides.

He had been home from Long Kesh Internment Camp all of two days, and with the exception of the Frontliners who called him a fool for getting caught, everyone treated him like he might break or produce a bomb. Liam wasn't planning on doing either. He wasn't about to give anyone an excuse to send him back to Lisburn, and as for breaking… well, he'd done all the breaking he'd ever do in the Kesh.

Even Mary Kate treated him differently, but that wasn't so bad. She treated him like a hero—and if heroes spent afternoons between Mary Kate's thighs, even if they went to hell for it, he supposed there were worse fates to be had. "Off for a walk," Liam lied. The flat's concrete walls pressed in more than he liked to admit.

"Again?" she asked. "You'll be careful won't you? Stay out of trouble?"

"Yes, Ma. I will." *At least as far as soldiers are concerned*, he thought. *Mary Kate's father might feel a wee bit different.*

"We're to Mass early tomorrow," she said. "Your father thought we'd do something nice after. For your birthday. A picnic."

Patrick Kelly was his stepfather, not his father, and Liam would've been willing to wager the idea was not Patrick's, but Liam had had his fill of confrontations so he let the lie stand. "What about the march?" Liam asked.

"We'll stay well clear of that. I told you about the Paras. Mrs. Foyle says there are sure to be more soldiers than usual and—" His mother looked away, uncomfortable. "Arrests."

Feeling tired, Liam stepped outside and rested his back against the closed door with a deep breath. He loved his mother. He did. He hated lying to her and didn't understand why he did it. That she approved of Mary Kate was obvious, having invited her over for cooking lessons multiple times while he was away. However, he was dead certain his mother wouldn't think much of how they'd been spending their afternoons. Guilty as he felt, he was also happy, even if the first time Mary Kate had let him make love to her he'd shamed himself by crying. She hadn't laughed, or drawn back as he feared she would. Instead, she pulled him closer and whispered soothing words until the tears stopped.

Afterward, she kissed him tenderly and then said, "I thought I was the one who was supposed to weep." Embarrassed, he'd looked away.

"I didn't mean to make you feel ashamed." She'd touched his cheek. "This means as much to you as it does to me. And that makes me love you all the more."

Standing now in the hallway outside his flat, he checked his watch and saw it was three o'clock. He took the steps two at a time and then loped down the street. Running had once been a pleasure; it had been the one school activity in which he had excelled and after three months of confinement it had become a physical need. It was cloudy and cold, and the wind was up, but he didn't realize he had forgotten his coat until he was halfway down the block.

Rounding the corner, he spotted her. A gust caught at Mary Kate's long brown hair, pulling it into her pretty oval face. When the sun was bright it brought out golden highlights in her curls. In the approaching storm she resembled a graveyard angel. One graceful hand captured the flying tresses and trapped them behind her ear. Her coat flapped open, and he saw she was wearing a new green dress. The idea that she might be wearing it for him provided a measure of warmth in spite of the cold.

When he thought about it he supposed he had always loved her—ever since the day he'd been playing with a football, bouncing it off a wall. He'd accidentally hit her with it and then laughed when she'd cried. In response, she'd blackened his eye for him. Even at age nine the wee thing had had a punch that would fell a mule. She was four months older than him, fiercer than any angel written in the Bible and every damned bit as beautiful.

From the tilt of her chin he knew something was wrong. His heart stumbled. Running faster, he brought himself up short when two men stepped out of the alley. Neither looked happy.

"Stop right there, son," Patrick Kelly said, holding up his hand. His big red face was redder than usual. Mr. Gallagher took a place next to Patrick.

Oh, Lord, it's her father, Liam thought. *Shite. He's pissed.*

Mary Kate closed the distance and threw her arms around him in a tight hug. Her face was wet and cold on the front of his shirt. He kissed the top of her head.

"Bridget told father." She buried her face deeper. "Don't know how she knew. I certainly didn't tell her."

"Shhh. It's all right," Liam said.

Patrick Kelly said, "Unhand the girl."

Ignoring his stepfather, Liam pushed Mary Kate behind him. He was more concerned with Mr. Gallagher. Liam had known him almost as long as he'd known Mary Kate, but at the moment the man looked as though he was ready to punch someone.

Please, God, don't let it come to that. I don't want to hurt him, Liam thought.

"I said—"

Liam lifted his chin. An icy raindrop slapped him in the face. "I heard you the first time, Father." Turning to Mr. Gallagher, Liam said, "I'm sorry, sir. You're well within your ri—"

"Don't be telling the man his rights," Patrick Kelly said. "We're here to see the proper thing done. And so it will be. You'll not see the girl again."

"I'm marrying her, if she'll have me." It was out before Liam had time to think.

Patrick moved closer and said, "Don't be a fool, son. She's only your fir—"

"Don't." Liam felt a twinge of terror as black memory tried to surface, but he shoved it down with all his might. A tingling sensation originating in his chest crawled down his limbs. He focused on the pressure of Mary Kate's arms and prayed it would go away. The last time he'd felt like that he'd done something terrible. "Don't. You. Insult. Her." He balled up his fists. The powerful, black beast in his head fought to free itself. He trembled with the effort to keep it back.

No. Don't. Please stop.

The color in Patrick's face drained away. Mr. Gallagher's eyes grew round with horror. Liam didn't know for sure what it was they saw, but he knew that look. He had seen it in the Kesh often enough, and now understood it had followed him his whole life. It explained why he had not been able to get work no matter how hard he'd tried—why Sister Margaret had been so insistent that he repeat his prayers exactly. It had nothing to do with his missing Protestant father. Something wasn't right in him, and everyone sensed it.

There's a devil in that boy, Sister Margaret had once said to his mother.

And it was getting worse.

Mary Kate's voice came from behind him, loud and clear. "I'll marry you, William Ronan Monroe Kelly," she said, using his full name as if she wanted all present certain of who she meant. Then she squeezed him tighter. "Never wanted anything more in my whole life."

The black hulking thing pressing for freedom shrank as the meaning of her words sank in. Liam stood a bit taller and let out a shaky breath. "I'm sorry. This wasn't how I wanted it. Was going to get work first and then a ring."

"It doesn't matter," she said.

"And just how do you think you'll live?" Patrick Kelly asked.

Mary Kate circled around Liam and tucked herself under his arm. "I've a job."

His stepfather made a disapproving sound in the back of his throat. "You'd expect your husband to live off you?"

"Worked well enough for you. How long was it last?" Liam asked. "Two years? Three? And to be sure it wasn't the only time."

"That's different!" Patrick Kelly seemed to have forgotten his fear. "Your mother and I didn't start our lives as beggars!"

"Is that so? Then why is it we lived off Granny for all those years?" Liam asked.

"Don't you drag out the family troubles in front of—"

"I'm sure I've not said anything Mr. Gallagher doesn't know already. Him and the whole of Derry."

"You fucking wee bastard," Patrick Kelly said. Moving closer until his nose was perhaps an inch from Liam's chin, he then cocked back a fist.

Some things never change, Liam thought. "That's right. I'm not your son," Liam said, turning his face toward the threat. He didn't blink. He knew he was a goner if he showed any sign of backing down. "This is between Mr. Gallagher, me, Mary Kate and my mother. As of this moment, you're out of it."

The sleet quit blustering and got serious, smacking the pavement with everything it had. Freezing rainwater poured over Liam; the only warmth in the world was Mary Kate at his side. She was all that mattered. Patrick Kelly didn't twitch. Fist held high, his rounded face was bunched so tight that a vein in his temple pulsed.

The tingling sensation was back. *Let it go,* Liam thought. *It would be so easy. No more sanctimonious speeches about a man's duty to his family. No more begrudging every mouthful of food. Dead easy. You know it. You've done it before.*

No. I didn't, he argued with himself. *It wasn't me.*

A big man at six feet two and sixteen stone, Patrick Kelly had once intimidated him, but Liam had learned a great deal in the Kesh, and one of those lessons had been that when a man was afraid of you, you used it to your advantage. If you didn't, you'd end up on the wrong side of a shed getting the shite pounded out of you.

Unease shifted behind Patrick Kelly's eyes.

"I said leave." Liam stared down that doubt until his stepfather looked away.

"That's it," Patrick Kelly said. "Don't you expect another damned thing from me."

His stepfather turned and stormed down the street, seeming to take the black thing in Liam's head with him. Liam released the breath he was holding and prayed the rest would sort itself out.

Once Patrick Kelly was gone, Mr. Gallagher spoke in a quiet voice. "Mary Kate, there's never been any stopping you." He sighed. "If you want to marry, your mother and I will consent."

"Thank you!"

She left Liam's side, and hugged her father. Liam felt the lack at once. Watching them together, he made up his mind. "Mr. Gallagher, sir?"

"Yes?"

"I wish to wait," Liam said.

"What?" Mary Kate asked. "After all this?"

"We have to. I don't want to ruin everything. It has to be right," Liam told Mary Kate. "For you."

Mr. Gallagher stared at him, and Liam felt himself being measured. Afraid the black thing would be worked into the equation, Liam looked away.

"I love her, sir," Liam said. "I do mean to marry her. I don't think I could live without her. Not after—" He stopped himself before he said anything he would regret and shrugged. "I'll do my best. For her. I swear. Everything I can. More. Give me a year. To find work. I'll leave if I have to. Head down south. She'll be safe."

"Leave Derry? Are you mad?" Mary Kate asked.

"Mad enough to marry you," Liam said, shivering with cold.

One corner of Mr. Gallagher's mouth turned up. "Welcome to the family, son." He held out his hand.

Liam took it. "Thank you, sir."

He swore to meet Mary Kate only while chaperoned until they married. And with that, Liam walked home, teeth rattling in his head and soaked through, only to find his mother standing at the front door, crying. A large laundry bag rested at her feet.

"Why did you do it?" she asked, holding out his coat.

He took it from her and put it on, thankful of the warmth. "I love her, Ma."

"Not that," she said, whispering so her voice didn't carry down the hallway to Mrs. Foyle's. "Always knew there'd come a day. Mind, I'd much rather you'd waited. What were you thinking? What if the girl is pregnant?"

"We'll marry sooner, I suppose."

"Simple as that, is it? You'll learn, my lad. You'll learn. And you'll stand by that girl too. You'll not have to worry about her brothers or her father. Oh, no. I'll break both your legs myself. No son of mine runs out on—"

She would too. He smiled. "Don't worry, Ma."

"She's a good girl, Mary Kate. She'll see you don't get into too much trouble." She put a hand to his cheek and looked down at the bag. "No. It's your father. Why did you have to press him?"

"He's not my father."

Her eyes flashed up at him.

Might as well, he thought. *I'm out anyway.* "If he was a Protestant, I don't care. Surely, I can have his name at least? Munroe is all I have."

"I'll not answer that question. Not now. Not here. Don't ask it."

"Who are you protecting?"

"You," she said, closing her eyes with a deep breath. "I want you to go to your Gran's for a while. I called her. She's expecting you."

"No."

"Just until your—until matters settle. You won't have to stay long. A few days. I'll talk to him. In the meantime, you're to go to confession tonight, or I'll hear of it. I spoke to Father Murray at the church. You've until six." His mother picked up the sack. "Look at you. Why did you have to go off without even a coat? You'll catch cold."

"I won't." Resigned to his fate, he took the laundry bag from her. Sadness welled up inside of him. He had only just gotten home.

"I'll see you tomorrow. At your Gran's." She hugged him. Her hair smelled of lavender as it always did. "I love you."

"Love you too, Ma."

She clung to him like he was going to vanish. "You're a good boy. You've always been so—no matter what anyone says." She whispered in his ear. "Packed your birthday present. Don't you go opening it until tomorrow." She let him go with a sniff and fled, slamming the door shut behind her.

Liam didn't move until his vision stopped blurring, then he headed for St. Brendan's. Before he did, he paid a visit to Patrick Kelly's car.

In for a penny. In for a pound, he thought.

"Bless me, Father, for I have sinned," Liam began, "It's been three months since my last confession."

"More like six," Father Murray said. "But who's counting? Well, outside of your mother."

"Got that impression did you?"

On the other side of the shadowy screen Father Murray shook his head. "I'm thinking I'll need a strong cup of tea for this one. You too. Come on. Mrs. Finney will have left the parochial house by now. We can talk in private."

"Thought I was here for confession?"

"Tell you what—you still feel like confessing afterward we can always come back."

When Liam met Father Murray outside the confessional, the priest glanced at the laundry bag. "Tsk. It's that bad, is it?"

"She's sending me to Gran's for a few days."

"Ah. I see." Father Murray leaned closer. "In that case, we'll have the whiskey. You'll have need of it before you face the old witch. Of course, don't tell anyone I said so."

Father Murray was one of the new ones, from a seminary in Dublin. His short hair was dark brown, and he wore a close-trimmed beard and black horn-rimmed glasses. Liam followed him out of the church, uncertain.

"Your mother says you're seventeen now."

"Tomorrow. Yes."

Father Murray gave him a long look. "Happy Birthday." In his soft Dublin accent it sounded like an apology.

"Right. Thanks."

They reached the parochial house, and Father Murray let him inside, heading for the kitchen. Liam suspected his stepfather's entire flat could fit inside the front room. It smelled of furniture polish and antiques. Dark wood paneling gleamed in the afternoon light, and a green carpet runner muffled the sounds of their feet.

"Father Denton is at the civil rights meeting. Won't be back for a few hours yet." Father Murray opened a cabinet and brought out two bar glasses. "You had your supper?"

"No, Father."

Father Murray paused. "Strong drink on an empty stomach is not a good idea. Mrs. Finney made stew. Care to join me?"

Liam nodded. He had been unable to eat. In the Kesh, all he could think about was Mary Kate and food. Now that he was finally out, it seemed he could only manage to eat a few bites at each meal. "Thank you, Father."

They settled at the kitchen table with two steaming bowls of lamb stew and half a loaf of fresh bread. Father Murray prayed over it and then dug in. Liam picked up his spoon and checked the contents of the bowl for things that didn't belong.

"Is something wrong?"

"No, Father." Liam forced himself to put a spoonful in his mouth. It tasted lovely, but once swallowed it sank in his stomach like a paving stone.

"You were in Long Kesh."

Liam set the spoon back down, and held up his head but kept his eyes to the table. His throat closed shut.

"Sixteen is a bit young for that."

Listening to his heart pound in his ears, Liam waited.

"You don't have to say anything if you'd rather not, but you can if you'd like."

The table was scarred from years of use. Liam studied the polished swirling patterns of the wooden surface. Three of them together formed a face. It was screaming.

"I've a brother on the *Maidstone*, did you know?"

The prison ship, Liam thought. Shaking his head, he swallowed. He felt hollow except for that one mouthful of stew which gathered more weight until it anchored him to the chair.

"Marion Francis volunteered for the IRA when he was eighteen. Stayed with the Officials after the split. We're different, he and I. I don't believe violence solves problems. It creates them. But that doesn't mean I don't have sympathy for the cause."

"Didn't." Suddenly, Liam couldn't breathe. The memory of a boot on his back was overpowering.

Father Murray stared. "Didn't what?"

"Wanted to see Mary Kate. Was two o'clock. Saturday." Liam had to speak in short clips because he couldn't force it out any other way. He shut his eyes so he didn't have to see Father Murray's expression. "Aggro Corner. Didn't."

"Ah." Liam heard him whisper. "I thought not."

Liam focused on breathing in short shallow fits.

"So they put you away for being on the wrong street at the wrong time," Father Murray said. "That's hard."

Liam hadn't expected to be believed. He was certain his own mother thought he was lying.

Father Murray's chair scooted across the hardwood floor. Liam heard footsteps. The clink of crystal. A heavy glass thumped on the table in front of him, and the rich scent of whiskey burned his nose.

"To hell with it. We'll eat later," Father Murray said.

"Aren't you going to say God only gives us as much trouble as we can handle?"

"Do you want me to?" Father Murray asked. "Liam, there are some things in this world the Lord God doesn't have a fuck lot to do with. You ask me, that was one of them."

Liam's eyes snapped open. He had never heard a priest swear before. Mrs. Foyle had said the new curate had disturbingly modern ways, but then Mrs. Foyle didn't exactly keep up with current events. She—along with most of St. Brendan's—preferred to hear Mass in Latin and still ate fish on Fridays even though it'd been six years since Vatican II. A young priest with a degree in psychology had no chance at all of being accepted.

Father Murray said, "Surely we can arrange a stay of execution, it being your birthday. I'll call your mother. You can sleep here tonight."

Liam looked up.

"That's a Tyrconnell, man. Drink up." Father Murray drank from his own glass with his eyes closed and then sighed. "God bless Aunt Catherine. The Lord never made a more thoughtful woman." One brown eye opened, and he smiled. "I can see you've a bit to learn about whiskey. You don't like it, you can count it as part of your penance."

Uncertain, Liam picked up his glass. He'd had a pint or two in the pub with supper and had sampled whatever swill the prisoners brewed in the Kesh—enough to wish he hadn't the next day, but he'd never drank with a priest before. He took a sip. The whiskey tasted of oak and molten gold. It burned the inside of his nose and heated his belly, thawing the icy knot there in a flash. He wasn't certain if he liked it or not.

Father Murray nodded. "All right, then. One more to take the sting out, and then we'll talk." He poured another round and then capped the bottle.

After they'd both finished, he poured again and asked, "So. How long have you known Mary Kate Gallagher?"

Whether it was the whiskey or the change of subject, Liam didn't know, but the answer came off his tongue without a fight. "All my life."

"That's good. You been friends long?"

Liam felt himself smile. "Taught me to take down Sean McGowan in one punch when I was nine. I'd say yes."

"Got a lot of passion, that one." Father Murray stared at his empty glass. "Best ones do."

"What?"

"A man would have to be a damned fool to commit to the priesthood and not know what he was missing. Sacrifice in ignorance is no sacrifice at all." Father Murray sighed. "Her name was Mary too. Mary O'Brian. And I loved her with all my heart."

"You gave her up to become a priest?" Liam couldn't imagine anyone doing such a thing. If he even thought about it he wouldn't live long enough to cross the church aisle, and it wouldn't have been Mary Kate's father or her brothers or his mother that cut him down. It'd be Mary Kate.

"No." Father Murray filled the glasses again. "She died. Two months before we were to be married. We came up here to visit family. Went for a walk, and we were attacked. She was stabbed."

Liam felt he'd been gut-punched. "I'm… I'm sorry to hear it."

"Only told you so you'd know I'm talking from experience," Father Murray said and then emptied his glass. "Now. I'm supposed to tell you to keep your hands off her and that what you did was a terrible sin." He took a deep breath. "All I can say is I cannot fault you for doing something I don't regret doing myself."

This was not the conversation Liam was expecting to have.

"Had you told me you'd only just met, I'd have given you a tongue lashing that'd set you to thinking twice. But I saw you Thursday. Fresh off the bus from Lisburn. And I'm looking at you now." Father Murray paused. "She brought you back from the dead, that girl. She loves you and you, her. And that's something else altogether."

"Ma wouldn't think much of what you just said."

Father Murray nodded. "Yes, well, no disrespect to your Ma, but she's never been to the Kesh has she?"

Liam shook his head.

"There you are," Father Murray said. "There's something I should tell you. Ah, now. Don't look like that," he said. "It's only… Well, your mother and I discussed your situation when I first came here three years ago."

"And what did she tell you?"

Father Murray blew air out of his cheeks. "She said that your real father was gone."

"Did she tell you who he was?"

Getting up from his chair, Father Murray paused. Then as if searching for an excuse for having left the table, he got a glass from the cabinet next to the sink and filled it with water from the tap. He didn't turn around. "She didn't."

If the man weren't a priest, Liam would've sworn he'd just told a lie. Liam watched Father Murray drink, return the glass to the sink and then sit back down.

"I've been watching over you without your being aware. Don't worry. Your mother knows."

"You been spying on me?"

"I wouldn't call it that," Father Murray said. "Merely, taking an interest in your life. Making sure you got a fair shake at school—"

"You got to be fu—fecking kidding me."

"In general, attempting to keep you out of trouble."

"Why me in particular, Father?"

"You must be careful, Liam."

"Careful of what?"

Father Murray paused again. "The fighting. Don't get involved. The conflict is about power and money, not religion. And those things are not of God's realm."

Liam blinked. Father Murray seemed to be concerned he was going to volunteer. It wasn't that unusual for Catholics to have Protestant family members. Liam's uncle was a Prod. Now, it seemed, so was his father. By getting involved he would run the risk of killing his own, but if that was the worry, wouldn't it be better to know his father's name? Well, more than simply "Monroe"—if Monroe was his name at all. Why all the secrets? Why lie? "I never want to go back to prison, Father."

"There's no difference between Protestant and Catholic, you know. We're all the same. Peace is the only—"

"I'm not political."

Father Murray gave him a long stare and then seemed to come to a conclusion. He relaxed, settling in the chair with one arm draped on the back. "So, do you think you can eat now?"

"I'll give it a try."

"Good. I'll give your Ma a call then."

While Father Murray made the phone call in the other room Liam finished eating. Father Murray returned several minutes later and refilled the half-empty bowl, pouring another glass of whiskey without a word.

"I'll be drunk, I drink that," Liam said.

Father Murray said, "There's times when drinking means cowering and times when drinking can heal. Don't expect you to know the difference. I think in this case, I do. So, you'll have to trust me—if you can."

"This is some of that college psychology shite Mrs. Foyle goes on about, isn't it?"

Father Murray smiled. "That it is."

"Fair enough. Only wanted to be sure."

Hours later Liam found himself staring at the kitchen wall and sobbing while Father Murray listened to his confession. There was plenty he couldn't even bear to think about let alone speak of to a priest—Sanders, for one—but he confessed what little he could. He was sober enough to think himself weak for crying yet again but couldn't stop himself. When it was done, Father Murray absolved him of his sins, spoken and unspoken and then helped him stagger upstairs. Liam collapsed fully clothed on the bed and slept soundly and without fear or dreams for the first time in months.

Chapter 8

Londonderry/Derry, County Londonderry, Northern Ireland
29 January 1972

"I'm going to my mother's," Kathleen said, putting on her coat. "Give some thought to what I said." The children were outside playing. She'd made sure of it. All the years she'd been married she'd been careful not to fight in front of them. It wasn't always the easiest to arrange.

"Our whole life together he's been nothing but trouble. The rebellious wee shite," Patrick said. "He drove me to it, he did. He delights in making me angry."

"You're a man, and he's a boy," Kathleen said. "Between the two of yous who's the one should have better control of himself?"

"I'll not have the wee bastard in this flat ever again."

She stepped forward, getting as close as she could so he could be sure to know she was serious. He towered over her, but she wasn't letting that stop her—not this time. "Don't you ever call him that... that... word again."

Startled, Patrick's mouth gaped.

She used as much venom as she could muster. "You're as much as calling me a whore when you do. Fifteen years of marriage and five children. I'll not have that from you." She yanked her scarf from the peg on the wall. "Now. I'm to see that Liam is settled. He'll only be there for a day or two—"

"Woman, this is my flat, and I'll have the say of who'll be staying in it."

"It's man of the house, you are, and I'll not shame you. But you listen to me, Patrick Kelly. The day you married me you took my Liam for your own. You swore it would be so, and I'll not hear otherwise." She placed the scarf on her head and tied it under her chin with a jerk. "You will spend the time while I'm away cooling off, or there'll be no supper in this flat tonight. As it stands, there may not be anyway."

She turned and walked through the door, slamming it behind her. She stomped down the hallway and past her neighbor's open door. "Afternoon, Mrs. Foyle."

"Afternoon, Mrs. Kelly. Weather's up, is it?"

"Everything is fine," Kathleen said, attempting to ignore the feeling of being watched as she reached the stairs. The door gave out a thump as Mrs. Foyle went back inside her flat.

It was raining and dark when Kathleen entered the churchyard for the third time in a month. Having never had a means of contacting Bran before, she wasn't confident of it working. It had been a little over a week since she'd given Father Murray the coin, and yet, she felt like so much had happened since then. Her neck ached with tension from the fight with Patrick. She tried to put it out of her mind and made her way to the wall at the back of the churchyard, stopping under an old yew tree.

"Bran?" She called as loudly as she dared. "Are you here?"

Wind shook the trees and tugged at the umbrella in her hand. She re-situated herself and her umbrella to prevent being soaked further than she already was and hoped it wouldn't take too long for him to appear. She hadn't been lying when she said she was going to visit her mother. When she'd called to tell her that Liam needed the extra room for a few nights her mother had been less than pleased. She'd asked her how long it would be for this time and when given an indefinite answer had stated that the sofa was good enough for the likes of him. It was obvious Kathleen would need to smooth some feathers before he showed up, or the lad would be on the street.

"Bran? Please, come. I need you."

"And what is it you need me for, Kathleen?"

She suppressed a scream and then slapped him on the arm. "Damn you."

"According to your priests I'm already damned. Or is it you're adding more damnation upon my soul?"

"According to the priests you don't have one." She hit him a second time. "You'll be the death of me."

"No, Kathleen. Never," he said, stepping closer with wide open arms.

She moved her umbrella in front of her, using it as a shield and felt him bump into it.

"Now what did you go and do a thing like that for?" he asked. "And it laced with the iron, no less?"

Shifting her umbrella out of the way she saw he was holding a hand to his face, but he was smiling. She covered her mouth to hide a laugh. "I'm sorry."

"The things I suffer for love." His face grew serious. "Were you able to find out anything?"

"It came from a museum in London. They were more than a bit upset that it'd gone missing," she said. "It's lucky I am that I went to Father Murray with it, or I'd be on my way to Bligh's Lane or worse right now."

"I didn't know, Kathleen. I didn't."

"I know you didn't," she said. "But Father Murray had to do a wee bit of storytelling. He told them he'd found it in the church collection box."

"The priest lied for you?" Bran blinked.

"He's a friend. I told you."

"Did he learn anything else?"

"Was minted in the Tudor era. 1554. Those that are depicted on the front are Queen Mary and King Philip of Spain."

"It's Spanish, then?"

"No. English. She's Queen Mary. Bloody Mary. The one that killed all those Protestants."

"I don't understand."

She reached into her purse for the notes Father Murray had given her. "Queen Mary's father was King Henry the Eighth. The one who established the Church of England. The Pope excommunicated him for divorcing Mary's mother. Henry killed English Catholics who wouldn't convert. Mary didn't agree with her father. So it was when Mary eventually became Queen long after her father's death she abolished the Church of England. Burned three hundred Protestants for heretics, Father Murray said. It was then that the hatred between the Catholics and Protestants was born."

"Oh."

"After Mary died her half sister Elizabeth became queen. She brought back the Church of England. And that brought about more religious turmoil."

"What does a splintering within the new religion have to do with Ireland or the Redcap for that matter?"

"I don't know. It would make more sense if all this were about Oliver Cromwell. Was him that came to Ireland, declared Catholicism illegal and murdered the Catholics here. But he didn't come about until a hundred years later."

"So, the coin depicts an English Queen who burned three hundred people to death."

"Didn't you say the Redcap was English?"

"Aye. He is."

"Maybe he has a connection to Queen Mary, then."

"Maybe."

"Does that help?"

He tilted his head. "I'm not sure. It means something, but what?"

"It's all that could be got from it." She refolded the paper and stuffed it back into her handbag. It was difficult to hide her distress.

"You did well," Bran said. "Thank you."

"What happens now?"

He looked past her toward the street. "I wish I knew."

"Some great dark thing you are. Are you not able to foretell the future like the púca of Leinster?"

"Oh, Kathleen. That's not me at all. I'm no druid. Although, of late I wish I were."

"I'm sorry," she said. "You're doing what you can."

"Speaking of which," he said. "It's possible you won't be seeing me for a while."

"One of your battles?" She tried to hide her disappointment.

He nodded. "We've a chance at giving the Fallen a good rollicking. I can't tell you more. I wish I could."

"It's all right."

"You've not seen the Redcap?"

She shook her head. "Not at all."

His shoulders dropped, and he appeared relieved. "Well, then. It's possible he doesn't know about you. And I've been worried for you both for nothing."

"I should go." She kissed him on the cheek. "To keep you company until I see you next."

Happiness and surprise flashed across his features. "I love you, Kathleen."

"I love you too."

"I wish you would come with me. If we lose, things will go very bad in the mortal world."

"And how would you fight your war with me tagging you?"

He smiled. "You'd dress yourself in bronze and fight at my side."

"I'd do no such thing."

"Wish me luck then."

"I wish you all the luck in the world."

Chapter 9

Liam woke to warm sunlight on his face. Pale yellow walls gave the bare room a cheerful air. Sometime during the night, someone had taken off his boots and laid a blanket over him. The knowledge that someone—probably Father Murray—had done so without waking him filled Liam with dread. A jug of water, an empty glass and two white tablets were set out on the nightstand with a note written in careful cursive script.

Glancing up at the crucifix nailed at the head of the bed, Liam contemplated staying where he was. He didn't feel sick, but then he had yet to sit up. When he did, he was thankful of the aspirin and the water. The headache wasn't unbearable. He had only gone that far drunk once, and that had been in the Kesh when he had wanted to die.

Pulling off the shirt he'd slept in, he then gutted the laundry bag. He discovered a new sweater and a present wrapped in bright paper. The card taped to the wrapping was one of Moira's creations made from school construction paper, crayons and glue. She often told him that he reminded her of a shaggy black dog, and so that was what she had drawn. Something about it reminded him of the monster in the Kesh. He dropped it with a shudder.

The present turned out to be an old book. *Ma will never give up,* he thought with a sigh.

He had quit school the year before, Sister Margaret having made it clear that he was too stupid to bother continuing. At least he had learned his letters, but when he tried to read it was always with the feeling that he was playing a spiteful game of hide and seek, chasing vanishing words across a crowded page. He had often wondered why it was worth the struggle and with the exception of Mary Kate's letters, frequently didn't bother. His mother had other ideas.

Fanning the book, hand-tinted images of fairies and spooks flitted by.

He stopped when he came to a page marked with an old photograph of a young couple. The woman was younger and less worn by cares and hardship, but it was his mother just the same. The smile on her face shone out of the picture with openness he'd never seen in life. Her arms were wrapped around a tall man with thick black hair and light-colored eyes. The man's face was so much like his own that for a moment he thought it was. His hands shook as he flipped the picture. It took him a while to puzzle out the inscription.

Kathleen and Bran 1954

"Bran. My father's name is Bran Monroe?"

The church bells pealed, giving him a start.

I'll be late to Mass, he thought. Still, he couldn't tear his eyes from that face. There was something savage about it in spite of the happy expression. Feral. When he noticed the page the photograph marked he spied an illustration of a fierce black dog with demonic eyes. Shivering, he snapped the book shut and crammed it back in the bag. A loud knock came from the door. Liam snatched up a clean white shirt and stuffed his arms into it. The knock sounded again.

"Liam?" Father Murray asked.

Liam finished buttoning the shirt and pulled the new sweater over the top of it. "Almost ready, Father." It would have to do. He had already outgrown the Sunday suit his mother had bought six months ago. He wouldn't have another until next fall.

"I have to ask you a question," Father Murray said. "It's urgent. May I come in?"

When Liam spied Father Murray's face, he stumbled back. The priest's jaw was set, and there was an angry line between his eyebrows. "Did you go near your stepfather's car yesterday?"

Liam swallowed. It wasn't smart, but he couldn't bring himself to lie to a priest. "Borrowed a flashlight from the boot. Didn't want to go to Gran's. Thought I'd need it if I was going to stay in one of the derelicts on Williams Street. Was going to give it back. I—"

"The RUC are waiting outside the church. Your stepfather has filed a complaint."

"For a flashlight?"

"Someone smashed his car windows with a brick and then kicked in the side. He says you did it in retaliation for throwing you out," Father Murray said. "This is serious, Liam. They'll put you away again."

"I can't go back! I won't!" Liam paced the room. His heart slammed against his breastbone, and he trembled with the need to run, but Father Murray was blocking the only means of escape. "Please, you can't let them!" Liam whirled and emptied the laundry bag. Finding the heavy silver flashlight, he tossed it on the bed. "There. Give it back. They can't. Not for that. Please?"

"Did you or did you not vandalize your stepfather's car?"

"Do you think it matters?" Liam looked away, trying to remember. By the time he had gotten to the car he had been angry. The tingling had returned, and there had been a moment when he thought about kicking in the side, but he hadn't done it.

Had he?

You don't exactly remember what you did to that guard either, he thought. The image of a word written in blood and flesh surfaced. A voice pleaded in his head. *Don't. Please stop.* He shuddered and combed his hair with his fingers as if to wipe brick dust from them. "I didn't."

"You won't go back. Not if I can help it," Father Murray said. "Stay here. Someone will bring up food later."

"What about Mass?"

"Mrs. Organ's funeral is this afternoon. A private service can't be arranged until after the march," Father Murray said. "You'll be safe. Just… stay away from the windows."

Liam sat on the bed and attempted to gain some sort of control over the terror and anger. He resented being confined. At the same time, he knew he should be grateful he wasn't on his way back to Lisburn. "Thank you, Father." He forced gratitude through clenched teeth.

"We'll get it sorted out. Don't worry." Father Murray shut the door and hurried down the stairs.

Liam paced. He wanted to believe Father Murray, but dread had a vise grip on his chest, and he couldn't breathe. Quietly opening the door again, he gained a measure of relief. Then he turned to organizing the laundry bag and attempted not to notice that his mother had packed all the clothes he owned. When that was done, he stared at the book resting on the bed. Touching the black leather cover as little as possible, he stole the photograph from between its pages.

Next to his mother, his father's clothes were old but well-tailored. His glossy hair was wild and brushed the tops of his shoulders. Neither rich nor poor, he didn't have the look of a man used to work. He certainly wasn't a farmer. At the same time Liam couldn't imagine anyone who looked like that living in a city. While his mother's arms were clamped around his waist in possession, he rested one comfortable arm across her shoulders, taking pleasure in her presence but not bound by it. Although the picture was old and his father long gone, Liam placed his thumb over the smiling image as if that might help hold the man to his proper place.

At the sound of footsteps on the stairs, a bolt of terror ran Liam through.

He dropped the photograph on the bed and was still deciding whether or not to confront whoever it was in the hallway when Mary Kate appeared. She held her hand out in front of her in the universal sign of a toy gun and squinted, aiming.

"I've come for you, Liam Kelly. Surrender with your hands up."

"Don't make a joke of it." Crossing the room in four strides he caught her before she could enter.

She stood on her toes and kissed him. In a flash, he became uncomfortably aware of the proximity of the bed. Images from previous afternoons ran mad in his mind. It wasn't easy, but he pushed her back. "I promised your father," he said, trying to ignore the electric shiver running up his thighs.

With a wicked smile, she took one step forward. He hopped back, afraid if he touched her again his resolve would vanish like so much mist.

"Well, isn't this interesting," she said.

"Have some mercy, will you?"

"Say please."

"Please."

"Say 'I'm an idiot for putting a brick through my stepfather's car window.' Shite. Sometimes I wonder if you think at all."

"Didn't do it. I swear."

She gave him a hard look, and he held her gaze for what seemed an eternity before she sighed. "All right. I believe you," she said, backing into the hallway. "I'm going on the march this afternoon, and I want you to go with me."

"Can't leave. Father Murray said the RUC—"

"Your stepfather withdrew the complaint."

"What? How?"

She shrugged. "Didn't hear. Your mother and Father Murray both took him aside after Mass. Whatever it was they said, it must've been good. Don't think I've ever seen your stepfather apologize quite so sincerely before."

Liam's legs felt weak. He wanted to sit before he fell down, but the only place to sit was on the bed, and he wasn't about to do that.

"Father Murray said you should get something from the kitchen. Then we can go," she said.

"Have you not heard? Mrs. Foyle said the Paras will be at the march," he said. "And they'll be out for blood."

"And how would she know?"

"How do you think?" he asked. "She heard it from Mr. O'Brian who heard it from Mr. Porter. He's got a radio. Listens in on army channels before the marches." He sighed. "Ma told me what happened at Magilligan last Saturday. Paratroopers had to be stopped from beating protesters to death.

I'll not have you near those bastards."

Instead of being shocked or frightened as he expected, she put a hand on her hip. "Oh, so you think you can order me about?"

"I'm not ordering—"

"This march is for those who've been interred without trial. That means you, Liam Kelly. You and the rest of them that's still being tortured in that freezing hole. If you won't stand up for yourself, that's fine. But you'd let the others rot without so much as a word against it?"

He saw her standing there with her eyes shining and knew he was lost. "I'll go."

"Good."

"But you have to leave. Now."

She tilted her head in a question.

"I promised your father. I intend to keep my word."

"What? Do you think for a moment I'd ravish you in a parochial house?" she asked. "A girl could go straight to hell for a thing like that." She winked. "You've no worry. Sean is in the kitchen. Making a note of how long it's taking for me to get you downstairs too, no doubt. Let's go."

He paused. "Your brother?"

"Only one of them," she said. "Why?"

Liam felt his face heat up. "He didn't care for me much before. Now that he knows I—"

"Do you think for one moment Sean is going to kick the shite out of you in Father Murray's kitchen?"

"No, I suppose not."

"I should think," she said with a smile, "he's got manners enough to wait until you're outside."

Sean Gallagher was three years older than Mary Kate and worked down at the docks. His hair was the same sandy brown color as his sister's. Although Sean was short, he was powerfully built and was—Liam was certain—the brother who'd taught Mary Kate to punch. Sean stood glowering at the bottom of the stairs.

"*Thóg tú do am,*" he said.

"I wasn't up there for that long," Mary Kate said, hopping down the remaining steps.

"*Tá se mo chinneadh,*" Sean said, and then turned on Liam. "*Cad a rinne tú thuas ansin?*" His brows pushed together in a suspicious line, and the tone of his voice was harsh.

Since he didn't have any Irish, Liam decided it was best to stay silent. He glanced at Mary Kate.

"Sean, you're being rude."

"*Níl gaeilge aige a chór ar bith. Tá an bastún mór ag stánadh consúil iasc. Conas a feidir leat a phosadh rud mar é?*"

Mary Kate said. "Keep it up, and I'll tell Laoise I saw you with Nóinín last night."

"*Ní bheidh tú,*" Sean said.

"I would," she said. "I may do it anyway."

"*Níl,*" Sean said.

"*An Bearla,*" she said.

Sean sighed and stepped back, allowing him to pass. "Just remember," Sean said. "I'm watching you."

In the kitchen, Mary Kate heated leftover stew and then poured it into a bowl while Liam watched. She set it on the table in front of him. "Eat every bite."

"Now who's ordering who about?" Liam asked.

She smiled. "If I'm to be your wife you'd best get used to my looking after you."

Sean let out a snort from the hallway.

"Thought I was to look after you," Liam said.

"That's not the way my mother tells it," Mary Kate said. "Eat."

He ate to make her happy and felt better for it. When he was finished she washed the dishes and set them to dry. He couldn't help smiling as he looked on, imagining the future with them in their own flat. As birthdays went, he decided this one wasn't too bad.

"We're to meet mother and father at Bishop's Field. We'll come back for your things after. Then we're walking with you to your Gran's. Just in case Patrick Kelly decides to file another complaint."

"I won't go to Gran's," Liam said.

"Sure, she doesn't like you much, but where else will you go?" she asked. "Your stepfather may have called off the Peelers, but we both know he won't allow you back in his flat. Maybe I can talk Bridget into letting you stay with her and Gerry, if you'd rather. But with the new babies—"

"Fine. I'll go to Gran's."

Sean stuck his head into the kitchen. "Are you two going to argue all day? It's nearly three."

"Grab your coat, Liam. We can't be late. We go and do that, I'll be locked in my room for a year."

They passed several barricades and check points on their way to Bishop's Field. BAs and Saracen Armoured Personnel Carriers filled the streets. A military helicopter passed overhead. Derry was being invaded. As they crossed Waterloo, Liam yanked Mary Kate from the path of a speeding Saracen. It braked suddenly and the passenger side door swung open. A paratrooper leaned out, his beret the color of drying blood. When the Para smiled, Liam thought he saw teeth sharpened to points in a wizened face. The creature was staring right at him with burning red eyes. He'd seen that face before.

Aggro Corner. The day he'd been arrested.

The tingling sensation returned, and the beast that lived in the back of Liam's head shifted. *Enemy*, it said. *Danger. Kill it.*

"Going to blow your fucking head off," the Para with the sharp teeth said, pantomiming the action with two fingers and a thumb. "See you soon, dog."

Liam blinked in shock. A normal-looking Para slammed the door, and the vehicle sped off down the street. Sean made an obscene gesture at the Saracen.

"Did you see that?" Liam asked.

Mary Kate tugged him by the arm. "They're only trying to intimidate us. Bastards."

No, he thought. *Did you see that thing? It wasn't human.* Seeing monsters. The tingling. The memory loss. He was beginning to question his sanity, but if he said anything Mary Kate might leave him. "It's working then."

"Never mind them. It's just a short walk and then we'll listen to some speeches." She looped her arm through his. "You mentioned something about a wedding. Any idea when it might be?"

Sean snorted, and Mary Kate slapped him on the arm.

Locating Mr. and Mrs. Gallagher among the thousands gathered at Bishop's Field wasn't easy. Television and radio crews recorded the crowd as they laughed and chatted. Were it not for the banners he would have sworn it was a festival day. The sun was high in the sky, and there wasn't a cloud to be seen, making the bad feeling in his stomach all the more incongruent. He took a deep breath of cold air and tried to relax, but the beast was still there, muttering dire warnings in the back of his brain.

"Mother!" Mary Kate pushed through the crowd, dragging him with her. Her palm was sweaty, and nervous energy fueled her voice. "We're here!"

Mrs. Gallagher was in her Sunday best—a brown plaid coat with a hat and tall boots to match. "There you are."

Liam hung back, uncertain. Mrs. Gallagher studied him as if she were really seeing him for the first time. "Well? What do you have to say for yourself?"

"Good afternoon, Mrs. Gallagher," Liam said, feeling this was some sort of test.

Mary Kate moved next to her, the pair of them forming a judge's line. "What do you think, mother?"

"He isn't much to work with," she said. "Tall. That's good. The rest is all elbows, knees and hair."

"Mother!" Mary Kate said. "Don't be cruel."

Mrs. Gallagher opened her arms with a smile. "Come give your future mother-in-law a hug, son. I'll not bite."

"Don't you believe her for a moment," Mr. Gallagher said and winked. "She has very strong teeth. As does her daughter."

Mary Kate seemed to relax.

"Your father has good news," Mrs. Gallagher said, pushing the hair out of Liam's eyes. "Notice came in the mail yesterday, but it got delivered to Mr. Rooney next door."

"What?" Mary Kate asked.

Mr. Gallagher grinned. "We've been awarded a house. Finally. In the Creggan."

"That's wonderful," Mary Kate said, "Just in time for me to move out."

"Congratulations," Liam said.

"Ten years waiting. Didn't think it'd ever happen," Mr. Gallagher said.

Officials climbed up into the coal truck at the front of the crowd. One of the men brought a microphone to his lips. It didn't seem to be working. His voice was lost in the noise of the crowd.

"That's Bernadette Devlin," Mary Kate said, pointing to the pretty brunette at the back of the coal truck. Mary Kate knew he didn't pay attention to politics, but that didn't stop her from explaining. "Did you know she's only twenty-five? Elected when she was twenty-one. The youngest member of Parliament in history. I'm going to be just like her."

Liam shook his head, feeling a blush burn on his cheeks as Sean frowned at him. "You'll have to go to university first."

"I'll pass exams. You'll see. And you'll go with me."

"You know I can't," Liam said.

"No one can stop you from going back. You could catch up. You're not stupid. Sister Margaret. What does she know?"

Not wanting to disappoint her, he nodded.

The coal truck moved down Williams Street and the crowd with it. People sang. Others shouted slogans. Liam thought Mary Kate might be right, that he had worried for nothing—until they reached Aggro Corner. That was when he saw the troops on the roof of the abandoned shirt factory and along the wall near the Presbyterian Church. Something wasn't right. Unlike the BA regulars, the paratroopers—Liam spotted their red berets—weren't wearing riot gear. In sniper positions, their guns were pointed at the crowd. Why? Even he knew the IRA was taking the day off, and he had purposely avoided the subject. It gave Liam a chill. As the coal truck sped past Aggro

Corner, chaos pressed in. A group bolted down Williams Street, shouting, and he and Mary Kate were carried along with them. Rocks bounced off corrugated iron nailed to the fronts of the burned-out buildings.

"I don't like this," he said to no one in particular. He couldn't have explained why. The situation wasn't any worse than usual—less so, in fact—but the Paras frightened him. Perhaps it was because this was the first time he'd been near Aggro Corner since his arrest.

"We're not supposed to be here. We were supposed to go to Rossville Street," Mary Kate screamed over the crowd. She stumbled. "Liam!" She grabbed for his hand, and he folded himself around her in an attempt to keep her from getting trampled.

"We have to get out of here," he shouted in her ear to be heard. Then he pulled her up, steadying her.

A man's voice over the loudspeaker made an announcement. "This assembly may lead to a breach of the peace. You are to disperse immediately."

The crowd let out a roar and rushed the barricade. A volley of stones, bottles, boards, anything close to hand shot into the air aimed at the soldiers. Liam grabbed Mary Kate and held her to his chest as they were propelled closer to McCool's Newsagent and the barricade. In the crush, Liam heard the growl of a diesel engine. The pavement shuddered under his feet and then a flood of water smashed into the man standing beside him, driving him to the ground. Liam was soaked. Riot guns went off. Protesters scattered, and he was able to see the water cannon lumbering down the street. Two CS cloud columns drifted toward the barricade. The troops were laughing and cheering.

With the crowd dispersing, he was able to pull Mary Kate a few steps in the direction of Chamberlain Street.

Someone somewhere shouted in a sing-song voice, "Where is your brother, taig? Where is your Da?"

"Don't you laugh! Don't you dare!" She jerked her arm from his grip and snatched up a paving stone from a pile of rubble. "Bastards!" She threw it with all her might.

"Mary Kate! Stop!" He dashed after her. More CS gas canisters bounced and clattered in the street, spewing a fog of peppery smoke in their wake. Liam put a hand over his face to keep from breathing it in. More riot guns thumped and flashed in the smoke. He'd lost her. Rubber bullets whizzed past. People screamed. Cried. Then Mary Kate trotted back to him in the mist, holding a handkerchief over her nose and mouth. She stuffed a wet cloth into his other hand, and he smashed it to his face. Breathing in vinegar, his eyes watered. Nearby, someone threw up.

Have to do something, he thought. *Get her out of here.*

He tied the handkerchief over his mouth and nose like a television bandit from the Wild West. Once it was in place, he grabbed her arm again. When she struggled he pulled her up against his chest and half-carried her. "We're going home."

"Those bastards! They can't treat us like this! They laughed! They've no right!"

He got her as far as the first doorway before she kneed him in her frenzy. He released her at once and stooped with his hands on his knees, blinking back the pain.

"What's wrong?" she asked. "Is it the gas?"

"If you're planning on us having children one day I'd suggest you not do that again."

She put both hands over her mouth, stifling a horrified laugh. "I'm so sorry."

A window hissed open and a woman's voice shouted from above, "Girl, get your young man out of here before he's taken."

He looked up.

"Purple dye. You're covered in it. They'll know you for a rioter for sure. Hurry up. They're coming." The woman slammed the window shut.

Mary Kate said, "Oh, Liam, your new sweater. It's ruined."

People jogged past. Some of them were sobbing. Even more flooded the narrow street. In a moment there wouldn't be room enough to run. Again, he grabbed her hand, and they trotted together. He heard panicked screams and glanced behind. *This isn't happening,* he thought. *It can't be.* A large group of Paras charged down the street. Saracens brought up the rear. One stopped, disgorging troops who snatched men from the crowd. He heard gun fire and couldn't tell which direction it was coming from. The sound was different from the riot guns. Sharper.

"They've killed a boy on Rossville!" A woman screamed as they passed Eden Place. Tears streamed down her face. "A little boy! Shot him dead. In the back. I saw it."

He wanted to stop and help her, but the soldiers were closing, and he had to get Mary Kate somewhere safe. More shots. More screams. Something thumped him hard in the back. He stumbled. *Rubber bullet,* he thought. *Only a rubber bullet. If it were real it'd hurt worse. Right?* He slowed. It was hard to breathe.

A man shouted, "They're killing us!"

Mary Kate grasped Liam's arm with both hands tight enough to bruise, and then someone slammed him against the brick wall. Through the pain he saw Mary Kate throw herself on a Para, knocking his red beret off.

"Let him go!"

The Para turned on Mary Kate. He swung the barrel of his gun, hitting her in the face. Drops of blood dotted the concrete in slow motion. Mary Kate collapsed. The Para stood over her, holding his rifle like a club.

"No!"

The Para looked at him. His face shifted, and he grinned. It was that same wrinkled face. The same teeth filed to sharp points. The same red glowing eyes. "Hello, dog. The mac Cumhaill is a long way from here. Your master won't help you now."

I've gone mad, Liam thought.

"Is she sweet, your plaything?" the creature asked, its voice like gravel. It sniffed the air over Mary Kate who was bunched up and sobbing on the pavement with her hands over her head. "I smell your spunk. You've had her. Shall I shoot?" It pointed the rifle.

Liam flung himself over Mary Kate. He heard the creature guffaw and then the blows came. From a long way away he heard Mary Kate screaming. *Please God, let him shoot me, not her,* he prayed. *She's going to be an MP. She'll save us all. I can't even read.*

"You should've stayed in Long Kesh." The creature switched from hitting to kicking. More laughter. Others joined in. Liam was cocooned in dull pain.

I've lived through this before, he thought. *Won't be so bad.* Then something smashed into the back of his head, and it all went black.

Chapter 10

Malone Prison
Malone, County Antrim, Northern Ireland
August 1972

A blast of cold moist air stung Liam's cheeks and penetrated his coat. Malone wasn't much different from the Kesh—more structured, perhaps. Another hastily converted WWII facility, it was slightly less crowded and somewhat cleaner. There were fewer internees, and the prisoners were more hardened. All appeared to be paramilitaries of one stripe or another. Squatting with his back against the hut he shared with thirty others, he pulled his anorak tighter to no avail. A game was taking place in the football pitch, and shouts echoed off the tin buildings. A loud thump reverberated through the corrugated metal at Liam's back. Assuming it didn't involve him, he didn't bother looking down the narrow path. Instead, he wished himself invisible.

He was new to Cage Seven and as such, sitting alone was dangerous. One of the others might happen along at any moment, but he was having one of his bad days, and the narrow spaces between the nissen huts were the closest thing to privacy available. The corroding tin wall wasn't much of a view. However, there weren't many alternatives since Cage Seven was located in the center of the prison. Looking out through the chain-link fence would only mean seeing yet another cage and other prisoners—which was fine if you wanted to trade or needed news of the outside, but Liam had had his fill of news from the outside.

Mary Kate had been accepted at Queen's University. She would be leaving for Belfast any day now. A confusion of emotions crowded his skull. On one hand, he was proud of her, but he was angry too. She was off living her life. A life he couldn't share through no fault of his own. Then there was the fear. Compared to Derry, Belfast was a metropolitan city, and she would navigate it without the support of her family and more importantly, without him.

An image of Mary Kate tossing chunks of pavement stone at BAs sprang to mind, and a reluctant smile crept across his face.

Perhaps, it's not her I should worry for, he thought.

Crunching footsteps snapped him out of his reverie. A stocky man whose square face was framed in a neat brown beard settled in the gravel next to him. Reaching into a pocket, the man said, "My name is Jack." He held out a cigarette and a lighter, "Yours?"

"Liam." He accepted the proffered lighter with a pounding heart and lit the cigarette.

Gazing down the path toward the game, Jack pocketed the lighter. "Been watching you, Liam."

Liam focused on the end of his cigarette in an effort to disguise his fear. He had kept to himself to prevent trouble, and more importantly, to keep a tight rein on the beast that lurked so close under his skin. He'd had nightmares of what would happen if the thing got loose again, but every day it became more difficult to maintain control. Twice during questioning at the Holywood interrogation center it had almost slipped free. He was proud of having managed to keep from harming anyone in spite of how far he'd been pushed. Luckily, he wasn't in Holywood anymore. At Malone the BAs patrolled outside the walls, not within them, and so for the most part he'd been left alone. In return, he had done his best not to draw attention. His first week at Malone had been spent doing what was expected without complaint or comment. He got up when he was told, participated in cleaning the barrack when it was his turn, kept the boiler full of water for the tea as assigned and otherwise walked the grounds as the others did. Everything was going to plan.

Until now.

In spite of the repercussions, it was obvious the prison guards at Malone didn't exert any special effort to segregate Republicans from Loyalists, let alone Official IRA from Provisional; however, based on snatches of overheard conversation, he had surmised the men in Cage Seven were mainly Provos. A few of them seemed to know one another from the outside, and based upon what he'd overheard, Liam was relatively certain the man next to him was the OC—Officer in Charge.

"You're not participating in the game," Jack said. "Are you well?"

"No, sir. I mean, yes, sir."

Jack examined his face long enough to make Liam nervous. "I suppose an eye like that would make the idea of football less than appealing."

Liam carefully touched the bruise. His left eye was still tender—a parting gift from a BA as he had boarded the helicopter that had taken him from Holywood to Malone. Three days ago the eye had been swollen shut, and he'd worried about losing his sight, but he had been blessed with easy recoveries before, and this time hadn't proven different. The eye seemed to be healing well with no change in his vision.

"You've not been to class either. Nor have I seen you chatting with any of the others. We're not criminals—no matter how hard the British try to make us so. We're Prisoners of War. As such, we've rules here. Not their rules," Jack said, obviously meaning the screws. "Our rules. Is there something you need to tell me?"

Liam shook his head. The temperature between the huts dropped as blood drained from his extremities, and every muscle tensed. There had been a Loyalist—a self-proclaimed member of the Ulster Defence Association among the prisoners at the start of his stay. The UDA man had apparently lasted two weeks before his mouth broke his nose for him—and then some. Liam had seen what the Republicans had left in the hut the next morning. He'd watched as the screws had carried the remains off on the stretcher. It had been his third night at Malone, and the image had left an indelible impression. Liam was no Loyalist, but that didn't mean Jack knew it. Without moving, Liam checked the space between the buildings for obstacles; although, it would only delay the inevitable. There wasn't anywhere to run to.

"Frankie thinks he may have seen you in Holywood a month ago. Where are you from?"

"Derry, sir."

"Ah," Jack said, "And what are you in for, Liam from Derry?"

"Was on a march. Anti-internment. Was picked up. BAs said I was rioting."

"And were you?"

"No, sir," Liam said. "Only been out of Long Kesh a few days. Didn't want trouble. Still don't."

Jack nodded, but his face didn't lose its hardness underneath the smile. "And why were you sent to the Kesh?"

Liam shrugged. "Watching the Frontliners throw rocks on Aggro Corner."

Jack whistled. "You're one poor luckless bastard. But I suppose when it comes down to it, we all are."

There was a shout and a thump. The football slammed into another hut.

"As I was saying," Jack continued, "We've rules here, and participation is compulsory."

"I'm not political. Only want to get back home to—"

"Doesn't have to be sport," Jack said, his face growing softer. "Although, it's likely we'll only have the ball a few more days. The BAs are due for their regular tour, and it'll probably need more than a patch after they've done with it. You should attend class tomorrow. We're reading Shakespeare—*Hamlet*, to be precise."

"Shakespeare?"

Jack grinned, and Liam saw it was a real smile this time, devoid of judgment or calculation for the moment. "You were expecting a lecture on the sudden and violent release of mechanical or chemical energy from a confined space?" he asked. "Sorry to disappoint, but I earned my degree in literature, not chemistry. Although, if you've never read *Hamlet*, the end is rather violent. The descriptive 'explosive' might be a bit of a stretch, though."

And that was how Liam had met Jack Rynne, secondary school teacher from Belfast and volunteer for the Provisional IRA.

Jack was proven right about the BAs' tour. The next night Liam woke to the bang and rattle of the hut being unlocked. The lights came on and someone shouted, "Go to the wire!"

Assuming the situation was much the same as in the Kesh, Liam stayed as he was until the hut OC said to comply. At that, everyone went out in the cold and lined up against the chain link fence while the BAs ripped through the contents of lockers and tossed bedding. As the hut was given the go over a second set of BAs went down the row of prisoners and conducted a body search. Dressed only in his kacks, Liam attempted not to show his nervousness, but when a man was pulled from the wire and beaten he began to shiver. Not wanting to be known for a coward, he stared ahead and hoped no one would notice.

"It'll be all right," the man next to him said. Liam had noticed him before. He had a nasty scar running through his eyebrow and half down his cheek. "Nothing out of the ordinary. Be over with soon. After they've had their fun."

Liam nodded and waited his turn, fingers hooked in the steel links and staring into the next cage. When his time came the BAs weren't particularly rough about it, and it was over with quickly. An hour and a half later, everyone was told to go back to their huts and the locks were replaced. It took some time to sort out the cots and the bedding, but eventually everyone got back to sleep.

Seven-thirty came terribly early the next morning.

"*Maidin mhaith,*" a blond prisoner said with a grin.

The man with the scar said, "Oh, fuck you, Jimmy."

Half-awake, Liam asked, "What did he say?"

"Good morning," the man with the scar said. "It's too fucking early to be that fucking happy. Particularly after last night."

With little interest in much else and no real choice in the matter, Liam decided classes might not be so bad. Eight months of prodding from Jack,

Mary Kate's optimism, his own obstinacy, and a large number of strategically invested cigarettes managed to get Liam through fifth year. Knowing full well the Gallagher family's position on his lack of Irish, he'd also been picking up what he could from the other prisoners. It wasn't easy. There weren't many fluent speakers even among the staunchest Republican prisoners, and most of the common prison vocabulary consisted of words he wouldn't have used in front of Mary Kate, let alone her mother. However, he was able to glean a few phrases. To show off, he decided to surprise Mary Kate during her next visit. He entered the room with its rows of folding tables and chairs. Other prisoners sat opposite their loved ones and friends, talking quietly. It didn't take him long to spot her. She stood up and waved. She was wearing a short brown skirt and a corduroy jacket with a sheep fur collar. It looked new.

Sitting down across from her, he could hardly contain his excitement. He hoped he would get it right the first time and without hesitation. "*Dia dhuit, a Maire Cháit. Ar mhaithleat dul amach?*" *Hello, Mary Kate. Would you like to go out?* He hoped she wouldn't press on much further as he'd just run through the extent of his hard-earned vocabulary—unless she wanted to talk about the weather, of course.

She leaned across the table and trapped him in a fierce hug. "Oh, Liam. That's wonderful!"

The guards burst from their corners and yanked him away from her. Everyone stopped what they were doing to stare.

The guard with the red hair said, "Visit is over."

Liam said, "We've a half hour!"

"You, shut your cakehole," the red-headed guard said. Liam recognized him as the one Frankie called "Gingernut." He had a reputation for being strict, particularly if there wasn't any profit in being otherwise.

Gingernut turned to Mary Kate. "Go on. Get on home."

"What did we do?" Mary Kate asked.

"No fucking Irish," Gingernut said, forcefully shoving Liam across the room.

Liam staggered into the wall. "I won't do it again! I'll tell you what I said! I only asked her—"

"I don't give a fuck," Gingernut said.

Liam patted his pockets for anything he could give the man but wasn't quick enough. The guards dragged him through the door. Furious, he fought them with everything he had.

Liam opened his eyes and found himself on an infirmary cot. Jack was at his side, sitting on the floor. Liam wasn't surprised. When the doctor wasn't on duty other prisoners took on the role. Jack's face was a sketch in concern. "Which guard did this to you? I'm filing a report."

"I'm done." Fervor passed through Liam's clenched teeth. He wanted to scream his conviction—he didn't care who would hear, but the agony in his sides stopped him. His ribs were broken. The words came out in a fierce whisper instead. "I'm joining up."

Jack leaned close. "This isn't you. It's only the anger talking. You'll calm down—"

"Fucking mean it."

Gingernut had ordered a cavity search, and Liam couldn't stop them from carrying it through. It'd taken three guards to hold him fast while it was done, and they'd laughed and made lewd comments in the process.

With a deep breath, Jack settled on the floor and brushed dirt off his knee. His shrewd brown eyes scanned the infirmary walls until at last he said, "Truth is, I wouldn't have you, son. Not in my brigade."

"Why not?" *He knows,* Liam thought. *He knows about the monster. They transferred someone from the Kesh. He's heard the stories.*

Reaching into his coat, Jack pulled out a note. "Can you tell me what that says?"

Accepting the slip of paper, Liam opened it. The words were written in blue ink—in cursive. It was then that he understood it wasn't the monster that Jack had heard about, but something else. Shame burned Liam's face with the force of an unexpected blow, and he turned his head. Before he knew it, the heat of embarrassment became a tingling sensation in his chest which crawled down both arms and gathered in his clenched fists. Liam wanted to punch Frankie for not keeping his word. For not keeping his mouth shut. That's what he got for trusting the likes of Frankie. After all the months of careful self-control, Liam was on the verge of ripping something apart. Anything. He wanted to smash the note in Jack's smug face. He wanted to run. Only he couldn't run; he was stuck in the infirmary with two broken ribs because he'd been too stupid not to fight the guards. *Too stupid—*

I won't, he thought. *Won't have another goddamned teacher tell me I can't do something. Fuck teachers. Fuck Jack.* "Mike Cusack can't read, and he's in. What does that have to do with anything?"

Jack nodded. "Mike Cusack is a good man." A long pause stretched out, and for a moment Liam didn't think Jack was going to continue, but then he sighed. "We don't need more heroes to die for the cause. If the British could be repelled with a wall built of dead heroes, Ireland would have been free long ago," he said. "The Brits are getting smarter. Look around you. They're filling up the prisons with Republicans so fast they can't keep up.

So, they dump us in improvised shite holes like this. If we're to survive, we must change too. We must think." He poked an index finger at Liam's bruised head.

"You won't have me because I'm stupid."

"You're far from that, I promise you," Jack said.

"Then why?"

Gently placing a hand in the center of his chest, Jack pushed him back down on the cot. "Calm down, son. Don't hurt yourself after Murphy went to all the trouble of patching you up."

Liam closed his eyes, and the moment he did, he recognized the tingling sensation for what it was and how far it had gone. The monster was dangerously close, and if he didn't do something quick he'd lose it, and Jack would be the one to pay the price, not the fucking screws. Grabbing the iron cot frame under the covers with his right hand, Liam fought for control. Inexplicably, metal seemed to help. Not always, but enough that touching bars and aluminum walls had become a habit when he was angry or upset. He focused on the canvas-covered iron under his palm. He couldn't let the beast go. Wouldn't. *Stupid.* Doing so now would only prove him unfit—although not for the reasons Jack thought. Liam was dead certain that no matter what the English said, Provos didn't recruit monsters.

He bit down on his anger, and hissed for air through his teeth. Pain shot into his head from his bruised jaw, giving him a nauseating headache.

"Suppose we did take you," Jack said. "What of the others? Their lives will be in your hands just as yours will be in theirs."

"Frankie told you."

"He didn't." Jack raised an eyebrow. "I've been in secondary education for twelve years. Do you not think I'm capable of noticing differences in students' handwriting? Not that the differences are that subtle in your case."

"Fine. I'm stu—"

"Still, I couldn't think of how you were managing to read out loud in class," Jack said. "Waited two weeks and watched for a pattern. Then I had it. Frankie would kick you just before you'd read. That was clever. Had me thinking he was pushing a reluctant student. Hell, you must have memorized whole chapters to pull it off." He sighed. "So, I keep asking myself, what's stopping you? You're certainly not lazy. There are far easier ways of muddling through. Perhaps it's a lack of sufficient motivation? I don't know. Regardless, you'll have to work it out. Get through your O-Levels without cheating. Do that, and I'll recommend you myself."

"I can't."

"You can, and you will. Not for me, and not for the cause." Jack shook his head and sighed. "But because if you don't you'll lose that girl of yours.

And from what I've heard, you don't want to go and do that."

Liam took long, slow breaths, pain warning him to take care. He wanted to listen. He had to listen. The prickling sensation began to recede along with his anger.

When he had told Mary Kate he was thinking of taking fifth year, she had given him a kiss that had kept him up nights for a week. It had been why he had stuck out the classes, no matter how badly he wanted to quit. She only thought him a little slow. She didn't know he was practically illiterate, and he never wanted her to know. While there was no real shame in not being able to read where he came from—Bogside was full of men who couldn't—Mary Kate and her family held education in high regard, and she was at Queen's University, surrounded by learned men who weren't in prison and weren't fakes and liars.

"I'll do everything I can to help, Liam."

Turning to face the wall again, Liam swallowed. "I'll do it."

"I was hoping you'd say that."

Less than a week later, two of the guards who'd put Liam in the infirmary met with bad ends. One was shot by a sniper in the car park outside the prison, lost a leg and his job in the bargain. The other burned alive in a house fire. When Gingernut vanished the rumors started up again—mistreat the scrawny kid from Derry and bad luck is sure to follow. The prison *scéal* had it that Gingernut had been in a terrible car accident and had broken both legs. He wouldn't be walking for months, and thus, wouldn't be back at Malone for some time. None of the prisoners were sorry to hear it—Liam in particular.

When he was released from the infirmary, he was glad of it. The place was filthy and stank of death. Most of the time there was no doctor, only Murphy who'd once been a medical assistant at a hospital in Belfast. Two prisoners died while Liam was recovering. One expired in the cot next to him and no one came for the body for two days. Liam had to pull the covers over the man's head himself. He didn't know a proper prayer for the dead. So, he said an "Our Father" and hoped it'd be enough. The other died on the way up to the treatment room. The guards abandoned the dead man in the stairwell, and since Murphy hadn't been able to make it back to the infirmary for almost a week the body wasn't removed until the stench became unbearable. Liam begged Murphy to let him go back to his cage, and as soon as he could move without wanting to scream, Murphy relented.

Liam returned to his school work, spending most of his time in the study huts with Frankie. It took him the remainder of his stay at Malone to pass the exam without cheating—more than two years—but pass he did, and when Liam was released in February of 1975, Jack kept his end of the bargain. Six weeks later, the Provos arranged for Liam to begin work as a cab driver in Belfast.

When he got the news he called Mary Kate. He was in the kitchen, and his mother was just around the corner in the sitting room, watching television. It was the best time to call. The little kids were outside playing, and his stepfather wasn't due home for a whole hour. He could hear Eileen in the next room listening to her Bay City Rollers records. A muffled version of "Angel Baby" filtered through the wall for the third time in a row. He waited while one of Mary Kate's many flatmates called her to the phone.

"Liam? Has something happened?"

"I've good news."

"What is it?" She was shouting to be heard over her flatmates who were arguing over whose turn it was to make a call. It sounded like there were fifteen of them and all of them were hopping mad.

Les McKeown was permitted to reach the end of his song and then doomed to repeat it for a fourth time. Liam wished Eileen would let the damned album go to the next song.

"I've work," he said.

"That's wonderful. Look, can I call you tomorrow?"

"No," Liam said. His heart was now pounding in his ears fit to compete with the ruckus on the other end of the line. "I've a question to ask you. It's important."

"Are you sure it can't wait?"

"I'm sure!"

His mother appeared, giving him a look that said, *Do you have to shout?*

"Will you give me a half moment?" he asked Mary Kate. "This is not the kind of question you rush."

His mother blinked.

Mary Kate paused. "Hold on." Her hand must've gone over the receiver because he heard muffled screaming and then everything went quiet.

"Okay. You can ask now."

He swallowed. "It's about the work. I've a cab. The job is in Belfast."

"Oh." Mary Kate sounded disappointed. "Are you coming here?"

"Yes," he said. His heart was really going at it now. Was she unhappy about him moving to Belfast? Is that what he was hearing? Had she met someone and simply not told him? "I was wondering if you'd…." His voice gave out on him.

"If I'd what? Liam, I can't hold up the line. It's not my day for the phone and—"

"I was wondering if you'd… still want to marry me." He got the last out in a rush.

His mother screamed.

"What?" Mary Kate asked on the other end of the line.

"Marry me. Do you still want to marry me?"

There was only silence on the other end of the line, and his heart stopped jumping about and then dropped somewhere around his ankles. Between his mother's hysterical cries he thought he could make out what sounded like weeping.

"Mary Kate?" he asked. "Is something wrong?"

"I thought you'd forgotten."

It was his turn to gape. "I said I wanted to get work first. I've work now. Have you, have you met someone?"

"No. Oh, Liam."

"No, you won't marry me? Or no—"

"Yes! I mean, no, I've not met anyone. Yes, I'll marry you!"

His knees turned to jelly. "Oh, thank God."

"What did she say?" his mother asked.

"She said yes, Ma. She'll marry me."

There was an entire chorus of squeals on the other end of the phone. "When?" Mary Kate asked.

"When would you like? It'll have to be soon if we're to have it at St. Brendan's. But if you'd rather—"

"Let's set it for the moment I get home from Uni for the summer. I don't want to give you a chance of getting away from me again."

"When?"

"A calendar! I need a calendar! Hurry!" He heard a chorus of giggles and shuffling and pages being flipped. "Here. May. Got it. All right. How about the 11th?"

"Sure."

"What did she say?" his mother asked.

"Can you not wait until I'm off the phone?" he asked her.

His mother's lips pressed together in a hard line. "I must know. How am I to get the planning started?"

"The 11th of May," he said. "It's a Sunday."

"No. No. No," his mother said. "Not May!"

"Ma says it can't be May."

"What? Why not?" Mary Kate asked.

"She wants to know why not?"

Frowning, his mother said, "May is a terrible month to get married. It's a bad omen, it is. I'll not have it."

"Ma says—"

Mary Kate sighed. "I heard her. You tell her this is our wedding, and we're getting married on the 11th of May. Liam, it has to be. I don't want to wait. We can't wait. We've waited long enough."

"I know. I know." He moved the receiver from his mouth. "Ma, it has to be the 11th of May. Please. It means a lot to Mary Kate."

"Marry in May and rue the day," his mother muttered. She sighed. "She's the bride. It's her wedding."

Liam decided he didn't care what his mother said. He was twenty years old, and it was one of the happiest days of his life.

Chapter 11

Liam found Father Murray in front of the parochial house. The priest was on his knees and digging in a flowerbed under a window. The sun was out, and it was warm. Liam had gone for a run earlier and as a result felt more relaxed than he had in some time, and yet the tension between his shoulder blades wouldn't let up. He didn't understand it. This was without a doubt one of the happiest times of his life. Still, he couldn't sleep, and his stomach had been in a knot for three days. He was happy to see Father Murray enjoying the weather, though. The air smelled fresh and clean with a hint of the ocean. Liam decided he was going to miss Derry when it came down to it. For a moment he wondered if Belfast was going to be as beautiful in the spring.

"Hello, Father."

Father Murray turned, looking over his shoulder. "Ah, it's you, Liam. How are you on this fine day?"

"I'm well. You're in a good mood."

"I am," Father Murray said, returning to his digging.

"Do you have a wee bit of time, Father?"

"Is it going to require vestments?"

"Not at the moment. Well, eventually, yes. Mary Kate and I are getting married, Father. And I was wondering if you'd do the honours."

Freezing, Father Murray didn't move for what seemed a whole minute. Then he set the little spade he was holding deep into the earth. He didn't turn around. "Married."

"Yes, Father."

"You're quite sure about this?"

"There's never been anyone else. You know that."

Father Murray took a deep breath and released it. "And what does your mother say?"

"I've not seen her from the minute I told her. Spends her time with Mrs. Gallagher, and they've been on the phone with Mary Kate. I think between the three of them they've the thing planned already. As I understand it, all I'm to do is show up, and if they had a way to make a plan of that, they'd have done that too."

Turning at last, Father Murray dusted off his hands. "I'm sensing a bit of frustration."

"I spent three years in Malone, having almost no say over virtually anything you can name. So, why is it I feel I had more control over my life then than I do now?"

Father Murray smiled. "Let's have a drink."

Liam followed Father Murray inside. Standing on the runner, Liam looked into the sitting room. Father Michael glanced up from the book he was reading and nodded a greeting. Light from the window reflected off his reading glasses.

"We'll go to the back garden," Father Murray said, placing a hand on Liam's shoulder. "That way we'll not disturb Father Michael."

They went through the kitchen, stopping long enough to collect two glasses and a bottle and then exited to the back garden. Father Murray sat on the bench in the shade of the ash tree. Liam breathed in the scents of flowers and recently turned earth and instantly felt better. The garden was a good idea. He put a hand against the ash tree while Father Murray poured.

"It seems I'm forever drinking your whiskey," said Liam.

"Not to worry. I don't get much use out of it otherwise." Father Murray held up a glass. "Here," he said, "for the nerves."

"Frankie said women live for this shite and that I should get used to it."

"Who's Frankie?"

"A friend. From Malone. He's my best man."

"Ah. So, you did get a say in something, I see."

"That and in you, I'm hoping. Mary Kate wants you to marry us too. But Mrs. Gallagher is set on Father Michael doing it, and Ma won't go against her." Liam drank the whiskey and was feeling much better by the second short. "You've been a friend to us, Father. I'd rather it were you."

"So," Father Murray said. "You're marrying Mary Kate."

"I am."

"Are you thinking of having children?" The question sounded uncertain. Father Murray's expression was unreadable.

"We are, Father," Liam said. He hesitated to say the rest. He wasn't sure how Father Murray would react. He knew exactly how his mother would handle the news—she wouldn't, and Mrs. Gallagher would no doubt feel the same. "Mary Kate is thinking she'd like to wait until after she's done with Uni."

Father Murray nodded. "And what do you think?"

"I don't really know. I mean, I'm not in a rush, but…." Liam shrugged. "I want to get my feet under me first. Be at the job a while. I got a job, you know. In Belfast."

"Congratulations."

"Thank you, Father."

"That's quite a lot of change all at once."

"Don't I know it," Liam said. He didn't say that half the reason he'd been awake at night was worrying over the volunteering, what it meant and what would be expected. He couldn't tell anyone what he'd done—not even Mary Kate. The IRA was an illegal organization, and as such, membership meant serious prison time. Never mind there was a truce on and had been on and off since January, but it wouldn't last.

"How are you holding up?"

"Well enough."

"But?"

"It's my stepfather."

"Is there something I can do?"

"It's nothing I can't handle," Liam said. "But he won't lay off. And it's getting to a point where I have to spend most of my time away from the flat when he's around. It's worse when Ma isn't there. Calls me jailbird and such when he knows she won't hear. As if he knew fuck all about anything. Ah. Sorry, Father."

"I understand your anger. Have you tried talking to him?"

"Talking? To Patrick? Are you mad?"

"You never know, Liam. Talking can go a long way to resolving problems. Maybe he's upset that you're leaving—"

"Oh, right. More like not leaving soon enough."

"This is a big change for him too. Maybe he's feeling threatened by the amount of attention and time your mother is devoting to the wedding."

"I don't care."

"Promise me you'll be as patient with him as you can."

Liam sighed and shut his eyes. "I will, Father." He set the empty glass on the wooden bench. "So, do you think you can marry us?"

"I would be honored," Father Murray said. "However, I would like to speak to Mary Kate before I make it definite."

"Yes, Father. Sure, Father. Whatever you say, Father."

"Calm down," Father Murray said. "The wedding is a whole three weeks away."

"That isn't nearly soon enough."

Mrs. Foyle's organ music filled St. Brendan's Church to the brim, threatening to push the very roof off the building. It was so loud that the windows rattled, and Liam fought an urge to prop one open only to let out some of the excess noise before the building collapsed around one and all. It hurt his ears, but he knew she was playing out of a favor for his Ma and was only giving it her best. So, he kept the wincing to a minimum.

Dressed in a new yellow suit, his Ma sat in the front pew with Patrick. She'd already cried half her makeup off and was clutching Patrick's arm tight enough to bruise. She sniffed and smiled up at him with an expression that made him want to hug her. This was it, she'd told him the night before, she was losing her little boy to the wider world. Never mind, that he'd been away in prison for a good part of his life. He wasn't going to come home at all anymore and complain of school or fight with his stepfather. She was happy for him, and proud, but everything would be different. The flat would be emptier without him. He'd tried to console her, but it hadn't exactly worked.

Sitting next to her, Patrick stared straight at him. His stepfather's face was as expressionless as fresh concrete. To Liam's surprise, Patrick had paid for a night at a small inn on the edge of town. Liam was grateful but found it hard to believe the burst of generosity wasn't due to coercion.

"Stop your fidgeting, will you?" Frankie said. He'd been released from Malone two weeks after Liam and had driven up from Ballymurphy just to be in the wedding. It'd been natural to ask him to be best man since he'd been Liam's closest friend for the past three years, but now he was doubting the wisdom in the decision for the fifteenth time.

"Why is she not coming out already?" asked Liam.

"Because she bolted from the church. Her mother's on the way up to tell you. Only she can't get past the crush of cousins."

Liam's heart stopped. "She did?"

"Shite, Liam," Frankie said. "It's in a state, you are. It's not even any fun having a joke."

Standing next to them in a row, Father Murray cast a censorious glance at Frankie. The rest of the church was busy watching for the bride.

Liam leaned in close and whispered so Father Murray couldn't hear, "Fuck you, you tosser."

Frankie whispered back, "How is it you landed in a family with so many single women in it? Attractive too, you lucky wee fuck."

It was then that Mary Kate entered the church, and Liam forgot all about

Frankie. She was wearing her grandmother's wedding dress, and the daisies under the veil matched the daisies in her bouquet. Her hair was partially up and curls were set about her face and draped down her shoulders. She looked like Brigitte Bardot. He'd always thought her beautiful—well, since he was old enough to think of such things—and now, she was more than that, and she was his. She could've chosen to be with a fine, educated man with a bright future, a surgeon or barrister. All he had to offer was to be the wife of a Belfast taxi driver.

He felt someone elbow him in the side.

"Close your mouth," Frankie said. "You'll have her think she's marrying an idiot. And then I'll have to step in and—" He straightened his tie. "On second thought, keep your gob open."

Liam closed his mouth. When the time came he kneeled next to Mary Kate in front of the altar. He couldn't help thinking that their future was in his hands now. The knowledge of it weighed on him, settling into his shoulders. For a moment he couldn't breathe, then he snuck a glance at Mary Kate, and she winked at him. He felt better at once. The heaviness hadn't vanished, but it seemed to matter less—to have become more comfortable. He held himself straighter while the Mass droned on around them, knowing it would be one of the most important moments of his life. Father Murray had insisted on a full Mass, and it seemed to take forever. Liam's knees ached, and he repeated his vows a bit too loud. His hands were shaking so hard that when he moved to put the ring on Mary Kate's finger he dropped it but caught it before it hit the ground.

"Sorry," he whispered.

"It's all right," she said. When it came her turn she grabbed the wrong hand and try as he might, he couldn't get her to let it go. So, he let her put it on the wrong finger and then switched it to the correct one while no one was looking. The rest was pretty much a blur, but at last the Mass ended, and Liam kissed her in front of the whole church. He walked down the aisle with her hand in his and went out the door with a big grin on his face.

The reception was at Mary Kate's family's house in the Creggan, and it went as expected with one exception. Once the traditions had been observed and the drinking was well under way, Father Murray appeared at his side.

"Mary Kate, might I have a moment with your husband?"

Mary Kate said, "Sure, Father."

When Liam stood up he stumbled. He hated beer, and Frankie thought him downright unnatural because of it. Liam insisted he wasn't a teetotaler, but Frankie never took him at his word, and therefore had made it his duty to see to it that Liam's glass was never empty.

Mary Kate asked, "Are you all right?"

"I am," Liam said.

"Let's get some water into you and let it mix with the whiskey," Father Murray said.

"I can hold my liquor, Father."

"I'm sure you can," Father Murray said, "but at the moment you're holding yours, Frankie's and possibly half of Derry's as well. Come on."

It took a great deal of concentration to make it across the room and outside. Looking down at the steps, he knew he wasn't going to make it to the street—let alone go for a short walk.

"Sit," Father Murray said. "I'll be back with the water."

"Thanks, Father."

The weather had been fine all day—an omen excellent enough to make his mother happy. He breathed deep and stared up at the night sky. Cloud patches obscured the stars. He didn't have much in the way of friends in Derry, and he certainly wouldn't miss his stepfather. For a moment, he wondered what Belfast was going to be like. He'd never been except when he was on his way to or from a prison. He wouldn't know the city, and he wouldn't know anyone but Mary Kate.

The door behind him clattered.

"Here you are," Father Murray said, handing him a glass of water. "Drink up."

Liam emptied the glass and then set it down on the step. "Is there a problem, Father?"

Father Murray sat next to him, the empty glass resting between them. "No."

"Then why is it I've a feeling you've something to tell me that I'm not going to like?"

"I hope not." Father Murray smiled. "I'm being transferred to a parish in Belfast."

"That's good news, Father. Which?"

"I don't know yet."

Liam waited for the real reason for Father Murray's chat. There was a long pause.

"A family is a big responsibility," Father Murray finally said.

Nodding, Liam said, "Was thinking about that earlier."

"Good," Father Murray said. "You'll keep in mind what I've told you? About staying out of trouble?"

"Yes, Father." *As much as I can,* Liam thought.

"I heard an unpleasant rumor about your taxi association. The one that you'll be joining."

"Did you? What was it?"

"I understand that the owner might hold certain political views."

"Have a look inside the house behind you, Father. Most of them as lives in there hold certain political views, including my wife."

Father Murray sighed. "You can't get involved."

"I need to support my family," Liam said, "There's not many would hire a man who's done three years in Malone. It's what I could get. I told you I'd stay out of it as much as I could, but if the trouble comes to me and mine, what am I to do?"

"Christ said to turn the other—"

"They can do whatever they like to me. They already have," Liam said. The rest was something he'd been meaning to say for a long time, but had been afraid to offend. At the moment, however, the fear was gone, or maybe it was the drink talking. It didn't really matter which. "I'll take the insults and the beatings and the shite living accommodations and the RUC or the fucking army kicking in my door whenever they like and live on because that's how things are. But anyone so much as touches Mary Kate… that I won't stand for. I can't. You understand? God gave her to me. I don't know why. I certainly don't deserve her. But for as long as I have her, I'll protect her and our children with my life's blood. I'm sorry, Father, if I've disappointed you, but that's the way of it."

Father Murray took a deep breath. "You haven't, Liam. May God watch over you both."

"You too, Father," Liam said, feeling a smile creep across his face. "Anyway, there's a truce on. Isn't there? Still, you should be careful yourself. Belfast isn't like Derry, I understand. It's a lot tougher on hippies like you." He felt Father Murray thump him gently on the back of the head.

"Oh, go on, you. Get back inside and get serious about embarrassing yourself in front of your in-laws. It's traditional."

Chapter 12

The West Belfast flat he shared with Mary Kate may have been small and shabby, but it was their own. All things considered, they weren't doing too badly compared to some of their neighbors. He and Mary Kate had his earnings—or would the moment he got settled in his work—as well as her Uni grants which covered the books and tuition. Sitting at their rickety kitchen table loaded with mechanic's manuals, Liam had spent the last hour cleaning the cab's sparkplugs with petrol and struggling with frustration and anger. A glance at his watch told him Mary Kate would be home soon. He wiped his hands on an old rag and prepared to clean up. She hated it when he worked on engine parts at the table, but there wasn't anywhere else he could manage it. Nonetheless, he needed to watch himself. She'd been moody and strange for the past two weeks, and he didn't want to end up in another row.

A small oil painting depicting docked fishing boats hung on the wall opposite. The painting was a wedding gift from his half siblings, although he suspected his Ma had selected it for them. The painting was tasteful and completely out of place next to the thumb-tacked posters he'd collected of local bands. Most of the bands were shite, and he changed the posters frequently to Mary Kate's dismay. They were reminders of upcoming shows he wished to attend. Trapped in a cab for long stretches of time, he had quickly become sick of what was played on the radio and had started making tapes using Mary Kate's old record player—not the best recordings made, but it beat the hell out of the radio. Static beat the hell out of Telly Savalas. The bald fucker couldn't even sing. He read the verses to the music for fuck's sake. Bloody awful, but there it was. Number one on the charts. Sometimes he wondered at the sanity of his fellow human beings.

He looked again at his watch. There'd been a shooting on Sunday, a sixteen-year-old Catholic boy. A BA had gunned him down inside of a car.

It was the twenty-second death of a Catholic civilian since the start of the
IRA truce and tensions were running high. Liam hoped there wouldn't be
another student protest because if there was she'd be late, and he'd end up
worrying himself sick that she'd been nicked.

Relief and love twined themselves around his chest when the door burst
open as expected, and Mary Kate entered, dropping her books onto the
sofa. The usual copy of *The Torchlight* landed on top. She looked sick and
ran to the washroom. The wire brush still in his hand, he followed her, but
she shut the door in his face. He bit back his anger. It was the fourth day
in a row she'd come home ill.

"Sick again?" he asked, trying the handle and finding it locked.

"Go away."

"Enough of this, Mary Kate. You have to go to the doctor." The sounds
of her retching on the other side made him want to throw his shoulder
against the door—to hell with the consequences.

"No," she said, between watery coughs. "We don't have the money, and I
can't miss class. Anyway, you don't go when you should. Why should I?"

"That's different," Liam said. "I'm calling Father Murray."

"No, you're not."

She and Father Murray had had some sort of fight a few days before, and
she had insisted she wasn't speaking to him ever again.

"Dammit! What do you expect me to do?" He slammed a fist against the
door. For a brief moment he considered calling her mother and thought
the better of it. That would be as much as admitting he couldn't handle
Mary Kate, and he wasn't about to do that. Father Murray was the only
friend he had in Belfast.

Father Murray it was.

Liam left the wire brush in the bucket with the plugs and went to the
kitchen to wash his hands which were starting to burn. He glanced down
at the bucket. The flat stank of petrol, but there was no help for it at the
moment. He went out the front door and ran down the stairs—all three
flights—and got to the phone just as Mrs. Black, their neighbor on the
second floor, hung up the receiver.

"Thanks, Mrs. B.," he said.

"Is something wrong?" She was a short middle-aged woman with brown
hair and habitually wore a wispy blue scarf. Since he'd seen her collecting
her mail in her housecoat several times after early morning runs, he was
certain she slept in it.

"Nothing serious. Mary Kate has a cold, I think. Maybe the influ-
enza." He started dialing the number Father Murray had given him the
previous week.

"Summer colds are the worst. I'll just go up to see her."

"There's no need of that, Mrs. B. I've got it in hand."

"Hello?" Father Murray asked on the other end of the line.

Mrs. Black headed up the stairs, muttering to herself about new husbands not knowing shite about anything.

"Thanks, Mrs. B., but she'll be fine." He called up after her but she was already gone.

"Hello? Liam? Is that you?"

Sighing, Liam turned back to the phone. "Yes, Father. It's Mary Kate. She's sick."

"Do you need someone to take her to hospital?"

"No, no. Nothing like that," Liam said. "At least, I don't think so. But I need you to talk her into going to the doctor. She's being stubborn."

There was a short pause. "Don't you think this is something best resolved between the two of you?"

"Father, please. I tried. She'll not see reason," Liam said, pinching the bridge of his nose. "Can you come by tonight? Don't think she'll have the energy to put up a fight. She's throwing up her lunch and possibly breakfast too by the sound."

"I'm on my way."

"Thank you, Father." Liam hung up the phone and took the stairs at a run. By the time he got to the flat Mrs. Black was already sitting next to a rumpled and weary-looking Mary Kate.

"She's fine," Mrs. Black said. "I'll just go get some peppermint tea." She patted Mary Kate's knee.

"Father Murray's on his way," Liam said after Mrs. Black was gone. "Do you have a fever?"

"It's only something I ate," Mary Kate said. She got up from the sofa.

"Sit down," Liam said. "I'll make the dinner, then."

"You're planning on serving ham baps is it?"

"You're in no shape to be cooking. Sit."

She put a hand on her hip. "I'll not speak to him, you know. I don't care what the pair of you do. It isn't going to work."

"I said, sit."

Her eyes narrowed and her lips formed a straight line. He suppressed an urge to kiss her. If she was feeling well enough to argue then she would probably be all right.

"You promised to love, cherish and obey," Liam said. "So, make with the obey."

"William Ronan Munroe Kelly, don't you dare take that tone with me."

There was a knock on the door, and Mrs. Black entered, carrying a cup.

"Here's the tea, dear."

"Thank you, Mrs. B.," Mary Kate said. After glaring at him she sat and accepted the cup.

Liam went to the kitchen to finish the cleaning and then start on the dinner. He packed up the manuals and dumped them onto the bed in the next room. Then he moved the bucket of petrol and plugs into the bath and pulled the curtain. Getting the motor grease and petrol from the table was a bit tougher, and it occurred to him that he should be more careful in the future.

Mrs. Black asked, "Are you certain you're not—"

"Thanks for the tea, Mrs. B.," Mary Kate said. "I'll come by tomorrow and drop off the cup."

There was a spate of fierce whispering. Curious, he looked over to the sitting room. Mary Kate had Mrs. Black by the arm and was leading her to the door.

"I'm not," Mary Kate said. "Definitely not." She opened the door, gently pushed Mrs. Black outside and turned the lock.

"Definitely not what?"

"Having a case of summer pneumonia."

"Oh." He sighed and went into the little kitchen. "Still, you look a bit weak. Why don't you have a lie down? Drink the tea. Relax. Take a wee nap."

"I don't know if I feel like eating a bap tonight."

"What else can I make for you?" He peered around the wall and saw she was lying down. "I can boil water with the best of them. Had quite a lot of practice, you know. As many hours I had on the boiler at Malone, you may even call me a professional."

His humor didn't even get so much as a smile.

She sighed. "Let me just stay here for a minute. I'm feeling better already. It'll pass."

"I'm sure it will."

"No doctors, Liam."

"I heard you. How about some beans? I can heat a can of baked beans. Or soup? Thought I saw a can of oxtail somewhere. I think."

When Father Murray arrived Liam had both the beans and the ham baps ready. Mary Kate was sitting up and looking quite a bit better after her nap. She was still angry. That was obvious by the silence, and her reluctance to join them at the table. Liam pulled out the chair that wobbled the least and offered it to Father Murray.

"We were going to have a fine soufflé, but Bernadette Devlin dropped in," Liam said in an effort to lighten the mood. "On her way to the People's Banquet. And so, Mary Kate gave it over."

Mary Kate slugged him on the arm.

"Are wives supposed to be this abusive, Father?"

After dinner, Liam went down to the car park, opened the taxi's hood and got down to the business of replacing the plugs. Father Murray would need time to work on Mary Kate, and it was just as well to be out of the way. Liam tried to focus on what he was doing and not whatever it was they could be talking about—let alone whatever it was they'd fought about before. Mary Kate was being tight-lipped about the whole thing. Liam couldn't shake the feeling he'd done something to upset her. It had all started a few weeks ago when he'd noticed her missing in the middle of the night and found her sleeping on the sofa. She wouldn't explain no matter how many times he asked her why.

Leaning inside the hulking engine compartment, he lost himself in motor grease and engine parts. At some point, he found himself humming. Working on automobile engines certainly had its frustrations. One bleeding knuckle and a burn on his left hand attested to that—the burn being the result of an unwise attempt to pull the plugs when the engine was still warm. However, there was something soothing about engines too. They were generally not much of a mystery—unlike wives, apparently.

A stray memory of his stepfather tinkering on Sunday afternoons gave him pause. He stopped humming, and his hand tightened on the wrench he was holding. *The old bastard.*

Liam stared down at his battered knuckles and blinked. *No.* It was only that he'd had the cab a week and there was to be an inspection tomorrow, and he wanted to show he was eager to do a good job. That was all. He had nothing in common with—

"Liam?"

Banging his head on the inside of the taxi's hood, he cursed in Irish.

"Didn't mean to startle you," Father Murray said.

"It's all right, Father." Liam rubbed the hurt out of the back of his skull and was about to make a joke when he saw Father Murray's face. "What's wrong?"

"I'm not medically trained, but you were right. Mary Kate needs to see a doctor. She agreed to let me take her tomorrow. After class."

"I can't take off. There's the training and an inspection and—"

"Don't worry. We'll call you after the appointment is over."

Liam nodded and sighed. "What can I do for her? I feel I'm letting her down somehow."

"Just make sure she gets some rest," Father Murray said. "And don't do anything that will worry her."

"Yes, Father. Thank you."

"I'll talk to you tomorrow. Thanks for the dinner."

"You're welcome."

Liam finished with the spark plugs as fast as he could, started the engine to check that all was well and then shut it off, locking the taxi for the night. By the time he got up to their flat he found Mary Kate crying. He gathered her in his arms as gently as he could. "Love, what is it?"

She shook her head, sobbing.

"Oh, it can't be as bad as that," he said. "Only a wee visit to the doctor. Right? I can't go with you, but you'll be fine. Father Murray will see to it—"

That only seemed to make things worse. She buried her face in his chest.

"I'm sorry," he said, feeling helpless to solve the problem. He waited until she was done, wiped the tears from her cheeks and kissed her. To his surprise, she kissed him back—long and hard, and before he knew it they were both lying on the floor, and she had his shirt off, and he had her bra undone. He was starting to think everything was really going well when she stopped him from reaching inside her pants.

"We can't," she said.

"Are you still sick?"

"I don't think so."

He kissed her again as a convincer. She was sufficiently motivated to unbutton his jeans and then pushed him away.

"We can't."

"Come on, Mary Kate. Have some mercy. It's been a whole two weeks. And you feel so good."

"No." She bit her lip and looked on the verge of tears. "Please."

She was afraid. He could see it in her face. So, he rolled away from her at once. "Tell me what's wrong. Please. I'm so tired of being shut out. Is it something I've done?"

She looked away and sighed. "I think I'll go to bed now. Can you... Will you hold me?"

He went to sleep with her snuggled up on his chest, and his bollocks aching, but he was that worried for Mary Kate and prayed that the doctor would find out whatever was wrong—that she'd be all right. It wasn't easy. He couldn't bring himself to trust doctors, but there wasn't an alternative. There'd be someone to help her, he told himself. Had to be. She was going to be all right.

He dreamed of the infirmary at Malone—of lying there with his ribs broken and unable to move without screaming, and her in the cot next to him. She was staring at the ceiling with empty eyes and whispering to him with blue lips that didn't move.

"I told you not to call Father Murray."

He woke with a scream clogging his throat and a hand gripping one of the bars in the iron headboard with all his might.

"Name is Oran MacMahon." The stocky taximan sitting next to Liam put out a hand. There was grease under his fingernails. "What's yours?"

"Liam Kelly." He took Oran's big rough hand and shook it.

The taxi association building was not much more than an old warehouse, but there were makeshift offices facing the street. The walls didn't reach the ceiling and thus, didn't block out the noise of the inspections or the business being done. The place smelled of dirty concrete, iffy milk and engine grease. The tea was fine enough, though.

"You're new," Oran said, and Liam caught the Dublin in his voice.

"This is my second week," Liam said, gripping the edge of the steel chair with his left hand. Everything had been blissfully normal for two months. Never once a sign of the tingling nor the monster under his skin, but now it was back. Everything seemed to be falling apart just when it was supposed to be perfect. "You?"

"Been a mechanic with the association for a year. My brother, Bobby, and I. We have our own shop. You banjax them. I fix them."

The voice that Liam associated with the creature from the Kesh whispered in the back of his brain, *Danger. Kill it.* It made tracking the conversation difficult. He picked up the Styrofoam cup filled with tea and sipped. "That's good."

"Married?"

Kill what? Liam thought back, *Surely not the mechanic?* "I am. Been so for two months."

"Newlyweds, is it?"

Liam nodded. "My wife is a student at Queen's University."

"You must be proud."

"I am, at that. You?" *Danger.* Liam gripped the chair harder with his left hand. Things were bad enough. *Shut it.*

"Married too. Four children. Although, they eat enough for an army." Oran studied him. "Is something wrong?"

"Mary Kate. My wife. She's sick. A friend—" *Not a friend. Danger. Kill—* He put down the cup and shut his eyes to blot out the voice. *Can't have a fucking moment of peace.* "—took her to see a doctor."

"That's a shame," Oran said. "Is it serious?"

"I don't know, yet. My friend is supposed to call as soon as he has news. But he doesn't have this number."

"Ah, well then. Let's get you out of here," Oran said, standing.

"What? I have to wait for the inspection."

"I've a feeling you've passed," Oran said with a wink. "I'll be back with the keys, and then it's back to your flat for a beer."

"We don't have any beer."

Oran shook his head. "Then that's the first order of business. For you can't sit through a wait like that without a bit of something to tide you over."

Liam watched Oran stride out the door and into the back of the warehouse. He was back with Liam's keys in ten minutes.

"You'll take me back here in the morning, yes?" Oran asked. "We've more inspections to finish."

"Sure," Liam said, thankful that he wouldn't have to be alone.

"Come on," Oran said. "There's a shop down the road. You fit to drive?"

Liam nodded.

"That's good. Because I can't."

"You're an automobile mechanic, but you can't drive? Isn't that a bit like a queer gynecologist?"

"Fuck you, you fuck." Oran grinned and tossed him the keys. "Show some respect for your elders."

"Ah, so, you don't drive because you're too decrepit. Is that it?"

"Go on with you."

Climbing into the boxy black taxi, Liam felt better to be heading home early. He probably wouldn't know anything until late in the day, but being close to the flat seemed like a good idea. He wished there was something he could do. *Anything.* But he never seemed to do anything right lately.

Must go to her. Now. Danger.

Shut it, Liam thought back. He slapped his hand onto the cold steel door and held it there until the chill burned the tingling sensation away and then turned the key.

Sitting next to him, Oran gave him a look. "You sure you're in shape to drive?"

"I'm fine. Where to?"

"End of the corner. Turn right."

Liam backed out onto the street.

"Bobby says you're from Derry, and you spent three years in Malone and another in the Kesh."

Taken by surprise, Liam paused. "Was interred three months in the Kesh. Not a year." Wary now, he glanced at Oran. "And how is it Bobby would know?"

"It's part of his job. And mine. Relax, will you?" Oran asked. He leaned in closer and smiled. "*Tiocfaidh ár lá.*"

Liam knew that phrase. Anyone who'd been interred knew it. All Republicans knew it. It meant, *Our day will come.* If Oran was a Peeler it meant he suspected Liam for a volunteer. *Ah, fuck. Not this too. Not now.* His heart hammered at his breastbone. "What did you say?"

"I'm in your unit, you idiot," Oran said. "Never mind the beer. Let's get you home."

When Liam pulled into the car park and cut the engine, Oran hopped out.

"Third floor, right?" Oran asked.

Feeling uncomfortable, Liam asked, "You know where I live?"

"Of course, I do." Oran lowered his voice. "I'm in your fucking unit. So, what'll you have? It's on me."

"If you know that much then you'd know what I fucking drink."

Oran leaned inside the cab. "I've not been watching you quite that long."

"Cider."

"Fair enough," Oran said and then walked down the street.

Liam went up to his flat and grabbed the clean teacup. Then he went down to Mrs. Black's to return it in the hopes that she might have heard something. It turned out she hadn't. She promised to come get him if she heard anything at all. He returned to the flat and paced until there was a knock on the door. It was Oran who carried a bag containing drinks and crisps. Another man was with him. He was taller than Oran and older. Liam guessed he was in his fifties. Where Oran was affable this man was hard—even sullen. His eyes made Liam think of a predator.

"Liam Kelly, this here is Éamon," Oran said. "He's a friend."

"Oh." *That's brilliant. Stand there with your gob open. Some impression you're making,* Liam thought. He stepped back and allowed them in.

"Éamon here is our Lieutenant."

Éamon gave himself a quick tour of the flat, opening the doors to the washroom and then the bedroom and looking inside each.

"It's only us," Liam said. "There's no one else at home."

"Good," Éamon said. "We're here to talk business."

The shopping bag crackled as Oran emptied its contents onto the kitchen table. "You want one, Éamon?"

"Tá."

Oran tossed a can, and Éamon caught it before settling on the sofa.

"What about you, Liam? Are you ready for a pint?" Oran asked.

"Sure." He accepted a bottle and then settled on one of the kitchen chairs, leaving the sofa for Oran and Éamon.

"Have you been briefed on your unit?" Éamon asked.

"Was told I'd be contacted and would learn about my assignment then." Liam shrugged in an attempt to look more at ease than he felt.

Éamon took a long pull from the beer and then nodded. "Been through the training already?"

"I have," Liam said. Frankie had come up from Ballymurphy and taken him away for a few days under the guise of his stag do. Four nights rough camping in the rain and cold wasn't his idea of fun, nor was being shouted at by self-styled drill sergeants, but it had to be done. Of course, Frankie did manage to include one night of revelry at the end, and put in a good effort at ruining him. They'd turned up at his mother's house stinking properly of the drink. It'd taken two days to recover. His mother had given him shite for a week.

"Good." Éamon nodded.

Oran opened the crisps bag with a loud crunch and crackle of packaging and dropped himself on the sofa next to Éamon. "How long you been driving?"

Liam blinked. "The black hack? I told you. Two weeks."

"In general," Éamon said.

"Had my license about a month."

Éamon blew air out of his cheeks.

"Hold on, now," Oran said. "He'll do. I've seen him."

"I'm the one says whether or not he'll do." Éamon frowned. "What is HQ thinking sending us a green recruit?"

Liam tightened his jaw against any declarations of fitness. He didn't know what any of this was about. Sometimes it was best to sit and wait things out. He'd learned that from Jack in Malone. He sipped his pint, feeling the tension in his neck and back.

Oran looked over at him and smiled. "We can give Bobby a go at him for the driving. What do you think?"

Éamon nodded. "Yes. I think that would be wise."

"Driving?" asked Liam. "I'm to drive?"

Oran smiled. "Theoretically, we're to be in the business of raising funds for the cause. Once the truce is over, of course."

"What?"

Oran leaned in closer and whispered, "Bank robbery. You're the wheelman."

"What?"

There was a knock on the door. "Mr. Kelly?" The voice was young and male.

Oran and Éamon froze.

Heart slamming, Liam got up and went to the door but didn't open it. "Aye."

The boy on the other side said, "You've a phone call. Downstairs. Auntie Katherine said I was to come get you."

"Thanks." Turning to Oran, Liam said, "I have to—"

"Go on," Oran said.

Once again, Liam ran down the steps and found the receiver dangling from its cord. He snatched it up. "Hello?"

"Liam?" Father Murray asked.

Danger. "Is she all right?"

"She's going to be fine. Just fine."

Kill—

Sod off, he thought at the voice. The hand holding the receiver was shaking. "Thank God. What was wrong?"

Father Murray paused. "It was a virus. A bad one. Look, they want to keep her in hospital—"

"Hospital? She's in fucking hospital? You said she was going to see a doctor not—"

"She's fine. It's only a precaution for one nigh—"

"Which hospital? Tell me. Where is she?"

"They're only going to keep her overnight and then she'll stay with her Aunt Katie. Here in Carrickfergus."

"Carrickfergus? Why the fuck did you take her up there? Isn't that a Protestant town?" *Danger. She's in danger. Kill it. Find her.*

"Calm down, Liam."

"I'll not calm down. I'm sick of everyone telling me to be fucking calm," he said, banging his fist on the metal shelf below the phone. He grabbed the edge and held on.

"Will you trust me?"

"What kind of a fucking question is that?"

Father Murray sighed. "She said to say that you're only starting your life together, and you've the taxi business to start. She doesn't want you to see her like this. She doesn't want you to worry—"

"It's too fucking late for that."

"I understand," Father Murray said. "Look, she wants to stay with her Aunt Katie until the worst of it is over. Then she'll be home again."

Liam tried to absorb what was happening. He searched his memory for an image of an Aunt Katie from the wedding and couldn't place her, but he'd been drunk that night and the Gallaghers were a much larger family than his own. He was lucky to keep track of her eleven brothers and sisters, and he'd grown up with most of them. He hit the shelf a second time. It left a dent.

"Liam?"

He grabbed the shelf again. His knuckles were white. "I'm here."

"She's going to be all right. I promise. They've given her some medicine, and some fluids. She's sleeping. She's doing much better already. I've a friend here. She'll be safe. I'll stay and keep an eye on her for you. You needn't worry. She's in good hands. The best."

Danger—

Shut it. "Thank you, Father."

"She'll be home soon, and better than ever. You'll see. Now, go on. Get some dinner in you. I'll call again tomorrow."

"Thank you. Goodbye, Father." He hung up the phone and stared at the graffiti scrawled on it, but not really seeing it. Father Murray was right. She'd be fine, and she'd be home in a few days. Liam let go of the shelf, went upstairs and shared a few pints with Oran and Éamon.

Mary Kate came home three days later as promised. He met the two of them on the street in front of the apartment building. She exited the car, pale and weak, and Liam had to suppress an urge to crush her in his arms. Afraid of another misstep, he waited for a signal from her as to how he should react. Father Murray slammed the door of his old VW Beetle with a thump and then pulled a small suitcase from the back.

"Oh, Liam," Mary Kate said. "I missed you so much."

She put her arms around him, and after a while he lifted her up. She felt too light, but she was warm and kissed him on the lips.

"I've got the bags," Father Murray said.

Liam started to carry her up the stairs.

"What are you doing?" she asked, laughing.

"What do you think?"

"I'm not an invalid."

"Not at all," Liam said. "You're my bride, and I'm seeing you home proper. Stop wiggling, or I'll drop you, and I hear that's bad luck."

"Bad luck, indeed. You'll have us both in hospital," she said.

"Aye, well, then. Think they'll let us kip together?"

He took her up all three flights of stairs, over the threshold and into the flat. He was breathing heavy by the end of it, and she laughed the whole way. He didn't let her go until he'd placed her on the sofa. His back and arms felt ready to give out, but it was a good hurt. Father Murray stayed for a cup of tea and then left. He seemed subdued and distant and watched the two of them together with an expression that Liam could have sworn was regret. He decided the situation must have brought up a painful memory, and so, attempted to keep the exuberance down to a minimum until Father

Murray left.

Mary Kate slowly recovered, but the way she moved it was clear she was in a great deal of pain. He did what he could to help without bringing too much attention to what he was doing since whenever he'd slip and show his concern she'd become angry. From time to time Liam caught her weeping. It was hard going, and sometimes the tension between them was bad enough that he wondered if they should've married at all. He was miserable, but then so was she. He spent as much time as he dared outside the flat, tinkering with the taxi or talking to Oran or Father Murray. Oran claimed that the first year of marriage was the hardest and that eventually things would sort themselves out. After a month of abrupt mood swings, arguments and sudden dashes to the washroom she eased back into her old self again. Hopeful that Oran was right and the worst was over, Liam attempted to put the incident out of his mind.

Chapter 13

Andersonstown, Belfast, County Antrim, Northern Ireland
September 1975

Liam stood in the queue outside of The Harp and Drum, holding Mary Kate's hand and breathing out mist clouds. Tugging at his scarf so it would cover the back of his neck, he hoped they wouldn't have to wait long. It was fierce cold and the damp was in the air. He noticed Mary Kate was shivering, put an arm around her and pulled her close. She allowed him to keep his hand on her waist and seemed to be in a good mood. The Harp and Drum was much like any other Belfast pub, but it boasted a private club in the basement that featured up-and-coming rock acts. They were waiting to see The MacMillian Five, a band he'd heard about from a passenger a few days before. Supposedly, the drummer had once played with Bad Company, but Liam often heard talk like that from musicians and most of it was shite. So, there was no way of knowing whether the band would be any good. However, there was a crush to get in, he had enough in his pocket to buy a few pints, and it seemed Mary Kate might be amenable to a bit of fun after if he played her right. All in all, that was a good omen for the evening.

Glancing over his shoulder he noticed the two men in long black coats, hanging around a shop across the street. He'd first seen them when he and Mary Kate were three blocks from the pub. Both wore flat caps and scarves pulled up over the bottom halves of their faces, and appeared overly interested in the crowd gathered in front of the pub. Liam would've been concerned about a Loyalist attack but for the fact that he could've sworn one of them was wearing a priest's collar. He didn't like the look of either man, regardless.

Enemy, the black thing in Liam's head whispered.

Without thinking, he put a hand inside his pocket and grasped the steel lighter he'd taken to carrying. Mary Kate had painted a tri-color on the side and had declared it the People's Lighter by way of a joke when he'd refused to loan it to her the night before.

"Are you not going in?" the big man at the door asked.

Liam paid the man, and he and Mary Kate went down the narrow steps into the club. The room was small, smelled of stale cigarettes and old vomit, and the bare concrete walls were wet with condensation. The bar positioned on the left wasn't much more than a counter top with a couple of barstools stuck in front—not that he could've grabbed a seat anywhere. The place was packed. The stage at the front of the room took up half the space, and young people holding various drinks milled close to the platform which was apparently a tight squeeze for five musicians and their gear. At the moment, the Stones were blaring out of the speakers, and Mick Jagger was bemoaning the fact that he didn't always get what he wanted.

"Let's go over there," Mary Kate shouted in his ear.

Liam nodded, and he took her hand, pushing his way to the back of the room through the crush of long-haired men and their dates. With so many people crammed into such a small space it was warm in spite of there being no heat. He loosened his scarf. By some miracle he located an abandoned table—a tiny round thing made from furniture scraps. There were no chairs but at least they wouldn't have to hold their drinks the entire night.

"What'll you have, love?"

She grinned. "I'd like a short. Make it Bushmills."

"That's my girl." He wove his way back through the crowd to the bar. It took a while to get the barman's attention, and by the time he returned to her he had to tell some drunken tosser to bugger off and get away. It almost came to blows and would have but for the tosser's friend.

"Taximan," the friend said, pointing to Liam. "Black Hack."

The tosser stared and swallowed. "Oh, right. Very sorry, sir."

The pair of them vanished into the crowd.

Mary Kate shook her head. "I tried to tell him I had a date, but he wouldn't listen. Why do they always have to hear it from another male?"

Liam reached over and pushed a curl from her face. "Can't blame him. It's fucking beautiful, you are." He let his hand move down her back and then a bit lower. He moved closer and spoke into her ear. "I don't suppose there's any chance of me getting you drunk and removing your—"

"Liam!" She slapped his hand away from her thigh and tugged down her skirt, but she was smiling and it gave him hope.

The band began playing, and by the sound, they weren't half-bad. The guitarist had delusions of Jimmy Page. So, Liam sipped his whiskey and watched the crowd. A few of them seemed to be unaware that Ziggy Stardust and the whole peace and love scene was dead, and that if it was dead anywhere it was definitely West Belfast, but he supposed there wasn't any harm in giving it a go. Liam was getting into the music and starting to relax when he spied the two men from outside. Neither had unbuttoned their coats or taken off their scarves. They seemed to be glaring at him in particular, but it was difficult to tell.

Danger. Enemy. Get away. Must leave.

If they were UVF—Ulster Volunteer Force, and the two of them had guns, they'd have a hell of a time bringing them up in this crowd. On the other hand, if they were planting a bomb—

Leave. Must leave. Get out of here. Now. Before they come for us.

Liam's heart staggered and then raced. He turned to tell Mary Kate that they needed to go when he spied Father Murray.

"What's he doing here?"

"Who?" Mary Kate asked.

"Father Murray. He's over there. Do you see him?"

Father Murray had moved up to the bar and was speaking to the shorter of the two men in the wool coats.

"Maybe he likes rock music," Mary Kate said and shrugged.

"Do you think so?"

The shorter man began arguing with Father Murray and gave him a shove.

"Stay here. I'll be right back." Liam didn't wait for her answer. He made his way to the bar.

"—not in support of your little experiment."

Father Murray shouted back. "Then the Prelate will have to bring it up with Bishop Avery himself."

The taller man touched the shorter one on the shoulder and then bobbed his head in Liam's direction. His eyes were hard. Father Murray turned around.

Enemy. Kill them. Rip their throats out. Now. For once Liam didn't violently disagree with the thing in the back of his head. "Are these men bothering you, Father?" Liam asked, fist at the ready.

"Why, hello." Fear flickered across Father Murray's scholarly features. "There's no problem at all. Liam, I'd like to introduce you to Father Dominic and Father Christopher. We're from the same Jesuit Order."

Neither man looked anything like a priest. If anything, they reminded Liam of certain sentenced prisoners from Malone—the ones known for trouble of the worst kind. Father Dominic, the shorter of the two, had a long scar across the bridge of his nose. He didn't seem the sort you'd want to make angry, and by the look of it, Father Murray had just made him very angry indeed. Nonetheless, Father Dominic gave a grudging nod by way of a greeting as did Father Christopher. Father Christopher gave the impression that he thought Liam was something less than human.

"What the fuck are you looking at?" Liam asked.

Father Christopher said, "Go to hell, demon."

"What did you call me?" Liam asked.

"They were just leaving," Father Murray said, placed a restraining hand on Liam's shoulder. He spoke to Father Dominic. "Please give the Prelate my regards."

"One day," Father Dominic said, shoving a finger at Father Murray's chest and making him stumble, "you're going to be very sorry for this, Joe. Very sorry, indeed. You've gone soft."

"I'm flattered by your concern for my well-being," Father Murray said.

The pair shoved past, bumping into Liam on the way out. A blinding flash of pain shot through Liam's shoulder, and Father Murray put out a hand to steady him.

"You should go back to Mary Kate and enjoy your evening," Father Murray said.

"Who were they?"

"No one you need worry about," Father Murray said. "But if you should see them again… stay away from them. And call me. Understand?"

"Why?"

"I have to go," Father Murray said. "We'll talk about this tomorrow."

Liam got the impression he was in a hurry to get outside and that there was some unfinished business. "All right, Father."

Father Murray moved toward the exit and ran up the stairs. Liam glanced over at Mary Kate to make certain she was well. She appeared to be enjoying the music. He thought again about Father Murray being shoved and decided to risk going outside for a bit. Father Murray was firmly in support of non-violence which, to Liam's experience, didn't work well when the opposition was firmly in support of the opposite. He stopped to talk to the man watching the door.

"Need some air. Getting back in a problem? My wife is still inside."

The big man looked at him, exhaled a cloud of cigarette smoke at the ground and shook his head.

"Thanks, mate." Liam rushed up the stairs. Scanning the street, he didn't see Father Murray or the other two priests. He was about to head back down the steps when he heard someone shout. It came from somewhere on the right. He turned and jogged that direction, but before he reached the corner he spied them fighting in an alley. It took him a moment to register that that was indeed what was happening. Liam looked around until he spotted an old board in some rubble. He grabbed it, hefted it and moved closer. What he saw next gave him pause a second time.

Father Murray wasn't getting a good kicking as Liam had thought. All t the fuck are you looking at?" Liam asked.

r Christopher said, "Go to hell, demon."

at did you call me?" Liam asked.

y were just leaving," Father Murray said, placed a restraining hand
m's shoulder. He spoke to Father Dominic. "Please give the Prelate
ards."

e day," Father Dominic said, shoving a finger at Father Murray's chest
aking him stumble, "you're going to be very sorry for this, Joe. Very
indeed. You've gone soft."

n flattered by your concern for my well-being," Father Murray said.
pair shoved past, bumping into Liam on the way out. A blinding
of pain shot through Liam's shoulder, and Father Murray put out a
to steady him.

u should go back to Mary Kate and enjoy your evening," Father Mur-
aid.

ho were they?"

o one you need worry about," Father Murray said. "But if you should
hem again… stay away from them. And call me. Understand?"

hy?"

have to go," Father Murray said. "We'll talk about this tomorrow."

am got the impression he was in a hurry to get outside and that there
some unfinished business. "All right, Father."

ather Murray moved toward the exit and ran up the stairs. Liam glanced
r at Mary Kate to make certain she was well. She appeared to be enjoy-
the music. He thought again about Father Murray being shoved and
ided to risk going outside for a bit. Father Murray was firmly in sup-
rt of non-violence which, to Liam's experience, didn't work well when
opposition was firmly in support of the opposite. He stopped to talk
the man watching the door.

"Need some air. Getting back in a problem? My wife is still inside."

The big man looked at him, exhaled a cloud of cigarette smoke at the
ound and shook his head.

"Thanks, mate." Liam rushed up the stairs. Scanning the street, he didn't
Father Murray or the other two priests. He was about to head back
wn the steps when he heard someone shout. It came from somewhere
the right. He turned and jogged that direction, but before he reached the
rner he spied them fighting in an alley. It took him a moment to register
at that was indeed what was happening. Liam looked around until he
potted an old board in some rubble. He grabbed it, hefted it and moved
loser. What he saw next gave him pause a second time.

Father Murray wasn't getting a good kicking as Liam had thought. All

Chapter 13

Andersonstown, Belfast, County Antrim, Northern Ireland
September 1975

Liam stood in the queue outside of The Harp and Drum, holding Mary Kate's hand and breathing out mist clouds. Tugging at his scarf so it would cover the back of his neck, he hoped they wouldn't have to wait long. It was fierce cold and the damp was in the air. He noticed Mary Kate was shivering, put an arm around her and pulled her close. She allowed him to keep his hand on her waist and seemed to be in a good mood. The Harp and Drum was much like any other Belfast pub, but it boasted a private club in the basement that featured up-and-coming rock acts. They were waiting to see The MacMillian Five, a band he'd heard about from a passenger a few days before. Supposedly, the drummer had once played with Bad Company, but Liam often heard talk like that from musicians and most of it was shite. So, there was no way of knowing whether the band would be any good. However, there was a crush to get in, he had enough in his pocket to buy a few pints, and it seemed Mary Kate might be amenable to a bit of fun after if he played her right. All in all, that was a good omen for the evening.

Glancing over his shoulder he noticed the two men in long black coats, hanging around a shop across the street. He'd first seen them when he and Mary Kate were three blocks from the pub. Both wore flat caps and scarves pulled up over the bottom halves of their faces, and appeared overly interested in the crowd gathered in front of the pub. Liam would've been concerned about a Loyalist attack but for the fact that he could've sworn one of them was wearing a priest's collar. He didn't like the look of either man, regardless.

Enemy, the black thing in Liam's head whispered.

Without thinking, he put a hand inside his pocket and grasped the steel lighter he'd taken to carrying. Mary Kate had painted a tri-color on the side and had declared it the People's Lighter by way of a joke when he'd refused to loan it to her the night before.

99

"Are you not going in?" the big man at the door asked.

Liam paid the man, and he and Mary Kate went down the narrow steps into the club. The room was small, smelled of stale cigarettes and old vomit, and the bare concrete walls were wet with condensation. The bar positioned on the left wasn't much more than a counter top with a couple of barstools stuck in front—not that he could've grabbed a seat anywhere. The place was packed. The stage at the front of the room took up half the space, and young people holding various drinks milled close to the platform which was apparently a tight squeeze for five musicians and their gear. At the moment, the Stones were blaring out of the speakers, and Mick Jagger was bemoaning the fact that he didn't always get what he wanted.

"Let's go over there," Mary Kate shouted in his ear.

Liam nodded, and he took her hand, pushing his way to the back of the room through the crush of long-haired men and their dates. With so many people crammed into such a small space it was warm in spite of there being no heat. He loosened his scarf. By some miracle he located an abandoned table—a tiny round thing made from furniture scraps. There were no chairs but at least they wouldn't have to hold their drinks the entire night.

"What'll you have, love?"

She grinned. "I'd like a short. Make it Bushmills."

"That's my girl." He wove his way back through the crowd to the bar. It took a while to get the barman's attention, and by the time he returned to her he had to tell some drunken tosser to bugger off and get away. It almost came to blows and would have but for the tosser's friend.

"Taximan," the friend said, pointing to Liam. "Black Hack."

The tosser stared and swallowed. "Oh, right. Very sorry, sir."

The pair of them vanished into the crowd.

Mary Kate shook her head. "I tried to tell him I had a date, but he wouldn't listen. Why do they always have to hear it from another male?"

Liam reached over and pushed a curl from her face. "Can't blame him. It's fucking beautiful, you are." He let his hand move down her back and then a bit lower. He moved closer and spoke into her ear. "I don't suppose there's any chance of me getting you drunk and removing your—"

"Liam!" She slapped his hand away from her thigh and tugged down her skirt, but she was smiling and it gave him hope.

The band began playing, and by the sound, they weren't half-bad. The guitarist had delusions of Jimmy Page. So, Liam sipped his whiskey and watched the crowd. A few of them seemed to be unaware that Ziggy Stardust and the whole peace and love scene was dead, and that if it was dead anywhere it was definitely West Belfast, but he supposed there wasn't any harm in giving it a go. Liam was getting into the music and starting to

relax when he spied the two men from outsid[e] their coats or taken off their scarves. They seem[ed] particular, but it was difficult to tell.

Danger. Enemy. Get away. Must leave.

If they were UVF—Ulster Volunteer Force, and they'd have a hell of a time bringing them up in hand, if they were planting a bomb—

Leave. Must leave. Get out of here. Now. Before t[hey]

Liam's heart staggered and then raced. He turn[ed] they needed to go when he spied Father Murray.

"What's he doing here?"

"Who?" Mary Kate asked.

"Father Murray. He's over there. Do you see him[?]"

Father Murray had moved up to the bar and was of the two men in the wool coats.

"Maybe he likes rock music," Mary Kate said and

"Do you think so?"

The shorter man began arguing with Father Mu[rray] shove.

"Stay here. I'll be right back." Liam didn't wait for his way to the bar.

"—not in support of your little experiment."

Father Murray shouted back. "Then the Prelate will with Bishop Avery himself."

The taller man touched the shorter one on the should[er] his head in Liam's direction. His eyes were hard. Fath[er] around.

Enemy. Kill them. Rip their throats out. Now. For once Li[am] disagree with the thing in the back of his head. "Are the[y bothering] you, Father?" Liam asked, fist at the ready.

"Why, hello." Fear flickered across Father Murray's s[?] "There's no problem at all. Liam, I'd like to introduce you t[o] and Father Christopher. We're from the same Jesuit Orde[r]

Neither man looked anything like a priest. If anything Liam of certain sentenced prisoners from Malone—the trouble of the worst kind. Father Dominic, the shorter o[f] long scar across the bridge of his nose. He didn't seem the to make angry, and by the look of it, Father Murray had very angry indeed. Nonetheless, Father Dominic gave a gr[?] way of a greeting as did Father Christopher. Father Christ[opher] impression that he thought Liam was something less than h[?]

three priests were standing over a man lying on the ground. Father Dominic held a blood-soaked dirk. His coat was torn, and he held his left arm at an awkward angle. Liam smelled blood, and something else. Something that wasn't right. It stank of decay and long death. He knew the difference between fresh blood and old. He'd become familiar with both in the infirmary at Malone. The stinking black puddle forming under the man on the ground slowly expanded, and he saw Father Christopher lift his boot to avoid the stain.

What the fuck just happened? Am I really seeing this? Or have I finally gone mad? "Father?" Liam asked and regretted speaking at once.

Father Dominic whirled, brandishing the dirk. "Drop the weapon, spawn."

"Don't," Father Murray said. "He's an innocent, I'm telling you." He stepped in front of Father Dominic.

"Drop the club." Father Christopher placed a hand inside his coat.

Liam blinked. "What?"

"Liam, do as they say," Father Murray said, holding his arms out as if shielding him.

Father Dominic moved closer, causing Father Murray to shuffle backward in order to keep his position. Father Christopher edged toward Liam's left. Both exuded a professional menace that Liam recognized at once. A broken board wasn't much defense against a long knife—particularly when wielded by someone who knew what to do with one, but at least it was something. Drop the board, and he'd be at their mercy, and they didn't appear to have mercy on their minds. Liam worried about Father Murray getting in the way. The beast squatting in the back of his brain pressed for freedom to attack. *Kill all of them. Now. Now.*

"Liam! Please! The peaceful solution! It's the only way!"

Reluctantly trusting Father Murray, Liam dropped the splintered board and put his hands in the air. "There. It's done. I'm sorry," he said. "Thought they were attacking you. Who is that man? Why did they kill him?"

"That thing isn't a man anymore than you are," Father Dominic said.

He knows what we are. Kill him. "What?"

"Please, Dominic," Father Murray said, "put the knife away." He was so close now he was practically standing on Liam's toes. "I won't allow this. You know I won't. I can't."

Father Christopher folded his arms across his chest and frowned.

"If you continue, I will send in a report," Father Murray said. "And neither you nor the Prelate will like the resulting inquiry."

Sighing, Father Dominic's shoulders slumped. "Get him out of here."

"Come on, Liam." Father Murray tugged at Liam's arm.

"I don't understand."

"I'll explain everything," Father Murray said. "First, let's let them do what they must."

Crouching, Father Christopher reached into a pocket and produced a clear vial. He uncorked it and muttered something that sounded like Latin as he poured the contents on the dead man's head. Steam rose off the body.

Liam allowed Father Murray to pull him away. Priests were killing people in the streets. *Priests.* And Father Murray wasn't doing anything to stop it, but then, what could he do? "I thought they were attacking you."

"That's all right. I understand, but you needn't have worried. I had everything under control," Father Murray said. "For now, I want you to go back inside. We'll discuss this in detail tomorrow. Don't tell Mary Kate, whatever you do. It will only upset her."

"I won't," Liam said. "Father?"

"Yes?"

"What did he mean when he said that man wasn't a man any more than I was?" *They know about us. They'll come for us. We should've killed them.* Liam shook his head to dislodge the monster's warnings.

Father Murray cast a glance over his shoulder. "Overzealousness is a danger in any policing force."

"Father Dominic and Father Christopher are Peelers?"

"Of a sort, yes."

They stopped in front of The Harp and Drum. Electric guitar music wailed its way up from the underground nightclub. It was a good rendition of Elvis's "Jailhouse Rock." Liam shivered inside his coat. "Why did you let them kill that man?"

"Just go inside," Father Murray said with a pained expression. "We'll talk about this tomorrow."

Liam nodded, checking the empty street for trouble. "Be careful, Father. You should keep a little something with you. To protect yourself. Those two—"

"I'll be fine, Liam. Goodnight."

"Goodnight, Father."

Trotting halfway down the steps, Liam turned to watch Father Murray go. He tugged up the collar on his coat and walked down the street, a lone man in the darkness. Liam sighed and then re-entered the club. He found Mary Kate was still at the table and this time she was alone.

"You were gone for a while," she said.

He nodded. "Had a talk with Father Murray."

"That's nice," she said. "But you know, I've a problem."

"You do?"

"You see, this very attractive man made a particularly lewd suggestion. Something I'm sure my mother wouldn't approve of one bit," she said. "But I've been sitting here thinking about whether or not I'd take him up on his offer anyway. I've had two shorts, after all. Trouble is—" She showed him her glass. It was empty. "He up and vanished on me. I'm here all alone. I don't suppose you're interested in finishing off where he started?"

Liam raised an eyebrow. "His loss is my gain."

"Strange, that was my very thought."

He went back to the bar, reassured by the return to normalcy, ordered two more shorts and got serious about seducing his wife. The band got better as they played and finished the set an hour later. Then he and Mary Kate staggered home together. He tried not to think about the two priests, and what they might or might not know about the beast living inside him. More than anything, he wanted to feel normal. He took Mary Kate's hand, and kissed it. If anyone made him feel sound, it was her—even if things had been a bit rocky of late. She didn't treat him as if he were a dangerous creature. She wasn't afraid of him. She trusted him, even believed in him. She stopped, got up on her toes, placed a hand on the front of his jeans and gave him a great scorcher of a kiss. That was enough to banish any unwanted specters of guilt, and gave him high hopes for a most interesting end to the evening, but the moment they entered their flat she headed directly to the washroom.

"Do you really have to do that now?"

"Yes," she said, slurring the word. "Def-definitely."

"You're going to tell me that you spent half the night giving me a hard-on the likes of which I've not had in a week, and you didn't check before we left?"

She placed the thermometer under her tongue and winked.

"You're fucking evil, you are," he said. "I should never have married you."

Putting her hands over her ears, she shut her eyes and hummed out of key. He went to the kitchen and found the whiskey they saved for special occasions. He supposed not being killed by a Peeler-priest was occasion enough and poured himself a glass. Then he went back to the washroom. She was squinting at the little mercury line. Ever since she'd gotten sick the thermometer had become an obsession—twice a day, every day, she took her temperature. He was beginning to really hate the damned thing.

"Well?"

A sly smile crept onto her face. "Oh, I don't know. It's hard to say."

"Why do you do this to me every time?" Liam asked. "Why can't we do things like we used to?"

"T-told you," she said. "I'm not getting preg—" She hiccupped. "—pregnant until I'm through Uni."

He sighed. "Couldn't we risk it the once? Please?"

"No."

"Fine. Well? Is it to be the headache or not?"

She bent over the sink and tilted the thermometer into the light with exaggerated care. Her short skirt rode up on her hips, giving him a nice view. It was then he noticed she wasn't wearing any underpants. That was his Mary Kate — freezing cold outside and there she was. No pants. Because she knew exactly what that did to him.

He tossed back the last of the whiskey and set the glass down. "Jesus, Mary and Joseph, will you please—"

She turned to face him with a knowing smile. "Will I please what?"

"Give me that damned thing. I'm going to fucking break it."

"No!" She jerked the thermometer away, laughing. He tried to get it from her, but drunk as she was the lithe minx somehow managed to keep it just out of his reach.

He tried another tactic and faked a grab for the offending glass wand and then threw his arms around her. "Got you now." Picking her up, he carried her out of the washroom and then threw her onto the bed. It was a short toss as the end of the mattress wasn't all that far from the bedroom door.

"Stay-stay back," she said, holding up the thermometer as if it were some sort of talisman. "Foul fiend."

"Ah, well. That's where you've gone wrong," he said, kicking off his boots. "Saw 'Dance of the Vampires' once, I did. Turns out I have to believe in order for it to work. And if there's one fucking thing I don't believe in, it's that."

"Shite."

He dove for her.

As it turned out she didn't have a headache after all.

"Have you ever seen something you're certain couldn't possibly exist?" Father Murray asked.

Liam blinked. They were in the The Harp and Drum—only this time in the pub proper. There weren't many people around. It was in the middle of the day, and Liam was taking a short break for a few pints and some chips before the evening rush of fares. "Honestly?"

Father Murray nodded. "You've no need to worry. I'll not think you mad."

Gazing out the bull's eye pane at a watery version of West Belfast, Liam's thoughts wandered back to the times when he was sure he'd hallucinated—the day he was first arrested, the Kesh, that day when the thirteen died. He sighed. "Aye, I have."

"May I ask what it was?"

Liam decided to start with the least troublesome of the lot—not that he'd have talked about the Kesh. He'd never even told Mary Kate about that, and he had every intention of dying before ever speaking of it. "I saw a Para with teeth filed to points."

It was Father Murray's turn to blink in surprise.

"Saw him twice. The first time he wasn't a Para. Was in the crowd when I was arrested on Aggro Corner. The second time he said something mad and then fair stove my head in."

Father Murray frowned. "Have you seen him since?"

"No."

"What did he say to you?"

"I don't exactly remember. Something about the mac Cumhaill. Didn't make any fucking sense at all. To tell you the truth, I half-believed I didn't remember it rightly because he cracked my damned skull."

"Are you sure? Fionn mac Cumhaill? Mythical leader of the Fianna? Caught and ate the salmon of knowledge? Had two nephews that were turned into hounds by a vengeful fairy Queen?"

"Sceolán and—"

"Bran." Father Murray blinked and swallowed.

Liam shrugged. "I know what it sounds like." He hadn't put that together before. He knew the stories because his Aunt Sheila used to tell them to him. Had it been her way of hinting at his real father's name? Or was it something else? Did the whole family know all along, and him the only one who didn't? He'd searched the phone directories when he'd returned to Derry back in February. There was no Bran Monroe listed anywhere. Then came the training and the wedding and what with one thing or another, he hadn't thought of his real father in months. Either the man had no phone or was dead—most likely dead.

But why had both his mother and his Aunt used fairy stories to tell him about his father?

If that's what Aunt Sheila was doing at all. "You must think me mad," Liam said.

"That's all right. I asked, didn't I?" Father Murray sat in silence for a few minutes. He seemed disturbed, and it frightened Liam. Then Father Murray took a deep breath. "Do you remember when I told you about my Mary?"

"Your fiancée?"

"Yes," Father Murray said. "I saw something that night. Something the constables didn't believe. They insisted that I'd been drunk which only made matters worse."

"I'm sorry, Father."

Father Murray shook his head. "We were out for a walk, she and I. We'd just had dinner with my mother. It was a fine night, and I had her hand in mine. Then I saw this man standing in the walk. He was large and looked like he had a hump on his back."

Confused, Liam nodded anyway.

"He attacked me. He came right at me with these… these claws."

He knows, Liam thought and for a moment he couldn't breathe. He fished the lighter from his pocket and squeezed it with all his might under the table where Father Murray couldn't see. *What the fuck am I going to do? Either I'm mad, or I'm cursed. Either way, will he let Father Dominic kill me?*

"She screamed and threw herself in front of me. I couldn't stop her. It hit her instead. People came running, but before they did—" Father Murray sipped from his pint and whispered, "The creature sprouted giant wings and flew away." He reached inside his coat and pulled out a long charcoal black feather. "I didn't imagine it, Liam. And I wasn't drunk. If you want to know why I became a Jesuit, this is it."

Liam felt his mouth drop open. Reaching out with a finger, he stroked the feather's ragged vane and shuddered.

"That man last night," Father Murray kept his voice low. "He was a fallen angel. A demon. Dominic, Christopher and myself, we're members of the same Order. It exists to protect humanity from the Fallen. We fight in secret so that humanity can live without fear. Every one of us has lost someone. You'll have to forgive Dominic—"

"Fight, you said. You fight?"

Father Murray looked away. "In my own way. Yes."

"Father Dominic, he thinks I'm one of those… things?" Liam had trouble speaking the question. *Experiment,* he thought, *Father Dominic mentioned an experiment.*

"You're not. I know you're not. I've been watching you for years, Liam."

"Because you thought I was a—a Fallen?" He wanted to ask more but was terrified of the answers he'd get. If he were perfectly honest, he didn't want to know about the monster living under his skin—not any more than he already did, and he certainly didn't want Father Murray to know if he didn't already.

"You've no need to worry." Father Murray took another sip from his pint glass.

Liam tried not to show his relief.

"Father Dominic is very devoted to the Order, but he's been at war for a very long time," Father Murray said. "I'm afraid he sees enemies where they don't exist." He took the feather from the table and tucked it back inside his coat. "I'd consider it a great favor if you didn't tell anyone about this."

"It's not like anyone would believe me, would they?"

"The Order goes to some lengths to remain a secret. I've risked much in telling you what I have."

"You can trust me, Father."

"I knew I could."

Chapter 14

"Joseph, would you mind explaining what exactly you had in mind when you interfered with one of our field units?" Father Thomas asked, entering St. Agnes's parochial house. He closed his umbrella and shook out the excess water on the doorstep. He was an overweight man with piercing brown eyes and a large nose. As Bishop Avery's assistant, he was efficient and an excellent ally. He was also Father Murray's direct supervisor within the Order.

Accepting Father Thomas's hat and coat, Father Murray said, "It couldn't be helped."

Father Thomas arched a heavy eyebrow.

"Please, come into the sitting room. Have some tea. Let me explain," Father Murray said.

After assuring that the sitting room door was closed and the tea was satisfactory, Father Murray settled in one of the wing-backed chairs and prepared himself for what would come next.

"We can't bicker amongst ourselves, Joseph. We simply can't afford it."

Father Murray said, "I didn't intend to cause a disagreement. But they'd made a mistake in their intended target."

"Your pet project?"

"He's a peaceful lad."

"He's been imprisoned twice for rioting, is the probable cause of a death of one prison guard—"

"That was an attack by a rabid guard dog. You saw the report. The stories were proven to be only rumors. He had nothing to do with—"

"—and is now a member of an association with a decidedly Republican slant."

"He married into a Nationalist family. There's no crime in that. He's not involved in politics. He's non-violent," Father Murray said. "He understands right from wrong—even loyalty. He's not like the other children of the Fallen. Surely, Bishop Avery sees that?"

"Non-violent? He threatened Father Dominic with a club."

"He thought I was in danger. He put it down when I told him to do so."

Father Thomas took a sip of his tea and set down the cup. "Your position isn't popular among the Order."

"We must be certain of what we're doing. There are lives at stake."

"My point exactly. Human lives."

Father Murray sighed. "I understand my reputation among the Order—"

"Your loyalty and service aren't in question," Father Thomas said. "You've completed many difficult assignments in less than ideal situations and maintained your reason. Few can say that. However, some say this is the very thing that is affecting your judgment. You're too close to your subject."

"Compassion is what Christ—"

"This a war, Joseph."

"All the more reason to take care."

Father Thomas pinched the bridge of his nose and took a deep breath. "I will tell the others to keep their distance and let you do what you must. But no more threats. The Bishop won't tolerate the development of factions. Do you understand me?"

Staring into his cup, Father Murray nodded. "I want permission for another contact."

"What?"

"I've reason to believe it will be low risk."

Father Thomas gave him a worried look. "Why do I have the feeling I'm not going to like this?"

"Please. It's the next necessary step. He's already made contact once—"

"You've never reported—"

"I did. Years ago. It wasn't a direct contact, but close enough that I feel this is a good risk."

"Why now?"

"I received information yesterday that confirms there may be factions among the Fallen," Father Murray said. "We can take advantage of this situation. We both know we need every advantage we can get. Think of the intelligence opportunities alone."

Father Thomas sipped his tea. "Very well. Where?"

"Derry."

"I'll inform the bishop. But that report will have to be on my desk the day after your return, and you will take precautions. Do you understand?"

Father Murray nodded. "Thank you."

"If anything goes wrong you will terminate the contact, or call in the nearest field unit. No more dithering. Do you hear me?"

"Hello? Is Mrs. Kelly there?" Father Murray asked, speaking into the telephone. It was located in the hallway next to the room Father Andrew used as a study. It wasn't the most ideal situation for a delicate conversation, but luckily, no one else was home at the moment.

"Ma is here, but she can't come to talk to you," said the young female voice on the other end of the line. "She's in the bog."

A voice shouted in the background. "Moira!"

"Hello, Moira," Father Murray said and attempted to keep the laughter from his voice. "This is Father Murray. Perhaps I should ring back."

There was a clatter as he assumed the receiver was dropped. "Ma! 'Tis Father Murray!"

He contemplated ringing off but the receiver was picked up before he could do so.

"Hello?"

"Kathleen?"

"I'm very sorry, Father," Kathleen said. "Moira knows better than to say things like that."

"It's quite all right," he said, settling into the chair positioned against the stairs. "How are the children?"

"Fine. Just fine. Growing like weeds," Kathleen said. "And how are you and your family, Father?"

"Fine. Fine. Aunt Catherine had a cold, but she's over it now." He paused. "I saw your Liam yesterday."

"How is he? I speak to Mary Kate once a week, but he's not rang for two."

"He's fine," Father Murray said. "Happy. Busy too. I hear the taxi business is doing well. Will tell him to ring you right away." He wasn't sure how to approach the actual purpose of the conversation.

"Thank you, Father."

"There is something I need to speak to you about in regards to Liam."

"Is something wrong? Has he not been to Mass? Has he done something—"

Father Murray smiled. "No. No. It's nothing like that. I'm not sure exactly how to say this. Do you remember discussing his... father?"

There was a pause. "Yes. Of course."

"You said his name was Bran?"

"Yes, Father."

"Do you happen to know if he has a connection to someone who claims to be Fionn mac Cumhaill?"

Another long pause stretched over the telephone line. "I'm not sure I can discuss that over the phone, Father."

"I understand. Would it be possible to meet sometime during the week?" Father Murray asked. "I can drive up to Derry and stay for a few days. It's important."

"Yes. Certainly, Father. I'm free most mornings. The children are in school then, you see."

"Would this Wednesday morning be a good time, then?"

"Yes."

"I'll ring you as soon as I get there. We can meet at St. Brendan's, if you like." He hesitated. "I was wondering. When last we spoke you said you had a means of contacting him."

"I've not seen him in two years, Father." Her voice was tight.

"I see," he said. "I'm sorry. Discussing the topic must be very difficult for you."

She sighed. "It's actually a comfort to speak with someone who doesn't think I'm completely mad. Sometimes I begin to wonder whether or not I've imagined the whole thing. And then he comes back—" She sniffed.

"I'm so sorry," he said. "I didn't mean to upset you."

Laughing, she sniffed again. "It's quite all right."

"Have you tried to contact him recently?"

"To tell you the truth, Father, no. There hasn't been a reason. And... and I'd rather only do so when I must."

"I understand," he said. "I know this must be a strange question, but... has anyone else seen him?"

Her voice was almost a whisper. "Yes, Father. It's what made me so sure I wasn't mad at the first."

"Who?"

"My mother. Although now she'd never admit it. And my sister Sheila. The three of us used to go the pub together. Bran, Sheila and myself. Take walks. Listen to music. I've several photos. Sheila took them."

"That's interesting."

"I would've shown them to you, but I wasn't sure— Well. I wasn't sure I should."

He shifted in his chair. Bishop Avery would be very interested in photographs. Most of the attempts at such evidence ended in failure, possibly because the subjects weren't willing. "I would be honored if you would allow me to see them."

"Certainly, Father. I'll bring them on Wednesday."

He decided to take the chance. "Do you think it might be possible for me to meet him as well?"

She paused. "I don't know."

"It's only, I've so many questions, and it might help Liam."

"You're certain he's not in any trouble?"

"Nothing immediate. But there may be something, and I'd like to discuss it with you both if that's possible. As his parents."

There was another long silence, and he only knew she was still on the line by her breathing. "Kathleen?"

"I'll see what I can do, Father," she said, "but he isn't much in favor of the new religion as he calls it."

"The Church offends him?"

"It isn't that. It's—" She paused. "I think he's angry with priests. I don't understand why. He's been this way since first I knew him. He seems to think you're dangerous. I've tried to explain, but he only gets angry."

"I see."

"You're sure this will help my Liam?"

"Definitely."

"All right."

"I'll see you on Wednesday, Kathleen." He hung up the phone and went upstairs to pack.

The drive north was uneventful, although the roads were rough with the weather turning for the worst. The multiple checkpoints along the way proved both tiresome and nerve-racking. There had been incidents of false checkpoints being set up to trap Catholics, and since he was going north, he was forced to drive through Loyalist areas. However, he arrived safely in Derry on Tuesday afternoon, got settled in the visitor's room at St. Brendan's parochial house and then picked up the telephone. Kathleen told him everything was arranged, and so, he woke Wednesday morning and pulled on a sweater over his shirt in anticipation of the cold. She'd told him they were to meet in the church, but then would talk with Bran somewhere in private.

Father Murray pocketed his jet-beaded rosary as well as a vial of holy water. Then he checked his knife and snapped it inside the sheath strapped to the small of his back. He made certain the shape of it couldn't be discerned in the back of his jacket and then shrugged into his black wool coat. He didn't like the idea of going armed into a negotiation but knew Father Thomas was right. Taking unnecessary risks with demons was never a good idea.

Exiting the parochial house, he was slapped in the face with a rain-laden wind gust. He pulled his coat tighter and ran to the church. Kathleen Kelly was sitting in one of the pews waiting for him when he arrived. She was wearing a dark blue coat and a brown scarf over her hair. Her face was etched with worry.

"Good morning, Father."

"Good morning, Kathleen," he said. "Is everything all right at home?"

She nodded. "Everything is fine. It's only that I'm not sure this is such a good idea."

"It'll be fine," he said. "I only wish to talk."

She looked away and bit her lip. "I know, Father. I told him as much, but he doesn't like this at all."

"But he agreed to see me anyway?"

"Aye," she said. "I told him it was for our Liam." She wasn't telling him everything—that was obvious in her expression.

"Is there something I should be aware of, Kathleen? You seem nervous."

Shaking her head, she turned away. "We should get going."

"Is there some sort of danger?"

"Why would you ask such a thing?"

"I'm sorry," he said, trying to cover his fear. "It's only that I'm a wee bit disconcerted. I've never actually met a mythological creature before." *At least,* he thought, *not one I wasn't under orders to kill on sight.* The trouble was, while he was beginning to doubt the wisdom of such a position, hundreds of years of evidence declared it to be the right one. However, everything Kathleen Kelly had told him, everything he'd seen in her son, indicated otherwise, and he had to be sure.

She smiled and got up from the pew. "We should go, Father." She crossed herself and genuflected before turning her back on the altar, and they walked out together. The weather seemed to be letting up somewhat as she followed him to his car.

"Did you bring the photos?" he asked.

"Yes, Father. I have them with me." After getting into the old Ford, she dug around in her handbag and produced three snapshots.

The first seemed to have been taken on a hill. There was a blanket spread on the ground, and a young Kathleen sat on it next to a lanky man with wild black hair. The second was taken outside a pub. The young Kathleen was laughing as was the man in the picture. The third was of the same man alone staring out of a window, the light on his face casting shadows. It was a lovely shot, and Father Murray could see years of worry in the brooding expression. Studying each, he saw where the son was slight, the father was muscled. "He'll be easy to recognize, I see."

"Liam does resemble his father."

"He doesn't look terribly mythological," Father Murray said in an attempt to lighten the mood.

She rewarded him with a smile. "He doesn't, does he?"

"Let's get going, then." Father Murray handed the photos back. He turned the ignition key and then steered onto the road, heading west as she directed. He listened to the steady rhythm of the windshield wipers until they'd cleared the final army checkpoint on the edge of town and then asked, "Are you going to tell me where we're going?"

"We'll meet on a hill. I'll tell you when to stop."

He nodded, feeling more relaxed. It wasn't long before she told him to pull over, and they got out. He missed his umbrella at once, but she'd told him specifically not to bring one. Heart in mouth, he followed her up the hill. The top was crowned with old growth oak trees, and the clearing inside sheltered a ring of ancient standing stones. The stones weren't tall, only three or four feet high, and their weathered surfaces were covered in lichen. He wasn't sure he liked the feel of the place. While it had a peaceful quality it vibrated with power. He might even have called it holy were it not in the middle of a farmer's field. It smelled of freshly turned earth and growing things.

A wind rustled through the oaks, and rainwater splashed down upon them as if the trees were slow-moving dogs shaking the moisture from their fur. He heard something in the rush of the leaves. It sounded like a whispered name.

"Kathleen."

It gave him a shiver.

"Kathleen, my love."

"I'm here," she said. "I've Father Murray with me."

"I can see that," the voice said, gaining solidity. It grew hard as if it carried years of controlled fury. "Step away from him. Come to me."

Father Murray searched the clearing and didn't see anyone. Kathleen moved forward and hesitated. It seemed she didn't see him either. Father Murray tensed up. He was beginning to think that perhaps he'd made a terrible mistake.

"Here, Kathleen."

She started and then walked toward one of the oaks to the left. As soon as she was within arm's reach of the tree, a shadow moved from behind the trunk, and the man from the photos appeared. He looked older, and there was a grey streak running through his hair on the right side. He was dressed in the same belted long white linen shirt, pegged jeans and short black boots, however. He briefly looped an arm around her waist and kissed the top of her head. Then he positioned himself in front of her and drew a short sword made of bronze.

"Move into the circle, priest," he said. He was tall, and Father Murray could see where Liam got his height.

Father Murray put up his hands. His heart was shuddering inside his chest, and he was sweating in spite of the cold and damp. "I've only come to talk."

"And that is why you bring iron into this place? I can smell it upon you." His voice lowered to a growl, and his eyes flashed red. "I said, move into the circle."

All isn't lost, Father Murray thought. *He hasn't attacked—not yet.* Stepping into the center of the clearing, Father Murray glanced around him but didn't spy any other demons. "You would be unwise to kill me. I've been protecting your son."

"Why?"

"Because he's different," Father Murray said, stopping. "You know he is. He is why I'm here to talk."

"That's what I understand. But first I'll have you shed your weapons."

"He doesn't have any," Kathleen said. "He's a priest. Priests don't carry—"

"I love you, Kathleen. But keep your promise. Stay out of this. I know what I'm about," the creature said. "Priest, do as I said."

"I'll lay down my arms if you agree to do the same."

The Fallen smiled and his eyes glittered like the darkest rubies. "All right." Slowly, and without looking away, the creature bent down and laid the bronze sword on the grass. "I do this for Kathleen and the love I bear for her and my son. She had me swear that I would listen to what you have to say. Therefore, I'm oath bound to do so. But understand, I'd have sooner killed you for what you and your kind have done."

Father Murray nodded. He hesitated and then fished the bottle of holy water out of his pocket as well as the rosary.

Bran snorted. "I said your weapons, not your talismans. You may keep those."

Glancing up to see the expression on the demon's face, Father Murray was puzzled when he saw the creature didn't seem disturbed. He reached underneath coat and jacket and drew the knife. He heard Kathleen gasp. "There," he said, laying it upon the wet grass. "That is everything."

"You may call me Bran."

"Please call me Joe."

Bran nodded and then sat in the grass. "We shall talk, then, Joe Murray, priest."

Following Bran's example, Father Murray sat with his legs folded like an Indian holy man. *This is going well,* he thought. Kathleen rested with her back against the oak. She still looked worried, but at least now he understood her fears.

"What is it you want from me?" Bran asked.

"In part, I'd like to understand a few things. Ask some questions."

"You may ask."

"Who are you?"

Bran tilted his head, and his eyes narrowed. "Are you asking for my name?"

"I'm trying to understand as much as I can of your situation. Kathleen says you're a púca."

"It is what I am."

"You're a shape changer? A demon? A spook that haunts the lonely roads and topples drunks from horses? A vengeful animal spirit? Dark. Half man, half goat. You take the form of a great black horse and drown those who would dare ride—"

Bran laughed.

"Is something wrong?" Father Murray asked.

"Kathleen told me of an American film. According to it, I'm an eight foot tall white rabbit that wears a hat. Do I look like any of those things to you?"

Father Murray shrugged and felt a little foolish. "Appearances can be deceiving."

"Aye, well. You don't much look like a murderous religious fanatic. We all have our problems, I suppose."

"You don't take different forms?"

"Are you a priest?"

"Yes."

"Well, then. That just proves some things are what they seem."

"You're nothing like I expected."

Bran tilted his head again. "And what is it you expected?"

"You have concerns for the humans around you. Kathleen. Liam. The Fallen aren't known for such behavior."

A sneer pulled at Bran's mouth. "Fallen, am I? And yet, you consider my son to be 'human'?"

"His mother is human. He acts like a human."

"And tell me, what is it to be human?"

"We live, die, love, hate, fear. We destroy, but we also create. We hope—"

"And that is what makes us so different, you and me? I could say the same."

Father Murray paused. He remembered the portrait Kathleen had shown him in the car and thought about everything he'd seen so far in the man in front of him. *He's genuinely concerned for his family.* Father Murray sighed. "You're at war with us. With humans. What is it you fear? Why do you fight us?"

Bran blinked. "We do not fight mortals. We fight the evil you brought here to our land. The Fallen."

"What?"

"You heard me, priest. They came here with you. And to make matters worse, you've gone about telling all who would listen that we're demons. Us. Those that were here before you. Those whose land you walk upon," Bran said. "We, who've awoken from a long sleep to aid our people when most needed. And you and your ones killing us at every opportunity. Turning our own against us. And us fighting the same crossed war."

Father Murray felt his mouth drop open. "You're not Fallen?"

"The Good Folk. The Fair Folk. Fairies. Legends. Myths. Ghosts. Call us what you will, but call us demons or fallen angels at your peril," Bran said and then sighed. "I suppose it's the way of invasions. Did we not demonize the Firbolg when we first came to Ireland?"

"I don't understand. You say you're fighting for humanity?"

"It's what I said, you holy idiot. We don't want those things here anymore than you do. They corrupt everything they touch."

"Jesus, Mary and Joseph," Father Murray said, feeling sick. "You're saying that I—we—the Church has been killing allies?"

Bran said, "The only reason I'm here talking to you is the service you provided me and mine when you researched that coin. It wasn't much, but it was something. And you did it in spite of knowing who it was for. But most of all, I'm here because all this time you've watched over my son and never once harmed him."

"Proof. I have to have proof of this and get it to the bishop. At once."

"What could possibly change their minds about us after all this time?"

The moisture on the grass was seeping through Father Murray's coat and trousers. He shivered. "You could come with me. Talk to them."

"And be shot full of iron or carved to pieces on a dissection table? I think not," Bran said, gathering his things and getting up. "Enough."

"Wait," Father Murray said. "I've more questions."

"You're not here to talk. You're only here to collect information to use against us." Bran wiped his sword dry, sheathed it and then walked to Kathleen who stood up. "I'm no fool."

"Do you know Fionn mac Cumhaill?"

Bran paused and turned around. "Why do you ask?"

"Because your Liam told me that a creature with filed teeth attacked him the day he was first arrested. He said it mentioned the mac Cumhaill before it did so."

Stepping closer, Bran asked, "Did he wear a blood-soaked cap and hob-nailed boots?"

Father Murray tried to remember how the creature had been described, but he hadn't paid much attention, assuming it to be only a demon at the time. "He said it was dressed as a British paratrooper. That's all."

"Oh, no," Kathleen said, "a Para? You're sure?"

"What is it, Kathleen?" Bran asked.

"The Paras," Kathleen said. "They wear a beret. It's red. It's part of the uniform."

Bran clenched his fist. "The Redcap."

"What does this mean?" Father Murray asked. "Is it one of your ones? Are there factions? I need to know."

Bran turned to Kathleen and grasped her arms. "I'm so sorry. All this time. He hadn't moved against you. I didn't think he knew of either of you. I thought he was only after my men."

"That was years ago, and nothing has happened since," Kathleen said. "Maybe it's dead now."

"He's not dead," Bran said. "He's in prison. Biding his time. I should know. I put him there myself. And there he'll stay. I'll see to it."

Father Murray got to his feet. The back of his trousers were soaked through, and his teeth were chattering. "*There is more in heaven and earth, Horatio, than are dreamt of in your philosophy,*" he thought. *Maybe Shakespeare knew more than how to turn a pretty phrase.* "Is there anything I can do to help?"

Bran faced him, giving him a long judging stare. "You're serious."

"I am," Father Murray said. "I don't know you all that well but having met you... well, strange as you are, I think I believe you."

"Not killing any more of us would go a long way," Bran said.

"I'll talk to the bishop. Present the idea. Perhaps I can get a delegation together. Discuss a truce or a partnership. I can't promise they'll be open-minded, not at the start. But I can try."

Bran put out his hand. "I thank you at least for that."

Father Murray nodded. "Can I—I mean, would it be possible to contact you again?" He looked down at the offered hand and with only the slightest hesitation, took it. Bran's skin was cool but quickly warmed.

Bran gave him another long stare. "Perhaps, Joe Murray. Perhaps."

Chapter 15

Andersonstown, Belfast, County Antrim, Northern Ireland
October 1975

Exhausted from a long day driving and an even longer one working on the taxi's recalcitrant engine, Liam made his way up the three flights of stairs. He was filthy, covered in grease up to the elbows, and it'd been for nothing. In his attempt to make the bastard run better he'd managed to banjax the timing and would have to ask Bobby to drop by and help him in the morning. Liam didn't want to call Oran—as much shite as he gave Oran for not being able to drive, it'd be too embarrassing, and Liam simply wasn't in the mood. Bobby was the quieter of the two brothers and had proven to be a patient teacher and forgiving of mistakes. This was good because try as Liam might he couldn't work on an engine for longer than a couple hours without his hands going numb and getting a headache. He'd start dropping tools and then his temper would grow short. Happened every time, but Bobby said he could make a mechanic of him yet.

Throwing open the door, Liam was met with the welcoming scent of boiling chicken. His favorite. His stomach rumbled as he slipped out of his coat and tossed it onto the sofa.

Mary Kate peered around the kitchen wall. "The dinner is almost ready."

"That's wonderful," he said and sighed.

"Bad day?"

He went to the washroom to clean up, and she followed him.

"No more than usual, really," he said, using the soap to get rid of the first layer of grease. "Fucking choke on the carburetor giving trouble again."

She nodded, kissed him on the back of the neck and then left him to scrape off the grime. By the time he was done the dinner was on the table. She seemed distracted but happy as he sat down.

"Well, I've done it," Mary Kate said with a bright smile that cut him through.

"What did you do? Exactly."

"I've quit the Socialist Party."

He swallowed and put down his fork. "But you adore Bernadette Devlin." It had been a point of disagreement between the two of them since the beginning and had resulted in many heated discussions about politics over the past few months. She believed in socialism. He didn't. It didn't help that the Officials, who were Socialists, and the Provos, who were much less so, were having a merry go at one another all over the news. The Officials were in favor of the continued truce but the Provos were not because there'd been too many Catholics killed by Loyalist paramilitaries during the truce. The Brits weren't interested in real negotiations and enough was enough. Someone had to protect the civilians from the UVF and the UDA. Everyone knew the RUC damned well weren't going to do it because everyone also knew that most constables were also Loyalists.

She looked away and shrugged. "I'm tired of all the bickering."

"You're done with politics altogether?" he asked, his heart sinking.

"No," she said. "I'm considering one of the other student groups." She paused and whispered in Irish, "If I could, I'd join *Sinn Féin*."

He choked. He hadn't told her he'd volunteered; he couldn't. It was against the regulations, and the Provos could be quite strict when it came to the regulations.

Sinn Féin, he thought. *The political arm of the Provisional IRA. Did I let something slip? Or did someone tell her? If she's figured it out, what of the neighbors? Do they know too? Will the RUC come—*

"Aren't you going to say anything?" she asked.

With his heart slamming in his chest like a rubbish lid against pavement, he got up and laid a hand inside the empty steel sink. "What do you want me to say?"

"I won't get into trouble."

"You always say that. And you always do. The protests are one thing. Demanding fair housing and work and having a real vote. I'll support you. But what of last week and the riot? And the riot before that? You scared me half to death when you didn't come home. And for all that, I'm still paying Oran on the loan of the bribe money it took to get you out."

"No more stone throwing. I promise." Although his back was to her, he knew she was smiling. He could hear the edge of laughter in her voice. "Anyway, I was only sitting in the street this last time. I wasn't doing anything."

"That didn't stop them from killing Jim Wray! You were there! Remember? Thirteen dead! We heard the shots! Doing nothing didn't stop them from putting me away either! Doing nothing never stops them!"

"That's just it," she said in a quiet voice. "Doing nothing won't stop them. I have to do something."

He shut his eyes and slammed his hand against the bottom of the sink to drive out the prickling. Dishes clattered inside the cabinets with the force of the blow. "No, you don't! Not like this!"

He felt her hand on his arm. "Oh, Liam. I'm so sorry," she whispered. "I thought you'd be happy."

"Tell me you passed exams, I'll be happy! Tell me you'll be getting more money out of your grant, I'll be happy!" He turned to look at her, and she flinched away from him. It shot a bolt of guilt through his heart. He looked away to hide his eyes. "One day you won't be coming home from University. One day you'll be in a morgue. Should I be happy then?"

She switched to Irish. "It's a political organization. It's not like I'd be taking up a gun or making bombs."

He turned his head before his face could betray him. The IRA had been standing down since February, but he'd kept silent nonetheless. With the last series of killings and bombings it was obvious that the truce wasn't going to last—if it wasn't effectively over already. She let out an exasperated sigh and then stomped out of the tiny kitchen. He heard rustling noises. The tear of paper. When she returned, she waved a sheet of ruled notebook paper under his nose. There was a message printed on it; she always printed when she wanted to be sure he understood, and it never failed to humiliate him. He was shaking with anger as he read it.

I know, it said.

"All the more reason you shouldn't do it, Mary Kate."

She moved to the table where they ate their meals—when he wasn't working, or when she wasn't at Uni or a political meeting. Shoving the plates aside, she wrote another message. Pointing to the new note, her index finger landed in the center with a thump.

This time he read, *I support your decision. I wanted to show you how much. Is that wrong?*

He took the pencil from her and wrote in his big, slow scrawl made worse by tension, *When we have children. What of them? One of us has to be there for them. We can't both be in prison.* He said, "I forbid it."

Frowning, she took a deep, shuddering breath. He watched the storm brewing behind her eyes and knew it for a slammer. She grabbed for the pencil, and he jerked it back, then held up his hand to stop her.

She hissed in Irish, "Then maybe you should've thought about that before you lied to me! Before you went and volunteered without so much as consulting me! Forbid, you say? You've had no surprises from me, William Ronan Monroe Kelly. I've always been political. I come from a long line of

Republicans. If it's one of us that should be quitting, it's you."

He blinked at the force of her fury.

"Anyway, it's not me who'll be carrying a gun," she whispered, continuing in Irish. "It's not me who'll be in a morgue. You think I'm happy about that? You think I haven't thought of that from the moment I found out?"

He wrote, *How did you find out? Must know.* He underlined "must" three times.

Folding her arms across her chest, her chin acquired the familiar obstinate angle he had grown to love and dread all at once. He handed her the pencil and for a moment he thought she wasn't going to take it.

She wrote, *Elizabeth MacMahon told me. Last week.* Then she slammed the pencil onto the table, breaking the point.

His unit consisted of Éamon Walsh, Nial Healy, himself and Oran Mac-Mahon. Elizabeth was Oran's wife.

A knock exploded against the door, and Mary Kate yelped.

"Mr. Kelly? There's someone on the phone for you," a female voice from outside said.

Mary Kate slumped in relief and left the table to open the door. A short middle-aged woman with brown hair gathered in her usual wispy blue scarf stood disapproving in the hallway.

"He'll be right down, Mrs. Black," Mary Kate said. "Did they mention who they were?"

Mrs. Black seemed to be avoiding looking at him. "I didn't think to ask."

Liam pushed past. "Thank you."

"You're welcome," Mrs. Black said in a disparaging tone.

When he reached the third stair he heard Mrs. Black whisper, "Couldn't help hearing the ruckus. Did the brute hurt you?"

He ran the rest of the way and berated himself for shouting. Never mind what anyone might have overheard—and he had to be careful of that at all times. Bullying a woman was the kind of thing his stepfather would do, and he hated himself for it. No matter that Mary Kate had been just as angry. When he reached the payphone on the first floor, he snatched the dangling black receiver. "Hello? This is Liam Kelly."

"Ah, good. You're there. I'm to come get you." The voice on the other end of the line was pure Dublin.

Liam checked the area for anyone who might be listening then he whispered, "Oran?"

"We've a job. Now. Tonight."

Liam's heart dropped into his stomach. His first assignment and here he was already letting the others down. "Car isn't ready. Was adjusting the carburetor and—"

"Never mind that," Oran said with a laugh. "We can walk. What the fuck are you doing, man? You're the driver not the mechanic." And with that, he hung up.

By the time Liam returned to the flat, Mrs. Black was gone, and Mary Kate was sitting on the sofa among his automobile manuals, flipping pages and pretending to scan the images of intake and exhaust systems. He could tell from the way her lips were compressed that the argument wasn't over. He wanted to apologize, but he was too angry with himself to do it properly and even if he wasn't Oran would be there any minute.

He strode into the bedroom, stepping onto the bed in order to create enough space to open the closet. It was mid-October and cold. He needed something warm and preferably in a dark color. Scrounging through what little he had, he was able to find a navy turtleneck. His jeans would have to suffice. He pulled off the green long-sleeved shirt he'd been wearing and then retrieved the knit cap he'd prepared, tossing it onto the bed. He heard her step into the doorway.

"Don't you dare walk out on me," she said, fists at her sides.

He looked at her, helpless. "I have to go."

"I said—"

"This isn't because of the row," he said, hoping she'd catch on. "I have to go."

Another knock came. "Liam?"

"Oran's here," Liam said. "I have to go."

Mary Kate's hand flew to her mouth and tears formed in her eyes. "Oh, no."

Oran pounded on the door. Liam squeezed past Mary Kate, and headed for the cramped sitting room. "Keep your fucking knickers on. I'm coming, damn you!"

"Liam, wait!" Mary Kate ran from the bedroom with a small cardboard box in her hand. "I was going to give it to you for Christmas, but if you're—I want you to wear it."

He opened the box and found a silver medal inside; the figure in the center of the circular medallion was bristling with arrows. The image didn't give him a good feeling.

"The church only had three saints' medals for soldiers and none of them were St. Joseph. I couldn't give you St. Michael. He's for constables too. Didn't think it'd be right," she said. "And St. George is English. This one's St. Sebastian."

"Of course. The English would leave us the one plugged full of holes."

Mary Kate reached inside the box. "I had it blessed for you."

She fastened it around his neck with a sniff, then she kissed him. The medal clinked against the crucifix his mother had given him for his First Communion. She'd been adamant that he start wearing it as soon as he'd been released from Malone. He never understood why and kept it under his shirt. As far as he was concerned it only made it easier for the Prods to spot a target. He jammed the sweater on over his head and then pulled the knit hat on without unrolling it over his face.

"I love you," Mary Kate said. "Come back to me. In one piece. I'd like to have you whole when I finish giving you a good knock about the ears."

"I love you too," he said with a smile.

From outside he heard, "What are you doing in there? Giving the girl a shag? We'll not be gone that long. Newlyweds. Shite."

Liam grabbed his anorak and threw open the door. "Not enough time. I'd need a few hours to do her proper."

"It's a wonder you ever get anything else done, then." Oran tipped his hat at Mary Kate. A whole head shorter than Liam, Oran was almost ten years his senior and tended to sound as if he were twice that. "Your man is naught but a braggart."

"Hardly," Mary Kate said, and Liam felt her grab his arse. "Get along then. Save some energy for me. I've a feeling I'll be needing a ride later."

"Yes, Mrs. Kelly," Liam said with a bow.

"Does your mother know you talk to your husband like that in public?" Oran asked, shifting the toolbox he was carrying to his other hand.

"What?" Liam feigned innocence. "She's talking about the cab."

"She is, is she?"

"Needs me to take her somewhere."

Mary Kate struck a sultry pose in the doorway that would've put Brigit Bardot to shame. The top of her white peasant blouse slipped off one shoulder. "Aye, I do." She blew him a kiss and shut the door.

"In the cab?" Oran asked. "Remind me never to sit in the back."

"Can we hurry this along?" Liam said, discovering that turning away from the door was tougher than he thought possible. "I'd like to get back before she cools off."

Oran punched him in the arm. "Lucky bastard."

As they passed Mrs. Black's flat, he saw her door was open a crack. She peered into the hallway through the two-inch gap.

"Evening, Mrs. B," Liam said.

She slammed the door with a harrumph.

"What is she on about?" Oran asked.

Sighing as they stepped onto the sidewalk, Liam said, "We had a fight, Mary Kate and I. Mrs. Black thinks I hit her."

"Did you?"

"How could you even ask?"

Oran glanced away and shrugged. After a long pause, he said, "I like you, Liam, but sometimes you get this look about you. And I get the feeling I'd rather not see you crossed or riled."

Liam remembered Mary Kate flinching away from him in the kitchen. He nodded, feeling a heavy weight tugging at his shoulders. Happy as he was, there were times when he thought he shouldn't have married—not because of Mary Kate—but because of the monster living inside him. When he was with Mary Kate he often forgot about the creature altogether, and for that reason he hoped that she might have the power to banish it forever. Nonetheless, from time to time the thing would remind him of its presence, and he'd worry if there might come a day when it would slip from his control.

Again.

Never. I'd never let it harm her, he thought.

Mrs. Black's whisper echoed in his head. *Couldn't help hearing the ruckus. Did that brute hurt you?*

I'm not Patrick. I'm not at all, at all. Liam walked half the block in silence then said, "You don't trust me."

"Don't be stupid. I trust you with more than my life," Oran said. "I trust you with my family's."

Liam counted twenty steps. "Thank you."

"Think nothing of it."

He followed Oran, turning right at the end of the street and proceeding up the next block. New to the organization, Liam hadn't been issued a gun, and he wouldn't get one until Éamon was certain of him. Éamon had a reputation for discipline and caution. These were good qualities, Liam felt, particularly in an organization infamous for lacking both. However, at the moment Liam wished the man were a little less careful. Regardless of the ceasefire, he was walking into a dangerous situation unarmed. "Where are we headed?"

"The residence of one Mrs. Russell, widow," Oran said.

"The others will meet us there?"

"This one is just you and me."

Uneasy, Liam asked, "If I'm not to drive, what am I to do?"

"Carry this for a start," Oran said, handing off the heavy tool box. His brown eyes twinkled in the streetlights. "Are your carpentry skills as good as your auto mechanics?"

"Far worse, I suspect. Why?"

"Ah, well. It's not as if anyone will be asking you to build a church altar."

Liam began to suspect the evening's venture was some sort of test. It was clear Oran didn't intend to tell him much of anything by way of preparation. With a deep breath, Liam decided to return the favor and trust Oran. It wasn't easy. His stomach twisted into a fluttering knot.

"Why did you take apart the cab?" Oran asked.

"Bobby mentioned if I kept it in good condition, it might perform better," Liam said. "Also said there were small adjustments I should make to the suspension. It'll take turns better if I do. Of course, it'd be better to not use the taxi at all, but if we could afford better wheels—"

"Why would you go to all that trouble?" Oran glanced over at him.

Liam shrugged. "In case."

"Bobby said you were going with him next weekend to the Rally."

"Said he'd ask one of the others show me a few things. Thought if I prepared—if I knew what to expect—what to do, I'd be more likely to get us home. No matter what." Liam shrugged again. "In case."

"Interesting," Oran said with a considering look. "You know, we usually get the ones who would rather be anything but a driver."

"I won't let you down again."

Oran traced a circuitous route through various back gardens in order to avoid two BA checkpoints. Liam followed in silence. At last they arrived at their destination—a stucco building with a blue window box. Stepping through the white picket gate, Oran proceeded to what was apparently Mrs. Russell's front door. He knocked, and an old woman dressed in a colorless print dress answered. Grey hair curled around her grey face, and she gave Oran a closed look. A baby cried from somewhere inside.

"Yes? What is it you want?" she asked.

"I understand you had some trouble with your fence," Oran said. "We're here to repair it."

Liam looked to Oran, confused.

"What is this going to cost?" she asked.

"It'll cost nothing. Will you show us where the man damaged it last week?" Oran asked. "He sends his apologies and is saddened that he's unavailable to do the repair himself."

Mrs. Russell's face transformed into a warm smile, and she stepped back. "Bless you both. And him."

After ushering them inside, she shut the door and then edged carefully around them. The narrow hallway was crammed with knick-knacks and smelled of lavender and boiled cabbage. Last in line, Liam attempted to keep from knocking over the items on the shelves with the bulky toolbox. A young woman bouncing a sobbing baby stood on the stair. The lines of her face echoed that of Mrs. Russell's from an earlier time.

"Is something wrong, Mother?" Her eyes were round with fear.

"Go on upstairs, dear," Mrs. Russell said, "They're friends."

The young woman gave the toolbox a worried look before she vanished up the stairs.

Mrs. Russell led them through the kitchen to the back door. The scent of boiled cabbage grew stronger. "Did your man get away safe, do you know?" she asked. "I'd feel terrible if my fence was the cause of a delay—that it caused his family grief."

Oran smiled. "He's fine."

"Good. Good. Well, the damaged planks are along the left. The hole at the back was there before," she said. "Would you like some tea?"

"Yes, ma'am," Oran said, entering the back garden.

When she was gone Liam whispered, "We're here to repair a fence?"

Oran nodded, assessing the damage. "Is there a problem?"

"No," Liam said. "I never thought that…. It's only…. This isn't what I expected."

"Lesson one," Oran said. "The organization can't presume to keep the hearts of the people if we go blundering through their property like a bunch of BAs. Give me the hammer, will you? We'll start by removing the broken boards. Then I'll want you to hold the flashlight."

Liam didn't ask where the fresh fence slats stacked in the alley on the opposite side of the broken fence came from. He had heard the IRA had connections with the construction industry around Belfast. Materials went missing often enough that some construction projects were never completed, the company in charge having long since gone bankrupt.

During the course of the work, Mrs. Russell plied them with several pots of tea and homemade biscuits. The job took twice as long because Oran insisted upon repairing the hole in the back fence as well. It was late by the time they were ready to leave, and Liam couldn't help thinking of Mary Kate alone and worrying. Oran decided to risk the last checkpoint to save time on the way home. The wooden barricade stretched across the road, and on the opposite side of the street, cars were being stopped and their drivers questioned. As Liam and Oran approached, two BAs moved to meet them. Liam recognized both, having driven through the particular checkpoint several times earlier in the day.

The first BA took their identification. "Put down the box and open it."

Liam did as he was told, and the first BA sorted through the toolbox, not bothering to put things back where he found them.

The first BA asked, "You're William Kelly and Oran MacMahon?"

"Yes," Oran said.

Liam kept his mouth shut, but one hand curled into a fist. They damned well knew who he was. They'd checked his driver's license at least three times a day for two weeks—even the dimmest BA's memory couldn't be that short.

"What are you doing with that?" the second BA asked, kicking the tool-box.

Pointing to Liam, Oran smiled and said, "Fixing his Granny's fence."

The first BA straightened and stared into Liam's face. "I know you. You're that one that runs every morning."

And you're the one that sites your fucking rifle on me while I jog past, Liam thought. His jaw clenched, but he kept his gaze averted and shrugged.

"I should think even a Paddy would know how to run without practice." The second BA smirked.

Liam felt Oran's hand on his arm. "Easy, now," Oran whispered.

"Right. Up against the wall, you two. Arms and legs spread," the second BA said. "Don't like the looks of you."

Liam was shoved against the brick wall.

"Aren't our papers in order?" Oran asked.

The BA didn't bother with an answer and started patting down Oran. The bricks were rough against Liam's cheek, and he could feel the second BA's hand in the middle of his back. Shutting his eyes and gritting his teeth, he prepared himself to endure yet another search.

Chapter 16

Sitting behind the wheel of a stolen Ford Escort RS1600, Liam listened to his heart slam a bass drum counter-beat to the rumble of the engine. Even with the heat on it was cold. He blew into his hands and rubbed them together. The others were inside, presumably clearing out the bank vault. The alley behind the bank was bloody dark with the headlights off, but he planned to make the first part of the journey home without them anyway. Lights might risk unwanted attention, and he could see well enough without as long as he kept the speed down.

A black cat stalked its prey among the rubbish bins twenty feet away. He watched until it vanished behind a broken crate and then turned his attention to the instrument panel. Petrol. Oil. Temperature. Everything was as it should be. The engine gave off a steady purr—the result of new performance spark plugs and an adjustment to the carburetor earlier in the day. Nonetheless, his shoulders cramped and his knuckles were white on the steering wheel. When he dared release his grip his hands trembled. Closing his eyes, Liam took a deep breath against the weight of the pistol tucked in a holster under his jacket. The familiar smell of engine grease and plastic filling his nose was reassuring, and he told himself that the next thirty minutes would be no different than any normal drive home after an evening's work.

This was his first real job, and it was natural to be nervous. Afraid of letting everyone down, Liam had done everything he could to prepare, including several timed practice runs in his black taxi. Since the stolen RS1600 was the same model as the one he borrowed for rallies, he felt comfortable driving. Oh, the car had its quirks; they all tended to, but once the new wheels and sticky racing tires were installed, the handling was relatively consistent with the RS he'd been driving for the last six months. Escorts had the advantage of being common on the streets and were equipped with a powerful 16-valve engine—even the four-door models. In addition, Escorts were light and fairly easy to steal. Bobby had been an amazing source of information about such things.

Uncomfortable with forcing financial hardship on a hard-working Catholic family, Liam had lifted the current vehicle from a known UVF sympathizer near Shankill Road. Oran had helped, of course. It'd been a thrill to drive off in the black RS, imagining the owner's face when the bastard discovered it missing. After everything Liam had witnessed during the "cease fire" he didn't think anyone could blame him for stealing from a Loyalist—not even peace-loving Father Murray.

Another deep breath and Liam's confidence was bolstered. He felt pre-pared—ready to handle any situation that might arise.

Someone was tapping on the window.

Liam's eyes snapped open and in that moment he knew he was fucked.

"What are you doing here at this time of night?" A constable directed a flashlight beam through the glass, temporarily destroying Liam's night vision.

Placing a hand on the grip of his pistol, Liam rolled down the window and mentally ran through a list of plausible excuses to get rid of the man. He knew his orders, Éamon had been explicit, and it was against the training, but Liam hadn't killed anyone before. Now that he was faced with doing so, he hesitated. A gold ring on the constable's left hand glittered in the light reflecting off the car.

"This is no place to be sleeping it off, Mick. Your identification. Now. Then out of the car with y—"

Liam's heart stopped when the bank's back door slammed open and Éamon, Oran and Nial exited loaded down with heavy canvas bags. Oran and Nial's expressions would've been comical but for the situation. The constable reached for his gun in slow motion. Liam pointed his pistol out the window and then fired twice before the constable's gun cleared its holster. Bang-bang. The report was deafening from inside the car, and the recoil sent a shock up his arm. Struck, the constable dropped with a surprised look frozen on his face—a black dot on his cheek.

Rolling up the window, Liam tossed the gun onto the seat and then slotted the pre-prepared mix tape into the stereo. The car rocked with the force of the doors slamming shut. Someone shouted. No. Multiple someones—from inside the car and outside of it. Too late for stealth now. Feeling numb, Liam checked to see that the others were inside. Then he gunned the engine, punched play on the tape and flipped on the headlights. He heard the remote pop of gunfire. Something smacked hard against the back of the front seat, and then T. Rex launched into "Get It On." There wasn't time to consider what had just happened, to think about the dark, lumpy splash that had appeared on the wall beyond the constable or about the man's hat having been blown off his head. Liam released the brake and felt the tires slide as his foot mashed the accelerator a little too hard a little too fast. He automatically let up and rubber gripped pavement. The Escort was catapulted past the rubbish bins. Absurdly, Liam found himself hoping the cat was well out of the way.

A long high-pitched squeal came from the backseat. "JesusMaryandPatrickmanyoufuckingkilledhim!"

"Shut it, Níal! Let the man fucking drive!"

Liam vaguely understood the last had come from Oran as the car made a quick but smooth left turn at the end of the alley. Distant sirens told him they wouldn't have the streets to themselves much longer—not that they would anyway; it was time the pubs were letting out. He took a right, swerved around a parked delivery van and headed west. Sitting next to him in the front seat, Éamon leaned forward with both hands splayed on the dashboard. The hard lines of his narrow face were set in a determined expression. As planned, Éamon focused on the road, intent on scouting for trouble. He gave off an air of professional steadiness. A volunteer since the 1940s, nothing affected Éamon. Níal was another matter.

In spite of everything, a confident joy blanketed Liam. He loved driving. In particular, he loved driving fast. The only thing better was making love to Mary Kate. He felt uninhibited—even more so than when he ran. At the same time, his heightened awareness kept every obstacle in perfect focus. Some part of him took over—a creature that calculated by instinct in a foreign math of exact distance, speed and the potential reactions of the other drivers. The speedometer read sixty when colored lights fluttered in the rearview mirror.

"Make this fucking thing go faster!"

"I said let the man to his work!"

"No! Fucking stop! Jesus, Mary and—"

Under Liam's direction, the car danced and dodged around three cars and a taxi then rocketed through a red light at eighty-five. A second RUC prowl car just missed the rear of the speeding Escort and plowed into the side of the breaking taxi. Níal let out a girlish wail. The crash was huge, the sound cutting off both Níal and T-Rex. The song reemerged at the verse comparing a woman to a car. An image of Mary Kate dressed in black stockings popped into Liam's head, making him grin. He was whole. Absolute. The car responded to his eager joy with grateful precision. He decided this was better than the rallies. Far better. Next to him, Éamon's lips moved in a silent whisper.

The first RUC vehicle vanished from the rearview mirror. Liam assumed they'd been unable to get around the wreck at the intersection and had had to take a second route. He slowed, granting himself a moment to think. There was a checkpoint ahead and there would be no getting through that with constables on his tail. The RUC would've radioed the Army. Traveling further west into the Catholic area was predictable. Too risky. He had to come up with another plan. Something unexpected. *Now.*

Once, all he would've had to do was head for one of Belfast's "No Go" areas. As in Derry, the Catholics—angry and frightened after years of persecution and murder—had thrown up barricades and declared their neighborhoods off limits for the British Army and the RUC whose numbers swelled the ranks of the UVF and UDA when off duty. IRA patrols backed up the Catholic community's declarations with force. In Belfast, the "No Go" zones had persisted until last year. Now, there wasn't anywhere safe from the RUC, the British Army or the Loyalists.

Liam made a decision. He slowed to forty-five and executed a series of turns, heading north. By now the RUC would have guessed, and guessed rightly, that he had intended to hide in mid-Falls or Clonard or even Beechmont. They wouldn't look for him in Shankill or Crumlin, but the north had its own hazards. The Peace Line separated Shankill from the Upper Falls Road which meant he'd have to risk going further west. In addition, he didn't know the streets north of the Falls Road. Couldn't. No Catholic in their right mind drove a Black Hack through a Loyalist area—at least no one with intentions of a long life—but speeding through Belfast with the RUC, and soon enough, the Army, tailing was currently the greater danger.

Slamming on the accelerator, Liam ran the next light. Soon he was three blocks from his destination. He could just make out the twenty-five-foot-high wall made of brick and steel mesh built to keep the Loyalist Protestants separate from the Republican Catholics—the Peace Line. In the rearview mirror Liam glimpsed two RUC cars shooting through an intersection a block away—still heading west. Éamon's sharp intake of breath drew Liam's attention to the road ahead. It was then he saw he was about to rear-end a stopped car. The white car's bumper loomed huge, and his vision became a series of shuddering stills, each an ever-larger version of the doomed bumper. He switched from accelerator to brake and gave the steering wheel a calculated wrench to the left. The tires slipped but held at the last, and the passenger side mirror disintegrated with a sound like a gunshot. Someone screamed. He navigated the car down the sidewalk. Pedestrians leapt out of the way. Éamon's whispering gained volume, and Liam recognized the 'Our Father' with a shock. Éamon stammered it over and over at a pace that would have put any penance recited by a school boy to shame. He kept getting the last line wrong, and Liam had to resist an urge to correct him.

The car leapt back onto the street with a crunching jolt. Liam slalomed around four more cars with ease and then navigated west to avoid being spotted by BAs patrolling the top of the Peace Line. He'd driven to Highfield by the time he'd found a place to cross. Once there, he slowed even further. He couldn't venture far. If he did, he'd get lost and that'd be the end. A few blocks into Loyalist territory he found a suitable alley. Backing in and then stopping, Liam shut off the engine. The distant wail of sirens told him that the RUC were still on the hunt. There wasn't much time.

Níal shouted, "We're in the fucking Shankill! Are you trying to murder us?"

Staring straight ahead, Éamon said, "Keep it down, Níal. You'll stir the BAs and God knows who else." His voice was dead calm even if his face wasn't.

The shuddering purr of army helicopters fluttered in the distant sky.

Oran said, "Here are the plates and the screwdriver."

"Thanks." Liam took the items Oran handed over the back of the seat and checked the alley one last time before stepping out. Then he walked to the front of the car.

The ring. The man was married. Had a family, Liam thought. *No. Can't think about that. Not now. No time.* He concentrated on not dropping the screws. The sense of elation was gone, leaving him empty. Cold. He removed the front plate with hands that were strangely steady. Finished, he retrieved the old one and tucked it under his arm as he headed to the rear of the car.

It started to mist.

That was bad. The pavement would be slick. Icy. He'd have to make adjustments.

Mick. He called me Mick. Definitely Mick. Or was it "a mhic" meaning "sonny"? Shite. Was it the Irish or not? Did I just kill a Catholic man with a family? One or two Catholics were known to have found their way onto the force—a misguided attempt to curb the RUC's general inclinations.

The hand holding the screwdriver began to tremble.

Took the back of his head off.

A car door swung open, and Oran appeared.

Painted the wall with the insides of his head. Just like… just like that soldier did to Annette MacGavigan.

"Are you well, Liam?"

With the last turn of the screw Liam's stomach did a lazy flip. Old nightmares flooded into his mind in vivid detail, lending a garish crimson to the face of the constable he'd just shot. The old plates slipped from his numbed fingers and clattered onto the ground. His face and hands went cold and the back of his throat grew slick. Standing, he staggered three steps and then threw up into a rubbish pile. Blackness swirled at the edge of his vision. The ground tilted. He stopped himself from smacking his head into the brick wall with an outstretched hand.

"Pull yourself together," Oran said. "We need you, man. Éamon can't drive. Níal is fucking useless if it isn't a lock or a safe. I'd take over, but we both know I can't."

Liam noted a touch of panic in Oran's voice. Wiping vomit from his chin, Liam nodded and spat.

"Here," Oran said.

A white handkerchief contrasted against the black splotches in Liam's peripheral vision. He wiped his face. His mouth was coated with muck, and he spat again to clear it. He almost lost control of his stomach a second time when he felt a lump of vomit shift from the back of his nose to his throat. He didn't want to swallow but didn't have another choice.

Oran whispered, "You only did what you had to."

Spitting one last time before straightening, Liam's whole body trembled with the effort. *I've done worse,* he thought. It didn't help. No matter what else he'd done in the Kesh he hadn't murdered anyone. Sanders may have killed himself but that wasn't Liam's doing—not directly. The constable's surprised face stubbornly haunted the surface of his mind. Liam breathed through his mouth, unwilling to risk the stench of his own vomit. "Do we have any black tape? I think I put some in the boot."

"What for?" Oran asked.

"Bullet hole." Liam pointed above the bumper.

"Ah, well. It's not like that's all that unusual around here, is it?"

Liam opened his mouth to explain, but Oran held up a hand.

"I'll look. Get yourself together."

Oran opened the boot of the car and rooted around.

"Left side," Liam said, wishing Oran would hurry. If Loyalists spotted them their families would be lucky to have pieces to bury. "In the box with the petrol can." *It's good the bullet didn't hit that.*

Letting out a grunt, Oran said, "And here I thought you'd gone daft with all the preparations." He pushed the boot shut and tossed the tape to him.

Liam caught it one-handed. Feeling better, he unrolled the tape with a violent jerk and measured it against the hole. Too narrow, the tape wouldn't quite cover the damage with one application. A couple layers later, Liam checked his work. Judging it might pass in the dark, he stuck the last of the tape in place. He reached for the "Safe as Milk" sticker on the back window and paused. The front seat sported a ragged round hole just to the right of where he'd been sitting. He swallowed back a fresh bout of nausea and peeled the bumper-sticker from the rear window. Oran gave him a raised eyebrow.

"They'll be searching for a black RS1600 with the previous license number and the sticker," Liam said. "It's why I put it on in the first place. Conspicuous, it is. Now we'll be harder to spot."

"Ah, didn't think you were a Captain Beefheart fan, but I wasn't going to ask," Oran said. "Is that everything?"

"Finished," Liam said, crumpling the sticker and then tossing it onto the rubbish pile. He stuffed the old plates under some rags and straightened.

"And you're good?"

"I am," Liam said, hoping the lie would prove truth. "Mary Kate has an early political meeting in the morning. And she'll be worrying." He hopped into the car and cranked up the engine. Then he proceeded to trace his way back to the Falls at a more sedate pace. He got them to the Upper Falls Road without incident.

They weren't far from where he needed to drop Éamon and Nial when a prowl car pulled up behind them and shined a flashlight through the rear window.

Only going home after a few, mate, Liam thought. *Just like everyone else.* The thought was almost a prayer. Liam's fingers tingled on the steering wheel. After a long pause, the constable swerved around them and went on his way. Not long after, Liam stopped where Éamon directed him, and Nial and Éamon got out. Nial approached a rusted '72 model Escort parked on the street, unlocked the boot of the car and proceeded to transfer the bags. Oran helped.

Éamon leaned inside. "There'll be a report."

Liam nodded.

Reaching in, Éamon placed something on the seat. Three crisp twenty pound notes rested on black vinyl. Liam blinked.

"Am I allowed to take that?" He'd heard what happened to those that decided to help themselves to funds earmarked for the IRA. Sixty pounds wasn't much compared to what had been stolen from the bank, but no amount was worth a bullet in each knee or the head—certainly not an amount as small as sixty pounds.

"It's your share and will be noted in the record."

"Yes, sir."

There was a long pause, and Éamon stared as if he were seeing Liam for the first time. "Where did you learn to drive like that?"

"Bobby is into the racing. Rallies. Lets me drive sometimes."

"Good. Good," Éamon said. "You keep with that."

"Yes, sir."

Éamon straightened, settling into his standard military bearing and proceeded to walk away. If he did so a little more stiffly than usual, Liam couldn't blame the man. Instead, he snatched the sixty pounds off the seat and stuffed it into the pocket of his anorak. It was more money than he'd seen all at once in his life. Mary Kate was going to go ape. And maybe, just maybe if he wasn't too late getting home she might not have one of her headaches.

Oran and Nial finished unloading the bags and relocked the boot. Then Nial headed home with a wave.

"Where to, Mr. Knievel?" Oran said, climbing into the front seat.

"You got it wrong. He rides a motorbike."

"Could've fooled me."

"We're to a nice abandoned car park," Liam said. "We'll change the wheels and then have a bit of a bonfire."

"Looks like a late night."

"Are you telling me you can't change a tire all that fast, old man?"

Oran gave him an obscene gesture. "The cheek on the young these days. Set your barbs if you like. You'll change your tune soon enough. I'm the one with the whiskey."

At the car park, they loaded the stolen racing wheels into the back of Liam's black cab. Then Liam got out his wrenches and approached the RS1600.

"What are you doing?" Oran asked.

"The plugs are new," Liam said. "No sense in torching them."

"Leave them."

"They cost me, they did. Special performance ones for the racing, they are. And the Quartermaster won't reimburse for them."

Oran put a hand on his shoulder. "And what will the RUC think when they go to searching the burned out mess? 'Oh, look someone took the time to remove the plugs before they abandoned the car? Now, who would do such a thing?' The RUC are known to be a bit dim but even I should think they'd be looking into the garages after a thing like that. Leave them."

A great deal of whiskey and several hours later, Liam staggered up the apartment building stairs with Oran's help. It was about four o'clock in the morning, and Liam attempted to be as quiet as he could. Even so, Mary Kate opened the door before he'd gotten out his key. Dressed in a short white nightgown, she didn't look pleased. All hopes of a proper welcome home evaporated when she sniffed and scrunched up her face in disgust.

"Evening, love." Liam gave her what he hoped was his most charming smile. It didn't have the desired effect, however, particularly after he tripped over the doorstep. Oran just about yanked his arm out of its socket pulling him back to his feet.

"And where have you two been? The pubs are long closed," she said, stepping back. "Don't lie. I spoke to Elizabeth two hours ago. She said you've not been home."

Oran steered him to the sofa and then dropped him. Liam bounced once on the cushions, and the apartment whirled as Mary Kate closed the door.

"We had a bit of trouble," Oran said. "Dr. MacMahon thought it best to administer a drop of something to numb the pain."

"A drop? More like a gallon." Mary Kate moved closer and gasped. "Oh, shite. Is that blood?"

"Not his," Oran said, pushing the anorak off Liam's shoulders.

"No. Wait." Words slid through Liam's teeth and off his tongue before he could give them proper shape. The apartment spun in a new and interesting direction.

"What is it?" Oran asked.

It took three tries, but Liam was finally able to produce the pound notes from his pocket before Oran removed the jacket. "Ish for you, Mar—Mary Kate."

Her eyes widened and then narrowed. "Where did this come from?"

Oran said, "A bonus for a job well done."

Thou shalt not kill, Liam thought and flinched. "T-twenty ish for Oran. Owe. Owe him. Last of… bribe money." Liam laughed, and drunk as he was he knew he didn't sound good. Barking mad, he must be. *Barking.* He snorted. *Job well done. Did that BA get a bonus when he shot Annette, I wonder? Did the Paras after they gunned down the thirteen that Sunday? A bonus along with a grand medal from the Queen.* "Oh, shite," he said. "I think I'm going to be sick again."

Oran helped him into the washroom where he lost whatever whiskey remained in his stomach along with anything he'd eaten in the past month. He was too weak to get off the floor when it was done. So, Oran and Mary Kate cleaned him up and dumped him into the bed where darkness blissfully ended all possibility of thought. Before the blackness completed its work he heard Oran say, "He'll be in a bad way tonight. If he's not right after that, you call me."

Chapter 17

Andersonstown, Belfast, County Antrim, Northern Ireland
December 1975

Liam woke disoriented and feeling worse than he had in his whole life—including the times he'd landed in the Malone infirmary. The yellow light filtering through the bedroom curtains was bright enough to sink molten shards into the back of his brain. Pans clattered in the kitchen, a signal that Mary Kate was home. Judging by the force she put behind each blow she wasn't in a good mood. For the first time since he'd been with her he wished he were dead. The agony in his head had grown too big for his skull and was threatening to crack it open like a baby pterodactyl splitting its eggshell. He couldn't remember why he hurt so much. Sitting up, he instantly wished he hadn't and groaned. In a flash, Mary Kate was at his side with a glass of water.

"Here," she said, her face tight with worry and fear. "This will be what you're needing."

He blinked, considering whether or not his stomach would accept such a thing without rebellion. *Drunk. I was drunk.* "What are you doing home?" His voice was no better than a croak, and he decided he sounded every bit as bad as he felt.

"It's half past one," she said. "We've eggs. Sean always wanted a Belfast fry after… well… Said the grease did him a world of good. Are you well enough to eat?"

The thought of grease made everything worse. "No."

"Oh."

In careful motions for which he was profoundly grateful, she sat on the edge of the bed and held out the glass. He took it and drank, inwardly swearing never to touch the drink again. She seemed to hold herself away and wouldn't look at him. Her pretty lips were set in a tense line. She didn't leave, only sat there while unspoken questions curled in the air between them. When no gentle touch on the shoulder or head came as it always did when he was sick, his heart ached enough to compete with his head. He'd had nightmares of hurting her—dreams of blood and screaming. *Did the monster get free? What have I done now?* He found himself searching for bruises on her face, her arms.

"I… called in for you," she said, the fear in her voice sparking terror in him. "Told them you were sick."

Right. It'd been Friday when he'd come home from—*I killed a constable,* he thought. *Does she know? Is that why she's acting like this?* "Have you seen the paper?"

"Didn't buy one. Wasn't in the budget."

"Can you borrow it from Mrs. Black?"

Mary Kate looked away but not before he saw the lie plain on her face. "I asked earlier, but she'd already used it for fish guts."

He thought, *She's seen something and isn't telling me.* Finished with the water, he lay back down and rolled away from the pain in his chest.

"Won't you be getting up?"

The light was too strong; it etched images into the back of his skull with acid—images he wished nothing more than to forget. The surprised look. Lumps of wet darkness on brick. Annette MacGavigan's bloody hair. Jagged flaps of skin. *Thou shall not kill.* He pulled a pillow over his agony-filled head.

"All right. Rest then." Her dread seemed to drain her concern of warmth. "I'll have the dinner for you in a few hours. You'll be wanting it then."

He listened to the door shut and forgot everything for a time. When he woke next it was night, and Mary Kate was talking to someone.

"I don't know what manner of creature you brought home yesterday, but that isn't my husband."

Liam's heart froze.

"Calm yourself," Oran said. "He's taken it hard. He's a good man, and you can be proud of him no matter what they're saying on the radio and the television. He saved us all."

Jesus Christ, what are they saying? Was the man a Catholic? Did he have children?

"I'm not talking about that. It's something else," she said. "He… does things in his sleep. Makes sounds. Growls. Something else, I…." He heard her whisper but couldn't understand what she said.

"There has always been something a bit off about Liam as long as I've known him, Mary Kate. You been married to him for what? Almost a year? And you've not noticed before now?"

"That creature isn't the man I married. Liam is sweet. Loving. He certainly doesn't growl or… or…."

Liam pulled the pillow tighter over his head to shut out her words, but it didn't do any good.

"You're fooling yourself. He's got something in him all right. Something dangerous," Oran said, his voice dropped to a low murmur.

"You don't believe that, surely?" Mary Kate said. "Old tales. Used to scare children."

"I do, and you do too. In the dark. At night. Tell me you don't," Oran said. "I'm from Dublin. Lived there until Bobby and me came here for the cause. But my grandfather was a farmer. He told us the stories, and I know what I see when I see it."

"Oh, go on."

"My grandfather met one once. Neighbor asked him to stay with his wife one night while he went for the doctor. Grandfather ran down the road. Was met with a young man at the crossroads, he said. With a fiddle and a bow and eyes that glowed red. Played a tune of such sweet sadness he'd never heard in his life nor ever did again. Walked slow, he did. Prevented my grandfather from doing anything more than the same. Before they reached the house the young man told him the Fair People had claimed the good woman for their own. He told my grandfather not to worry, and then left off the road. She was dead when my grandfather arrived."

"Listen to Liam singing with his tapes in the taxi, and you'll know he has no talent for the music. Even if they were real, that's proof enough he isn't one of them."

"His eyes aren't right. You've seen it. I know you have."

More than my eyes, Liam thought. *I never told her. I let her think I was normal. I married her with a lie between us.*

"That's just a trick of the light," she said. "Like as not my eyes go red from time to time if my mother's Polaroids are any proof."

"You didn't see. The way he drove."

"I've been to the rallies. There's others that are better, but they've the money, and they've been at it longer. My Liam is good at the racing. He loves it. There's nothing off in that. Nothing… fey."

Oran's voice lowered. "No one drives like he did that night. I've never seen the like. What he did… Was too fast. Don't think I'm complaining. I'm thankful beyond measure. But we should've been caught. The RUC had us dead to rights. Even Éamon says so. We should've cracked up. We should've died. Between the RUC, the Army helicopters and the check points I don't know how he did it."

"You were frightened—"

"Anyone would've been. Éamon believes. Although, he'll never admit it now. Why do you think he paid your man that bonus? You don't anger one of the Good People. It's a wonder we didn't end in a lake, drowned—like all do who are taken for a wild ride. Only this was no black horse. Was a black car."

"That's ridiculous."

Everything was quiet for a time, and then Oran asked, "Do you need me or Elizabeth to stay with you? Do you think he's that bad off? Are you afraid?"

A second silence stretched out between his question and her answer. "He'll not harm me, my Liam. Not even like this." The doubt in her tone bruised his heart.

"You can always go to Mrs. Black's," Oran said. "If there's need."

Oh sure, that'd be just grand, Liam thought, feeling the bands around his chest squeeze. *The meddling old bag would just love that.*

"No. I'll be fine."

Liam heard a thump as the front door was opened.

"Where are you going?" Mary Kate asked.

"There's nothing can be done tonight," Oran said. "I'll be back tomorrow. With a priest."

What does he think a priest is going to do? Drive out the demon inside me? He tried not to think of Father Dominic and Father Christopher standing over the dead man. The edge of another mad laugh forced itself against the back of his throat like vomit. If anything could've been done to get rid of the demon short of killing him surely Father Murray would've done it, had he but known. *Little experiment.*

He knows, Liam thought. *Even the whole of Derry knew. It's why everyone was so careful. Everyone but those who didn't believe.*

Within moments of the door closing he heard Mary Kate sobbing in the next room. The sound of it drew him out of the bed and through the bedroom door before he knew it. He found her sitting on the sofa with her hands covering her face.

"Mary Kate?"

She looked up at him with eyes swollen and red. For a moment he couldn't breathe.

"Do you need something?" she asked.

He stood where he was, shirtless and still dressed in the stained black trousers he'd been wearing since Friday morning.

She sniffed. "Well, what is it?"

He sat next to her and hesitated before gathering her in his arms. Gently. He didn't want to frighten her further. More than anything he wanted to comfort her. Reassure her. She was wooden at first, but then relaxed. Soon, he felt warm tears trace cooling paths on his bare skin.

"You'd gone from me," she said, not lifting her face. "I didn't know what to do."

Say it. Tell her. Now. While there's still time, he thought. *But she'll leave me. And then what'll I do?* "I love you."

"I love you too. Don't frighten me like that again."

"You're not angry?"

"Terrified." She blew out a loud sigh. "Was sure you'd gone mad."

"No. At least I don't think so. Well, no more mad than I am already."

"Good."

More than anything he needed to lose himself in her. Forget. Hold her and never let go, but after everything that had happened he wasn't sure she would allow it. "I... I need you."

"Oh." She sniffed and looked into his eyes, pleading. "I need you too."

He kissed her long and hard, then picked her up off the sofa and carried her to bed.

Church bells echoed through the Falls Road, calling the faithful to Mass. He lay on his back in the warm bed with Mary Kate's head anchoring his chest. It was a sin, missing Mass in order to make love to your wife, but it was a good sin. *The best sin.* Her fingers played with the hair curling in the center of his chest. It tickled something fierce. He twitched and felt her smile in response. The smile stoked a comforting glow that burned out all the bad feelings. He didn't want to move or think, happy in animal contentment.

Animal. Can't wait any longer, he thought. *It has to be done.* "There's something I must tell you."

"Don't." She laid a finger on his lips. "I know. About the constable. It's all over the papers. The radio. The telly. I don't care. Sooner or later it was going to come to killing. I knew, even if you didn't. Three of my brothers are volunteers. All of my uncles. Father too if Mother would let him," she said, "You only did what you had to do. That constable had to have known. He'd have felt the same, were it you and not him."

I wouldn't be so sure, he thought.

Someone knocked on the door.

"That's probably Oran," she said, getting up and throwing on her clothes. "Get dressed. He'll have brought a priest."

"Don't need a priest. I need to tell you—"

She paused in the doorway, her light brown hair stuck out in disheveled tufts minted gold by the late morning light. Her eyelids were puffy from sleep, and she'd slept with her mascara on. It made smoky smudges around her swollen eyes. A short blue dress hung crookedly on her slender body, and her feet were bare. She looked damned beautiful, he decided. She always did in the morning. On second thought, she looked beautiful no matter the time of day or night. *You've got it bad, you have,* he thought.

"You'd have a priest in the place, and you in the clothes you slept in? Where are your manners?"

"What clothes? I seem to recall some brazen bird tore the trousers right off my—"

"Hush now. They're right outside." Blushing, she closed the bedroom door.

He let out the breath he had been holding and stood up naked on the bed to open the closet. Most of what was in it belonged to Mary Kate. He selected a clean shirt and dug into the chest of drawers for a fresh pair of jeans.

Minutes later he found himself facing a man in his mid-sixties with thinning hair, brown eyes and a wide mouth set in a square jaw. No one spoke. Everyone was paying more attention to the tea cooling in their cups than each other. Liam didn't know this priest that Oran had brought into the flat, and if he expected him to spill everything to a complete stranger, then Oran didn't know his arse from a drainpipe. Losing patience with the air of expectancy in the tiny room, Liam stood up and announced that he needed to give the taxi a wash. Father Kearney displayed a disturbing tendency toward perseverance and asked if he could help. Unable to object without angering Mary Kate, Liam agreed.

It was too cold to muck about with buckets of water and suds, but he'd committed himself. He collected an old towel, filled two buckets with water from the outside spigot and approached the taxi with the priest at his heels. The taxi shone black in the car park. It had been imported from London along with the others in the fleet, he supposed because black cabs were the most efficient. It was a great hulking box of a car with seating for six in the back and space for two more up front with the driver. Filling it with fares was dead easy. Often the buses wouldn't run their routes for weeks due to a riot or a bomb, but the black taxis always did. Without the black hacks many in the community wouldn't be able to feed their families, and Liam was proud to be part of the service.

The instant Liam plunged his hand into the cold water he decided washing the entire car might be a bit ambitious and settled for cleaning the wheels. The taxi didn't need a washing anyway—that was obvious. Since he didn't own it he tended to be careful with it. By insisting on helping, Father Kearney had called his bluff. Deciding to give the interior a once-over afterward for show if for nothing else, Liam knelt and began soaping the front driver's side wheel. Father Kearney hovered like an army helicopter.

"Oran tells me you were in the Kesh."

Liam paused to allow the electric charge of shock settle before going back to what he was doing. He gritted his teeth. *Why tell the fucking priest about the Kesh? It's none of his damned business.* After their initial meeting, he and Oran hadn't discussed the past, and when he thought about it, the organization must have informed Éamon too. How much everyone really knew about his stay in Long Kesh gave Liam a shudder. "Served a few months. Was in Malone three years."

Father Kearney nodded. "Sorry to hear it. What for?"

Liam sighed. "Is it important, Father?"

"Not particularly," Father Kearney said. "You're from Derry?"

"Mary Kate and I. Yes." *As if you couldn't tell from my accent.* He finished with the first wheel and squatted in front of the second with his shoulders tensing. He didn't know why he resented the old priest's questions. He supposed it was because Oran had specifically sent the man to prying.

"How long have you been in Belfast?"

"Mary Kate has lived here since starting at Queen's University. Four years. She's studying to be a solicitor. I've been here since we married a year ago last summer." *There. Is that enough to keep your trap shut for a bit, old man?*

"Newlyweds, then?"

"Yes."

"And how is it?"

Liam turned to look up at Father Kearney. What sort of an answer was he fishing for? "It's good, Father."

"No troubles?"

"No more than usual, I suppose."

"And how is she holding up to the stress?"

"What stress?" Liam's heart slammed against his breastbone like a battering ram. *The stress of being married to a demon?*

Father Kearney squatted next to him and whispered in Irish. "I'm what could be officially termed an army chaplain. If any such thing were official."

Liam blinked. "Which, Father?" he asked in Irish. "The army or the chaplain?"

"In this case? Both, I think." He winced and stood. Returning to English, he said, "Now, are you going to finish up with this farce and find somewhere to sit and talk like civilized men? All this is a bit hard on an old man's knees."

Rinsing off the wheels, Liam emptied the buckets and then opened the rear of the cab. "Get in."

"Why not the front seat?"

"If the cab is going to double as a confessional, Father, the back makes a hell of a lot more sense."

"Ah," Father Kearney said, "Yes." He climbed in without further protest, although he cast an uneasy look at the street.

Thinking Oran had probably told Father Kearney about the wild ride, Liam settled into the driver's seat and turned the key. "Don't worry, Father. I promise to keep to the speed limit."

"That's good, then."

Liam steered the taxi out of the car park and into the street in silence, trying to work out what he would say—if he would say anything at all. When Father Kearney showed no sign of cracking, Liam offered him a boon. He switched to the Irish again. "Army chaplain? So, the Church is secretly in support of the cause, then?"

"Ah, no. If they knew, I'd be removed. I'm a volunteer."

Liam paused. "Don't most chaplains carry guns?"

"I operate strictly in a non-violent capacity. My purpose is to tend to those who don't."

"This is a bit... out of the ordinary, Father."

"Isn't it?" Father Kearney asked. "But it's what I was called to do. Was a time when the Church turned its back on the IRA. Priests weren't allowed to grant the sacraments, did you know?"

Liam nodded.

"I'm here to see it doesn't happen again."

"Ah." Liam drove four blocks before continuing the conversation. "Begging your pardon, Father, but I don't know anything about you. You could be an informer for all I know."

The rearview mirror framed Father Kearney's shrug. "Caution is an admirable quality. And surely this wouldn't be considered a traditional confession by any means, but anything you say is protected by my vow just the same."

For a moment, Liam thought of Father Murray—although, Father Murray had nothing in common with the man sitting in the back seat. Father Kearney wasn't gentle. If anything, his eyes were fierce. He claimed to not carry a gun, but Liam wasn't sure it was by choice.

"I'm not permitted to discuss anything with anyone," Liam said.

"Not even in a confessional?"

"Don't know. Never asked."

"It is your choice, then, my son. I can't force you."

Liam drove a bit further, avoiding looking into the rearview mirror. He wanted to speak to someone—had to, when he thought about it. At the same time, he couldn't imagine walking into St. Agnes's next Saturday and telling Father Murray.

"I kill... did for a man."

"I'm listening."

"While robbing a bank," Liam paused. "Don't suppose you've a standard penance for that, do you?" The madness was there again, tickling at the back of his throat.

"Was it in the line of duty?"

"What?"

"Were you under orders?"

"For which, Father? The robbing or the killing?" Liam choked back a laugh. *Steady on, man. You don't want Father Kearney telling tales to Oran or Éamon or HQ.*

"Tell me what happened."

Liam kept the story as vague as he could. Father Kearney made the appropriate listening sounds without interrupting except when needing clarification. When Liam finally stopped talking he found he'd driven halfway to Lisburn. He drove farther south a few blocks in silence.

"So, that's why Oran came to me," Father Kearney said. "You're the one shot that constable."

Liam's face heated. "You can go ahead and tell me what I already know."

"And what is it you already know?"

"Was a Catholic, wasn't he?"

"Protestant, actually," Father Kearney said. "Had a wife. Two children. Girls. Both in school. Does that help?"

Father Murray's voice echoed in Liam's head. The words were from the time he'd beat the shite out of a Protestant boy for calling him a stinking taig. *We're the same, Protestants and Catholics. You're never to think any different. This is important, Liam. Never do that again, you hear me?* And that was true enough, Liam knew. His uncle was a Prod, wasn't he? And Uncle Sean was a kind man, so he was. Therefore, he hadn't done anything like it again without severe provocation. *Until now.* "No, Father. I can't say that it does."

"And what would've happened if you hadn't killed him?"

Liam paused. "We'd be on our way to prison, I suppose. But like as not, we've all seen that before. At least those little girls would still have a father."

"And the organization wouldn't have the funds you collected."

"Sure."

"There'd be less money to pay for equipment, to pay volunteers like yourself, to provide for the protection of Catholic families," Father Kearney said. "As well as four less volunteers to shield them. Four volunteers who would've had to endure questioning and thus, risk betraying the entire organization."

Liam swallowed.

"Let me ask you something," Father Kearney said. "Why did you volunteer?"

Liam hesitated. Admitting to the killing and robbing was bad enough, but to answer now was as much as admitting being a member of an illegal organization and that meant going back to Malone or worse, the Kesh, for serious time. The Brits had revoked political status, and the news coming out of the prisons was that conditions were worse than they'd been before. He decided if Father Kearney was an informer he was probably done for anyway. "The truth, Father? I'd seen enough, lived through enough… well…. Was the red anger. Officer spotted it right off. Told me to reconsider. After a time I did. But then I thought about Mary Kate. In Belfast. Alone. With no one to keep her safe. But she was willing to take the risk. To fight back against the whole system in her own way. Then I thought about when I got out. We'd be married, God willing, and have children one day. And did I really want my son to see what I've seen? To live as I have? To be beaten and shut up in prison or shot?

"The long and the short of it, Father, is… I did it for him. And he doesn't even exist. Is that mad?"

Father Kearney said, "I shouldn't think so."

It was very quiet in the cab for a time.

"According to the Church, there is such a thing as a justified war," Father Kearney said. "In order for there to be peace, sometimes someone must make a stand for those who can't stand for themselves. Negotiation is the first moral option, of course. So, we attempt peace time and again. But the British are never serious about negotiations. They've demonstrated that. It's on their heads."

I don't know what manner of creature you brought home yesterday, but that isn't my husband.

Demon. Fallen.

"You're a soldier. You're not a chauffeur. Soldiers kill for their country," Father Kearney said.

He… does things in his sleep. Makes sounds. Growls.

I did it for my son. And he doesn't even exist. Such shite. Will you listen to yourself? "Do soldiers rob banks too, Father?" Liam tried to keep the bitterness out of the question but found he couldn't. Glancing at the rear-view mirror it was clear he needn't have worried.

"In your case, I'm afraid they do."

And what if I have to do for someone again? Will the monster grow stronger until there's nothing left of me? Ever since Liam could remember, he'd feared becoming like his stepfather. He hadn't understood he had the potential to be something else. *Something worse.* He tightened his grip on the steering wheel and waited for what was next.

"You only did your duty, hard as it was," Father Kearney said. "Say five 'Our Fathers' and a rosary for the dead man and his family." He made the sign of the cross as a blessing and to signify the end of the confession. "God forgives you."

But Liam knew differently. That dead constable's face would stay with him to the end of his days. The day it didn't would be the day Father Dominic and Father Christopher would come for him, and Liam had the feeling that they wouldn't be alone. Father Murray would be right there beside them.

Chapter 18

Andersonstown, Belfast, County Antrim, Northern Ireland
March 1976

"Come on, Mary Kate," Liam said. "I told Bobby we'd be downstairs. They'll be here any minute." It was Saturday morning, and Bobby was taking them to another road rally—the first of the new year, and Liam couldn't wait to get out of Belfast and have some fun.

Something clattered to the floor in the washroom.

"Dammit!"

"You're beautiful," Liam said. "Let's go."

"All right, all right." She emerged, wearing flares and a brown turtle-neck.

Light brown hair draped over her shoulders and down her back in silky waves. She had decided to stop cutting it, and he couldn't help but approve. She grabbed her handbag and coat, and they locked up and headed down the stairs, making it to the curb just as Bobby drove up. Oran was to ride in the back with Mary Kate and Elizabeth, and Liam would be up front with Bobby so they could talk about the race.

Bobby threw open the driver's side door and hopped out. Where Oran was stocky with straight blond hair, Bobby was slender with bushy brown hair. One wouldn't have thought them related but for the brown eyes and strong chin. "She's all yours," Bobby said, rounding the front of the still-running car.

"I thought you were driving?" Liam asked.

Bobby climbed into the passenger seat. "If you're going to drive today, you might as well test out the road conditions."

Taking the wheel with a grin, Liam eased into traffic and headed north. Bobby knew the location, and Liam followed Bobby's directions the whole way. They had to get out of the car for a search several times at various checkpoints on the way out of town, but it was the only black mark on an otherwise beautiful morning. The sun was out and the road was relatively

151

dry. He accelerated into the turns while judging the grip of the tires on the pavement. A herd of sheep afforded an excuse for quick braking. The RS1600 responded with joyous grace and precision. He rolled down the window and let the air push against his arm until Mary Kate complained of the cold. Then he turned up the heater, leaving the window open just an inch or so. It wasn't as good but it was good enough. He felt alive at the RS's wheel in ways he never could inside the sluggish taxi. By the time they arrived at the rally site Liam felt content and whole—the long months of mundane existence since the last race, since the last bank job, were blown from his mind. He was alert. Ready. And although he'd never done a timed run before, he was sure he would win.

Hopping out of the car, he gave Mary Kate a quick kiss for luck and then watched her follow Elizabeth up the hill. They would locate a good spot to view the race and then set up the picnic. He and Bobby would join them once the queue order was established. While Liam looked on, Elizabeth unfurled a blanket and then spread it out on the grass. Mary Kate bent over to get the tea from the hamper and Liam felt a smile pull at the corners of his mouth. Bobby went to check in with the rally organizers, get their queue number and a copy of the route map.

"How do you feel?" Oran asked.

"Fucking brilliant," Liam said, stretching. "I want an RS of my own. I really fucking do. But Mary Kate, she doesn't like the idea. Thinks I'll start crashing through checkpoints for a lark."

"It's not as if they could catch you, you know," Oran said. "Oh, now. Don't give me that look. I know you've more sense than that. She should too. You're fucking born for the racing."

"Ah, go on."

Oran leaned over, glared at the lumpy man standing next to the red Porsche parked two cars over and then smacked Liam on the shoulder. "Go show that posh fucker what West Belfast is made of." Then he walked up the hill to join Elizabeth and Mary Kate.

"Hello, Kelly. Feeling lucky today?"

Liam turned around and found himself face to face with the Porsche's owner, Gerry McDonald. "Aye. I do."

"You'd best watch yourself in that cheap bucket of bolts," Gerry pushed a pair of big white sunglasses up the bridge of his nose. He was wearing white leather racing gear with red stripes to match his car. "That piece of shite looks like it might fall apart on you."

"What's with the outfit?" Liam asked. "Thinking of joining Elton John on a tour later?"

Gerry grabbed him by the front of his anorak and shoved. "Sod off."

Liam struggled to free himself, but couldn't. Gerry outweighed him by quite a lot. "Let go of me." His arms and legs were already tingling, and his jaw tightened.

"Listen, you little gobshite," Gerry said. "You're only driving today because I was feeling charitable. You don't have a membership in the club. You can't even buy your own fucking car. That means you don't fucking race unless I say so."

Gritting his teeth, Liam glared at Gerry and lowered his voice. The prickling had gotten bad enough that he could feel it on his tongue. "I said, let go of me."

Gerry dropped him and stumbled back with a gasp. His face was pale. "Liam—"

"Everything's fine, Bobby. Gerry here was only wishing me luck." Liam took a step forward just to see Gerry retreat a second time. "Weren't you?"

"I—I was. Yes." Gerry smoothed his long brown hair back from his face. "Yes. Ah, good luck." He practically ran to his car.

"I'm not sure that was such a good idea, mate," Bobby said. "The bastard has a long memory."

"The fucking ballbag asked for it."

"You'll not get into the club without his say, Liam."

Liam took a deep breath and put a hand inside his pocket. His fingers brushed against cool metal—his lighter, and to his dismay he realized Bobby was probably right. "Sorry."

"For fuck's sake, you should have more self-control," Bobby said. "To be sure, he's a fucking wanker, but he's a fucking wanker with shady connections in Dublin, if you get my meaning. Don't be for winding him up too much."

"I said I was sorry."

"Come on," Bobby said. "Let's empty the boot and then get something to eat. We can go over the map."

According to the queue, Liam would go before Gerry and his Porsche 911 Targa. Liam was uncomfortable with the idea of Gerry being behind him. However, the weather was turning and if Liam waited much longer the club might cancel his run. While they'd had their picnic and had watched the others go through their runs, it'd started to rain. Three cars skidded off the road. One rolled over. No one was hurt, but Liam got the feeling that it had been a close thing. As his turn approached, he gulped the last of his tea, snatched another kiss from Mary Kate and took his place in the queue. He had too much nervous energy to stay in the car. So, he paced alongside of it. When the driver in front of him took off, Liam jumped back into the

RS and pulled forward. Gerry moved up as well with too much force and tapped the rear bumper of Bobby's RS.

"Fucking bastard!" Liam unbuckled his seatbelt.

"He's only arsing around!" Bobby grabbed his arm. "*Ná dean breallaire baoth diot féin!*" *Don't make a bloody fool of yourself.* He tended to slip into the Irish when he got excited.

"But your car—"

"This beast will hold. We've no worries," Bobby said. "Now, settle down, or the bastard will have you too rattled to do what I know you can."

Nervous, Liam reached into his pocket.

"You know where we're going," Bobby said. "You can do this. I know you can. But this is your first. So, it's all right to take it slower than you think you can."

Liam nodded. "The rain."

"Aye. The rain."

The Starter moved next to the car as well as the Timer. Looking into the window and at Liam, the Starter put up his hand and signaled with his fingers. *Ready. Steady. Go.*

Slamming the accelerator, Liam adjusted to the grip of the tires in the damp and was able to avoid sliding. It was a good start. The first turn came up fast, but he did as Bobby had told him and took it slower than he wanted. He was rewarded by not slipping into the ditch two others had landed in before.

"Good. Very good," Bobby said. "Now watch the next one, *a cara.* It'll be the fucking bitch. Once you're out of it, push her hard as you can without losing control."

Liam rounded the next turn faster than recommended, and Bobby gasped, but Liam knew the tires could take it, and take it they did. He punched the accelerator, and the RS leapt eagerly at the road. He didn't look at the speedometer. Didn't need to. He could feel the weight of the car around him, and the way the wind caressed its steel body, the grit of the road beneath the wheels. His arms and legs were tingling again, and the beginnings of a headache haunted the back of his brain, but he ignored them. The only thing that mattered was the road and tearing down it as fast as the car could stand. Bobby was yammering something about road conditions and another turn in Irish. Liam didn't really hear the words. They registered somewhere in his subconscious and collected there for future reference. He and the car were one. He knew what she could take and what she couldn't—more than Bobby ever could. If asked later, Liam wouldn't have been able to explain why he knew. The knowledge was there, resting in the front of his aching head, solid as stone.

A turn loomed ahead. There were skid marks where the previous car had flipped and lost control. By this point, Bobby's English was long gone as well as his proper Irish, and he rattled off a long series of swear words in Gaeilge. Liam smiled, but the smile faded as he felt the tires give. He willed the car to stay on the road. Still, it slid. He steered into the skid and concentrated with all his might. *You will stay on the fucking road. You will stay—*

Bobby's swearing stretched out into a scream.

—on the fucking road, you fucking bitch—

The tires on the passenger's side of the car went over the edge of the pavement, and something thumped. There was a loud bang, but the driver's side wheels grabbed.

—you fucking whore. Hold!

And then he was through the turn, and the car rocketed down the straight-away toward the second Timekeeper. They roared past. The Timekeeper waved his hands in the air. Liam reluctantly mashed the brakes several times, slowing the RS, and as he slowed he could sense the wheels on the driver's side felt more and more wrong.

By the time the car limped to a stop Bobby was laughing like a madman and blathering. When he finally calmed down enough to remember his English, he said, "Jesus, Liam! That was fucking brilliant! Wild! *Níl fhios agam conas—* I don't know how you did it! We were goners for sure. I swear to God."

Liam started shaking. He felt like he'd just downed half a bottle of whiskey in one go. "We were fine. I knew we'd make the turn. I knew it."

Bobby hopped out of the RS and ran to the Timekeeper. He grabbed the clipboard and whooped. "Beat that, you fucking wanker and your fucking wanking Porsche!"

Getting out of the car, Liam bent over and grabbed his knees. He was dizzy. He laid his palm against the RS's door to steady himself. *Thank you, you beautiful bitch. Thank—* Then he saw the remains of the front tire. It was shredded. His stomach did a lazy flip. "Ah, Bobby. I think you need to see something."

Bobby came running, still holding the clipboard. The Timekeeper was right behind him, obviously wanting the record sheets back. "Liam, you have to see the time!"

Swallowing, Liam straightened. "Bobby, I'm sorry. Your tires. Fuck, look at the wheel."

Bobby finally looked where he was pointing. "Oh."

"I'll pay you for a new one, I will. Tell me how much, and I'll pay you for it. I'm so sorry."

"What the fuck are you apologizing for? It was a race, mate. And I think you fucking won."

"What?"

"It's not over yet. Gerry, that fucking bollocks, has to go through, but he'll not beat you. Not with that time. This is fucking beautiful, I tell you. I've wanted this for so long."

Annoyed, the Timekeeper snatched the clipboard from Bobby and walked back to his spot. Using the radio to tell the Starter and the first Timer that everything was ready, the Timer got back to business.

"But the wheel," Liam said. "It's completely banjaxed." It was warped, curving outward like a bowl, and the rim was flattened. He hadn't even known that was physically possible.

"We've another. Pulled it out of the back to lighten the load before the race, remember? And I can borrow a second from my cousin Michael. He's over there. You'll get home. What the fuck are you worried about?"

"I wrecked your RS."

"And I'm telling you it's nothing that can't be fixed. It's expected. It was a fucking race," Bobby said. "Come on. Let's get up the hill before Gerry starts his run. If he rolls that fucking Porsche trying to beat you, I want to see it. Hell, I want fucking photos."

Bobby made certain the RS was well out of the way and then the both of them jogged up the hill to join the others. They got there in time to see Gerry start. Liam stumbled when Mary Kate grabbed him in a fierce hug.

"I thought you were gone," she said. "You scared me half to death."

Oran was grinning. "That was fucking amazing, that was. Makes me want to get my license."

"Oran MacMahon, you'll do no such thing," Elizabeth said.

They watched the red Porsche make the first three turns, but when Gerry hit the last bend too fast, he slid straight off the road and into a tree. It took three men and a chainsaw to get him out. Gerry hollered the entire time about them damaging his Porsche. Liam didn't understand what the fuss was about. The car was a lost cause. At the last, Gerry stumbled out, cursed and took a swing at the farmer who'd cut him out. The first Timer and two of the other club members had to hold him. There was a cut on his head, and he'd bled all over his white leathers.

"If the fucking rooster hadn't fit out that thing with a racing cage, he'd probably be dead," Bobby said, punching Liam on the shoulder. "Lost his sense trying to beat you."

When the times were tallied, Liam was declared the winner. Bobby almost couldn't contain himself. "Do you know what this means?"

"Not really," Liam said.

"You set the club record," Bobby said. "The record. They have to let you in."

"But I can't pay the dues, and I don't own a car."

Bobby smiled. "Ah, well. Maybe we could work something out."

"How?" Liam asked.

"Put in an hour or two a week at the garage for a start," Bobby said. "We could use the hand. Doesn't matter. It's worth it to me having you in the club. Show that fuck it takes more than money to win."

"I don't know," Liam said.

"Tell you what. You and Mary Kate drive the RS home. Talk it over. Think about it." Bobby tossed the keys, and Liam caught them. "Michael and me, we got the wheels and the tires sorted. Me, Oran and Elizabeth will ride home with Michael."

"Are you sure?" Liam asked.

"You set the fucking record, you wee fuck," Oran said. "Consider the drive home your prize."

"Take it easy on the way back," Bobby said. "I won't trust the suspension until I have her up on the rack and can give her a good go-over."

Mary Kate looked uneasy. "I don't know."

"Come on, love," Liam said. "It'll be grand. I'll show you how fun it is."

She sighed. "All right. I know it means so much to you."

Elizabeth, Oran and Bobby said their goodbyes with promises of a few celebratory rounds at The Harp and Drum as soon as they got back to Belfast. Liam opened the RS's door for Mary Kate, helped her inside and then trotted over to the driver's side. He climbed in and started the engine, then sat listening to its throaty rumble.

"Isn't that the most beautiful sound you ever heard?" he asked.

"Not really."

"Oh, come on, Mary Kate. It's a fucking RS1600. It's the closest thing to a race car I could ever own."

She folded her arms across her chest. "I know what it is. I saw you nearly roll the thing over into a ditch."

"I won't drive the RS like that. Not every day. Only for the racing."

Frowning, she stared out the passenger window. "You shouldn't drive like that at all. Ever."

"You never complained before." He backed up and pulled onto the road. Oran and Bobby waved goodbye, and he stuck an arm out the open window to return the wave.

"You were careful before," she said. "This time—this time you scared me. Was that what you were like that night—" She stopped herself and then whispered, "Oran said you took them on a wild ride."

"What?" *No one drives like he did that night.* He blinked. *I am that thing when I drive.*

Biting her lip, she looked as though she wanted to say something, and he had a terrible feeling he knew what. *I'll lose her.*

She sighed. "It sounds mad. All of it."

"Don't you mean Fey?" *Demon. Fallen.*

"Liam, don't."

"There's something wrong with me. I'm... not normal." *She knows. You lied to her. Just tell her already.*

"Not at all. There's nothing wrong with you. I-I'm afraid of what will happen."

"I was in control." *What if driving is like the killing?*

"No. You skidded. You almost wrecked."

"I kept it on the road. I knew what I was doing."

She turned to face him. "Did you? Did you really?"

She's right. You didn't. It did. But the thought of giving up driving was too terrible. "Accidents happen, love. There's fuck all I can do about that. Anyway, I don't understand what the problem is," Liam said. "You know what I do when I'm off on a job."

"I know. I know."

"Why is this any different?" he asked, and then lowered his voice out of habit. "At least there weren't any bullets or prowl cars or—"

"Stop it!" She slammed both palms down on the seat. "You and the other ones—you do what you have to. That's the way of things. I understand. It's for our future. For Ireland. But that back there, that was for fun. Liam Kelly, you nearly killed yourself for the fun of it!"

"I need it."

"You don't need it. You want it."

"It's like the running," he said. He could feel the headache coming back more fierce than before. It happened sometimes after a long day at the wheel. He assumed it was the pressure of dealing with the other cars and the press of time. "Sometimes I feel I'm going to die if I don't get out and move. Fast. I feel trapped. Like I'm being buried alive. This. Driving. It's like the running only better. I'm free."

"You're free when you're at home too."

"Not like this," he said, accelerating into a turn and easing the car gracefully around the bend without moving into the next lane. The weight of the car tugged against the grip of the tires, and it gave him the sensation of swinging on the end of a rope. "It feels... it feels so fucking good."

"Are you saying you're trapped when you're home with me?"

"What? No!"

"Because if that's what you're saying—"

"That's not what I'm saying at all!" His foot mashed the accelerator. His temples were throbbing. "Can't you feel it?"

"I understand that four years of prison has left you with a need to run," she said, "to feel like there's no one can catch you. Not even me."

"That's not true!"

"But it's running away. That's all this is. This need to go fast. And you can't run from the past. You can't run from whatever it is those bastards did to you in the Kesh and—"

"I'll not fucking talk about that." There was a double bend in the road. It twisted up a hill and down the other side, tracing a path along a lake. It was a beautiful sight, and he'd make her feel what he did by making the car dance. He'd make her understand, but his head ached enough to make him blind. *Out.* He had to get out. *Away.*

"You never talk about the Kesh," she said. "And I'd be fine with that but for the fact that every time you hear the fucking name you flinch or bolt out a door or run from me."

"I do not." *Coward,* he thought. *She's as much as calling me a coward.*

"You do. I don't care what it is you did in that place. It doesn't matter."

—to be your first. It was Sanders's voice, whispering up from the past. Liam pushed the car through the first bend as fast as he could and willed the rush of wind battering the wind-screen to blast the memory from his mind.

"I'll still love you," she said. "You don't even have to tell me what it was you did."

Isn't that sweet?

He whipped through the second bend, and the tires protested with a high-pitched squeal, but he didn't really hear it. He wasn't actually listening to anything but the voice inside his head. The shame was overwhelming—that, and the rage came with it. The crush of emotion was so vast it pushed the breath from his body. He wasn't so much seeing the road in front of him as the inside of that cell.

"Just stop running from it before you kill yourself."

You like it, don't you? I can feel it.

"No!"

The car soared over the crest of the hill and came crashing down onto the pavement with a jolt. He felt something in the undercarriage give away. Somewhere in the distance Mary Kate screamed.

I know what you are. I saw it the first time I saw you. And now you know it too. Sanders had been right. There was something terrible and unnatural in him. He'd responded. He'd—

The water.

He knew what to do. He'd drown it out of himself. Whatever it was that Sanders saw. Kill it. No one had to know. He steered the car for the lake and slammed the accelerator pedal to the floor. A car passing the opposite direction blared its horn. The moment the RS's wheels left the pavement he knew he'd made a terrible mistake. He mashed the brakes to stop it from happening but was too late. Mary Kate screamed as the car plunged off the bank and into the lake. The impact with the water came as a crushing jolt. His hands slipped from the wheel, and he smacked his head on something. Mary Kate's scream was cut off. Freezing water poured in through the half-open window. His mind muzzy, he watched uncomprehending as a waterfall was created from automobile glass and lake water.

Mary Kate coughed, and his brain snapped into focus at once.

Get her out, he thought. *Got to get her out.*

He shoved himself against the car door three times, but it wouldn't budge. The car was filling up. He didn't have much time. At the moment the car was floating but any second it'd start to sink. Mary Kate moaned.

Think, damn you!

He punched the seatbelt clasp and got it undone on the second try. He tried unrolling the window and got it for the most part before the handle broke off in his hand. Even more water rushed in.

"Fucking hell!"

The opening was wide enough. He could push her through. Turning to her, he saw there was blood on her face. He blinked. *I've killed her,* he thought. *I've fucking killed her.* The water was gushing in faster. It was at his hips now, and the car was sinking.

Not now. Get her out. Worry later.

His hands were freezing as he plunged them into the water and grasped the seatbelt clasp. By some miracle he got it on the first try. She slumped, but seemed to be coming around.

"Mary Kate, love. Go through the window. Do you hear me?" He pushed her toward the driver's side. His teeth were clattering in his head.

"What happened?"

Coughing and sputtering, he helped her through just before the car went under. He held his breath, but he'd not gotten a good gasp before the water closed over his head. There was a pocket of air along the ceiling, and he shoved his face against the vinyl covering the roof and gulped as much air as he could, then he half-swam to the window and slipped out. When he surfaced he saw she'd made it to the bank and two strangers were helping her out of the water.

"Liam is in there! You have to get him out!"

He swam to shore with his head pounding something fierce. Touching lakebed at last, he crawled across the rocks and mud with his vision pulsing with the beat of his heart. Focused. Blurred. Focused. *I almost killed her,* he thought. He looked back, and the RS1600 was nowhere to be seen. *Fuck. What am I going to tell Bobby?*

"You must sit down, miss."

"He'll drown!"

Liam used the last of his strength to drag himself up on his feet, then stagger to her. "Here, Mary Kate. I'm here." He dropped to his knees and winced as he hit the rocks.

"My wife went for a doctor," one of the strangers said. "Help will be here soon."

Mary Kate's hand reached up from between the Good Samaritans and grabbed his. "Liam!"

"I'm here."

The big man in the brown anorak moved aside so he could sit next to her. More than anything, Liam wanted to lie down and sleep, but his head was killing him, and he felt dizzy.

"You all right, sir?"

"Am."

Mary Kate started to cry. "I'm sorry."

"What have you to be sorry for?" Liam asked. "I'm the one to blame. Jesus. I'm sorry."

She sat up and threw her arms around him. "I didn't mean to upset you."

"I lost control," Liam said. "Was my fault. Let the anger get the best of me. I'll never do it again. I'll talk to Father Murray. There has to be something he can do."

"I thought you were dead."

"Shhhh. There now," he said, smoothing her hair. She was wet and shivering and so was he, but he did what he could to warm her anyway by pulling her tight to his body. "It's all right."

"The car—"

"You're alive. That's all that matters."

Someone brought a blanket and wrapped it around the two of them. He focused on making Mary Kate comfortable until help arrived.

"You'll have to get back to the driving again," Oran said. "You can't hold the wreck against yourself forever."

"I know," Liam said.

"It's been four months." Oran stared into his pint while the pub clientele shouted and laughed around them. "Éamon has been very patient."

"I know." Liam had just gotten off his shift for the day, and the headache thumping behind his eyes was one of the worst yet. He'd argued with

Mary Kate multiple times about getting in to see a doctor, but he'd held his ground. Eventually, the ache in his head died down and his vision was right again, but ever since the accident the headaches at the end of the work day had gotten worse.

Oran lowered his voice. "It has to be tonight."

"I know." Liam sipped from his pint. *To drive again. Really drive.* It'd been so long. *Will it be safe?*

"The job is in a few days."

"I know."

"Will you stop with the 'I know' already?" Oran asked. "You're starting to sound like a parrot."

"I know."

"You wee bastard." Oran shoved his shoulder. "You're sound, all right."

The sudden movement caused the ache in Liam's brain to crank up a notch. He took a long drink of cider and prayed the pain would fade.

"You don't look so good, mate," Oran said.

Liam shrugged. "Bit uneasy, is all."

"Everything good at home?"

Shrugging again, Liam said, "Hasn't been great since, well… you know. We get on each other's nerves."

"She'll come round. You both had a wee scare is all."

Liam nodded. He didn't tell Oran that he and Mary Kate hardly spoke to one another without it ending in a row. It'd gotten to a point that even the running didn't help. His head hurt too much, and he was sick of thinking about it.

"Elizabeth says Mary Kate is learning to drive."

"Aye."

"It wasn't your fault, you know. Bobby looked the car over. The fucking tie rod gave way. He feels terrible. You shouldn't give up the racing."

"I could have killed her."

"You didn't."

"I could have."

"How many times do I have to—"

"You weren't there."

"Maybe so," Oran said. "But I know you. And I know you'd never hurt Mary Kate. Not on purpose. It was an accident."

Liam looked away, his jaw tensing and his heart aching to compete with his head. *Not on purpose.* "Do you have a car in mind?"

"I do."

"All right," Liam said. "We'll do it. Tonight."

"Now you're talking sense."

Finishing off his pint, Liam stood up. "Think I'll go home now."

"Stay. Have a few more," Oran said. "Relax."

"Can't," Liam said. "Mary Kate will be home early, and I need to finish with the carburetor before she gets there. The fucking choke on that damned taxi gives me trouble once a week. I'd buy a new carburetor, but I'm paying Bobby for the RS."

"He said you don't have to. The insurance paid off."

Liam shrugged.

"All right," Oran said. "I'll meet you on the corner at eleven."

Getting into the taxi, Liam started the engine and headed home. Thanks to the choke, the engine died three times along the way because the idle was off, and it wasn't getting enough fuel in the mix. He wanted to hit something, anything, by the time he got home. His head was splitting already, and another hour with his head under the hood didn't sound remotely good, but it had to be done. He pulled into the car park and decided to grab some aspirin first. He locked the taxi and went up the stairs to the flat. When he opened the door he stopped and blinked. Mary Kate was there already, and she was wearing something that amounted to a few bits of gauze and some ribbon.

"Welcome home," she said.

He felt his mouth drop open.

"Are you going to shut the door?" she asked. "Or would you rather I caught cold?"

"Wha—" He swallowed and then shut the door. Through the fog of his aching brain, he tried to think of an anniversary date or a special occasion missed, but it was the end of July. There was nothing. "I—I—"

She moved close and put her arms around him. Suddenly, his headache was of much less importance. "I wanted to apologize for last night. Well, the last few nights, actually. All right. The last few months."

Ever since the crash, she'd been distant and quiet. He'd begun to think she was frightened of him, and it'd taken its toll on him. He'd started to wonder if she would leave him after all. The black thing living under his skin was becoming more and more of a problem. "Oh." *Fucking brilliant,* he thought. *She goes to all this trouble and all you can say is "Oh"?*

"There's something I need to talk to you about." He felt her press even closer so that her body just touched his.

"Ah, yes? What is it?"

"You were right. We should have a baby."

"What?"

"It has to be now. Please. Or it'll be too late."

He stepped back. "You said you wanted to wait. You wanted to finish school first."

"I've changed my mind. Please." She tugged at his shirt, pulling him to her. She unbuttoned it and then her nipples were hard points against his skin. He moved to push her away, but the feel of her in his hands gave him a rise.

"I want a baby. Your baby," she said. "Now."

"You want to be a barrister. You'll not finish if we do this."

She was tugging at the front of his jeans now. He felt the button pop open under her fingers. "I don't care."

"I do."

"Do you, now?" She gave him a wicked smile and licked his neck. It sent a lightning-quick charge through his body. When her hand probed inside the front of his jeans, suddenly nothing else mattered. "Do I have your attention?" she asked.

"Aye. You do, it seems. Firmly in your grasp." The familiar banter gave him a warm comfortable feeling that burned away all the long months of tension between them.

"Well, then," she said. "Would you rather spend the evening arguing?"

He decided that the taxi's choke could wait one more day.

Chapter 19

Paris, France
November 1976

A steady tap-tap-tap of dripping water echoed from the tunnels until one of the junior priests pushed the massive iron-bound door closed, leaving two priests to guard the catacomb entrance. Creaking wooden folding chairs and hushed whispers haunted the chilly room. For reasons of security, the Convocation of *Milites Dei* was taking place in a section of the Paris catacombs located beneath a famous cathedral. Father Murray glanced at the walls created from stacked human bones and shivered. One hundred priests from various European Archdioceses occupied the chairs, and at the front of the room sat a row of elderly men wearing bishop's skull caps, sternly facing the audience. Not all present wore priestly robes—some wore suits, depending upon how positively the Catholic Church was viewed in their area and how much freedom obvious members of the Church were permitted.

Father Murray scanned the low-ceilinged room and once again was hit with the enormity of the challenge before him. In all the years that he'd been a member of *Milites Dei*, this was his first Convocation, and it would more than likely be his last. It was both thrilling and unnerving.

The junior ranking priest who had closed the door now swung a thurible as he made his way down the center path between the rows of chairs. At once, burning frankincense blanketed the smell of damp, ancient rot and the press of too many people packed into a small space. As he watched, Father Murray caught the profile of a severe-looking woman when she turned her head. She was seated in the front row facing the bishops. Her brown hair was caught up in a tight French twist. He was about to ask Father Thomas if he knew anything about her when a bell rang and everyone in the room stood up for Cardinal Sabatini.

Father Murray felt a trickle of sweat trace an itching path down the center of his back.

"Are you absolutely sure you want to do this, Joseph?" Father Thomas whispered.

Nodding, Father Murray didn't speak. He'd prayed for guidance during the months before the Convocation and had come to the same conclusion time and again. The risks didn't matter, lives—whether or not they were human—did. He'd spoken to both Father Thomas and Bishop Avery and while both were supportive of an investigation neither were willing to risk anything further. Therefore, the responsibility of approaching the Convocation would remain firmly on Father Murray's shoulders.

After conducting a blessing for those present, Cardinal Sabatini began a discussion of the administrative aspects of the war—the casualties, the lack of new recruits which in turn led to an announcement regarding the addition of the Order of Saint Ursula to *Milites Dei*. The woman with the French Twist got up and approached the Cardinal in the midst of a whirlwind of objections.

"Silence!" Cardinal Sabatini banged his fist on the wooden table in front of him, his excitement making his Italian accent more prominent. "I will not tolerate disruption. This action has been ordered by His Holiness, the Pope."

Father Murray saw a pained expression flash across the woman's face. He wasn't sure if it was due to the reception or the Cardinal's tone. As for himself, Father Murray was stunned. *Milites Dei* had existed for centuries and had never before included females among its ranks—not even in an administrative capacity. It was considered too dangerous.

"The Order of Saint Ursula has been inducted into *Milites Dei*," Cardinal Sabatini said, "and will be treated as respected members. A small unit is to be assigned within each Archdiocese. The first will be based in the United Kingdom next year. Sister Catherine, you may speak."

"Thank you, Your Eminence." Sister Catherine's accent was American, and she was dressed in a conservative black suit with an ankle-length skirt. Even so, Father Murray found it difficult not to stare. She wasn't wearing makeup or jewelry but retained an understated beauty. Her build was athletic, and her stance, confident. "I speak for my sisters within the Order of Saint Ursula when I say that we intend to fulfill our duties and responsibilities as well as our male counterparts. We feel we have unique advantages—"

Someone coughed and another man laughed. To her credit, Sister Catherine didn't acknowledge either.

"—which will be a boon to the service. Thank you." She returned to her seat with a dignified nod of the head to the Cardinal.

"With that," Cardinal Sabatini said, "we turn to the respected representative from the Archdiocese of Rome."

Another long discussion resulted, this one regarding the state of the secrecy of the Order, supplies and various other administrative issues. Commendations were given to various members for bravery, but Father Murray's mind wandered to how he might approach the idea of a truce with the Fair Folk. As much as he'd prepared, he wasn't entirely confident. As the meeting drew to an end, Father Thomas elbowed him.

"This is it," he said. "Now or never."

Father Murray raised his hand. "Your Grace, if it is permitted, I would like to address the Convocation."

Cardinal Sabatini nodded his bald head. "You may do so, Father... ah...."

"Father Murray, Your Grace. From Northern Ireland."

"Ah, yes," Cardinal Sabatini said. "Please come forward. I understand you have been experimenting with the idea that some children of the Fallen might be... salvageable. A most controversial and dangerous position given the history of the Fallen."

Sweating, Father Murray stood up with his heart pounding in his ears. There was a metallic taste in his mouth. *This is it,* he thought. "Yes, Your Grace. It is my work with one such individual that brings me here today."

Cardinal Sabatini looked confused. "Yes?"

"Due to my interactions with the subject and those associated with him, I've come to the conclusion that he is not a son of the Fallen."

"He is human?" Cardinal Sabatini asked. "The Spotter was mistaken in his assessment?"

"Yes and no, Your Grace," Father Murray said. "I believe the Spotter was mistaken. However, he was correct in that the subject is not human. It is my belief that he may be a son of one of the Good Folk."

The line between Cardinal Sabatini's eyes darkened. "I don't understand."

"He is one of what the people of Ireland refer to as the Good Neighbors."

"A fairy?" An elderly bishop at the end of the row asked. His voice was crisp and British, and it framed a perfectly mannered contempt. "Fairies aren't real."

"I beg the Convocation's indulgence," Father Murray said. "But I believe that the Church may have been short-sighted in categorizing all paranormal entities as demons, ghosts or fallen angels. I wish to make a study—"

The room erupted in shouts and arguments. Several members stood up and were waving their arms. Not all the objections were in English.

Cardinal Sabatini pounded the table with his fist again. "Silence! There will be silence!"

The voices died away.

"Father Murray, you propose that fairies exist?" Cardinal Sabatini asked, looking down his long nose. "This is preposterous!"

"I merely request the Convocation's approval to investigate the matter. I feel it is important—"

"You waste our time, boy," the English bishop said. "Chasing fantasies of children. Next, you'll tell us leprechauns are real."

"But what if it is possible that these creatures exist? We might count upon them as allies in our war."

"I've never heard of anything so ridiculous in all my life," an American bishop said.

"If there is even a small amount of uncertainty," a bishop with a French accent said, "then I believe it is worth investigation."

"We must be cert—"

"No!" The English bishop stood up. "I won't stand for this ridiculous, childish—"

"Childish? It's childish to question whether or not we're making a serious mistake? Assassinating an entire people merely because we cannot admit to being wrong is beyond unethical," Father Murray said. "It's diabolical!"

The Cardinal was once again banging on the table in front of him. "Silence!"

This time it took several minutes for the room to grow quiet.

"Father Murray, you are to refrain from such outbursts," Cardinal Sabatini said. "The matter has been brought before the Convocation and will be considered. The presbytery now convenes this Convocation. Go in peace."

"That didn't go so well," Father Murray said, sitting down.

"What did you expect?" Father Thomas asked. "You practically called Bishop Wilkinson an advocate for racial extermination."

Father Murray said, "I suppose I could have phrased it better."

"You must watch yourself, Joseph," Father Thomas whispered. "You can't continue on this way. It won't work. You're committing career suicide. All for nothing."

"It isn't for nothing," Father Murray said. "I'm right. I know it."

"Well," Father Thomas said, "you'd best start proving it. Otherwise, we'll be facing serious problems. This isn't just going to come down on you now, but Bishop Avery as well."

Father Murray watched the delegates exit the room. A few of them glanced in his direction—most of the looks weren't friendly. The room was nearly empty when Sister Catherine stopped at the end of the row in which they were sitting.

"For what it's worth," she said. "I thought you had a point."

"Thank you," Father Murray said.

"Hope you have better luck than we've had," she said. "It took ten years to change the Cardinal's mind. And as it stands, my Order will only participate in an administrative capacity."

Father Murray felt his mouth drop open. "I thought—"

"It's for show mostly," she said, frowning. "We're to free up the men who will fight. Isn't that a kicker? Still, it's a start."

"Are you there?" Father Murray whispered to the trees in the back of the cemetery outside St. Agnes's Church, feeling ridiculous. "Bran?" It was dark under the frigid branches of the ash tree in spite of a full moon peering out from among the clouds. He'd made two attempts to reach Bran to no avail, and he was about to give up when a wind gust clattered the tree branches, and a chill crawled slowly down his back. He got the feeling he wasn't alone just before he spied movement near the big Celtic cross in the center of the churchyard.

"This had best be good, priest." There was no sign of Bran, only his voice floating hollow on the wind.

"I brought my proposal before Bishop Avery as promised."

"What proposal?" The voice was more solid now, but Bran still didn't make an appearance.

"The truce. It took some time but I was able to speak before the Convocation."

"And?"

Father Murray sighed. "It will take more time than I'd hoped. They refuse to believe you exist as separate entities."

Cold laughter echoed between the gravestones, containing layers of bitterness and anger that had been distilled for years—perhaps even centuries.

Moving nearer to the stone cross, Father Murray said, "I wish I had better news. There are those among the order who might support my position. But I need more time."

"Time is all that I have, priest. Regardless of what happens. You, however, are another matter."

"Let me bring Bishop Avery to you."

"No."

"The killing has to stop," Father Murray said. "There must be an end to it."

"There will be an end," Bran said. "It won't be one either of us will like. But there will be an end, I assure you."

"Please. Give me another—"

"You had your chance, priest. Do not call upon me again. I will kill you if you do."

Father Murray walked around the Celtic cross and found no one there. He laid a hand on cold limestone, the rough surface scratching his palm. "Please. We must not give up. For the sake of your son—if for no other reason."

The wind rustled the dead leaves among the graves.

"They know who he is. They know where he lives," Father Murray said. "Now that I've angered the Convocation, I don't know how much longer I can protect him."

"Was that a threat?"

Starting, Father Murray turned to see Bran standing directly behind him. His eyes glittered red in the darkness, and once more Father Murray wasn't sure he liked having Bran so close.

"It was meant only as a warning."

"A warning," Bran said, frowning.

"There are members of my Order who don't agree with what I've done. They believe I should have—" Father Murray stopped himself and swallowed. He may be on sacred ground, but he was far from safe.

Bran's eyes narrowed. "Speak, Joe Murray, priest."

A curious tingling sensation brushed against Father Murray's skin, and he felt a sudden need to continue. For a brief instant he recalled reading about the use of names among the Good Neighbors, and fear raised the hairs on his arms before he dismissed it as mere superstition. "Bishop Avery supports my decision regarding Liam as does my direct supervisor. However, there are those who are pressing for action."

"Execution, you mean."

I've said too much, Father Murray thought. "I'm doing everything I can. But I need help. Give me something—anything—I can take to the bishop to convince the Convocation."

"Your priests have killed us for demons since setting foot in this land. Centuries of murder. Is there any such proof in all the world to make them stop?"

"I must try." Father Murray let his shoulders fall. "The hopelessness of the fight doesn't matter."

A sad smile crept across Bran's face. "I understand."

Pausing, Father Murray said, "I grant you my word that I will not stand for further assassinations of the Fair Folk."

"You would go against your own in this?"

"I must act as my conscience dictates."

Bran stared, the flames in his gaze fading into mere sparks. "I am confused."

"Christ lived among the lepers and the tax collectors—"

"You would compare us to the weak and disreputable among mortals?"

"I'm sorry. That wasn't what I intended at all," Father Murray said. "I was attempting to—"

"You choose to follow the ways of your gods regardless of whether or not those among your elders believe as you do."

Father Murray paused and then nodded. "However, I am not sure how I can tell the difference between our mutual enemies and…." He let his voice trail off. He'd been searching for the distinctions between the Fallen and the Good Folk, but there was no information available. No comparisons had been made in all of the history of the Church. He had only the old stories, and those were rarely consistent. Most were obvious fabrications.

Bran shook his head. "You wish to know the difference between ourselves and the Fallen?"

"If I were able to show the committee a clear distinction then I could make progress. Otherwise, I've nothing but my intuition and that isn't enough."

"Interesting," Bran said, sitting on the top of a tombstone. "It is possible that a talisman might be arranged. However, its use would be restricted to yourself and no other."

"But that won't help me prove to the Convocation that a difference exists. Once again, they would only have my word."

"Your committee is not my problem. The safety of my own is, and such a thing could be used against us." Bran shook his head and sighed. "So, tell me. How is it you make a distinction between mortals in your wars?"

Father Murray gave the question consideration. "Uniforms. Language. Appearance."

One of Bran's eyebrows twitched upward. "I saw a man shoot another dead in the street while he was waiting for a bus. Neither one was wearing a uniform. And I'd swear both were Irish."

Sighing, Father Murray said, "Our current troubles are difficult to explain. The sides are less demarked."

"Aye?"

"There are those who feel Ireland should exist free from the English. All of Ireland. Not only the south. They are Nationalists," Father Murray said. "And the Loyalists fear such a thing and wish to prevent it from happening."

"Why?"

"As long as partition exists the Loyalists are the majority. They have power. The moment Northern Ireland becomes a part of the Republic is the moment they become a minority. They will lose their control. Their power. They fear being abused as they have abused."

"I see," Bran said. "And how is it you know the difference between these Nationalists and Loyalists?"

"It's difficult to explain. In part, it is divided along religious lines. However, the conflict has nothing to do with religion."

"But you are aware of the differences?"

"For the most part, I am."

"Not all of the Good Folk are to be trusted," Bran said. "There are those among us who work for the Fallen. I can't give you an easy answer for why any more than you can give me one."

Father Murray looked up into the sky. *God help me,* he prayed. "Nonetheless, this talisman would be a step in the right direction. I would be grateful for it."

"Then I will put my faith in you, Joe Murray, priest."

"When?"

"Soon."

"Thank you."

"I'm not certain it is a gift for which you should be thankful. Possession of such an item will make you many enemies," Bran said. "But you will have my protection as you grant your protection to my son."

"May I contact you again?"

Bran looked away and didn't speak for a long while. Father Murray heard a rabbit or a cat move through the hedge to his right.

"Aye," Bran said. "You are convincing, priest. You risk much. It is only fair that I should do the same. We, the Fianna, cannot win this war alone any more than mortals have a chance against the Fallen. It would be wise for us to fight together. Together there is hope."

"I'm glad to hear it."

"But take care where you use my name," Bran said. "And take care how you would use the talisman."

"I will."

Several days later there came a knock upon the parochial house door while Father Andrew was away. When Father Murray answered there was no one there. However, resting in the exact center of the mat was a round stone with a hole in the center. A leather thong was tied to it. Picking it up, he stepped out onto the walk and scanned the area. He didn't see anyone.

"Thank you," he whispered and went back inside to see what he could discover in his research about holey stones.

Chapter 20

Andersonstown, Belfast, County Antrim, Northern Ireland
23 December 1976

"Can't believe you took such a risk," Oran said.

"What better way? Delivered safe and whole to the man's own car park?" Liam asked. He sipped his whiskey and winked. Sitting at Oran's table, he was having a quick glass of Christmas cheer before heading home. A nagging thought had told him he should go home, but when Oran had held up the bottle of Bushmills and raised an eyebrow the matter had been settled. Elizabeth and the children were gone to her mother's, and Liam didn't know when Mary Kate might make another slip. One more round would lend him the courage to tell Oran the news. Every day for two months Mary Kate had exacted a promise not to speak of it but that morning before Liam had left she'd forgotten. It was an opportunity he couldn't miss.

Oran said, "Surely, you didn't walk from the Shankill?"

"You were the one saying the RUC was getting close," Liam said with a shrug.

"It's fucking mad you are. Leaving the car in front of a known Loyalist's house. One of the RUC, no less."

Liam smiled. "Did the man a service, I did. Gave the car a new set of spark plugs and a nice cleaning. This way, we don't have to burn it out after. And who knows? I might borrow it again. Already done all that work on the suspension. Owner couldn't possibly begrudge a few miles on the engine and some petrol."

"And did the RUC catch on?"

Waiting until Oran had taken a drink, Liam said, "Came for him this morning. Who'd have thought they had such a grudge against Captain Beefheart? One small sticker, and they go mad."

"You've gone off your nut."

"Maybe I have," Liam said. "It isn't the first time."

"What?" Oran asked. "You've done this before?"

"Just giving the RUC the guidance they need." Liam took another sip of whiskey. "Anyway, I've got some news."

"What news?" Oran asked, looking uneasy.

"Congratulate me."

"What for?" Oran asked. "Surviving your own foolishness?"

Liam grinned. "Is that any way to speak of someone's Da?"

Oran looked blank. "What are you on about?"

"Mary Kate. She's pregnant."

"But I thought you two were waiting?"

Liam shrugged. "She changed her mind."

Holding up his glass, Oran said, "Well, then. Congratulations, man. It's about damned time. Was starting to think something was wrong with your—"

"Don't even."

"How many tries did it take?"

"What makes you think I'd tell the likes of you a thing like that?" Liam leaned forward and grinned. "The first time."

Oran whistled. "Wait until Elizabeth hears of this. She'll be that jealous I got the news first."

"You can't."

"What do you mean I can't?"

"Mary Kate has some stupid notion that speaking of the baby will bring bad luck."

"She's going to have to say something sooner or later," Oran said. "Has she not told her own mother?"

Liam shook his head.

"What is she afraid of?" Oran asked, pouring another round.

"The Good Folk," Liam said. "She thinks they'll come for the baby. Never seen anyone so afraid of such a thing in all my life. Didn't even know she believed. And her at Uni."

Oran's face changed, and he stared down into the glass in his hand as if he were hiding his expression.

Liam asked, "Are you going to tell me you believe it too?"

Not taking his gaze from the glass, Oran frowned and then shook his head. "I don't believe that they'd come for your baby."

"Where do you think she got a notion like that?"

Oran glanced up at him. The glass shook as he lifted it to his lips and sipped. "Oh, pregnant women get ideas in their heads. Drives them a bit mad, the pregnancy. Don't tell Elizabeth I said so, I'll never hear the end."

Oran was a bad liar. The deception would've been obvious even if Liam hadn't overheard that long-ago conversation. Once again it occurred to him that Oran was frightened. Unlike the others, for the most part Oran didn't show it, but for the careful glance or the unspoken word here and there. Liam gripped the glass in his hand. His face burned and his knuckles went white. *Does everyone see it in me?* "I'm not what you think, Oran."

"And what is it I think?" Oran looked nervous.

"Heard what you said. After our first job. Well, you know. When I was sick, and you brought the priest."

Oran went a little pale. "I didn't mean any harm."

"I know you didn't," Liam said. "You were scared. Hell, I was scared too."

Setting down his glass, Oran said, "I love you like a brother. You know that, don't you?"

"I do."

"Doesn't matter to me what you are and what you aren't," Oran said. "You're my friend. And you're a good man. That's all I care about. Nothing else matters."

"I'm not—"

"Don't deny it. We've all seen you drive. Me, N*í*al and *É*amon. We know."

"You're telling me the lot of you think I'm some sort of—"

"*É*amon is of the opinion you're Lon Chaney, Jr.," Oran said with an incredulous look. "Says he got a report, you see. Some sort of rumor about you. From the Kesh."

A chill ran along Liam's arms, raising the hairs under the sleeves of his sweater. "Shite." How much did HQ know? Worse yet, how much had *É*amon told Oran and the others? N*í*al's watchful looks began to form an image in Liam's head that he didn't like—the image of the word "fairy" written in flesh.

He suppressed a shudder.

"Not to worry. We'd never tell. Not that anyone would much believe us if we did."

It was Liam's turn to gaze into his glass. When the skin on the backs of his arms started to prickle he got up from the chair, feeling a little sick. *Lon Chaney, Jr.* "I have to go."

"You don't have to worry. I told you," Oran said.

The need to run had overtaken Liam and grew powerful enough that he found himself quivering with it. *Must get home. Now.* He grabbed his anorak and shoved his fists into the sleeves.

"Will you be going to midnight Mass tomorrow?" Oran asked, looking worried. "Elizabeth wants to walk to the church together."

Unable to speak, Liam nodded and then threw open the door.

"We didn't drink a toast to the babe's health," Oran said. He paused and then added, "Later, then?"

Liam bolted down the stairs as fast as he could without tumbling. He burst through the apartment building's entrance and jogged home. The last of the warmth from Oran's flat faded, and he was left frozen and empty for the length of three breaths. Then between one lungful of air and the next the urgent need to see Mary Kate propelled him down the street. Concern became terror and terror exploded into panic. Something was wrong. Very wrong. The knowledge pressed bone deep in jagged shards—trapped inside the ice of his chest. He didn't know why or how he knew. He just knew.

He hadn't bothered zipping up his anorak. Cold moist wind tugged at the flapping coat and pinched his face as if unseen forces attempted to hold him back. *It's too late. Don't go. You don't want to see.* Reaching their building, he shot up the stairs without a pause. When he hit the second landing he was knocked down by three running men wearing masks. He smelled the blood as they thundered past, and he noticed something odd about their shoes but didn't consciously register what it was. Above, someone screamed, ripping his attention away from the men. Liam scrambled to his feet and took the steps three at a time. When he reached the last landing he spied Mrs. Black. She was standing in the hall just outside the door to a flat. *Our flat. Mine and Mary Kate's.* A scarlet stain in the shape of a smudged, deformed flower had bloomed on the front of her blue print dress. The ever-present scarf was gone, and her brown hair—normally so carefully groomed—stuck out in shocked angles. Her face was pale enough that her skin faded into the white paint on the wall beyond. She would have been invisible but for the round black eyes and gaping red-painted mouth. Her throat moved, and Liam was afraid she was going to scream again. He didn't want that. He knew if she did he would blow apart like a glass pane smashed with a stone. Taking charge, he grabbed her arm at the elbow.

"They killed her. They… they…"

Mary Kate will need to go to hospital. "Call Father Murray at St. Agnes's if the phone is working. Send for him if it isn't. Get him here. Now. I'll—" He released her and stepped inside the flat. The furniture, what little they had, had been wrecked. From the amount of blood covering the walls and soaking into the old sofa, he knew that Mrs. Black had to be right.

I should've gone straight home, he thought. *I knew it.*

Please, God. Jesus and Mary, please, let me not be too late, he prayed, cautiously moving forward step by step. He was certain all of the men were gone, but there was always a chance they'd left a surprise. A message had been scrawled on the wall. It blurred and then he blinked. It read: *We know who you are –UFF.* A bloody handprint had been placed just below the message; its shape like that of a BA's hand stopping a car. *The Red Hand.* They'd also left a coin in the center of the floor and drawn a circle around it in blood. Moving closer, he saw it was an old shilling—at least, he thought it was. He picked it up and pocketed it, thinking he'd ask Oran or one of the others about it later. Then he spied Mary Kate's shoe in the corner of his eye and turned toward it.

She lay in the doorway between the bedroom and the kitchen. She was on her stomach, hands clutching her belly beneath her. The print skirt she had put on for University that morning was soaked black with the blood.

So much blood.

I knew. I should've been home, he thought.

He was so certain she was gone that she groaned twice before he heard her. Rushing to her side, he gently rolled her over so that he sat with her head in his lap. Her face was bruised and splotched. He was fairly certain her nose was broken. At the edge of his awareness, clammy wetness seeped through his jeans.

"Mary Kate? I'm here. Say something. Anything."

"Bastards."

He wanted to hug her to him but couldn't risk hurting her further.

"Fucking UDA." It came out in a mumbling lisp. Her front teeth had been shattered. "Looking for you." She started to sob. "Oh, Liam, the baby. They—they—"

"Shhhhh, hush now," Liam said. "You're both going to be all right. Mrs. Black went for Father Murray. We'll get you to hospital."

"It hurts."

For a moment he couldn't speak past the lump in his throat. He took a breath and forced the words out. "I know. Don't move." *Don't take her from me. Please, God. Not her and the babe. Not now. I'll do anything you want. Please. You can't take her. It's Christmas.*

"I'm cold."

Moving as little as possible, he reached to the bed and pulled the rumpled blanket to the floor. He draped it over her as best he could. "There. You'll be warm soon."

"I love you." Tears streaked the drying blood on her face.

"I love you too." He kissed her on her forehead and blinked, suppressing a compulsion to hunt down the three men now while he had the chance of catching them. The black monster shifted in the back of his brain, but was otherwise quiet. He didn't understand why he didn't feel anything—not even the tingling in his arms. He should be grieving. He should be raging. But there was nothing in him at all.

"Always loved you," she lisped through her broken mouth. "Told Theresa Madden. Was going to marry you. Was twelve."

"Hush now. Save your strength."

She sobbed. "Don't want to die. I want to stay with you."

"You're not going to die. You're going to live."

He sensed more than saw someone move in the doorway, but didn't see anyone from his position on the floor.

"Why am I so cold?"

Where the fuck is Father Murray? The Church isn't that far. What if he doesn't come? What if she dies because I waited?

Mary Kate started having trouble breathing. Panic rippled through his body. He wedged himself under her until she was sitting up and then he wrapped his arms around her. He tried not to think of how sticky the floor was. His skin itched, and his face was cold. Her breathing eased. He rocked her slowly as if she were a fragile child.

"I'll not leave you alone again. I'll protect you. I swear it," Liam said, and then started to hum without thinking. Too late he realized it was that stupid Bay City Rollers song, "Bye, Bye, Baby."

A breathless laugh bubbled out of her mouth.

"What's funny?"

"You never did have the music."

Footsteps and voices echoed up the stairwell. Within moments Father Murray and Mrs. Black entered the flat. Father Murray's brown hair hung in his shocked face.

"Over here, Father," Liam said. "We have to get her to hospital. Can you drive the cab? I—I can't."

Father Murray nodded.

Liam reached into his coat pocket and held out the keys. His hand was stained crimson.

"I should do something." Mrs. Black asked, biting her lip, "May I call her mother?"

"Number is on the kitchen counter," Liam said, thinking he sounded too calm. "Call my mother too. If you would. Lock up, will you?" He clamped down on a laugh. *As if there was anything worth saving now.* He kissed the top of Mary Kate's head. He felt better, stronger now that Father Murray was there. "Mary Kate, love, brace yourself. I'm going to lift you."

"I love you so much." Her voice was sleepy.

He wrapped the blanket around her battered body and gently looped his arms under her. She gasped in pain as he straightened. Father Murray led the way down the empty hallway. The soles of Liam's work boots were slick with blood, and he concentrated on not slipping as he went down the stairs one at a time. *Too long. I'm taking too long. Shouldn't have waited.* He got her to the cab without any disastrous mishaps and tucked her into the back. He got in next to her once she was settled and then they were off.

"I knew it," he whispered. "Should've been home. I knew."

"What do you mean?" Father Murray asked.

Please, God, Liam thought. *I'll never touch a drop again. I swear it. I'll give up the cigarettes. Anything.* "I—I knew."

It couldn't have taken long to reach the hospital; it was only a few blocks away. He had a sense that Father Murray drove with speed and skill unexpected in a priest, but time had slowed. Mary Kate lay curled on the black leather seat, her skin glowing white in the darkness. Her eyes were closed, and he would've thought her asleep or dead were it not for the grip she had on his hand. Her lips moved, and he moved closer to hear.

"I'm sorry," she whispered.

"You haven't done anything to be sorry for," Liam said.

"I'm so sorry. For the baby. I shouldn't have."

He carried her into the hospital while Father Murray parked the car. It seemed to take forever for the nurses to take notice and even longer for them to bring a gurney. When he set her down Mary Kate cried out and clamped onto his hand with a surprising amount of force.

Liam smoothed the tangled hair off her face. "Shhh, you have to go with the doctors now."

"No. Please."

"I'll not be far."

Father Murray arrived just as they wheeled her away. A nurse handed Liam a clipboard and a pen. He stood, blank and empty, watching her retreat. The rubber soles of her white shoes squeaked on the grey linoleum. He glanced down at the clipboard. The text on the form shifted and scrambled before it blurred. *I can't read it. I didn't protect her, and now I can't even fill out the fucking forms.* The ballpoint pen in his right hand shook.

"Let me take that," Father Murray said. His voice was gentle and calming. "Come have a seat."

"Is she going to die, Father?"

"I don't know."

Liam allowed Father Murray to lead him to one of the square plastic chairs with steel legs that were positioned against the wall.

Father Murray reached into a pocket. "Here," he said, holding out a handful of black rosary beads. "It'll give you something useful to do."

The rosary felt warm in Liam's otherwise numb fingers. He closed his eyes and started praying in an urgent whisper. "I believe in God, the Father Almighty, Creator of Heaven and Earth." The words brought some measure of peace. As the antiseptic hospital smell penetrated the numbness he told himself that none of it was real. It was a bad dream, and he'd wake at any moment. "And in Jesus Christ his only son, Our Lord."

Outside, someone was crying. A woman. He could hear her through the glass doors. They must've given her bad news. Her wails pierced the walls and rattled Liam's nerves, breaking his concentration.

Somewhere a door swung open and hurried footsteps approached. "Father? Can I speak with you for a moment?" It was the doctor. Bright red splotches stained his white coat.

I should feel something, Liam thought. *Why don't I feel anything?*

Father Murray put down the pen and the clipboard. Glancing over his shoulder he said, "Will you be all right for a little while, Liam?"

Liam swallowed and nodded. Shutting his eyes again, he returned to his prayers. He pretended he couldn't hear the doctor whisper to Father Murray of what the three men had done to Mary Kate and that the baby was dead. He pretended not to hear Father Murray ask the doctor if he could enter the room to administer the Extreme Unction. The hairs on the backs of Liam's arms stood up on end, and his skin bunched in cold knots.

Mary Kate wanted to go home for Christmas. She wanted to see the Giant's Causeway. It was to be our first real holiday.

I should've come home. I didn't protect my family.

A fierce pain pierced his chest. The woman outside continued her cries, if anything they grew louder. No one was comforting her in her grief. It occurred to him that she was alone. It wasn't right for anyone to be alone with such news. He stood up, and the rosary fell from his nerveless hands. He would go to her, to the grieving woman. He'd comfort her.

He made it to the glass doors when he saw her standing on the walk. She was slender and graceful under the white old-fashioned dress. Long black hair curtained her face. He had placed a hand on the door's handle when her chin lifted, and he saw her eyes. They glowed pale, silvery blue. He saw it had started raining. Big fat drops slammed the pavement. Her skirts blew in a wind that didn't affect the nearby tree, and her hair floated, dry on the damp air.

"Liam," Father Murray said. "You must come with me."

"Can you see her?"

"Who?" Father Murray peered through the glass. "There isn't anyone out there."

Realization filtered through the haze.

"Come, Liam."

Liam didn't think he could move, but somehow he did. "I knew." He understood he must've sounded mad, but it didn't matter. He couldn't have stopped himself from speaking if he'd wanted to. "I knew it."

"She needs you." Father Murray's hair hung in disheveled clumps. He held out a hand. "She's lost too much blood."

"I'll go in, Father." *I should've gone home. I shouldn't have waited. I should've driven her to hospital myself. I should've risked it.*

They'd tucked her into a bed with blankets and someone had cleaned her face. Her skin was so pale it was tinged with green. The stench of disinfectant and drying gore spooked him, and for one alarming moment he was torn between his terror of hospitals—*must leave, must get out of this fucking place*—and his love for Mary Kate. He shuddered with the need to run. *Fucking coward.* How could he even think of leaving her in the awful place? Alone?

Her eyes fluttered open, and he snatched her hand to tether himself. Unlike before, her grip was weak. The reality of it registered in his brain and in a flash his terror was gone.

"I'm so sorry," she whispered. "The baby."

He buried his face in her chest and sobbed. He felt her hand on his head as if to comfort him. Her chest lifted once and then it was done. An instant and she was gone forever.

Liam felt someone tugging at him. He was hollow. Mary Kate lay still under his forehead, and no matter how he tried to convince himself he felt some small breath, some sign of life, there was none. Reluctant to see proof, he sat up and stared at the blank hospital room wall.

"Do you need anything from the flat?" It was Father Murray. "You can't go back. The RUC are there. Do you understand?"

Liam blinked twice before slowly nodding. Not caring. He heard a soft tapping at the window and saw a moth fluttering against the glass. Stumbling across the room, he reached the window and pushed it open. The moth flitted through the gap and into the night.

"I'll call for Mrs. Black. We'll take care of the arrangements. But we must get you out of here."

Shuffling toward the double glass doors like a sleepwalker, Liam was almost afraid he'd see the Banshee again, but the walk was empty. He'd somehow gotten to the cab. Glancing inside the window to the back seat, his emotions flooded in at the sight of Mary Kate's blood. Feelings slammed into him so hard he couldn't breathe or think. He caught himself with one hand on the glass; his reflection gawking back at him. The tingling ran up his arms and legs. Pain twisted inside his guts. His breath finally came but only in short gasps.

My fault. Should've been home.

Then they'd have had us both.

Took too long to get her to hospital. I should've taken the risk. I should have driven her myself.

"Liam?"

"Get back inside, Father." Liam didn't turn around. He was afraid of what might happen if he did.

"I—I must tell you something."

"I know what they—" He swallowed. The lump lodged in his throat hurt, but it was only another pain lost among a whole catalog of pains. "I know what they did to her."

"It isn't that," Father Murray said.

Liam wasn't sure how much longer he could hold himself together. Instinctively, he reached inside his pocket and found his lighter. *The lighter that Mary Kate painted the tricolor on,* he thought. He jerked his hand from his pocket and slapped it against the side of the taxi instead. "Get away, Father. Get away, now."

"You won't harm me."

"Please, Father. Go." Liam couldn't stand straight anymore. His guts were twisting. The pain was awful. It was the monster clawing its way to the surface at last.

"You aren't evil. Nor is whatever it is inside you. Evil isn't capable of love. You loved Mary Kate, and she loved you."

"Mary Kate didn't know. Never saw it," Liam said. "Father, please. You don't know what will happen. I can't control it."

"Let it come. Whatever it is. We'll deal with it together."

"No."

"What are you afraid of?" Father Murray asked. He paused and then seemed to come to a decision. "You're wrong, you know. She did see it."

Liam slammed his hand against the car door again. It wasn't working—not this time. Nothing was the way it should be. *I don't want to know this. Not now.* "You're lying."

"It wasn't long after you were married. She told me she saw something while you were sleeping. At the time, she wasn't sure what she should do. She came to me to ask whether she should stay."

A cold knot formed in Liam's stomach as pieces fit together in his head, forming an ugly picture. *We have to wait. Just a few years.* "It wasn't about finishing university. Wasn't about the money. She didn't want to have a monster's baby." The ground seemed to shift from under him. He staggered.

Father Murray didn't speak.

"That's the reason, isn't it?"

Taking a deep breath, Father Murray released it slowly. "We weren't sure of what would happen. She loved you. She chose to stay. And in the end, she loved you enough to have your child. This time. In spite of her fears. Isn't that enough? She believed you were a good man—whatever lurked inside you."

Liam stumbled, the tingling sensation forgotten. "She knew."

"Yes."

"You told her what I am?"

Father Murray paused and then nodded.

"But you didn't see fit to tell me?" Liam's heart went colder yet. "Why did you marry us?"

"At the time I hoped she could help you. Keep you from indulging your destructive side. And so I thought she did. Combined with proper guidance from me. I thought we had everything under control. But I was so wrong about—"

"What did you tell Mary Kate?"

Father Murray stared at the ground. "There's something I need to say, but you must be calm."

"What did you tell her?"

"She was pregnant when we talked that first time. God help me, I—"

"Pregnant? Wait. When?"

Closing his eyes, Father Murray said, "A month after you were wed. She came to me. Terrified of what she'd seen and more of what she carried. We... we got rid of it."

"She was sick. A virus. You said." Liam was cold, and he stood straight—the pain forgotten for the moment. "I remember. It was a virus."

"A doctor performed the procedure. It was handled as safely as—"

"You talked her into murdering our child?" *Oh, God. Jesus, Mary and Joseph, not this. Not now.*

"There wasn't a choice. It had to be done. Based on what she told me, based on what I thought I knew, the baby would only have been an abomination."

They'll take the babe from us. You'll not say a word, will you? It was clear who she'd meant now, and it hadn't been the fairies. Liam's teeth ground together, and he felt a snarl building up in his throat. The hairs on his arms were standing on end. "An abomination. Like me."

"No, no, you're not. I was wrong. You're different."

"And who is to say my children wouldn't have been the same?"

"I... I thought... at the time... we couldn't take the risk," Father Murray said. "What I did was wrong. So terrifically wrong. I know that now. I'm so sorry."

The chill in Liam's chest was gone—transformed into a terrible rage. "Why tell me this now?"

"You must be careful, Liam. You can't afford revenge, do you hear? You'll be executed. It doesn't matter that I was wrong. That you aren't one of the sons of the Fallen. You're one of the Fey. You're—"

"Get away from me!"

"You must listen."

The proper guidance, Liam thought and remembered all the wise things peace-loving Father Murray had said. *And all the while he believed not a word.* "Never come near me again, or I'll kill you. You hear?"

Father Murray's expression grew fearful.

A sharp pain lanced through Liam's chest. He held his breath until it passed. "Get the fuck away!"

"I don't think that's a good idea, son."

"Then stay and be torn apart. I don't fucking care anymore!" Liam listened to Father Murray's staggering retreat and desperately clutched onto his self-control until he was certain the man was gone. Then he slipped to the ground and let the monster come. There really wasn't any other choice. It was going to whether he let it or not. His senses changed in a last wrenching gasp of agony. His eyesight grew sharper. His sense of smell became so intense that he could see what he smelled. His hearing—

He would find the men that had killed Mary Kate. He'd find them and rip them apart one by one. He'd taste their blood, breathe in their fear and bathe in their screams. They would suffer for having touched her—for having raped her. He would rip and tear until nothing recognizable remained. Their families would carry with them the result of his grief for generations. None would prosper. None would make old bones. All would die of the violence their fathers had perpetrated. Red rage seared his veins—cooled for an instant by a single thought as a soothing voice from Derry filled his skull. It was Father Murray.

Vengeance is mine, sayeth the Lord.

No. It's mine, the monster thought back, shaking its head to rid itself of the words. *You hold no dominion over us, priest.* And with that, he sprinted—his sense of purpose guiding him through the confusion of sights and smells. When he got to the car park outside their apartment building he saw the RUC had indeed arrived. Shadows moved across a window on the fourth floor. In the car park, Mrs. Black stood alone in the cold answering their questions. The other residents cowered in their beds.

Mrs. Brown frowned and shouted, "We'd have called for you if you'd have done something about it!"

He kept to the shadows and wished himself invisible. It had worked before, in the Shankill. It wasn't reliable, but the stronger his emotions the more likely it was to work. He took a lungful of air and sifted its contents for the scents he had noticed before—sweat, blood—Mary Kate's blood—tobacco, ale, gun oil, wool, leather. He was surprised to find there were four trails and not three. The fourth contained old blood, not Mary Kate's alone. All four ran north and west.

To Loyalist territory.

Then he remembered the shoes. Polished to a fine shine, they were—marred only with blood and scuffs from their flight. A military shine. He looked to the men questioning Mrs. Black. *A constable's shine.*

It came as no surprise. The monster located the scents again and followed on four legs, not stopping until one trail vanished. The fourth. He paused long enough to set the spot in his mind and then continued on. He traced the Peace Line along its length until he could pass through, invisible. Buildings, store fronts, houses all slipped past. The passage of time became the passage of scents and colors. He didn't stop until he arrived at the end of the first trail.

He knew the house, or at least Liam did, nested in the hindmost part of the monster's brain. Most of all he knew the car parked out front.

Ah, now. Is that any way to repay the favor we've done you? We've half a mind to take the plugs back and a good portion of the engine with them, he thought. *After. After we've paid our call.* He went through the front gate headfirst, breaking the latch. It let out a small squeal as it bent back.

Lights glowed from inside the house. A woman was speaking, accompanied with the sounds of a fork scraping a plate.

It seems we've arrived in time for the dinner.

Wood gave way without much resistance as the monster threw itself against the door. He entered a small, shabby room with a black-and-white television and two padded chairs. The television, showing some sort of news program, was the only light in the room. A woman screamed from the kitchen. Something clattered to the floor. The monster roared its arrival. From his dark corner Liam urged it on.

A man ran into the room, his face bunched with anger in the flickering light until he spied what had broken into his house. He was dressed in a constable's uniform.

His anger became terror.

The monster leapt for the man's throat, knocking him flat. Its teeth ripped into the constable's flesh before Liam had time to think. The stink of urine. Warm salty blood flooded his mouth. The constable struggled, shrieking. Somewhere a gun went off. Once. Twice. Three times. Distant pain exploded in the monster's body. The woman screamed again and fled back into the kitchen. Pots and pans clattered to the floor. The constable made a last fight for freedom, shoving with futile hands—the gun lost. The monster lowered its jaws again and fell to its work. Dark liquid sprayed the walls in the cold blink of television light.

Sirens wailed. Outside, gunshots echoed.

The monster lifted its gore-stained face and sniffed. Others were on the way. It was time to leave. But there was one left. One who must pay.

The monster trotted into the kitchen, its toe-nails clicking on cold tile.

The woman was curled into the far corner, a skillet clutched in one hand, her skirts were rucked up around her thighs. She might have been pretty, but her face was drained of color, and her eyes were distorted with horror. They were green like Mary Kate's. In his distant place, Liam had a change of heart and implored the monster to leave the woman be. The monster panted a laugh and padded closer. The woman squeaked and held up the skillet. It wavered in the air, an ineffectual threat. *Stop. You have to stop,* Liam pleaded. *We can't do this. Please. She wasn't a part of it.*

We can. We will. For Mary Kate. Isn't this what you want? The monster paused, one paw above the woman's ankle. It slowly rested the pads of its foot on the edge of the woman's skirt, inking a print in blood on the cloth. Its foul breath huffed stray curls from her terror-frozen face. Shivering, she flinched and turned away. Above, the pan in her hand wobbled. The monster glanced up.

The skillet was made of iron.

Backing away, the monster left a trail of sticky crimson and then exited the house the way it came. It hurried along the streets. Sirens and lights invaded the night behind it. Pain throbbed in its shoulder, gathering force. It reached the other side of the Peace Line and limped to a group of buildings on the opposite side of the Falls Road. It left Liam quaking in agony in a filthy alley. He dragged himself from the grimy concrete and staggered to his feet. His left shoulder was immobilized with pain. He couldn't stand straight. Using all of his strength to will himself invisible, he retreated from the sirens and gunshots. Somewhere above an Army helicopter battered the air. Liam walked in fits and starts, pausing to lean against store fronts or brick walls to catch his breath. Consciousness flickered in and out. He didn't know how far he'd gone when he found himself blinking up at a night sky hemmed in by street lamps. The pavement was hard and cold beneath his back. It was snowing. A car approached, and unable to move, he prepared himself for death. The tire squealed to a stop inches from his face. The tread had been worn bald on the inside.

Needs an alignment. He felt a smile curl the corners of his mouth. Doors swung open.

"Liam? Is that you?" It was Níal. Oran was there too.

"Out of the way, you *amadán*. Of course it's him," Éamon said. "And still alive yet, in spite of Father Murray almost having run over him."

Liam groaned. He wanted to die. He didn't care how. He should've stayed at the constable's house until they came for him. He should've made them shoot him down. He should've—

Not until they pay, the monster thought. *Not until every last mother's son pays. We live until then, damn you.*

Chapter 21

Ballymena, County Antrim, Northern Ireland
March 1977

Rory Gallagher's *Moonchild* thundered out of the monolithic stereo speaker at Liam's back. In a drowsy haze, he allowed the guitar riff to vibrate through him as if he were no more substantial than sea mist. The music tickled somewhere inside his chest and threatened to bring him back to himself. He would've moved to prevent it but couldn't find the energy. Ultimately, he'd have preferred The Clash, or Iggy Pop—even the Sex Pistols would've better suited, but his current host, Jimmy, had no appreciation for punk music. Liam didn't mind. To be honest, in his current state he wouldn't have reacted if the Shankill Butchers rompered his skull in with heavy boots while carving him up like a side of beef. Liam was floating in a drug-saturated sea, and it was the best he'd felt since December. The nightmares had retreated, which meant he'd been able to sleep for the first time in months. He wasn't himself anymore. He was someone who didn't feel pain or rage or fear. Someone who didn't have the troubles Liam Kelly did—someone who lived with his uncle and mourned a young wife that had died of a long illness—not a wife murdered by Loyalist constables. Thanks to Father Murray and Liam's mother, who both insisted that he leave Belfast for his own safety, the new man Liam had become didn't have to think about which side of the street he walked on, or what he wrote on job applications. He didn't have to think about Mary Kate either, unless he wanted to, and right now, he wanted anything but.

Jimmy's sister, whose name he'd long forgotten, danced topless in the middle of the room. Liam was fairly certain she was unaware she had an audience, and he felt a little guilty for gawking. On the other hand, he recalled some vague argument over women's rights and the inequality of sexual norms imposed by a patriarchal society. It ultimately led him to wondering that if it were "liberating and revolutionary" for her to go about half-naked, was it equally so for him to watch her doing it? Or was

187

he supposed to ignore her? *A damned near-impossible feat if you ask me,* he thought. She had nice tits, and from what he could see of the back of her tight jeans the rest of her wasn't bad either. Sometime earlier she had made a rather "liberated and revolutionary" proposition, but then he wasn't certain she knew to whom she'd made it or even if it mattered to her. Women's Liberation was confusing and unsettling in the worst way. So, he'd resolved the matter for himself by refusing her. Of course, he hadn't been high at the time. Now, he couldn't have put up a fight—which, on second thought, might not have been so bad.

He closed his eyes, not wishing to watch her long brown hair glide across her silky skin. The truth of it was he didn't want her. He wanted Mary Kate with every cell of his body. He missed everything about her. The feel of her sleeping at his side. Her gentle snores. Her soft brown curls tickling his nose enough to wake him from a sound sleep even on nights when he needed it most. Her smile. The smell of her. At odd moments he thought he had heard her laughter, or he'd catch a glimpse of her in the corner of an eye, but all of it was a lie, and every time it happened it was as if someone had ripped a deep wound in his chest. The pain was raw enough to make him want to take a razor to his wrist, but each time he considered acting upon the idea something stopped him, and so, he stumbled on barely alive and wishing for an end. At times he couldn't breathe, couldn't move without wanting to scream.

Hard as he tried for his Uncle Sean, he hadn't lasted at the cigarette factory. One month in, it had become too much to get up in the morning and face the concerned looks of his coworkers. He assumed his uncle had told them enough to explain the erratic behavior—enough to keep them from asking too many questions. When Liam's supervisor had taken him aside to discuss the latest spate of tardiness, Liam had ended up at the pub. That's where he'd met Jimmy. Jimmy had seen something was wrong from the moment they had met. Drunk, Liam had told him there wasn't enough whiskey in the world. Jimmy had said he understood and that he had just the thing—had imported it himself from England.

Jimmy was a weedy twenty-year-old living off his father's money. Why he wasn't doing it somewhere more exciting than Ballymena Liam hadn't brought himself to ask. He didn't exactly care. There wasn't much he cared about these days. If he could, he'd stab enough smack into his veins to make him sleep for the rest of his life, but Jimmy was onto him and doled out the shite a bit at a time regardless of how much Liam begged. To Jimmy's consternation it never seemed to last as long as it should, but for now Liam was content. He was nothing and no one, drifting away and never returning to a world where Mary Kate was dead. *Worse than dead.* And he'd been the one to leave her unprotected. *Her and the babe.*

A hard kick knocked the thoughts out of his head. He looked up, expecting to see Jimmy's sister, infuriated at being ignored. Instead it was Oran, and he was scowling.

"Just what is it you think you're doing?"

Liam opened his mouth to tell him to fuck off, that he didn't belong in Protestant Ballymena, that he, Liam, was supposed to be in hiding, and he, Oran, should go back to Belfast where he belonged, but what came out was too weak to be heard above Rory Gallagher's guitar.

"This place is disgusting." Oran yanked him up off the floor. "Time to go."

"No."

"Oh, yes," Oran said, dragging him across a filthy shag carpet that had been new and clean not so long ago.

Jimmy blocked the hallway. "Who the hell are you? And where do you think you're going with Billy?"

"Billy?" Oran's frown furrowed deeper into his face. "*Billy* here is leaving your grand company."

"He owes for the smack. And he isn't going anywhere until he pays."

Oran let go, and Liam's head thumped against the wall, a picture rattled, and someone laughed—Jimmy's sister by the sound. *Oran will give up now,* Liam thought. He would leave him to fade into just another stain in the already stained carpet.

"How much?" Oran asked.

Praying that whatever it was that Jimmy wanted would be too much for Oran to pay, Liam stopped tracking the conversation. He got the vague impression that some sort of negotiation took place. He didn't care. He crawled back into the comfort of brain-numbing electric guitars. Time passed. He measured it in needles and promptly lost count. The next he saw Oran he was wearing a different shirt under his heavy coat, and once again Liam felt himself lifted from the floor. This time Pink Floyd's *Animals* swirled in the air around Oran's angry face.

"A bit of help for fuck's sake. For having lost as much weight as you have, you're heavy."

"Sod off."

Oran whispered in his ear. "Not an option, mate. You've only two. The first is coming with me. The second is a bullet, and I don't fancy gunning you down, you hear me?"

"Why?"

"Holiday is over. You're back on duty," Oran said. "It's pathetic you are. What did you do to your hair? Cut it in the dark with a machete, did you?"

"How did you find me?"

"Easy enough," Oran said. "Your uncle asked down at the pub when you didn't come home. Sent word to your mother. She sent a message to me, thinking I might know something. She's worried sick. You're lucky she didn't come looking herself."

Stumbling out the door with Oran, Liam cried out when sunlight bored into his eyes. He was coming down already. He could feel it. He tried to go back into the house, but was no match for Oran. Oran half-dragged him to an unfamiliar green car parked on the street, threw open the passenger side door and tossed him in. Liam smacked his head on the steering wheel. He actually felt the pain this time. That was bad. His bruised head exploded, and if he didn't know any better he would've sworn that at some point he'd been dragged down a flight of stairs feetfirst.

"For fuck's sake, man," Oran said, climbing into the car. Sometime in November, Éamon had decided that a certain level of redundancy was in order for their unit. Oran was the muscle, but it was time he should fill in as the wheelman if Liam couldn't. Oran had been driving since the end of January, and it was still a shock to see him behind the wheel. "The sight of you. You smell like a sewer. When was the last time you had a bath?"

"Should've shot me."

"Oh, cut your sniveling," Oran said. The car's engine roared to life, giving voice to his anger. "There's plenty lost family in the war. Don't see any of them filling their veins with shite. We've been patient on account of Mary Kate and how she was done. But now's the time it's over. No more of this. You hear me? HQ won't tolerate it."

"Where are we going?"

"Home. Belfast."

"Won't go back to the apartment."

Oran shook his head. "Afraid you're in no state to be trusted on your own, mate. First, you're in for a long chat with Éamon. After that, you'll be staying with me and mine."

"No."

"You'd rather live with Níal? Fine by me, but he can't cook, and by the look of you you'll want some nursing and feeding up. Especially after Éamon."

Liam pushed himself into a sitting position. Countryside flitted past the windows faster than he could track. It made him dizzy. "Didn't say nothing to anyone."

"Glad to hear it, mate," Oran said. "Don't much relish shooting you, myself. But sometimes the drugs do the talking for you. That's why HQ has the regulation. No drugs. Ever."

"Didn't. I swear it. Want to sleep first. Can't we wait to see Éamon?"

"If there's enough left of you after Éamon is done then you can sleep all you like."

Liam blinked. He'd known HQ wouldn't approve of what he'd done, but he hadn't thought about what that meant exactly.

"So, it finally sinks in," Oran said. "You stupid bastard." He slammed on the brakes and steered the car to the side of the road. It was clear he was new at the driving and didn't know how to handle himself. The tires slipped off the road before the car finally stopped. The windshield wipers screeched. Liam hadn't noticed the sleet. "Don't just sit there with that stupid look on your gob. Goddamn it, man. Do you not see the trouble you're in? I can't believe you did this. We trusted you. We thought you were up here to get yourself together. Not this. Éamon has orders. We all do. Do you know what that means now?"

Liam swallowed and nodded. The last of the heroin seemed to have faded away. He was freezing and wanted to be sick. "I'm sorry."

Oran snorted. "Well, if you're not, you will be soon enough."

"I'll clean up. I swear."

"And you'll stay that way, you hear?"

"I will. Never again. Not even an aspirin."

Oran gave him a judging look. The old Ford's engine idled, and outside, it started to snow. The wiper blades slapped away the flakes, but still they came until they built up into a small drift on the car's hood. "Well, I don't know it has to go that far." Dropping the car into drive and carefully steering back onto the road, the emotion on Oran's face transformed from anger to apprehension. "Didn't want this for you. You've been through enough."

Liam nodded, feeling sicker. His teeth clattered together, and he wrapped his arms around himself. He wished he knew where he'd left his coat. The pub? Jimmy's place? He couldn't remember. He didn't even know what day it was, or how long he'd been gone from his uncle's. It had to have been a while if Oran had come to get him.

"If it's any consolation," Oran said. "I don't think Éamon will be too hard on you. We all know what you been through. And well, there's the other reason."

"What reason is that?"

Oran gave him a sideways glance. "Like as not something real bad might come of it, you know?"

"I wouldn't do anything to—"

"I know you wouldn't. You know as well as I do that Éamon is just doing his duty. We all do what we must for the cause. But just the same. I don't think he'll take any chances."

"If Éamon's so fucking scared of me, why doesn't he just top me and get it done with?"

"Ah, well," Oran smiled and said, "as much trouble as you are, he still thinks you're the finest wheelman the cause has ever seen. And anyway, HQ isn't exactly flush with silver bullets. I mean, what else is certain to kill Lon Chaney, Jr.?"

Feeling somewhat relieved, Liam nodded.

"Nonetheless, you do this again you're a dead man. Whether Éamon is right about you or I am, doesn't matter. Given enough bullets I suspect we can make even the likes of you bloody uncomfortable."

"I won't. Never again."

"You'll want to," Oran said. "Just. Don't. Was bad enough burying Mary Kate. I've no wish to bury you too, mate."

"Would you like something to eat?" Elizabeth asked in a tired but concerned voice. She was hunched so that she could look him in the face, although Liam wasn't sure why anyone would want to do that at the moment. He'd seen himself. He looked like something out of a horror movie—not in the sense that Éamon seemed to think of him—more like the victim.

Liam shook his head, it made the headache worse, but he didn't want to speak. It hurt too much, and he was afraid his mouth would bleed again. He didn't want to put her to any more trouble. He'd already given her enough of that. He'd done nothing but throw up in a bucket from the time Oran had deposited him on the sofa sometime about two o'clock in the morning until the sun had came up. She was pregnant with Oran's fifth child, and she had enough to deal with.

"You have to eat something," she said. "I heated up some soup. You should try just a bit."

He shook his head again, shut swollen eyes and pretended to go back to sleep.

"All right, then," she said. "I'll leave you a glass of water. There's a straw in it. The soup is on the stove if you change your mind. You know where the tea is. I'm off to work now. Someone will come by soon. You'll be all right for a little while, won't you?"

He grunted and shivered. He felt her throw another blanket on him and then her footfalls went out the door.

Unsure of how much time had passed since the door had shut, he opened his eyes and waited to sit up until after he was certain she was gone. He really wasn't in that bad shape—all things considered. Éamon had been careful, and Liam had let him do what he must. Now that his head was clear, Liam knew he deserved it. He'd endangered Oran and the others. He wouldn't do it again, of that he was certain—no matter how much his blood itched and his bones ached. At least it was pain he could control. It was pain that wouldn't last forever, and twenty-four hours after his last fix, he already felt better than he had any right to if Jimmy's sister had been telling the truth. Nonetheless, his stomach muscles ached from being sick so much, and he was exhausted, but the nightmares had come back all the more vivid for having been quieted.

Liam didn't know how long Éamon would require him to stay on Oran's sofa, or how long Elizabeth would have to tell the children that Uncle Liam was ill and needed quiet. He did know that Oran and the others were planning another job and that he'd have to drive soon. Liam didn't know if he could, didn't know if he wanted to. Hell, he wasn't sure of anything much anymore—except that everything about Belfast reminded him of Mary Kate, and the monster living in the back of his brain wanted nothing more than to kill every last one of the men who had murdered her. The force of the beast's hatred frightened him. He understood now what had kept him from opening up his veins with more than a needle. The monster wanted to live, needed to live, and it would drag him back into consciousness and life whether he wanted it or not.

Someone knocked on the door. Liam considered not answering but thought better of it. It was Níal or Éamon come to watch over him of that he was certain, and if he didn't answer there'd be trouble. Shuffling to the door, Liam discovered Father Murray standing in the hallway.

Father Murray said, "You look like hell."

The monster stirred in the back of Liam's head, but he was too exhausted and sick to do much more than stumble backward. With nothing to stay the tide, memories of laughter and potential for happiness flooded in. He looked away and blinked. *We'd have had a child were it not for him,* he thought. *I'd have had something of her. A family.* "So, Oran has sent you to watch me has he?" Anger choked his voice.

Father Murray settled into a chair. "If anyone sent me it was your mother. She's worried for you, and I can see why."

"She could've come herself."

"The little ones are sick. She couldn't get away."

Liam retreated to the sofa, wrapped the blankets tighter around himself and waited for what was to come. There wasn't much avoiding it.

"Is there anything I can do?" Father Murray asked.

"Bring her back. Take back what they did to her and the babe. Take back what you did. Bring back our child. The one you killed. I should fucking kill you. And I would but I haven't the strength. So, babble at me as you will. I'm through listening."

Father Murray looked guilty, and his voice was barely above a whisper.

"We said the Mass—the Month's Mind—for them in Derry."

"I'd rather you didn't have to." Liam couldn't stop the rage, it seemed. He needed someone to lash out at, and Father Murray was handy.

The corners of Father Murray's mouth drew in tight. "I know what happened that night."

Liam was on his feet before he realized it. Father Murray stared as if he'd gone mad, and for a moment Liam thought he might have the energy for violence after all. *Not here. Think of Elizabeth and Oran.* He searched for a logical reason for having gotten up. Not hungry, but needing to get out of the sitting room, he went into the kitchen and poured soup into a bowl with shaking hands.

"It wasn't your fault," Father Murray said.

The pan slammed down on the stove and warm soup splashed onto his arm. *Another mess for Elizabeth to clean up.* "I don't wish to talk about it." He looked for a towel.

"All right," Father Murray said. "Let's talk about a constable slaughtered in his home the night Mary Kate died. Let's talk about the man's wife telling the RUC she saw a great black dog tear apart her husband before her very eyes."

Liam found what he sought and began wiping up the stove.

Father Murray entered the kitchen and whispered, "I know, Liam. The man's gun had been fired. We found you with a matching gunshot wound a few blocks away. We wouldn't have looked near the Falls Road but for Oran. He knew you'd go into the Shankill looking for revenge. And he was right, wasn't he?"

Automatically placing a hand on the stove's iron grill, Liam discovered its surface was still hot but not enough to burn—at least not in the way expected. A low-grade ache froze his skin. The tingling didn't recede but at least it got no worse.

"Why? After all you've done to stay out of trouble—why would you resort to revenge? Would it have made Mary Kate happy, you think?"

The beast in the back of Liam's head roared at the mention of Mary Kate, taking the agony in his head to new levels. "Don't you talk about her!" He slammed his other hand down upon the stove top to stem the rush of emotion and pain.

"I covered for you. Blamed it upon another. One of the Fallen. They won't be coming for you. Not now. And you damned well know who. But do it again, and I don't know I can stop them. You can't do anything like that ever again. Promise me."

"Go, Father. Now." Liam shuddered against the weight of all he was holding back. One of the iron rings came off the top of the stove, and he blinked before he realized it was designed to do so, and that he hadn't broken it. "Get out. Please. For fuck's sake. Before I do something else I'll regret."

Father Murray went out the door and turned in the hallway. His expression was filled with worry. "What are you going to do?"

The monster will have its way. And when we're done there'll be an end to it at last, Liam thought. He slammed the door in Father Murray's face without giving him an answer, dropped the iron ring on the floor and then ran to the washroom to be sick.

Oran, Elizabeth and the kids were eating their dinner when the telephone rang. Elizabeth exchanged polite greetings and inquiries with the other end of the line before she paused next to the sofa with a worried look.

"It's no trouble at all. Thank you, Mrs. Kelly. And the same to you," she said. "Liam, it's your Ma. Calling from Derry." She held out the phone receiver.

He shook his head.

"She's waiting to speak to you," Elizabeth said.

He rolled away from her to face the back of the sofa. The blow on his shoulder came as a shock. Rubbing the pain out, he looked up and saw Oran.

"Take the call," Oran said.

With some effort, Liam dragged himself from the sofa. He accepted both phone and receiver from Oran and then staggered barefoot to the washroom, stretching the cord as far as it would go. Then Liam looped the cord under the door. It wasn't quite long enough and left him sitting on the cold tiles with his bare back resting against the closed door for privacy—not the most comfortable position, but it would do.

"Liam? Are you there?" His mother's voice was filled with concern.

It didn't do much to stave off his resentment. "Aye."

"Father Murray says—"

"Don't want to hear it, Ma."

"And why not?"

"Because the fuck talked Mary Kate into murdering our child. That's why!" On the other side of the door, Liam heard a door slam. Elizabeth must have taken the weans for a walk to circumvent yet another dubious expansion of their burgeoning vocabularies. It was just as well.

"I don't understand. What—"

"Father Murray convinced Mary Kate to have an abortion when she became pregnant a month after we were married."

His mother gasped. "That's impossible."

"It is possible. Very fucking possible. When you consider Father Murray thought the babe would grow into a monster."

"You're not making any sense," she said.

"It's clean, I am," Liam said. "Will no one fucking believe me?"

"Watch your language, young man. I'll not listen to—"

"Why is it you never told me about my real Da?"

The question was met with shocked silence from the other end of the phone. Liam would've thought she'd rung off but for the sound of her breathing.

"Answer me, Ma. Why?"

"I told you. On your seventeenth birthday!"

"A photo stuck into a book is not telling me! It's avoiding the subject! Same as you have my whole life, Ma! Did it never occur to you that I should know what it is that I am? That having such a father might affect me in some way? That Father Murray might use that as an excuse to kill our child—Mary Kate's and mine?" Sweat felt slick on his skin and the rapid beat of his heart urged the pain in his temples into higher levels.

There was a muffled conversation on the other end of the phone. He assumed she was at his Gran's house—the only person with a phone who could afford a lengthy call to Belfast. She must've asked for privacy because a familiar disgruntled sound preceded a slamming door. After a few moments his mother spoke into the receiver at a whisper. "You seemed perfectly normal to me."

"Normal? I'm normal, am I?" His stomach twisted into a queasy knot. "Are you sure about that?"

She sighed.

"Tell me, Ma. Please."

She paused, and her hesitation only served to make him angrier. He spoke through clenched teeth. "I've a right to know the truth."

"His name is Bran—"

"I know that already. Bran Monroe—"

"The family name—Monroe. That, she made up. A lie. Your grandmother insisted. She told everyone that your father was in the British Navy. That he and I had run off together because the Church wouldn't marry us. And that your father died before you were born. Drowned, it was. That I'd come crawling back after. I was too young to fight her. The lie was the only way she'd allow me to keep you. The only way I could bring you into the house. Otherwise, they would've forced me to give you up. For adoption. I couldn't. I'm so sorry."

Liam swallowed the lump forming at the back of his throat. It was quite a lot to process all at once. *So. It'd all been a lie.* Nonetheless, it wasn't the whole of the truth, and he wanted all of it. He wouldn't settle for anything less this time. "Father Murray seems to think my Da is—" He closed his eyes and forced the question out past the pain in his head and the itching chill in his bones. It was the only way he'd know for sure. "He seems to think my real Da is some sort of… demon. Is it true, Ma?" The words sounded mad echoing off the practical reality of white washroom walls. The chill seeped through the seat of his jeans. He gritted his teeth to keep them from chattering and berated himself for not bringing a blanket from the couch but—

"Father Murray means well, but… no. Your father is not a fallen angel or a demon," she said, her voice gaining a measure of confidence. "He's Fey."

"He's mad?"

"No. At least I don't think so. He's one of the Fianna."

"What?"

"You heard me. He's a Fey warrior. He can change forms, so he can."

Liam felt suddenly dizzy as if someone had yanked a rug from beneath him.

"He can become an eagle or a horse. Many things. I've seen it. He's a púca. Like in the stories," she said.

The wolfhound at the Kesh, he thought. *Was it him?* "I'm—I'm Fey. Not mad. Fey."

"You're my son. You're human. No matter what they say."

"I'm not human, Ma."

"You are—"

"No, Ma. Listen to me. I'm like my father. Do you hear? Like the—like the stories Aunt Sheila used to tell. Shite. That's why she told me those stories, isn't it? She knew, didn't she? Gran knew. Father Murray knew. Did everyone know but me?"

"Don't do this to yourself—"

I could've saved her, my Mary Kate, if I'd but known. The knowledge of it slammed into his gut and threatened to force up the soup he'd consumed earlier. His own mother had lied to him.

She sniffed. The sound of it carried over the phone line. "You're my son. Nothing else ever mattered."

I could've saved her, he thought as the phone dropped from his hand.

"Liam? Liam? Please listen to me! I only ever meant to protect you!"

"That's all *I* ever wanted. To protect my family. You didn't tell me what I should've known. I could've saved her, Ma. Had I but known. I could've saved them both."

He let her tinny voice rattle off excuses at empty air until he gathered enough energy to slap at the phone and ring off. He'd had enough.

"Well," Oran said, "What do you think?"

It had been two days since Father Murray's visit, and Liam felt more focused than he had in a long time. His mother had attempted to speak to him several times over the past forty-eight hours, but he'd refused. There were no complications now—nothing holding him back. He knew what he had to do, and he would do it. Nothing else mattered. No longer lost, he had purpose. He stared at the blue Escort and frowned. "What do I think? It's an RS2000. That's what I think."

Oran said, "It's newer. It's better."

"I drive 1600s. I know 1600s. I know how they work. I know what to expect out of them. How hard I can push them. How much they can take. I don't drive 2000s."

Oran sighed. "Well, you'll drive this 2000 because that's what we've got. Would you rather drive your cab? It's what the others resort to, you know."

"Why didn't you let me get the car?"

"Because you're in no shape for it, that's why." Oran slammed the hood shut. "What the fuck's the matter with you?"

Liam paced the littered yard behind Bobby's mechanic shop, his work boots crunching gravel and old cigarette butts. The place smelled of discarded oil. He threw himself down on the old car seat the staff used for a sofa. It let out a whiff of mildewed vinyl. He picked up a small stone and threw it at the chain-link fence. The sky was an angry grey. "It's going to rain tonight. Pavement will be wet."

"Isn't it always?" Oran asked, sitting next to him on the bench seat. It tilted a little and then righted itself. "Won't have to worry about it for a couple of days yet."

Liam paused. He suddenly guessed what Oran must be thinking, and he didn't like it. "I'll need to take it out."

"Fair enough," Oran said. "You should get acquainted."

"It's got good tires on it."

Oran grunted.

"I hear the suspension handles better. I won't have to make any adjustments."

"How would you know?" Oran asked. "You been unconscious for at least a month."

"More like three."

"Right."

Getting out a cigarette, Liam then offered one to Oran. Oran accepted and lit the end.

Liam took a deep drag and then settled back, blowing out his nervousness in a small cloud of smoke. "It's going to be all right, you know."

"What is?"

"The drive," Liam said. "You don't have to worry about me. I'm ready."

Oran peered at him out of the corner of his eye. "Didn't say you weren't."

Selecting another rock, Liam tossed it at the fence. The metal links let out a ring, the stone bounced off and hit one of the junked-out cars Bobby used for parts.

"You're not wearing your crucifix," Oran said.

Liam shrugged.

"Blaming God are we?" Oran asked.

"Doesn't matter," Liam said. "I'm bound for Hell anyway."

"What the fuck are you on about?"

Sirens echoed off the buildings, and it wasn't until the shouts came from the front of the shop that Liam understood what was happening. He jumped to his feet and dragged Oran up with him.

"The fence. Come on," Liam said.

"But Bobby—"

"He's up front. Peelers have nicked him already."

Liam ran and jumped, grabbing the links and pulling himself up. The fence shuddered with Oran's weight, and Liam almost lost his grip. He reached the top, dropped down the other side and landed on his feet. Although constables were jogging up one end of the alley, he could easily outrun them. Oran might have trouble, but it was possible.

"Stop right there, you Fenian bastards!"

A scent drifting down the alley brought Liam up short—a scent that dredged up memories of a stairwell in December, of three masked men wearing constable's shoes. Liam stopped and put up his hands.

"What are you doing?" Oran grabbed his arm and tugged.

"Go! I'll keep them busy," Liam said.

Oran glanced backward. "We can both make it."

"I said go!" Liam jerked free.

"I won't leave you."

Someone shoved Liam from behind, and he fell and hit his chin on the ground, biting his tongue. Tears sprang into his eyes at the fresh burst of pain. Tasting blood, he was roughly searched. His hands were jerked behind him and the cuffs locked into place. He could hear Oran jabbering about his wife and kids and needing to give them a call. Liam had been taught to keep his mouth shut, but he assumed Oran had his reasons and knew what he was doing. For himself, Liam would follow orders. He'd made enough mistakes, and he wasn't about to make another.

The constables yanked him up from the ground. Liam turned to see his captors, risking a beating to get a visual to match the scent. He was rewarded with a glimpse of red hair and a narrow nose before he was slammed face-first against the chain-link fence.

Got you, the monster thought.

"What's your name?"

The constable on the other side of the table was balding, and his uniform coat fit neatly across broad shoulders. He had introduced himself as Detective Inspector Haddock in a Liverpool accent smothered with London. He stank of stale cigarettes and old beer, and it made Liam want to be sick. He sat on a hard wooden chair, his wrists trapped in cuffs and focused on the steel table in front of him. The detective was playing yet another pointless game with him—one of many Liam had endured over the past seven days. Detective Inspector Haddock knew his name already. The RUC had Liam's driver's license along with everything else that'd been in his pockets when they'd arrested him.

"I know you can talk," D.I. Haddock said. "Heard you squawk when Johnston gave you that thumping. So, you can just answer the fucking question."

Not going to talk. So, you can toss me back in the cell, thought Liam. *But you can't, can you? Time is up. If you were going to ship me off to prison you'd have started the process already. Right? So, this is just the last gasp before you let me go.*

D.I. Haddock slammed both fists down on the table, and Liam involuntarily jumped.

"Answer the question!"

Turning away, Liam thought of how the beast would resume its work. First on the list was the big ginger Peeler. Liam didn't need a name. Now that he knew where the man was stationed, tracking him to his home would be easy. Then would come the questions. Liam couldn't believe his luck. He hadn't even had to search the city—just endure a few days of shortened sleep and the occasional hiding. D.I. Haddock with his empty threats was not important. D.I. Haddock wasn't even worth worrying about.

"Fine, then. Don't talk, and we'll let you go. You've done your seven days. That's how this plays out, is it?" D.I. Haddock asked. "But there's more. See, here's the best part, young Mr. Kelly. I may know you didn't talk. And you may know you didn't talk. But your friends aren't going to be so sure, are they? And you're in enough trouble with them already, aren't you?"

D.I. Haddock grabbed Liam's arm and shoved his sleeve up, exposing the track marks inside his elbow.

"I don't know where you found heroin in this godforsaken country. I don't particularly care because frankly, I don't give a damn what you fucking Paddies do to yourselves," D.I. Haddock said. "But your friends do care don't they? And who's to say you didn't sell out for a hit? Maybe even a whole supply?" He set his teeth in a vicious grin. "Yes. That's right. I think maybe I should have someone contact you outside. Once a week. Be sly about it but not quite sly enough. Make sure they know. Make a few calls. Keep an eye on you. Maybe even leave you something for your trouble. Whether you accept it or not won't make a difference. It's their perception of the situation that matters."

Liam jerked his arm free and glared.

"Got to you, have I?" Haddock asked. "Yes. I have. I can see. Welcome to the rest of your life, you piece of shit. You think you can fuck with me? You're wrong. I can make bloody sure the last moments of your life are a living hell. And the nice part is, I won't even have to lift a finger. Your Fenian scum friends will do it for me."

Haddock lit a cigarette and blew the smoke in his face. Liam didn't move.

"Way I see it, this is your last chance." Haddock said, "All we really have to do is shoot you up and plant a kit on you. A pretty picture, that. One even a Paddy could put together."

Looking away, Liam listened to the sound of his heart. His whole body quivered with each thudding beat. *He's lying. He can't do it. He won't. He's a Peeler. It's a threat, that's all. Peelers are bastards, but he won't do it. Calm down. Don't show him anything. They've fucking revoked political status. You'll go in for good. Don't say anything. Don't give him anything. Don't—*

"Nigel!" D.I. Haddock reached inside his coat and brought out a zippered bag. "It's time!"

The door slammed open and a Peeler came in. Liam recognized him from the beatings. He was a few inches shorter than Liam and weighed at least twice as much. Of course, after two months of Jimmy's smack Liam couldn't have fought Oran's Granny. Constable Nigel Johnston had blond hair, a crooked nose and a really unpleasant right hook. He stepped behind Liam's chair and placed a meaty palm on each shoulder. Haddock unzipped the bag.

"Hallway is clear," Constable Johnston said, "We've fifteen minutes. No more."

"Time is running out fast," Haddock said, holding up a spoon. "Don't get the idea I don't know what to do. I worked narcotics for six years. Undercover." He set the spoon on the table and unbuckled his belt. Then he came around the table and looped the belt around Liam's arm and drew it tight. The detective's hands were cold.

"One minor infraction," Haddock said, "And they send me to this... shit hole. Fucking Belfast."

Liam watched in horror as Haddock cooked the heroin in the spoon using the cigarette lighter from the zippered bag. The syringe plunged into the cotton ball. Haddock's movements were efficient. Practiced. "Hold him tight, Johnston. Don't want him to wiggle and make a mess, now do we?"

Fear shot ice shards into Liam's stomach, and sweat trickled down his sides. *It's only a threat. He's not really going to—*

"This is high-grade smack. Shame to waste it on the likes of you. One last time," Haddock said in his terse accent. "What's your name?"

Liam tried to get up from the chair but was slammed back down at once. He wasn't in shape for a fight, and Constable Nigel Johnston knew exactly how to handle himself. Liam had learned that much the hard way.

Haddock held up the syringe. "Your choice," he said and then pinned Liam's left wrist to the steel table with the other hand. The needle stabbed down and sharp pain rocketed up Liam's arm.

"No!" He tried to escape, to dislodge the needle and failed.

"Too late," Haddock said, clucking like a disappointed school teacher. "You had your chance."

The heroin was still warm as it entered Liam's veins. Struggling, he didn't notice when the belt had been removed. Either Haddock had been none too gentle when he'd removed the needle or it'd been his own struggles, but blood dripped on the floor. Liam blinked, feeling dizzy. He had a whole inventory of bruises, cuts and a number of cigarette burns courtesy of Constable Johnston. Small pains. All of them vanished in a warm haze and then Liam's eyes fluttered closed.

"Oh, no. You're not sleeping here."

"Did you give him too much?"

"He's just being stubborn. Fucking Paddies."

Liam's head rocked back.

"Wakey, wakey."

"We've only four minutes, boss."

"Get him out of here."

Then movement. Grey tiles. A car. Ribbed vinyl upholstery sticky against his cheek. The smell of old cigarettes. Door open. Outside. Cold. Pavement. Steps. There were steps, and he was using the rail to keep himself from falling. Marveling at the cold steel in his palm and no pain. Water oozed from the sky in icy silver sheets, but he couldn't feel it. The warmth in his veins burned out all other sensations. The colors. Everything outlined in gold. Beautiful. A woman stood in front of him. She had dark wavy hair, freckles and amazing brown eyes. Her flower print dress bulged about the middle. Pregnant. She spoke but he couldn't make sense of the sounds she made. Pretty sounds. He sat, unable to go any further. His hand in a water puddle. Threads of bright red swirling in cloud-filled water. *Reflection,* Liam thought. *It's a reflection.* Red liquid stained the sky, and he wondered if it would rain blood. He thought of the plagues in the Bible and started to laugh. An angel came for the first born. Had it been a fallen angel? Someone screamed. Oran appeared. A dark bruise over his left eye.

"Didn't," Liam said, seeing the anger etch lines in Oran's face.

Oran's mouth moved, but again Liam couldn't make any sense of what was being said. His head grew too heavy to hold up. So he rested it on the walk and watched black patches form in the clouds. The inky spots bled over everything until there wasn't anything else.

Chapter 22

Andersonstown, Belfast, County Antrim, Northern Ireland
April 1977

A knife blade of pain shot up the inside of Liam's left arm and lodged into his spine somewhere between his shoulder blades. "*Mac an mhadaidh sráide!*"

"Stop jumping about," Oran said. "Let me change the bandage."

Seven-year-old Brian sat next to his father, his little face intent under thick brown curls. "What did Uncle Liam say?"

Oran jerked the dressing free none too gently, taking parts of the scab with it. Liam pressed his lips together to keep from screaming something else little Brian would regret repeating.

"Never you mind," Oran said. "Why don't you go outside and play?"

"It's raining," Brian said. "What's wrong with his arm?"

"Then go finish your homework," Oran said.

"Finished already," Brian said. "He got measles? Is he going to be sick again?"

"Go play with your sisters!"

Looking hurt, Brian stood up and then retreated into the next room.

"Sorry," Liam said.

"Watch yourself," Oran said. "Elizabeth hears the little ones repeat one more phrase the likes of that one, we'll both be looking for new lodgings. Had a rough enough time with her over the last bout of this."

Liam's throat constricted, and he looked away.

Tying off the new bandage, Oran said, "You've done some less than brilliant things on occasion but nothing this stupid. Was the drugs that tempted you, you'd have been more careful about it, I'm thinking. Cagey. Said so to Éamon, myself. Christ, your arm is a mess."

Liam changed the subject. "What about the job? Is it still on? What are we going to do?"

"Nothing, mate," Oran said. "Not a damned thing. You'll go back to your

204

cab, and I'll see to the shop. Someone has to run it while Bobby is inside. You were right. Should've had you lift the wheels."

"But—"

"They're watching us. Can't do anything out of the ordinary. Not for months—maybe even a year. We're out of the war for a time, you and me."

Thinking of the ginger-haired constable, Liam inwardly disagreed. *Wait until I get my strength back,* he thought. *Then we'll see.*

Stopping his taxi, Liam let Mr. Gower and his sons out and waited for Mrs. Burney to get in. "Where to, Mrs. B.?" Since the taxi was now empty Mrs. Burney's destination would determine the taxi's and any subsequent passengers would be dropped or picked up along the way.

"My sister's bakery on the Springfield Road. The bus isn't running today because of the bombing. Poor wee Kevin. Ten years old. Bombing an Easter parade. What's the world coming to?"

"How's the McMenamins getting on?"

"Not well at all," Mrs. Burney said. "Such a tragedy. Will you be going to the funeral?"

"Aye."

"Still, we must go on."

"I'll get you to your sister's, Mrs. B."

His arm was taking its time healing, and it ached with every gear change or sudden move. He wanted to grab a cup of tea from the thermos Elizabeth had been kind enough to provide, but he needed to concentrate. The cab was new to him. Although most people would argue that one couldn't tell one black hack from another, he knew the difference. The new cab hadn't been as well maintained as his cab had been. It had a looser clutch and tended to hitch in second gear. Even the seats were worn-out and could use a bit of cleaning. At least the carburetor was in decent shape. He made a note to himself to give the cab a wash when his shift was done. It was warm enough. He could give the entire car a thorough go over. Maybe even get the little ones to help. It'd keep them all distracted for an hour or so, and grant Oran and Elizabeth a bit of much-needed privacy.

Liam glanced in the rearview mirror in preparation for merging back onto the street.

Detective Haddock stood just behind the cab, one step from the curb. His lips pulled back into a vicious smile. He waggled his fingers by way of a wave hello.

A surge of hatred poured through Liam, his fist tightened on the gear shift knob, and he checked an urge to slam the car into reverse. This was the second time that fucker had appeared in the past three hours.

"Is something wrong?"

"No, Mrs. B.," Liam said. "I'll have you to the shop in no time." He rolled down the window and gave Detective Haddock the two fingers.

Mrs. Burney gasped. "What are you doing?"

"Sorry, Mrs.," Liam said. "Was signaling we could take two more passengers."

She glanced at the interior of the empty cab which had space enough for at least five more and harrumphed in disbelief. Haddock just grinned and waved again. Oran had said not to react to Haddock, but Liam couldn't help himself. The day before, two undercover constables had gotten into his cab and tried to offer him an envelope full of smack. He'd told them to stuff it. Luckily, two passengers signaled they wanted a ride or there may have been blows—or worse. Frightened by the prospect of being forcibly shot up again, Liam had explained what had happened to Oran. When he was finished, Oran gave him a nervous sideways look that Liam didn't like. The whole situation was getting to him, and Liam began to second-guess everything he did—worrying over what it must look like to Oran. He knew it only made him look guiltier, and understanding that this was what Haddock wanted made him hate the bent Peeler more than ever.

He drove while Mrs. Burney talked about her daughter's upcoming wedding. Attempting to calm himself after the encounter with Haddock, Liam made the requisite noises of agreement and pretended to listen while he thought about his preparations for the evening ahead.

It'd taken several tries, but he finally had been able to make the change from human to monster and back at will. Locking himself in the washroom hadn't been the smartest idea as it had turned out. The transition hurt like anything, and he'd come back to himself to the sound of Oran pounding on the door. Once inside, Oran had searched the washroom and then checked Liam's pupils. Liam understood why. That was, after all, the reason he was staying there. However, he was getting damned sick of the arrangement, and he was certain Elizabeth was reaching the end of her patience as well. He needed his own place, but that wasn't likely to happen anytime soon with Detective Haddock and his friends making their appearances. Not that Liam looked forward to the vulnerability of living alone, given his history with Haddock.

Accepting his fee from Mrs. Burney, Liam breathed a sigh of relief as she made her way to the bakery's door. She latched onto Mrs. Lawson at the entrance, machine gun blasts of chatter rebounding off the glass and through the open cab window. No one was waiting for a ride. As he continued on down Springfield Road he popped in his new favorite mix tape.

Everything was planned. He'd go into the car park to tinker after dinner. He did it most nights well into the evening. Oran wouldn't think it unusual, and once Oran grew bored with watching out the window—sometime around eight-thirty if the past two days were any indication—Liam would pay his visit to the ginger constable. Oran would discover him missing—that was inevitable but he could explain he'd needed a walk and accept whatever punishment came as a result. As for the killing, he would have to be careful. He couldn't afford to be caught by Father Murray or his friends—at least not until every one of the men who'd murdered Mary Kate were done for. After that, Liam would welcome Hell. He was sure it would be Hell. He hadn't been to confession, let alone Mass, since December. The closest Liam could bring himself was to walk to the church and stand outside while Oran and his family attended Mass. Liam wasn't afraid of any priests coming for him. He hadn't done anything to which the Church might object. Well, not yet. *Not lately.* Nonetheless, he couldn't bring himself to go through confession. Come to think of it, did the spawn of fallen angels or the Good Folk even have souls? Suddenly, he almost regretted running off Father Murray before he'd asked the question.

Liam stomped on the brakes to avoid hitting a man standing in the middle of the street. The cab skidded to a halt before he understood who it was.

D.I. Haddock. Again.

Foot twitching on the brake, Liam would've run the man down but for the passengers waiting at the curb. He glanced out the window and noticed two of the three men were unfamiliar. That didn't mean anything, but it didn't put him at ease either. The third one he couldn't rightly see as he was standing behind the others with his back turned, but he was a big bastard with blond hair and didn't give Liam a good feeling. The men climbed into the back of the cab as expected. However, Haddock yanked open the passenger front door and slid in next to him before he could ask where they were headed.

"Hello, Sweetheart," Haddock said. "Glad to see me?"

Liam ignored the electric bolt of fear that exploded in his stomach and set his jaw.

"Oh, come now. You'll have to get this bitch going or someone really will take notice," Haddock said. "Don't worry about stopping for anyone. You're full up. Isn't he, boys?"

"Yes, boss."

Liam glanced into the rearview mirror and recognized Constable Nigel Johnston's face with its crooked nose.

"Just so you don't decide to get creative," Haddock said. "Johnston there has a .38 pointed at you. It will make a rather large hole in the seat before it makes another rather large hole in you. Shame to muss the car, but you have to break some eggs to make an omelet I hear. Drive."

Setting his jaw, Liam put the car in gear. Sweat trickled down his back. Paul Simonon's drawl buzzed out of the cab's tinny speakers. *An' if I get aggression I give it to them two time back. Every day it's just the same with hate an' war on my back.*

"What utter shite." Haddock switched off the radio in disgust, nearly ripping off the knob in the process. "Now. Aren't you going to ask what it is I want?"

Liam searched the street for an excuse to stop, but there was nothing. His heart hammered out a rapid bass solo. "You going to arrest me?"

"Knew all along you had a pretty voice," Haddock said. "Just a matter of the right motivation, it seems."

"Well?"

"Ah, now why would I go and do a thing like that? Especially since we have our little agreement," Haddock said.

The street was vacant of passengers just as Haddock had said it would be.

Bastards, Liam thought.

"Give him the envelope," Haddock said.

A familiar brown envelope appeared over Liam's left shoulder. He made no move to accept it. A red light forced him to stop the taxi. He considered getting out, but abandoning the cab would've brought down even more trouble, and on top of that the likelihood of escaping before Johnston blew his head off wasn't exactly high.

Haddock grabbed Liam's wounded arm. "Take your fucking medicine."

Liam snatched Haddock's wrist with a snarl and twisted. The tingling associated with the monster flowed under his skin. *Not now. I say when it's time. Not you,* Liam thought. "Let me go before I rip your throat out with my teeth." He felt something hard and cold press into the back of his head.

"Let the boss go. Now."

Haddock's face was pale, and he drew back the instant Liam released him. The car behind them honked, signaling the light had become green.

"You said was only the appearance that was important," Liam said shifting and then pushing the accelerator.

Anger flooded color back into Haddock's expression. "What the fuck are you on, Paddy boy?"

"Fuck you."

The barrel of the gun was shoved farther into the back of Liam's head.

"Answer the boss."

"What's he fucking care?" Liam asked, leaning away from the Peeler in the back seat.

"Take the envelope, you Fenian bastard, or I'll let Johnston splatter your brains all over the wind-screen," Haddock said.

Liam took the envelope.

"Good boy," Haddock said. "Bet your Mum is right proud of you."

"At least I know who she is," Liam said. "Unlike you."

Haddock punched, and to Liam it felt like his jaw had exploded. The cab bounced off the curb, and for a moment it was difficult to see. He blinked watery eyes, maneuvering half-blind and somehow managing to avoid running into any of the other cars or pedestrians in the process.

"Don't you wind me up! Don't you dare! I'll fucking break you in two!" Haddock held his breath. After a moment he slowly let it out. "Let that be a lesson to you. Pull over here."

Happy to be rid of Haddock, Liam did just that. He wiped blood from his lip with the back of a hand.

"We'll be seeing you," Haddock said and slammed the door.

The other three got out of the back, laughing.

Fuckers, Liam thought. He got out his handkerchief and daubed his lip until it stopped bleeding, then crammed the envelope in the glove compartment. *One day I'll repay you in kind. Maybe tonight.* He slammed the glove box shut and then hit the dashboard four times while the monster inside him raged to get out. When he'd calmed down enough to drive he finished his route. At the end of the day, he navigated the safest path to the river. It was a bad area of town, and it was foolish of him as a Catholic to go near there after dark, but he couldn't think of anywhere else he could safely dump the smack. Standing on the concrete re-enforced bank, he stared at the murky water.

Don't have to get rid of all of it, he thought. *Just one hit. Could be real careful. Use a vein in my foot. Between the toes. Oran won't look there. Just one hit.*

Then he remembered how potent the smack had been, how lovely the high, and thought why toss it at all? But where would he hide it? He couldn't bring drugs into Elizabeth's home. Wouldn't. Not with the weans. Never. He wouldn't repay her and Oran that way.

The cab.

First place Oran would look, Liam thought. Take that one hit tonight and then what? He glanced to his left and saw a group of toughs gathered in a tight knot a block away. They were drinking and seemed not to have noticed him, but that would change soon. *Oran is sure to be wondering where I am. Knows when my shift ends. So, turn up late with dilated pupils? That's a fast track to a bullet in the brain, that is—assuming I survive being half out of my mind in this place. And even so, where am I going to find a needle on the bank of the Farset? No, I have to get rid of the shite. No one for the road. Not even half.*

In the distance, a gun went off. It could've been a car backfire, but he doubted it since most cars didn't sound anything like a Kalashnikov. He opened the envelope, looked inside and almost laughed. Haddock had supplied everything. Just in case.

Of course. Fucking bastard.

It took every ounce of will Liam possessed, but he emptied the envelope, threw the lot in the Queen's channel and ran back the cab. Racing for Oran's flat, he struggled with a deep desire to go back to the river. It would be suicide in more ways than he could count, but that didn't matter to the hunger. Somehow, he managed to get home, though. Everyone was at the dinner table when he opened the door. Elizabeth gave him a leery stare, but when he didn't stagger or show any other outward sign of the drugs or drink she went back to eating.

"Where've you been?" Oran asked.

"Bit of trouble with the cab," Liam said, mentally kicking himself for taking too long. *So much for getting free of Oran tonight.* "Fixed her up just fine. Should check on it after dinner, though. I'll wash up."

Oran got up from the table, blocking his path. "Mind if I check your pockets first?"

"I wasn't... I'm not...." Liam sighed and put his hands behind his head—half in imitation of a police search and half to hide the fact that his hands weren't dirty with grease. "Go ahead."

Oran looked hurt and remorseful. "It isn't like that."

"I know," Liam said, feeling his face burn while Elizabeth watched. Suddenly, he was very glad he'd made the right choice, as hard as it had been. "I've given you reason enough to mistrust me. Check my eyes too if you like."

"Eat your dinner, youse," Elizabeth said to the children. "Stop your gawking."

Liam waited while Oran gave his pockets a cursory check and then returned to the table, embarrassed. Elizabeth's mouth was tight with tension while she stirred the contents of her plate. Liam couldn't avoid hearing her fierce whisper as he went to the washroom to rid his hands of nonexistent grease.

"This has got to stop. Think of the children."

After dinner Oran followed him outside to have a look at the cab while Elizabeth put the little ones to bed. There wasn't anything for it. Liam knew he had to come clean. Even if he had no intention of doing so, Oran knew enough about cars that he'd know a bad lie, and Liam was sick of lying. Oran knew he was covering for something. That was obvious by his expression. It was best to just come out with it and be done.

Lifting the car's hood, Oran leaned in for a closer look.

Liam took the plunge. "I lied about the cab breaking down," he said. "Haddock was at me again today."

"Is that where you got the lip?" Oran straightened and blew air out of his cheeks. "Told you to ignore the bastard. What did you do?"

"He was in my cab. Him and two others. He… he…" Liam paused. *Get on with it. It's half out already.* "He had heroin."

"What happened?" Oran asked in a hard voice, his eyes squeezed into a squint. "Tell me. Exactly."

Liam told him everything right down to throwing the lot in the river and wishing he hadn't. "Sorry I lied to you, but I couldn't. Not in front of Elizabeth and the little ones. You get enough shite over me as it is."

Oran's shoulders drooped. "That's all right."

"He's not going to stop, you know," Liam said. "Don't know how much more of this I can take. That was fucking close."

Oran nodded. Liam tried to puzzle out his expression but couldn't.

"Wouldn't blame you for putting one in my skull right now," Liam said. "I'm a weak spot. The bastard will keep pressing. You going to tell Éamon?"

There was a long pause, and Liam searched Oran's face for some sign of what to expect.

"No," Oran said, seeming to come to a difficult decision. He looked extremely uncomfortable about whatever it was. "I'll not tell Éamon. And I'll not shoot you either."

Liam didn't know why he was relieved.

"There's… someone I can talk to. Take care of it," Oran said.

"Of Haddock, you mean?"

"Aye."

Liam nodded. "I could do it." He really could. He was already prepared to do for three others. What was one more? And if there was a Peeler who needed his throat ripped out Haddock was the one.

"You're in enough shite as it is, mate."

"I suppose I am at that."

It started to mist.

"Better get inside before we're soaked, and Elizabeth is on us for tracking the damp on her clean floor."

"Oran?"

"Aye?"

"It'll be all right, won't it?" Liam found himself asking. After everything that had happened, after Mary Kate, after Ballymena, after the last arrest, after Haddock—he wanted to be reassured like a boy gone to his big brother with a nightmare. He'd made mistakes, and everything he knew, what little of it that remained, was so fragile. It could break apart, and he would break apart with it in ways he never imagined before.

"It will," Oran said, and even though Liam knew it was a lie he was grateful. "Come on. We'll have a couple of pints."

Liam thought about his original plan for the evening. He could go inside with Oran. They could have those pints, maybe even get a bit drunk and everything would blow over. Liam wanted it more than anything, but that would mean the men that had murdered Mary Kate would live one more night, and he couldn't bear the thought. "Would it be all right if I went for a wee walk? I... I need to think."

Oran gave him another long, hard look. "Give me your word this is not about going back to the river."

"I swear. It isn't. I'll not go anywhere near there."

Liam listened to the rain as it gathered force, the moisture grouping together to form ever-larger drops. Oran turned up his collar.

"What if Haddock comes after you again?"

"I love the little ones. I do. And you. And Elizabeth, no matter what she thinks of me now. But I can't breathe in that place. I'm being watched every second. My skin crawls with it."

"Was that or top you," Oran said in a quiet voice. "Was the only choice HQ gave us."

Liam shook his head with a sigh. "You made the wrong choice."

"I didn't! You're my mate!"

"I'm grateful you took the chance, Oran. I am. But I'm a liability to the cause now. HQ was right."

Oran snorted. "Liability? Where did you learn such shite language?"

Liam's chest ached, but it was a bearable pain unlike before. Guilt and relief hit him in the moment of realization that he no longer felt like dying at the mere touch of her memory. "Mary Kate. She wanted to be a solicitor, remember?"

It was Oran's turn to shake his head.

"Please. I need to be alone. For an hour or two. To prove myself. To gain your trust again. I have to. I can't live like this. You can't watch me forever."

"I can if Éamon says I must."

"Not if you're to keep your family. And I'll not have you lose Elizabeth over me."

Oran paced along the side of the cab. "You're something else, you are.

Present me with all the reasons why I should kill you and then ask me to trust you."

"It works out, I won't ask again for a week. It doesn't, and Haddock shows up again, you can top me and be done. Has to be that way."

"Hell of a chance." Oran slowly filled his lungs. "Could wait until Haddock isn't a problem anymore."

"We both know you can't tell Éamon about Haddock."

Oran stopped pacing and gave him that guilty sideways look. "What do you mean?"

"You tell Éamon, and I'm good as dead. They'll not go so far as to top a Peeler over the likes of me. Better, easier to do what should've been done in the first place."

"No!"

"Don't you lie. This is war. I'm a security risk. And that bastard Haddock knows it. He'll not stop until I break."

"You won't. I've seen you! You're strong!"

"That's bollocks. Wasn't you told me all that hard man shite was pointless bravado? Everybody breaks."

"The hunger strikers at Portlaoise haven't broken."

"I look like Martin Ferris to you?"

Oran smiled. "Aye, well, you're skinny enough."

"That is not funny."

Looking away, Oran sighed.

"Give me this. We'll figure out what to do about Haddock after," Liam said.

"All right," Oran said. "One hour. No more. We keep this between you and me. Get back on time."

"I will. Promise."

"Right," Oran said, looking at his watch. "Don't make me regret this."

Liam started across the car park. "I won't. Thanks!"

Oran leaned on the cab as if to take shelter under the hood, checked his watch a second time and then lit a cigarette.

Trotting down the street, Liam couldn't contain a sense of euphoria. It was all he could do to keep from breaking into a run, but the monster brought him up short. There was work to do, serious work, and there wasn't much time. Liam made his way to a closed-off alley and then gave himself to the change. It hurt—it always hurt but seemed to take less time than it had in the washroom. *Practice makes perfect,* the monster thought and dashed off out of the alley.

It had been a risk following the ginger constable from the police station the day before. Any number of things could've gone wrong—like Oran finding out about the shorted work hours, but the gamble had paid off. The ginger constable lived in Crumlin. Liam would have sworn it was part of another city altogether, perhaps even another part of the world. The walk-up flat was located on a street populated with playing children and smiling young couples watching over their offspring. There had been no fear in any of the faces. No furtive looks. No thinly disguised vigilance for the slightest sound or the stranger, just children playing unafraid of the parked cars. One boy actually kicked a can he found in the street—no child in West Belfast would've taken a chance. While Liam gaped, the monster had grown restless. All he'd wanted to know was where the constable lived and that question was answered.

Now he traveled on all fours, and it was nighttime. With the wet pavement under the pads of his feet and the quarry near, the monster didn't consider what would happen if the ginger constable wasn't at home—it simply wasn't an option. He glanced up at dark clouds backlit by a full moon and huffed out a chuckle of anticipation. He could almost taste the salty blood of revenge. In a burst of enthusiasm he ran ever faster and arrived at the ginger constable's door in record time. There were no gardens, no fences, no gates on the ginger constable's street. All was quiet, the happy children having long since been tucked into their warm, safe beds. The number twenty-three glittered in mist-laced moonlight like a beacon. Pausing to listen, the monster could hear more than one male voice rumble from behind the door.

Isn't alone, Liam thought from his corner of darkness.

Too bad. Should've picked another night for a pint with his mate, the murderer, the monster huffed and ran a paw down the door, scraping paint and wood in long curls with his nails. *Knock, knock. Who's there? The big bad wolf.*

When no one answered the monster threw a shoulder against the door. The voices grew silent.

Ah, now. That's better, the monster thought. *Little pig, little pig. Open up, or I let myself in. And I'll huff, and I'll puff—*

That's not how it goes, thought Liam.

It does now.

Someone approached the door. "Who's there?"

The yellow acidic smell of fear soaked through two inches of wood. *Now you're playing the game,* the monster thought and thumped again. The door rattled on its hinges.

Footsteps shuffled. Whispering. Caution was understandable. It was late, and no one was expected. The 'Ra had been exacting a toll among the Peelers over the past few months. So, who was to say the 'Ra hadn't decided to target gingers in particular?

"I said, who's there?"

The monster eased back, taking a position along the wall and just under the front window. When the door swung open he rocketed through and knocked the hall's occupant to the floor. The man landed with a grunt. A cricket bat dropped from his hand. The monster's enormous paws jabbed into the man's chest and stomach. The instant he was certain of his footing the creature shoved his muzzle in the man's face and took a deep breath.

Boot polish. Cigarettes. Beer. That horrible cologne some fool marketing executive had named High Karate six or seven years back. The monster grinned at the unexpected bonus. *Now, now. Isn't that interesting? Two for one.* He sneezed to get the foul cologne out of his nose. Beneath him the second constable trembled, and a thin whine escaped his throat.

"Get it off me."

"W-what the fuck is that?"

"I don't know! Kill it! Get it off!"

"That thing is fucking huge!"

The monster basked in the constable's fear for a moment before he lowered his snout and licked the man's cheek. The cloud of fear grew more intense. *Good. So good,* the monster thought. *Perhaps I'll take a nip here or there. Maybe I'll rip a line low in your stomach, Peeler. Watch you crawl the hallway with your intestines trailing behind.*

Sounds of items being upturned from the kitchen.

Enough, Liam thought. *He's looking for a weapon. Finish. Now. Kill him. While there's time.*

Don't be a spoilsport.

One of the happy young residents of the street is sure to have heard the screaming. It wouldn't take long for a prowl car to arrive. *Do it. Now. Now. NOW.*

The monster ran a clawed paw down the middle of the constable's chest. It resulted in a series of long screams. Warm blood oozed between the monster's toe pads. He felt something give way under him, and the constable's innards parted in a warm gush. The monster was wading in the man's intestines now. More screams. Looking up he spied the ginger constable standing in the hallway. He was holding a gun. The barrel was shaking. The monster lifted a hind leg and urinated on the man beneath him, daring the ginger constable to shoot.

"Get away! Off, you big bastard!" The ginger constable fired.

The monster felt wind from the bullet's passing on his left ear, then he leapt from the remains of the High Karate wearer and landed in front of his last target.

"No! Oh, God! No!" The ginger Peeler scrambled, retreating to the kitchen.

The monster followed. A shelf crashed down in front of him, then a door opened and the ginger constable was out into the back garden. The monster climbed over the debris and burst through the door, knocking it off its hinges.

The fenced yard was empty.

Nice try. I can still smell you, you bastard.

Something clattered and a grunt came from the fence in front of him. *Got you now.* The monster let out a howl.

Sounds of running. Jumping, the monster hit the top of the wooden fence and dropped down to the other side. The ginger Peeler was dashing through a small park and dodging children's play equipment as he went. One of the swings let out a high-pitched squeak as the chains swayed with his passing. Beyond the park was a dense nest of trees. The constable was making for the safety of the tree line. The moon rode the clouds, casting the entire scene in bluish light. Approaching sirens echoed in the night. Liam thought of the constable inside the flat. Was he dead yet? Should he make sure? Careful. He was supposed to be careful. Another man found mauled to death by a wolfhound certainly wasn't being careful. What was he thinking?

There are others of our kind. The monster inwardly shrugged and continued pursuing his prey. He caught up to the ginger constable on the bank of a tiny stream.

"Mum told me about you," the ginger constable said, his teeth clattering together. "When I was little. You—you can't cross streams. Running water." He stepped on a stone and slipped, splashing into the stream. "I'm safe." He laughed and there was an edge of hysteria to it. "Guns don't stop you. But running water does." This statement didn't cause him to lower his shaking gun. His foot touched the opposite bank.

The monster edged to the stream and sniffed. It was true. The man's scent trail vanished where he'd crossed the stream, but that was as far as the myth went to Liam's experience. If he were one of the Good Folk—the monster huffed a laugh at the name—he was of the sort that enjoyed water. Ignoring the rocks, the monster set a paw into the stream.

"No. You can't. Mum said. Mum would know. Was from Ballymena, Mum was. Her people were in with the Good Neighbors. Means I am too." The ginger constable's eyes weren't seeing, that much was clear. Nor was he talking to anyone present.

"You won't kill me. Can't. Don't matter what she said, that Fenian slut."

The monster stopped—three paws in the water now.

"She caused trouble, that one. Roused up the others. Started riots. Filthy Catholics should stay where they belong. Would have but for her. Had to shut her up."

The monster stared the ginger constable in the eyes, willing more answers from him. *What did she tell you?*

A choked laugh fell from the ginger constable's mouth. "She... she said we'd be cursed. She said her husband was a... a monster. Said he'd come for us. One by one. Rip us apart. John said it was a lie. Said her husband was just 'Ra scum. But she wasn't lying, was she? You're him, aren't you? You came for John and now you're here for me and Alex. You got Alex, but you won't get me." He reached into his shirt and brought out a stone tied around his neck with a cord. When he held it up, the moonlight shone through the hole in the center. "See? My Mum gave this to me. Talisman this is. Look through and you can see them, she said. Fairy Folk. Only I can see you without it, can't I?"

The monster placed all four paws in the water now.

"Shouldn't have done it," the ginger constable said. "Said she was pregnant. Shouldn't have done it. I'm sorry. But they're always pregnant, aren't they? Catholics. Breed like fucking rabbits. So, John laughs and says let's check to be sure."

Moving closer, the monster's rage burned more fiercely than before. He focused that hate until it shone bright red from his eyes. *Kill you. Now.*

"I'm sorry. You can take the stone. You won't hurt me. I'm sorry. So sorry. We shouldn't have done it. We didn't know. Never again. Offerings. I'll give you whatever you want. Anything."

Reaching the bank where the constable stood, the monster reared back on his hind legs, and standing, he towered over the ginger constable. A misshapen shadow poured over the terror-stricken face. The whites of the man's eyes were bright in the darkness.

"Oh, God. Jesus, I'm sorry. Please."

Images of Mary Kate lying in her own blood on the floor sprang to mind—of holding her in his arms while she shivered in pain. He remembered the feel of the gore soaking through his jeans. The smell of the hospital room. *I don't want to die. I want to stay with you.*

The echo of her last words was all he needed to push him past the hesitation. *I'm so sorry. The baby.*

The man's screams were cut off in one satisfying crunch. Blood exploded in the monster's mouth, and the warm copper taste of it filled his nose, his brain, his world. He shook his head back and forth worrying the constable's corpse like a dog with a rag. For a time Liam only knew the taste, smell and feel of blood. When he came to himself again, the monster was standing in a shredded mess of meat that had once been the ginger constable.

Lights flickered in the trees and voices of those who searched called out to one another.

Hour. One hour, thought Liam. *How long have I been here?*

He got down on all fours and ran through the stream to rinse the gore from his paws, and then bolted for Oran's flat as fast as he could. When he was within a block of the place he ducked into the same alley as before and changed back. His clothes were wet and a little worse for wear but that couldn't be helped. He got up from the pavement and headed for the car park at a brisk walk. Oran was almost exactly where he'd left him, but was now wearing a jeans jacket to keep off the rain.

"Two minutes to spare," Oran said with a relieved smile.

"I'll take that pint now." Liam needed something to wash the taste of blood from his mouth.

"Oh, aye?" Oran asked. "We'll have to be quiet about it then. The little ones are asleep."

Liam woke from dreams of Mary Kate to the sound of someone kicking in the door. He had time to sit up and throw off the covers before the men were upon him, and a black cloth bag was forced over his head. Someone tossed him his clothes, and after he was dressed his wrists were cuffed behind his back. The children were crying. There was a scuffle—involving little Brian from the sound. In the confusion he could make out Oran shouting and Elizabeth screaming. Who were the men? The Church? The RUC? Loyalist paramilitaries—the Ulster Volunteer Force? The 'Ra finally come to settle accounts?

"Sit down, Mrs.," a man's voice said. "No harm will come to you and the little ones."

Blind, Liam was dragged out of Oran's flat. The door to a van thundered open, and he was thrown inside. He flipped over onto his back to sit up, and something big and heavy landed on top of him, hitting him in the groin.

"Fuck!"

"Sorry," Oran said, rolling off him.

When Liam could breathe again he could make out the scents of three others in the back of the van besides himself and Oran. All gave off nervous energy. In pain, Liam had already lost track of which direction they were headed.

"What's going on?" Oran asked.

"Shut up."

A series of thumps and shouts followed, which Liam assumed was Oran receiving a violent kicking.

Right then, Liam thought. *Not a sound.*

Oran let out a moan and everything got quiet again. The men settled back into their places once more. Liam closed his eyes and attempted to conserve his wits and energy for whatever was to come. The van drove for quite a long time. Exhausted and with little else to do but worry, he let the hum of the engine lull him into a light doze.

He came to when the van's door rolled open. It was daylight, he could tell by the weak light the coarse weave of the black bag permitted. They were in the country far from the city. He could hear birds. Chickens. A cow lowing. *A farm, then?* It was difficult to smell much beyond the inside of the bag on his head. Once more he was half-dragged from the van. Rough hands grabbed him—one pair at each of his arms—and walked him across grass. He tripped over an obstacle and then stumbled across wooden planks. A door slammed, and he was pushed to the floor. His arms ached and his wrists were burning with cold. He needed to piss.

"Stay there, if you know what's good for you."

Liam nodded.

"You've been quiet. That's good. You might live," a second, deeper voice said. The sound of its mild approval was gravelly and coated with phlegm. The stink of old cigarettes was heavy in the air.

A heavy smoker, thought Liam. *Not a Peeler. Peeler would've thrown his weight around already. Definitely not Haddock and his boys. Not the Church. They wouldn't have taken Oran too, would they? Loyalists then. UVF or UDA—Ulster Defence Association. But what if they're ours? The Officials or Provos?*

Oh, Christ. Don't let it be something I've done.

Someone in the next room screamed.

"Oran?"

"Shut up!"

Liam was punched in the face. He ducked his head in anticipation of more blows. Nothing happened. But Oran continued to howl in pain. His voice climbed to ever higher, more desperate pitches. Liam thought he'd go mad. He tried to give himself to the monster, but the monster wouldn't come. His wrists ached. The cold in them bone-deep now. *The cuffs,* he thought. *Steel is part iron. Is it the steel, then?*

Just when he was sure he couldn't take any more, the screams stopped. Oran was sobbing now. Nothing else for a few minutes. A clicking. A pop. Somewhere flame roared to life. Liam knew that sound and shuddered.

A blowtorch.

Again the screams.

"What do you want from us?" Liam asked. "Who are you?"

"I said, shut your gob and wait your turn!"

This time he was kicked five or six times before they let up. Anything was better than listening to Oran being tortured. It went on like that for hours. Oran's cries. The beatings when Liam couldn't stand hearing anymore. He waited for them to ask him questions, but they never did. Whatever it was they wanted they kept at Oran. Liam lost track of time. He needed to use the toilet something terrible. When he said as much one cuff was undone and the bottom of the bag on his head was arranged so that he could see to piss into a bucket. Later, he was given water and part of a ham bap. Unsure of how long he'd be held, he ate as much as he could stand and fought to keep it down. They took a break from torturing Oran, and when they didn't come for him, Liam slept.

Hours later, it was dark. When a match was struck to light a lantern Liam bit back a scream. He needed to piss again but didn't want to draw attention to himself just yet. Somewhere outside his hood the men ate their dinner. Roasted meat. Chicken, by the smell. His stomach rumbled. Whiskey made the rounds. He heard the slosh of the bottle and caught a whiff of it. Whoever they were, they seemed a solemn bunch, intent on the job but not enjoying it.

That's something, Liam thought. *Maybe not UVF or UDA.* Those bastards would be enjoying themselves. It's what they did. Not this bunch. Not a single Catholic joke or jibe. *The Officials or Provos then. But if they're Provos, why torture Oran when I'm the one Haddock got to? Why not just top me and go home? Surely Oran keeping me alive when he shouldn't have doesn't deserve this kind of punishment?*

When dinner was over footsteps approached. Liam's heart did a slam dance inside his chest. *Is this it? Is it my time now?*

"The boys say you've been asking after your mate."

The hood came off his head. He blinked in the lantern light. Ten or eleven men were in the room—a big open kitchen. White lace curtains. Most were sitting around a table. All were dressed in shades of khaki green. *Paramilitaries. But which?* He dropped his gaze to the floor before he spied any faces.

"Let's go see him."

Two men brought Liam to his feet and led him into an empty bedroom. It reeked of blood, sweat, piss, shit and the lingering odor of burning flesh. The first thing he saw was Oran blindfolded and slumped in a chair, blood staining his clothes. The second thing was Éamon sitting in the corner next to a propane tank, an ArmaLite rifle in his lap. The sudden jolt of recognition and understanding loosened Liam's knees.

This is my fault, he thought.

Ignoring Éamon, Liam went to Oran. They'd used the blowtorch on his fingers one by one. Liam fought to keep from getting sick. He touched Oran's lower arm—gently so as not to hurt him. The skin was warm. Oran jerked with a moan.

Not dead, Liam thought. *That's good. Right?* "Oran? Speak to me, mate."

"He's no mate of yours. Nor mine," Éamon said from his corner of the room. His face constricted with rage. "He talked to the RUC. Worse. Fucking British Intelligence. MI5."

"No," Liam said. "He was protecting me. From Detective Haddock. The bastard was after me. It's because of the drugs. Fucking Haddock would've got to me, but Oran said he was going to have him killed. Said he'd call someone."

"He called someone, all right," Éamon said. "He called Haddock."

"He wouldn't."

"He did. British Intelligence got to him. Through his family. Through you. Doesn't matter. Oran gave up the whole operation. You. Me. Níal. The shop," Éamon said. "We were supposed to think it was you that squealed. Only we're not that stupid."

"I didn't say anything to anyone."

Éamon stared. "Glad to hear it." His face was hard and cold. This was an aspect of Éamon that Liam hadn't seen before, an aspect Éamon reserved for the enemy. "Time to prove it."

One of the others unlocked Liam's cuffs. The bone-deep ache that had numbed his fingers was gone in an instant. If there was a doubt in his mind about steel being a problem for the monster it was gone now. A pistol was shoved into his hand. He wrapped stiff fingers around the grip and looked to Éamon.

"Shoot him," Éamon said. "That's an order."

"What?" It was a stupid question, but he vomited it up nonetheless. He went cold and light-headed as all the blood in his body seemed to drop into his feet.

"Think on it as an object lesson," Éamon said. "Look hard. This is what happens to those that betray the cause. You take the drugs again—just one more time—and what happens to you will make this look like a nice Sunday afternoon chat. Now. Shoot him."

Liam swallowed. "I can't."

"You will, or I'll have another go at him with the blowtorch and then top you myself."

Stalling, Liam took a deep breath. "Not here. Outside. I don't want his last sight to be the inside of this fucking room. And I want to talk to him. Alone." He felt the monster stir somewhere in the depths of his subconscious.

If Liam didn't know Éamon he would've missed the fear that flashed across his features. "Fine. But I'll be watching you. One wrong move and you're done."

A man wearing a balaclava over his face roused Oran with a bucket of water. He woke, shouting for Elizabeth.

"Oran! It's me. I'm here," Liam said.

The man in the balaclava unlocked the cuffs that had been securing Oran to the chair at wrists and ankles.

Oran blinked in confusion. "What's happening?"

"We're going outside, mate," Liam said. "Can you stand?"

"Aye." Oran got to his feet. He was unsteady but could walk with a little help.

It was cold and dark outside, but the moon was still full and bright in the sky. The house was far enough from Belfast that Liam could see the stars. They were beautiful, more beautiful and brighter than he remembered seeing before. A forest pressed in against the stone fences. He'd been right. They were on a farm—probably somewhere along the border. It made sense. All the screaming and gunfire in the world wouldn't bring the Peelers out here—well, not right away. The trees and grass and the hedges were brilliant with moonlight. Somewhere roses bloomed. He could smell them. It was peaceful. Fitting. Suddenly, he was glad he'd asked them to let him take Oran outside. He stopped when they reached a rock where Oran could sit comfortably and then waved the others off. True to his word, Éamon waited a short distance away, ArmaLite rifle at the ready. Liam wondered if he'd gone so far as to load it with silver bullets and then he took off Oran's blindfold.

"Thanks." The word was mushy in Oran's mouth.

Liam realized they'd been at his teeth and shuddered. "Want a smoke?"

Oran looked up. His eyes were glistening with tears. He knew what was up. Liam could see it in his face.

"Sure." He nodded.

Patting his pockets, Liam discovered he'd left his cigarettes and lighter at the flat. He called out to Éamon and the others and in short order he had two cigarettes and a lighter. He waited until Éamon had left. *At least Éamon is being decent about it,* Liam thought. *In consideration for time served.* He stopped himself from laughing like a madman.

Oran couldn't use his hands. So, Liam had to light the cigarette and put it in his mouth for him. Liam handled the cigarette for Oran when it was obvious he needed the help. They took a few puffs in silence, both preparing themselves for the horrors ahead. Liam understood he couldn't flinch. Wouldn't. It would make things worse for Oran, and Oran had been through enough. He'd be quick about it when Oran was ready. One shot. Painless as he could make it. No fuss. Done. Fuck Éamon. He'd take an hour at it if he had to.

"Everyone breaks."

"Oh, Oran." Liam's vision went blurry, and he looked away.

"Told you. Doesn't matter. They'll find something. Just a matter of time. Fucking Peelers. Everyone breaks. You… you have to hold out as long as you can and hope they quit before you do."

"Who was it done this to you? Who got to you?"

"I'm glad it's you," Oran said. "And not him." He nodded in Éamon's direction. "Something's not right about him."

"What do you mean?"

"Knew everything," Oran said. "I called him when you went out walking. They didn't have to… to…."

"Christ," Liam said, feeling his insides turn to water. "Are you sure?"

"Dead certain. He's in with Haddock. He doesn't know I know, or we wouldn't be talking, I'm thinking. Would've told the others but they're probably in it too. Watch yourself."

"I will." *I'll do more than that,* Liam thought.

"Don't tell Elizabeth. Don't tell her it was you killed me. She won't understand. Tell her— Tell her I fell in a fire fight. Don't tell her I talked. Let her think—"

"I know. I will."

"And you'll look after Elizabeth and the weans? You know, grant them what you can? Good lives, that sort of thing?"

"For fuck's sake, what are you on about?"

Oran indicated he wanted another puff from the cigarette, and Liam put it between his bloody lips. When the cigarette withdrew Oran turned his head and let out a great cloud of smoke.

"You're one of the Fair Folk. Only you're not like they say. My Da always told me to stay away from them. Said they never did a good turn without a bad one right behind. But that's not you. You're different. You're more like us than them. You're a good man."

Liam shook his head and thought of the monster. "You've never seen—"

"Do what you can for my family. Please. It's all I'm asking. I can't." Oran choked. "I can't see after them. But you can do it for me. You can protect them. Keep them safe. Don't let Brian join up. Give him a good job. A good long life. Please."

"I will," Liam said. Whether it was true or not that he had the magic—didn't matter. Oran believed and that was what counted.

Oran let out the breath he was holding. "Good." He closed his eyes and licked swollen lips. "One last thing."

"Anything."

"Haddock. Was Haddock got to me."

"Then he'll pay for what he did," Liam said. "I'll see to it. He'll die screaming."

Oran nodded. "Thank you."

Both cigarettes were down to the filters. Liam dropped them on the ground and stamped out the embers.

"I'm ready now," Oran said.

Liam took a shaky breath and nodded. *I don't want to do this.*

"Tell Elizabeth and the weans I love them."

Liam's cheeks were cold, and his throat was tight. It was hard to get out the words, but Oran needed to hear them. "I'll tell them."

Closing his eyes again, Oran sat up straighter. "You've been a good friend. Don't blame yourself. I'm glad it's you."

"Do you...." Liam coughed. "Do you want it in the heart or the head?"

"Heart first. Then the head. Just in case. Just... don't miss. Don't think I could stand it if you did."

Liam raised the pistol and aimed. The point wavered. He tried to steady it. He needed to be accurate at this moment more than he ever needed it in his life. Holding his breath, he pulled the trigger. The bullet hit Oran in the chest. Then Liam followed it up with the second shot before Oran could register the pain. Liam's vision blurred even more, and he was thankful he couldn't see what he'd done.

Oran slumped and began to slide off the rock. Liam caught him, easing the body onto the ground and then checking for a pulse. When he found none, he folded Oran's damaged hands over his chest.

First Mary Kate. Now Oran. Is every soul I love going to die because of me? "Goddamn it, Oran." He stood up and screamed. "Goddamn it!" He threw the gun as far as he could. It landed somewhere in the trees. His breathing came in great gasps. The hair on the backs of his arms prickled. The ache in his chest grew so great that it consumed his whole body.

Éamon and two men came running. By the time they arrived Liam was writhing on the ground.

"What's the matter with him?"

"Son of a bitch," Éamon said. "Oh, Christ. Oh, Jesus. Shouldn't have.

Had to. Oh, Christ."

When the monster rolled onto all fours Éamon was halfway to the farmhouse. Ignoring the two men for the moment, the monster bounded straight for Éamon. Éamon was ready. He got off four shots from just inside the doorway before the monster caught him. The scent of super-heated silver floated on the air.

Chapter 23

Andersonstown, Belfast, County Antrim, Northern Ireland
April 1977

"Where are the little ones?" Liam asked and leaned against Elizabeth's doorframe as he gulped for air. He had no idea how many miles he'd just run. Stooping and then gripping his knees, he wasn't sure how much longer he could remain upright. His legs throbbed with expended energy. The stitch in his side hurt like hell, and his skin was gritty with sweat, soot and old gore. When he registered his question had been met with silence he glanced up to see if Elizabeth was still at the door.

Her face, already blotchy from hours of crying, now had lost what little normal coloring it possessed. The contrast made her freckles even more noticeable. "I sent them to school. Where's Oran? Is that blood? Oh, Jesus—"

"Please, can I come inside?" Liam looked over his shoulder, checking the empty street. He hadn't been spotted yet, but then Peelers didn't give dogs much notice—even when they were larger than average and a bit mucky. A gasping man in blood-soaked clothing was quite a bit more notable even in this part of town.

"Y-yes."

He staggered past her, shut the door and drew the curtains.

"Where's Oran?" Her voice grew brittle as panic took over.

"Don't know how best to tell you this," he said. "But Oran is—"

She charged him like a mad bull and then slapped his face. "Don't you dare! My Oran will be home soon!"

Liam's cheek stung and then grew warm. The monster shifted in the back of his brain. *Stupid cow.*

She's been given a shock, Liam thought back at the monster. *People do stupid things when frightened.* There was no telling how soon the Provos would turn up, and turn up, they would. Subtlety be damned. "He's dead. I wish—I wish I could tell you different. I do."

"You're lying! He's alive! He promised!" She flew at him again, fists slamming into his chest. "This is your fault! He'd have been out but for you! Said he was safe. Said you were lucky. Lucky! It isn't fair! You're alive, and my Oran is dead! You're nothing but a bleeding addict! You got nobody! Goddamn you! It isn't fair! Jesus Christ, why wasn't it you?"

Reeling under the blows, he grabbed her wrists and held her while she sobbed into his blood-stained shirt. He didn't allow her words to sink in. Rather, he distracted himself by preparing the lie he'd tell in keeping with Oran's last wish. For now, he'd endure her grief, and if that meant more abuse, he would take it and gladly. It was the least he could do for her. *For Oran.* Eventually, her cries quieted, and her quaking stopped. Suddenly, she jerked back as if realizing who had held her. Her eyes were wet with hate.

"You tell me what happened. You tell me right now."

"The other night—"

"I know about the other night. They was here for you, weren't they? Was you and those damned drugs! He protected you! I wanted you out! I told him! Put him out on the street before he takes you down with him and us too."

Liam looked away, blinking and nodded. It was better than any excuse he could think up. "You're right. Was me they came for." The vastness of the lie barely fit through his lips.

"I could kill you! Goddamn you! I knew it!"

"Told them I was clean. Oran stood for me. They were going to let him go," he said. "But then the BAs came."

"What?"

"Must've been watching the place. Maybe somebody talked. I don't know," he said, pushing his hand through his hair. He needed to keep to what would be found so that when the Provos came to talk to her they wouldn't destroy everything. "They set fire to the place. Oran and I, we were almost out of there. But the BAs stopped us. They shot him. Didn't want to leave him, but he made me. He wanted you to know what happened."

She staggered backward to the sofa. The sheets and blankets he'd used only a day or two before were gone. It wasn't his bed anymore. It was only a sofa. Her sofa.

"Was brave. Didn't beg or nothing. Died protecting us. But there were too many of them. They killed everyone. I was—I was the only one got away."

Covering her face, she sank to the couch. "I don't want to hear anymore."

"He said he wanted you to know he loved you."

Her hands dropped from her face. "Shut up!"

"But—"

"He didn't love me! Not enough! If he had, we'd be in Dublin. Safe. And he'd be alive!" She stood up, her face pinched into a mask of rage. "I never wanted to come here. I told him he was mad, and he'd only end up dead. He promised me! Well, I was right! Oh, Christ, it isn't fair!"

Liam didn't know what to say. "Oran believed in the cause."

"To hell with the cause! Stupid fucking war! What are we to do now? What am I to tell Brian? Your father died for the cause? So he can volunteer when he's old enough? And die too? It never ends!"

"Oran didn't want that. Wanted a good long life for him." It was out of his mouth before he'd thought about what effect it might have on her.

Elizabeth paused and blinked. Her face was now an unattractive mix of bright red, orange freckles and colorless white. Snot ran from her nose, mixing with the tears.

His skin itched with dried blood, and he didn't think he could stand her staring. "I… I need to use your bog. Must clean up before I go."

"You're leaving?" Her voice was quiet. Defeated.

"I am. I'd stay. Help set things to rights. But I don't want to bring—"

"Good."

That one word cut Liam deepest of all. It drove home everything she'd said in one short syllable. Then the agony of seeing Elizabeth's face became too great, and he fled, slamming the washroom door behind him.

Liam watched the street as a chilling rain numbed West Belfast's jagged wounds. A clump of sullen teens loitered on the corner, smoking—most hadn't seen the inside of a school building in months or even years, he assumed. Two women with grocery bags crossed the street to avoid passing too close. One of the youths shouted something unintelligible and the others laughed. With no hope of a future to keep them in school, the gangs were worse than the paramilitaries if anyone bothered to ask Liam. At least the paramilitaries had a more significant cause for violence than boredom, and they didn't prey on their own. He looked on as the gang finished up their smokes and then moved farther east. Relief loosened a knot in his shoulder. He'd have to leave soon and didn't like his comings and goings being observed, especially now—not that it actually mattered when he thought about it.

He'd passed the summer in the abandoned building. Mary Kate had been dead and gone eight months, and he was still alive. It was late August now, almost September. Gazing down at the street through the boards nailed across a broken window pane, Liam longed to be as empty as the house around him. Winter in this place was going to be unpleasant. About all that his current residence had to recommend it was the view, and if he were a sniper it provided an ideal vantage point, but that was all. With no electricity, the place was far from warm. Little more than a husk, the plumbing was gone, and every window pane was broken. The devastation was not the result of war, but of brutal practicality. The Housing Authority ordered it to prevent squatting, which was precisely what he was doing.

He wasn't the only one. A family of twelve, the Currans lived in the walk up at the opposite end of the row. Of course, there wasn't much risk of prosecution for squatting in this part of Belfast, and they were also fortunate to have electricity in addition to a roof over their heads. However, it was the only house on the row with power and as a result Liam didn't have any other neighbors. Naturally, the Currans concerned themselves with the Electricity Service's collection agents about as much as they did the Housing Authority's. No meter reader was foolish enough to enter the Catholic areas of West Belfast's ghetto—being marched out at gunpoint tended to get the idea across rather efficiently.

Up the 'Ra, Liam thought.

A man with long blond hair made his way down the street. He was memorable for both the length of his hair, which reached down to the middle of his back, and his imposing build. It was the third time Liam had spotted him in a week, and that alone made Liam nervous. But for the hippy-length hair, he would have taken the man for one of Father Murray's assassins. He certainly walked like someone who knew what they were about. He was both out of place and familiar at the same time and reminded Liam of the photo his mother had given him long ago—the one he still kept in that battered book at the bottom of the olive green laundry bag containing what little remained of his life.

He resisted an urge to run downstairs and confront the blond man out of curiosity. The monster in the back of Liam's brain seemed to know him and was reassured by his presence. Liam didn't know what to make of the situation. He told himself repeatedly that it didn't matter. The only thing that did was killing Haddock—but not before extracting information from him on the last of Mary Kate's murderers.

Noting the time, Liam got up from the window and went to the fireplace. Then he tossed another half-rotten timber into the fire and began the process of making tea. Haddock would be on his way home from the station soon, and Liam planned to be standing at the man's door when he came home. It had taken months to locate Haddock's latest residence. Twice Liam was certain he had the man dead to rights only to discover Haddock had pulled up stakes. The bastard was too damned careful for a regular Peeler, and even if Éamon hadn't said so, Liam would've known Haddock for MI5 on that alone. If Liam were concerned about life after Haddock's death, he might consider that a dilemma. For one thing, the 'Ra wasn't in favor of freelancers and generally came down hard on that kind of thing. Although, the British government was going to have a hell of a time blaming a wild animal attack on terrorism—not that a little thing like concrete evidence had stopped them before.

Gulping hot tea, Liam heated his hands on the cup. The foul stuff scalded his mouth but succeeded in warming him nonetheless. Without the assistance of sugar or milk, the reused teabag produced a liquid that wasn't even remotely satisfying, but it formed the bulk of his diet aside from toast and whatever the monster ate.

He avoided thinking of how much he wanted a hit, but the urge remained. It lived like a rat in the pit of his stomach, gnawing at his insides. Heroin would stop Elizabeth's words from replaying in his head. Heroin would make being alone with his thoughts more bearable. Heroin would keep the memories of Mary Kate at bay, but he had to stay clean. He wouldn't have the strength or clarity of mind to top the last murderer if he didn't. Every day was a struggle, and he often wondered why he bothered. Elizabeth had been right to ask God that question. Why the fuck had he lived? No one was sure to miss him were he to die. *Certainly not Elizabeth.*

His appetite hadn't returned, and his living conditions hadn't done much for his appearance either. Thus, no amount of talk could convince her he was off the smack. It didn't matter to her that the 'Ra didn't restrict its activities to running off meter readers. It didn't matter that as far as Liam knew Haddock was the only source for any illegal drug in Belfast. She was convinced he'd always be addicted, and perhaps she was right. The last time Liam had seen her he'd promised he would kill those responsible for Oran's death. She had only given him that stare and then explained to him in very firm language that she didn't give a damn about revenge. She wanted him out of her family's lives. *Forever.* Frankly, he couldn't blame her. Everyone he cared about seemed to die in particularly nasty ways. Best he steer clear. *Best for the poor weans.*

He did everything he could for them, anyway—which wasn't much, all things considered. He left food and money on their doorstep when he had it, often not bothering to take any of it himself, and while she waited until he was gone to open the door, she obliged him by not throwing any of it out. Where the money came from he wasn't certain. Stolen from a Peeler or a BA, he assumed. With no reason to enforce control over the monster that lived inside him, the thing came and went as it liked. Sometimes he watched events from the far corner of his own brain, but more frequently he didn't bother. He didn't want to know what the monster did. Living with the knowledge of what he'd already done was bad enough. So, he lost himself in the flood of sensation. It was the only relief from his thoughts—the closest thing to drugs to which he had access.

Glancing around the empty room, Liam realized that about all he'd leave behind was an old mattress, two blankets, the contents of his kit and a few bits of crockery. He supposed he should be sad about that, but all he could think of was that there'd be an end to the pain. To be sure his mother would grieve if she wasn't already, but that'd be about all, and it wouldn't be for long. She had other children to live for.

There came a sound from downstairs and because he wasn't expecting it, it took several seconds to register that someone was knocking on the front door. Liam paused. Whomever it was seemed determined. They weren't going away. He went to the window with the intent to tell them to bugger off and stopped.

A priest.

The priest was alone. He knew him for one even though all he could see was the top of the man's grey flat cap. For a moment Liam wondered if it was one of the Church's assassins, but then the man looked up, and Liam recognized Father Murray.

What the fuck is he doing here? A blast of super-heated rage roared through his veins and then vanished, leaving him emptier than before.

"I know you're in there. You have to let me in. I'll not leave until you do."

"Leave me be," Liam said. He felt weary as if the moment of rage had used up the remaining energy he'd had.

"I understand your anger—"

"Take your fucking psychology and shove it up your arse." Liam moved away from the window and went back to his tea. He could hear Father Murray pacing on the front step. The man finally went away, to Liam's relief, but then reappeared at the back garden several minutes later. The back door was broken, and peering out a rear window overlooking the garden, he spotted Father Murray tugging at the boards nailed to the doorframe. Liam cursed and went to the top of the stairs.

"This isn't helping your situation," Father Murray said, his footsteps thundering in the house below. When he appeared at the bottom of the stairs, shock registered on his face before it evolved into pity. "What have you done to yourself?"

Liam sat on the top step. "What does it fucking matter?" His voice sounded rough from lack of use.

"Of course it matters."

"What do you want, Father?"

"You must leave this place. Come with me. We'll get you cleaned up and—"

"No."

Father Murray sighed. "I'm so sorry. For everything. I should've talked to you. I should've told you. All of it. In any case, you seemed well enough without my interfering."

"Without your interfering? You told Mary Kate rather than allowing me to do it!"

Father Murray looked away. "There was a danger. I thought there was. I thought I had to."

"Are you implying I might have harmed her?" Liam banished images of the car crash and looked away.

"The Fallen thrive on war and torment. They tempt men into committing vile deeds. Fallen angels can't be reasoned with. Bloodshed is the only way they can be stopped."

Liam paused as several clues fell into place at once. "Were you meant to kill me?"

"By the time I found you, you were already a boy of thirteen. I pleaded your case before the bishop. It was easy to see you weren't like the others. I documented everything—"

"Wait," Liam said, thoughts rushing too fast in his head to track. "Already? You kill babes?"

"The spawn of—I did—I don't anymore," Father Murray said. "Please. They know you're in the area."

"Let them come. At least they know enough to do the job right. 'Ra don't know shite. Like as not they'll send someone with fucking silver if Éamon was anything to judge by."

"I'm serious. You must leave."

"I've nowhere else to go, Father."

"Come with me, then. Please."

"And how would that be any different from handing myself over to one of your death squads?"

"I'll hide you."

"And why would you do such a thing?"

Father Murray sighed. "Your father isn't one of the Fallen. You're both Fey. It was all a terrible mistake. I've much to make up for."

"Is there a proper penance for murder then, Father? A few 'Our Fathers.' Say the rosary once or twice, and we're both in the clear. Is that it?" Liam saw Father Murray wince.

"You aren't one of the Fallen, and I can't stand by and allow them to kill you for one—no matter what."

Liam recalled the night in the alley when he'd seen the two priests standing over a dead man and understood that Father Murray wouldn't be able to stop the Church's assassins. Rather, by standing in the way he would only be putting himself in danger. In spite of everything, Liam wasn't sure he wanted that. *Let no one else die because of me. Please,* he thought. *Let there be an end.*

Again, he was reminded of his Aunt Sheila's stories of fairy men stopping priests along dark and lonely country roadways, the questions about the end of the world. The stories made sense to him now in ways that his Aunt Sheila could never have understood. Or perhaps she had and that's why she'd told him the stories to begin with.

"What happens to me when the end comes, Father? Is there a special Hell for the Fey, or am I already in it?" He found himself laughing, and he didn't like the sound.

"Don't do this to yourself."

"I'm afraid, Father." Liam sighed and pushed both hands through his filthy hair. "I'm afraid somewhere along the line I went a bit mad." The skin along his arms prickled.

"I can help you."

Reaching into his pocket, Liam brushed his fingers against his lighter. Before he withdrew his hand he felt something else there as well. *The coin.* He fished it out of his pocket, needing something to hold onto that wasn't associated with a happy memory, but he was trembling, and it slipped from his fingers. It rolled down the stairs.

Father Murray caught it, glanced at it, paused, and then examined the coin more closely. Anxiety registered on his face. He came up the steps and perched on the stair just below. "Where did you get this?"

Liam said, "One of the men who murdered Mary Kate left it for me to find. Only I don't know why. Doesn't have any Loyalist meaning, at least none I'm aware of. Fucking bastards."

"Why didn't you show this to me before?"

"Wasn't important."

Fear was plain on Father Murray's face now. "The night she died—Did you see a man in a blood-red cap? The one you told me about seeing before. Did you see him again?"

Thinking back, Liam tried to dredge up memories of the men who'd knocked him down in the stairwell. As often as he'd tortured himself with images of that night he could only remember three men in that stair-well—not four, but four had been there, he knew. He'd known from the trail he'd found outside the apartment building. The fourth trail, stinking of old blood, had dead-ended. He hadn't considered what it might mean at the time. Had the same creature he'd seen before, the one from Aggro Corner and Bloody Sunday, participated in Mary Kate's murder? What did it all mean? He shivered. "No, Father. I didn't see any such man."

"May I keep this?"

"Certainly. It's done me no amount of good," Liam said. "But what is it?"

"A shilling from the Tudor era. Mary Tudor, to be exact."

"What's that got to do with me and Mary Kate? Why did I see that creature before? What does it want from me?"

It was Father Murray's turn to look away. "I'm not entirely sure. But I'll find out. And when I do I'll tell you everything."

Liam nodded. For some reason he couldn't explain he felt better for having seen Father Murray. It wouldn't change anything, Liam knew, but at least someone was aware he was alive—someone who didn't wish him dead or simply gone.

"When I come back for you," Father Murray said, "will you consider leaving with me then?"

Pausing, Liam decided the lie was best. He knew if he didn't, Father Murray would never leave, and he would run the chance of missing Haddock again. "Sure, Father."

"Good," Father Murray said, and got up from the stair. "I'll return within an hour if I can."

Liam watched Father Murray go and mentally said goodbye for the last time. Then he went back to the fireplace, banked the coals just in case and then grabbed his hat. When he was certain Father Murray was gone, Liam sprinted down the stairs, changing form as he ran down the now dark and deserted street. The change came easier now, only problematic when he considered what he was doing. He almost enjoyed it—the short stab of pain, the flood of amplified sights, sounds and scents, the feel of grit under the pads of his feet. Grass was heavenly as was the running under the shadows of trees and the pursuit of the prey. The Hound relished the feel of warm flesh and blood in his teeth—the taste of fresh death. *Running.*

The rain had stopped, and the sun had buried itself in the horizon, extinguishing the sparks of life in the damp earth. He rounded the corner and loped past gutted buildings and the remains of an old barricade. He checked the street but didn't see any sign of the blond man. A pair of young priests proceeded down the walk in tandem. The vigilant way in which they moved spoke more of Inquisition than funeral procession. The closest church was four blocks in the other direction. What were priests doing here? One of them had a scar running across his nose.

Father Dominic and Father Christopher.

The monster caught himself before he could skid into a parked car and pretended to sniff at something underneath the vehicle. *You've been careless and led them right to us,* Liam thought from the back of the monster's brain.

Or perhaps your Father Murray was followed, thought the monster. *We should have dealt with all three sooner. We've you and your squeamishness about killing to thank for this.*

A car door slammed, sending a quake through the Ford's metal frame and giving Liam a start. He looked for the sound's source and saw Father Christopher standing next to the car. His closed fist rested on the dented door.

"We've been looking for you, demon," he said, holding a double-edged, four-foot-long sword in his right hand. Liam blinked. He'd expected the Church's assassins to carry guns, not swords. Swords belonged in the medieval deserts of Jerusalem and were carried by actors in American films. They weren't seen in Andersonstown in the hands of priests.

Leave it to the Church to stick with tradition regardless of practicality, the monster thought.

The priest inched closer and a powerful cloud of dread smashed into the monster, making him stagger. He was afraid, now. He couldn't have said why. His heart slammed against his breastbone, and his limbs trembled. He panted with the fear. Then there was the smell. It overwhelmed his snout with the stench of ancient power. The stink was so thick that the back of his throat clogged with it. *We must get out of here,* Liam pleaded with the Hound.

It is they who came to us.

"Something gave us the impression you might be in the area." Father Christopher reached inside his coat and held up a chewed RUC badge.

The man was a Prod, the monster thought. *Since when does a Catholic care?*

Was? Liam thought. *You killed him?*

"Time to die, demon." Father Dominic stepped from around the front end of the Ford and flipped back the folds of his long coat to draw his dirk.

Breathing in great gasps, the beast stepped backward into the street and slipped on a patch of ice. At that moment Father Christopher brought his blade down. The monster whirled and tore into Father Dominic's leg. The sword missed its mark, biting uselessly into the pavement. Boot leather shredded in the monster's jaws as he bore down on Father Dominic's ankle. With a shake of the head the monster felt a satisfying bone snap. Blood gushed into his mouth, and Father Dominic screamed in pain.

"Demon!"

The only demon here is the one you've made. The Hound opened his jaws, and Father Dominic tumbled onto the ground, his foot dangling at an unnatural angle. The monster sensed movement at the edge of his vision and ducked just as Father Christopher's blade swept the air. Steel nicked the Hound's right ear and unbelievable pain shot through his whole body, felling him before he understood what had happened.

Get up! Liam thought, *Move!*

Father Christopher lifted the sword for another swing. The monster rolled and then staggered to his paws. His limbs felt rubbery, and his blood burned.

The blade, Liam thought. *The blade is poisoned. We must get out of here.*

No! Not until they're dead, the monster thought back and then balanced on his hind legs. He swayed. His ear was numb, and half his skull felt like it'd been hit with acid. Furious at being weakened so easily, he roared and swiped at Father Christopher's chest. Claws flayed skin, snapped bone, and a spray of gore hit the monster in the face. Blinded, he lunged at Father Christopher headfirst, hitting him square in the stomach. Father Christopher dropped with a grunt, and a clear-pitched ring sounded as tempered metal crashed to the pavement.

Christ. They're priests, Liam thought. *I can't do this. Let them go. Please. For fuck's sake!*

Them or us. The monster shook his head until his vision cleared. Father Christopher's arm was clearly broken at the wrist and a ragged wound gaped in his chest. He scooted toward his lost sword while the monster looked on. Warm crimson melted patches in the frost. *They will only come back for us. Bring others.*

I don't care, Liam thought. He fought to emerge from the dimness—to wrench control from the monster. *Mother of God, I'll not do this. I. Will. Not.*

The monster dropped to all fours and howled in frustration. The prickling sensation that signaled the start of the change crawled its way down his limbs. *No! It isn't finished!*

Liam pressed all the harder until he found himself lying on the cold pavement, blinking.

"Demon!"

He pushed himself up from the ground. His right ear throbbed in time with his heart, and his palms smarted in the grit. When he was on his feet again he saw that Father Dominic was also upright, steadying himself with one hand to the parked car. The other held the dirk.

"I'm not finished with you," Father Dominic said, breathing heavy.

"Doesn't matter. I'm done with you." Liam combed blood-soaked hair from his face with one hand. *I did it,* he thought at the monster. *Shoved you back into the dark, you fucker. As far as I've gone, at least I have that.* He shuddered with the relief and almost laughed. He heard metal scrape concrete and saw that Father Christopher had at last reached his weapon.

Father Dominic slammed his hand on the car's hood. "Fight me!"

I fucking did it. And done once, I can do it again. Breathing out a jittery sigh, Liam said, "Get Father Christopher to hospital."

"Coward!"

"This ends here. On my say."

"I'll hunt you down," Father Dominic said. "I don't care how long it takes."

"And I'll protect myself when I must, but I've no war with you," Liam said. "I'm no demon. I'm—I'm Fey." He turned his back to Father Dominic and walked away.

"Come on, you great bastard! I'm here! Come and get me!" Father Dominic's voice echoed off the buildings.

It began to sleet, and Liam shivered. He knew he was only putting off the inevitable. The monster raging in the darkness at the back of his brain was right. Father Dominic wouldn't stop, but Liam decided he'd face that problem later. For the moment, only Haddock and the end to his vengeance for Mary Kate was important. He sprinted across the street, using as much speed as he dared muster on the ice. In his rush, he forgot to check the road first, and the squeal of tires brought him up short. A black taxi skidded a circle across the slick pavement. When it slowed to a stop, the driver waved a fist out the window of his cab and cursed.

Sorry, mate, Liam thought and continued north.

The sky was full black and he was out of breath and soaked through when he arrived at Haddock's place.

At last, Liam thought. *Soon it will be done. At least no one else will have to die.*

The monster whispered back from the darkness, *Will you stop your whinging, you wee girl?*

Liam checked the house. A car was parked in the garage, but the lights inside were off, and no one answered the door when he knocked. Hoping he wouldn't be disappointed again, he located an alley within sight of Haddock's house and prepared himself for a wait. Lighting a cigarette, he pulled up the hood of his anorak. The warmth from the long run was starting to wear off, and he shivered with his back against a wooden fence as sweat cooled under his coat. The sleet had stopped but the humidity remained, and a mist hung in the air. He watched bus passengers come and go. Children played football in the street. He fought an urge to pace. *Patience. We're probably in for a long wait.* When Haddock walked up with a grocery sack in one arm, keys jangling, Liam almost missed him.

What kind of mad bastard walks home in the weather when he owns a car?

Briefly, Liam considered assassinating Haddock in the street, but that wouldn't get the information Liam needed about the mysterious fourth man. Haddock vanished into the recess protecting the doorway from the street. The door slammed, and the lights flipped on. Liam paused long enough to consider the situation. He hadn't shaved in quite a while, and his hair had grown out. Haddock might not recognize him. The monster pushed for action. Crossing the street, Liam then knocked on the door. The light inside the front room shut off at once. A television flickered through the windows. The porch light seemed suddenly bright. Haddock's shadow moved beyond the peep hole.

"Who's there?"

Liam didn't answer, only knocked again.

From the other side of the door he heard the sound of a bullet being chambered.

"I asked for your name, Paddy. And I suggest you give it. This is a .45. It'll blow a hole through this door and you."

"Liam Kelly."

"One step back, if you please, Mr. Kelly," Haddock said and then paused while Liam complied. "Ahh. Knew they hadn't fried your skinny carcass. What the fuck do you want?"

Words formed on Liam's lips before he knew what he'd say. "The medicine." He let himself shiver. "I'm dying for it. Tell you whatever you want. Just—"

"Oh, shut your fucking sniveling!"

There was another long pause, and Liam wondered if his act had been convincing. Of course, if he was honest with himself he wasn't entirely certain it'd been an act.

"Are you alone?"

Liam said, "You think the 'Ra would provide me an escort after what I've done?"

"The farmhouse. What happened?"

"Open the door, and I'll tell you."

Yet another long pause stretched out. The sounds of children playing in the street filled in the silence. Liam's teeth chattered. For a moment he thought Haddock wasn't going to allow him inside. Liam considered busting down the door but knew he didn't have the strength. He'd been starving himself too long which, now that he thought about it, had been a bad idea. Haddock was tough, and he'd need everything he had to best him. *Too late now. Doesn't matter if I make it through, so long as that fucking bastard doesn't.* There was the front window. If Liam was going to make enough noise to rouse the whole estate he supposed a bit of glass wasn't going to matter.

"Get back. Turn round, and put your hands against the wall. Do it. Now."

Liam paused.

"Be a shame to put a hole in the door just to rid myself of one pathetic sod, but I'll do it."

Turning, Liam put his hands up against the wall. He heard the door open, and before he knew it he'd been slammed face-first against the bricks. Cold steel pressed against the back of his skull.

"Don't you move."

Liam's heart jumped as Haddock conducted a quick search. *Doesn't matter what he does,* Liam thought. *Get inside. Ask about the fourth man. He's MI5. He'll know. When we've got what we want then he'll get his.* The monster wasn't in favor of delay. He wanted to end it now. Gritting his teeth, Liam willed himself still, but when a cuff circled his left wrist he jerked. An explosion of pain erupted in his right kidney.

"I said don't fucking move."

His right arm was yanked down to the small of his back to be trapped with his left. Cold burned into his flesh. *The cuffs.* He felt Haddock's hand on his bicep. Liam's stomach clenched, and trembled. *Trapped. The cuffs. Can't shape-shift.* Haddock said something but the fear was so bad Liam couldn't make out what.

"Are you deaf? I said get inside."

Liam was pulled from the wall and shoved through the door. He tripped and fell onto the horrible shag carpet. The door thumped shut. Liam was able to roll onto his side before Haddock landed the first kick.

"You stupid fuck," Haddock said. "What makes you think I'd waste anything on you?" The toe of his shoe slammed into Liam's back twice and once in his arm. "What the fuck will I get out of it?"

Through the pain Liam heard a click and the lights came on. The room was bare but for a lone sofa, television and an old coffee table littered with bits of wire. A frayed poster of a naked blonde woman stared down at him. It was the only decoration on the bare white walls.

"Farmhouse. Tell you about the farmhouse," Liam said. "You said you wanted to know. Take the cuffs off. I'll tell you."

"How about I leave them on, and you tell me anyway?" Haddock kicked him twice more.

"All right! I'll tell you!"

"Out with it, you stupid fuck."

"Was a fight."

"Tell me something I don't know," Haddock said, circling. "Two years I worked on them contacts. Worked my way up the chain one by one. Two years in this lousy shit hole. Gone in an afternoon. You tell me why!"

"Éamon was working for you, wasn't he?"

"I'm the one asking the questions, you piece of shit."

"Were after Oran. Never asked me anything."

"Go on."

"Oran told them about Éamon. Éamon went crazy. Started shooting up the place. That's all I know."

"Give me the rest, damn you."

"I don't know! Spent most of the time with a bag over my head. I swear. I don't—"

Haddock kicked him hard in the thigh, and Liam screamed.

"Don't you lie to me," Haddock said. "I'm supposed to believe you brought down the operation. You. A stupid Mick who can't even bloody read for Christ's sake."

Liam spit at Haddock and missed.

"I can see we'll have to get creative." Haddock strode out of the room and into the next.

Liam had a bad feeling when he heard things being turned over in the kitchen. He pulled at the cuffs on his wrists. He writhed on the floor until he could leverage himself against the sofa. With that, he was finally able to get to his knees. He was about to stand when Haddock re-entered the room.

"Now, now. We can't have you rabbiting off just when things are getting interesting, now can we?"

Haddock punched him twice in the stomach. Liam couldn't breathe. Wheezing, he was dragged to the coffee table. The cuff came off his left wrist and then he was anchored to the table's leg. He glanced down and saw that Haddock had looped the cuff inside the metal bracket between the leg and the tabletop.

"There," Haddock said. "That's better. And here you weren't even going to wait to see what I have for you."

He began placing objects on the table—a lump of tin foil, a syringe, a spoon and a lighter. Liam started to relax, but then Haddock left again. A door slammed in the back of the house. Noises from outside. When Haddock returned, what he held in his hands made Liam's guts turn to water. A small blowtorch.

"Let's handle this like your friends would, shall we?" Haddock asked. "It's something your slow Paddy brain will comprehend."

"You don't have to. I'll tell you anything you want."

"I know you will," Haddock said, reaching inside his jacket and pulling out a small black zippered bag. "And then you'll tell me the truth."

"Look, I could go back. Get you some names."

Haddock shook his head. "We both know that's not possible. They probably have the same questions I do. And will ask them just as hard." He unzipped the black bag and brought out a compact and lethal-looking chrome knife.

A scalpel, Liam thought. *Oh, Christ.*

Two scalpels from the black bag clicked onto the table. One was slightly longer and more lethal-looking than the other. Haddock re-arranged the items, aligning them in a neat row just as Liam had seen him do with pens and a notebook at the station before the long-ago interview.

"I'm not without mercy. Be a good little junkie, and you might get your medicine."

Liam licked his lips and tried to control his breathing. *Focus,* he thought. *You have to focus. Get yourself out of this.* He stared at the tin foil.

"That's right," Haddock said. "Now. Just in case you decide to display a selfless streak, I've done my research. Read your file. You've a mother. In Londonderry."

Liam's stomach turned to ice.

Haddock laughed. "So easy. Éamon at least presented a challenge. No family, you see. None he cared much for. Was smart. Kept it that way. Knew family was a liability in this business. Only he made one little mistake. He took money from someone he shouldn't have. Oh, he was sly about it. Waited a good three years before he spent it. But spend it, he did. On that stupid farm."

Grabbing Liam's arm, Haddock yanked him upright.

"Now," Haddock said. "The farm. What happened?"

"Brought us there. Asked Oran the questions."

"You've already said that," Haddock said and reached for the first scalpel.

"They tortured him. Oran," Liam said. *Shouldn't have let him cuff me. Should've let the monster have him. Questions or no.*

Haddock stood up. Bending over, he placed Liam's left hand on the carpet and then stomped on it. Pain shot up Liam's arm, and he cried out.

"You're not trying hard enough," Haddock said.

He took the scalpel and cut at the shoulder of Liam's anorak. In a moment the sleeve was gone as well as the shirt underneath. The furnace hadn't had time to heat the house and cold air prickled Liam's bare skin. White fluff floated across the carpet. The steel cuff numbed his right wrist. *Cold. So cold. Got to get it off my skin. Can't change. Can't—*

"I suggest you talk faster." Haddock leaned closer and touched a curved blade to Liam's bicep.

"Éamon ordered me to shoot him! Oran! I killed Oran! In the field. Near the trees."

Haddock paused. Blinked. "You shot the only friend you had?" His mouth stretched into a slow smile and then he let out a loud guffaw.

Enough, Liam thought, feeling his anger rise. He searched the floor for anything that might help. Spying the ripped sleeve lying on the carpet next to his knee, the last of the fear vaporized beneath his rage. His left hand tingled beneath Haddock's shoe. Liam breathed in gasps as the change fought against the cold iron in the cuff, adding to the hurt but lending a certain clarity. "You've read my file. You know the stories." His voice sounded suddenly calm in his own ears.

Haddock continued laughing. "Éamon said you're a werewolf. What superstitious rot."

"You want the truth? I'll tell you. I ripped Éamon's throat out. Killed the others too. Tore them apart with my bare hands. Then I set fire to the house. There was no fight. There was only me."

Haddock stopped laughing. He was seeing something that didn't make sense—that was clear. He took a step backward, uncertain. The scalpel was still in his hand. Liam snatched up the shirt sleeve and stuffed it between his wrist and the cuff. The freezing burn stopped at once, and the monster stirred.

"You want to know why I'm here?" Liam asked. Rage coursed through his body in electrified ripples. Black claws sprang from his fingers. He couldn't change completely, not with the cuff on his wrist, but he could change enough. Gritting his teeth, Liam slammed a fist down on the tabletop with all his might. It collapsed. "I made a promise to Oran before I shot him." The words had some difficulty moving over his teeth. His jaw didn't feel quite right in his head anymore.

Backing away toward the kitchen, Haddock's face had become a pasty mask of terror. "Stay away from me."

Liam stood up and then ripped the cuff from his wrist. "I'm here to keep my promise. But first, I've questions. About my wife's murder. Four men were responsible. At least two came from your division. I want the names. All of them."

Haddock drew his pistol. The gun was steady in his hand.

"You honestly think that's going to save you?" Liam asked, feeling the beginnings of the change prickle his skin. "You saw the report. It didn't save Éamon. It didn't save any of them."

Haddock turned and bolted into the kitchen. Before the door swung shut Liam saw him grab what looked like a radio from the counter. Keys jangled again.

The car.

The monster sprinted after Haddock, passing a sink filled with fertilizer and plumbing supplies. *Fuck the questions. Ask another Peeler.* Haddock couldn't get away—not after everything the monster had been through. He didn't care what he'd have to do to see the man dead. The back door banged. The monster followed after, leaping upon Haddock before he'd reached the car port. Haddock flipped, then punched him in the face. The monster's nose broke with a crunch. His howl echoed off the buildings. Haddock was up again and through the gate, but he'd dropped the radio. Without thinking, the monster picked it up. Pain made his eyes water.

Isn't a radio, Liam thought. *It's a transmitter.* Suddenly an image of the kitchen sink came to mind. *Fertilizer. Wiring. Car. A car bomb.*

Liam didn't stop to think of why Haddock had been building a car bomb. There wasn't time. Haddock was backing out into the street. The car flattened a stray football. Children trotted out of the car's path, cursing. A woman ran from an open door. She screamed at the children to get out of the street. Haddock was getting away. The monster roared. He had to do something. *Now.* He would do it. He would kill him. *NOW.* The monster gripped the transmitter in its claws. A child saw him and shrieked.

No, no, no, NO! The children!

Ignoring Liam's protests, the monster pointed the transmitter at the car and pressed the button. He turned his back to the car before it went off. Numb, he was slammed down onto the pavement face-first. He hit the ground and rolled but didn't feel it. For a moment there was no air, only bright orange light and peace. No sound. Then nothing. Liam woke just as something hard smashed into him. His back felt like it was on fire, and the monster was gone. Coughing, he rolled onto his side. It wasn't easy. The pain was terrific, the worst he'd ever felt in his life, but he needed to see—had to see that Haddock was done for. He couldn't lie flat. Something prevented it. So, he levered himself up off the ground with an elbow and almost passed out with the effort. An eerie silence had descended upon the world. Smoke was everywhere. Movement. Flames rising out of the twisted wreckage that was once Haddock's car. Broken glass. A house on fire. He relaxed to the pavement. The agony in his back and chest made it next to impossible to breathe. Something lay next to his head. He turned his face and saw it was a woman's shoe.

It was filled with blood.

Jesus Christ. The woman. I killed her. The pain flooded in, and he closed his eyes to shut out the worst of it. When he let himself look again someone was standing over him. Someone dressed in a long black coat over the top of glittering chainmail. The figure bent closer, and Liam realized he'd seen the face before. But for the hair, he looked quite a bit like Bran as he'd appeared in his mother's long-ago photograph. His golden hair fell long past his shoulders to the middle of his back. The man's eyes glowed red as he stooped and touched Liam's shoulder.

It's the devil, Liam thought, *come for his own at last.*

Chapter 24

Londonderry/Derry, County Londonderry, Northern Ireland
September 1977

"Tell me what happened, Sceolán." The first voice was angry and hard. It echoed on air that felt cool and damp. "He looks like a roast boar with the skewer still in."

"Was an explosion." The second voice, presumably Sceolán, was upset but more controlled. "What are you going to do? He'll die with the iron in him."

It took a few seconds for Liam to register that the entire conversation was in Irish. The next thing that came to him was that nothing smelled of home. He knew without thinking that it lacked modern scents—diesel exhaust, the day-to-day grit from modern violence and rubbish left to rot. People. The air smelled sharp and clean like an ancient forest after a good rain. It smelled of stone. Its moist coolness caressed Liam's burning skin. He came to understand he was in a cave. Again, he knew all this without knowing why. Pain was everything. It sucked away every coherent thought. He lay on his side with half his face touching soft fur, the only comfort in a world of torture. His left shoulder was immobilized with a fierce bone-deep cold. The pain was a great smothering wall of agony that wouldn't allow him breath. He was freezing, and the shivering only intensified the hurt. He wanted another blanket. He needed to tell his captors he was awake but couldn't get enough air to make sound. A weak moan escaped his lips, and he forced his eyes open. Firelight flickered off rough stone walls.

Liam thought, *I've died, and this must be Hell.*

"We'll send for the mortal healer. Let her deal with the iron."

"He won't last that long," said Sceolán. "It's too close to his heart."

"Then I'll do it."

"You'll be poisoned the moment you touch it."

"I'll last until you get back. He won't."

"There's the iron on his wrist too. You won't be able to—"

245

"He's my son, Sceolán. I have to try." A shadow passed over Liam and then he saw the owner of the voice, and although there was grey in the black hair and the face was older, he knew it at once from the photo—one of the few things he'd kept with him and now was gone with the rest.

"Would that I could do something for the pain," Bran said. "But I don't have that power."

Liam forced out one word. "C-c-cold."

"He's awake," Bran said. "Bring me a blanket. Fresh water. Then go."

Someone moved on the edges of Liam's awareness.

Bran reappeared. "Everything would be easier if you went back to sleep," he said. "I'm sorry to put you through this."

"Good luck," Sceolán said, and Liam felt the weight of a blanket on his legs. Slowly, warmth penetrated the cold, and his shivering eased somewhat.

"Same to you," Bran said to Sceolán. "Get back as soon as you can. Leave no trace. We don't want the Redcap here."

"And what of Finnabair's claim? What will you do?"

"Nothing. She is Connacht. Consider the source."

"This is serious," Sceolán said. "If a connection should be made between you and—"

"I've never been to England in my life. You know this to be true. And do you honestly think I'd force myself upon a maid?"

"No. But Finnabair—"

"Is spreading lies. The Redcap is mad, and she with it. The riddle of the coin is false. That he exhibits no weakness to iron's poison should be proof enough. He's no relation," Bran said. "There is no time for this nonsense. Go. Before it is my real son's undoing."

Sceolán stooped, and Liam caught a glimpse of long blond hair. "May Danu smile upon you, little brother." And then he was gone.

A surge of pain shoved Liam's eyes closed and for a moment he wasn't aware of anything around him. When it passed he saw that Bran was still there, but now he was holding a warm cloth to the shoulder wound.

"I'm sorry that it has taken so long for us to meet. It is good your mother relented at last. A geas given by a woman of power is a terrible thing," Bran said. "And I could not go against it. No matter I wished otherwise. But I've been watching over you as best I can."

New questions ran rampant through Liam's mind. *Geas? What the fuck is he on about?* But agony prevented his voicing any of them.

Bran set the cloth into a bowl. "I need to remove your shirt. What I can of it. I'll try not to hurt you more than I must."

Liam shut his eyes. The only reason he wasn't screaming was because he couldn't get enough breath. He endured Bran's gentle motions as he unbuttoned the shirt. When the time came for the cloth to be peeled from Liam's skin he blacked out. He resurfaced as Bran was washing dried blood and soot from his arm and chest. The water felt cool, and it produced another bout of painful shivering. Liam wanted to tell Bran to stop but couldn't.

"There's a piece of steel lodged in your shoulder. I can't pull it out. I've tried. I'll have to cut it out, or you'll die," Bran said. "If it helps, I have done this before. For my men. When we've no healer. I've the whiskey for the pain and to clean the wound but that's all. Ready yourself."

A cup was pushed against Liam's lips, and he had to tilt his head to drink. He gulped as much as he could stand without choking, spilling some of it on himself and the fur under him because of the awkward angle. Fresh pain was added to the agony as alcohol dripped down his neck and onto his chest.

"I'd lay you flat to get a better look at what I'm doing, but your back is badly burned, and I don't think I should." Bran sighed and put a hand on his arm. "I can't put this off any longer. Scream if you've the need. There's none here will shame you for it. Are you ready?"

Feeling muzzy and distant, Liam nodded. Bran went away for a few minutes and when he came back Liam caught the scent of heated metal. Bran set a lamp near enough for Liam to feel warmth from the flame. The bronze blade in Bran's hand was blackened from the fire. He dipped it in a clay bowl and it hissed, sending a cloud of burned whiskey into the air. Liam felt a gentle touch as Bran held his shoulder again and then the cutting began. Liam had thought the previous pain had been the worst he'd endured.

He was wrong.

"Am I dead yet?" The words fell out of Liam's mouth in a hoarse whisper. The oppressive pain remained but now seemed to have localized in his left shoulder as well as his back from the top of his skull down the backs of his thighs. The piercing cold in his chest was gone, but his right wrist was numb, and when he attempted to move his hand it wouldn't respond. Blinking in the near darkness at red-tinged cave walls, it was difficult to focus. The fire had been allowed to burn down to the coals, and the scent of burnt wood and smoke was thick. He was still on his side on top the furs with blankets on his legs. He was naked and cold but was afraid to move lest he spur the pain into fresh life. There was movement in the darkness, and a clay cup touched his lips.

"Drink this." It was Sceolán. Liam blinked and saw that streaks of blue stained Sceolán's face. "You'll feel better."

Liam drank the water without thinking. It tasted sweet and clean although it hurt to swallow. He hadn't realized how dry his throat had become. He choked and for a moment he thought he might be sick. The mere idea of retching was enough to make him flinch.

"I'll return with the surgeon," Sceolán said, switching to English. He stood up. "She's with Bran now."

"Why?" Liam asked.

"He burned his hands pretty badly, digging that shite out of you."

Liam thought, *I didn't ask him to do it.*

The surgeon came, or someone Liam assumed was the surgeon. The last time he'd seen a doctor he'd been in Malone, and after seeing what had passed for medical care in that place he decided he'd rather die than see another. She certainly had the self-possessed authority he remembered as well as the air of disdain. *Fucking doctors.* She poked and prodded him while muttering about the state of his back and the hack job done on his shoulder. She cleaned the burns which took some time even though she was none too gentle about it. When she was done she brought out a pair of what looked all the world like bolt cutters from a cloth bag.

"Now for the hand."

"You'll not take it," Liam said. The freezing numbness in his right hand had gone deep through the bones and all the way up to his elbow. Something told him it wouldn't be long before it reached his shoulder, but he didn't care.

"This isn't for your hand, you idiot," she said in her broad country accent. "It's for the cuff, it is."

Sceolán arrived with a lamp. "You should do as she says. Otherwise, this time tomorrow she'll have to take the hand. But if you'd rather it be so, it's up to you."

Liam gritted his teeth and with a great deal of concentration was able to move his arm. Sceolán held it straight and at the proper angle so that the surgeon could get a good purchase with the bolt cutters.

"There's a lad," he said.

"I'm not your fucking—" Sharp pain accompanied a thump-snap as the cutters were brought to bear, and the cuff fell off his wrist.

"He's a foul-mouthed piece of work," she said, and sighed. "Well, he's one of youse. The rest is up to him. I've done all that I can in this filthy place. If you want anything more from me you'll have to get him to hospital. Watch him. Close. He still might take a turn for the worse."

Is she fucking joking? No painkillers? No fucking antibiotics? Typical god-damned doctors, Liam thought.

"Good enough," Sceolán said. "And my brother?"

"He'll be right by tomorrow."

"Thank you."

"You're welcome. Is it the usual, I'll have?"

Sceolán nodded. "The usual. Aye. You will."

"Why is it always a call in the middle of the night from you lot? There are times when I wish my Grandmother had never made that bargain no matter the lives it saves," she said, getting up off her knees.

"You wish to be rid of your Grandmother's gift?" Sceolán asked.

She shook her head with a rueful smile and sighed. "I'm sorry. It's been a bad week." She looked at her watch. "I've my hospital shift at five. I'm getting too old for this shite." She walked away without another word.

"Get some sleep," Sceolán said and followed the surgeon, taking the lamp with him.

Liam lay alone in the darkness, wanting to flip onto his back in spite of knowing that such a thing would be a very bad idea. Any movement at all was agony, even breathing, but his muscles were stiff, and he needed to stretch or change position. Something. The sensation of pins and needles in his right hand—the return of feeling—distracted him soon enough, and while he didn't think he'd ever sleep again, sleep he did.

Morning came to the sound of stealthy movement and the rich scents of coffee and cooking meat. Liam opened his eyes and saw Bran crouching near the fire. Liam's stomach growled.

Bran glanced over at him. He seemed nervous. "Breakfast?"

Liam shut his eyes. The pain had quieted to a consistent level that he could almost ignore if he didn't move too much. Unfortunately, with that came the memories of the explosion—the aftermath. Images ran through his mind of the young woman running out of her house, yelling at the children, telling them to get out of the street. *The bloody shoe.*

I killed her. I didn't mean to. Was that bastard Haddock we were after. Only Haddock. I didn't mean to—

The thought of the children in the street sent a chill through him that stopped his heart. *Were any of the little ones hurt? Did she get them away? Christ, what if I killed them too?*

He rolled onto his back and agony blasted the last of his thoughts from his consciousness.

The sensation of falling woke Liam with a start. He now found himself in a soft bed. Once more he lay on his right side, but now there were tubes filled with clear liquid attached to his left arm. The pain was only vaguely present, and as a result he was comfortable and warm inside a thick cocoon of white thermal blankets. The room didn't belong to a hospital or prison infirmary. The familiar scent of lavender, cabbage and old age floated on the air—not disinfectant. He also detected pipe smoke and knew it didn't belong. Yellow sunlight filtered through white curtains covering a small window. There was a crucifix nailed above the door with a scrap of red cloth tied to it. The walls were papered with tiny blue flowers, and he recognized the pattern at once. He was at his Gran's house in Derry—her best guest room if memory served. The one he'd never slept in regardless of the many times his mother had sent him to stay. It'd always been the sofa in the sitting room for him.

A small wooden table cluttered with various medicines was positioned near the bed, and a steel armature held a plastic IV bag. Both were incongruent with the photos of relatives past and present on the walls and shelves, and if he hadn't known where he was based upon the wallpaper, he'd have known it for the photos.

The door opened and Father Murray entered, carrying a tray with a steaming bowl balanced in the center. It smelled of chicken, and Liam's mouth watered.

"Why am I here?" he asked, willing his stomach to stay silent.

Father Murray said, "We're far enough away from Belfast that I think you're safe for the moment."

"Was in a cave. With my real father. Was it a dream?"

"He found you after the… accident. You were with him for a time. But you wouldn't heal. So, he brought you to me." Father Murray set the tray on the edge of the crowded table and then grabbed a cushioned chair from against the wall.

"Why here? How? Gran hates me. The very idea of her letting you keep me here—"

"I didn't convince her. Bran did."

"You should've let me die."

Sitting in the chair and balancing the tray on his knees, Father Murray frowned. "Why would we have done such a thing?"

"What is it you want from me?"

"You can eat some of this broth for a start."

"I don't want it."

"How long has it been since you last ate?"

"It doesn't matter."

"Are you attempting to starve yourself to death?"

Liam didn't say a word.

"We've all of us made mistakes," Father Murray said. "It's a burden to live with for certain, but it must be done."

"Why?"

"Because our time isn't yet finished. Only the Lord can make that decision."

"I'd like to know one goddamned thing that ever was my decision."

Father Murray put down the spoon. "All that anger. You should let it go. Do something with the life you have. You've already lost so much."

"You don't know a fucking thing about me. Not anymore. Don't pretend you do."

"Perhaps I don't," Father Murray said. "But the young man I knew wouldn't have let anyone or anything keep him from doing the right thing."

"Mary Kate was the strong one. Not me."

Father Murray set the tray on the edge of the table and then picked up a pipe from amongst the clutter. "That isn't true." He put a finger inside the pipe's bowl to clean it out. Then he placed an ash tray on the floor next to the leg of his chair. "Have you forgiven her yet?"

"Who?"

"You heard me. Mary Kate."

Liam's thoughts flashed to the baby, the one she'd never told him about. The one she'd killed. He felt guilty for it at once. "I don't need to forgive her for anything."

"You don't blame her for dying?" Father Murray reached inside his jacket and brought out a tobacco pouch. He fussed with his pipe for a while then lit the tobacco with a match. There was a slight tremble in his fingers. He took two puffs and closed his eyes for a moment. The pleasant smell of pipe smoke drifted on the air.

It suddenly occurred to Liam that Father Murray might be right. There was a reason he'd never come back to Derry, a reason why he'd never visited Mary Kate's grave. He could have asked Oran for permission. *Oran.* Liam closed his burning eyes. *Poor Oran.*

It hadn't only been that he was unwilling to accept that she was dead. Had it? He was angry with her, bloody furious, in fact. Even so, he hated himself for it. It wasn't right. She'd said she was sorry with her last words. He was certain she'd meant the first child, not the last. She wanted to be forgiven. Needed it. And he hadn't forgiven her, had he? Her only fault had been in believing what Father Murray had told her, in doing as the Church had directed her to do. Was she really at fault?

Yes. Every bit at fault as he was for all those he'd killed for the 'Ra, and for revenge— *The woman in the street. Oh, Jesus. The children*— Everyone had their regrets. Everyone made mistakes.

Some more terrible than others.

Something in his chest loosened. "It isn't as if Mary Kate asked to die."

"No, but still, she left you. Alone," Father Murray said. "I've lost someone too. I understand what that's like."

"Do you, now? Do you also know what it's like having the Church convince your wife that you're demon spawn, and your children are too monstrous to live?"

Father Murray tapped out his pipe and left it in the ash tray. He wove his fingers together and stared at his hands. "I'm truly sorry for that."

"I don't want your fucking apology!"

"You don't have to forgive me. I won't ask you for that. It's too much," Father Murray said. "You don't have to do anything. But do you think Mary Kate would've wanted you to waste your life like this?"

Father Murray stopped talking and filled his pipe a second time. He returned to smoking in silence while Liam shut his eyes, determined to remain silent. The edges of his eyelids gathered moisture that threatened to spill onto his cheeks. It only made him furious. Why couldn't everyone just leave him be? Why couldn't he have one damned thing as he wanted it? The petulance in the thought didn't escape him, but it only enraged him further.

"The Church has made a horrific mistake. And I've done vile things in its service." Father Murray sounded uncomfortable and tired—as if the words he spoke came at great cost. "Life is so diverse. There are more creatures, more entities than the Church acknowledges. Ghosts, demons and angels. Not every supernatural being falls in those categories," he said. "I can't let the killing go on. I won't. And that is, I believe, the reason I still live. I must. In spite of all the terrible things I've done. There isn't anyone else."

Suddenly, Liam's mouth felt very dry. "What are you saying?"

"I'm saying beings that should never have been harmed have been executed because the Church is unwilling to admit its policies are wrong. I'm saying," Father Murray said, "I'm no longer working in support of those policies."

"You're no longer a priest?"

"I've not left the Church," Father Murray said. "Although, I'm not entirely certain of what would be made of my current beliefs. Nonetheless, I'm doing what I can. I discussed my discovery with the bishop before I resigned from the Order. He remained unconvinced, I'm afraid. But I made the attempt."

"You tried to get them to stop murdering babbies?"

Father Murray nodded. "The archbishop said that even if it were possible that other magical beings might exist, none were listed in the Bible and therefore weren't to be considered part of God's plan."

"The platypus isn't listed in the Bible, Father. Does that make it worthy of execution?"

A small smile appeared on Father Murray's face. "A tidy argument, that. But the problem runs deeper. Were the Church to acknowledge that other supernatural beings exist outside of standard Christianity, two facts would become immediately apparent. One: if other powerful entities exist then other religions—non-Christian religions—might contain valid truths, and therefore, may be legitimate in general. And two: that the Catholic Church has participated in genocide for centuries."

Liam blinked.

"As much as I wish to believe otherwise, the Roman Catholic Church isn't likely to adapt its policies. Not in this. To do so would threaten the very existence of the Church.

"Nonetheless, I've been observing the Order's targets on my own. The ones in Belfast. I've been identifying. Categorizing. If I am reasonably uncertain of the status of suspected Fallen, I've attempted contact and issued warnings. However, both my inexperience and my being a priest have meant my success rate hasn't been all that high. I can't say as I blame anyone for not listening to me." He took a deep breath. "I've been praying for guidance. Assistance. And I think I may have just gotten my answer."

"Why not merely stop being a priest?"

"My belief in God and my vocation aren't in question."

Liam frowned. "But what of everything that goes with it? Don't you owe an allegiance to the Church?"

"The Church has made drastic policy changes in the past—the recent past in particular. Just because it isn't likely to doesn't mean it's impossible."

"But after what you just told me they'd excommunicate you."

Father Murray nodded. "I suppose they would." He took a deep breath. "I need your help, Liam. To protect those who need protection. From the Order."

Flipping onto his back, Liam felt the ghost of his former pain. He scanned the walls and found himself staring at a framed photo. It was taken sometime around 1966 before the war began. His mother was smiling and holding baby Eileen. He saw himself at age nine with thick shaggy hair and a sullen expression smoldering on his face, turning from the camera to unsuccessfully hide a black eye. The three of them were standing in front of St. Brendan's. It'd been Eileen's baptism, and Patrick Kelly was nowhere in the picture—nowhere near the church, in fact. Liam remembered that day. It was the day he understood that no amount of trouble he caused, no amount of complaining, angry fits, pleading or attempts at reason would make a difference. His mother had married Patrick Kelly and whether or not Liam accepted him didn't matter anymore. His half sister had destroyed everything. His mother belonged to Patrick Kelly, and he, Liam, had lost her forever. It was the first time he'd understood he was alone—really alone. It had taken him years to forgive Eileen, but in the end he'd done it. She couldn't help being born any more than he could.

Protect others from the Church's assassins. It was a noble cause but then so was the Irish Republic. Liam looked at the battered and angry boy in the photo and felt sad.

"Can I ask you something?" Father Murray asked.

"Can't stop you." It was a whisper. The words barely squeezed past the pain in his throat.

"Why are you wearing that crucifix?"

Touching the silver at his neck, Liam considered his answer. Lies were easy. Lies would mean he wouldn't have to know the truth himself, but he'd already thrown away one opportunity to tell the truth when it could've made a difference. He wasn't sure he was ready to lose another. "Was a gift. From Ma. My First Communion. The St. Sebastian medal Mary Kate gave to me for my birthday."

"An odd choice. I thought the IRA went in for St. Joseph."

Liam blinked. He considered denying it but no longer saw the point. In any case, if Father Murray were going to turn him in he'd have done so already. Liam repeated the words he'd heard and read to himself hundreds of times over the years. "*Whoever reads this prayer or hears it or carries it, will never die a sudden death, nor be drowned, nor will poison take effect on them. They will not fall into the hands of the enemy nor be burned in any fire, nor will they be defeated in battle.*" He looked to Father Murray. "Maybe Mary Kate knew it'd be endurance I'd need, not protection." Once again he thought about lying but decided not to. "Everything was gone. And… I needed something to hold on to."

"So, you turned back to the Church."

"I've not set foot inside a church since the day Mary Kate died."

"Oh. I see."

"It isn't much, but it's the very last of myself that exists, Father. The last part of me that was before the fucking monster came. Everything else is gone."

Father Murray leaned over and cleaned out his pipe into the ash tray sitting on the floor next to the big green chair. He filled the pipe again and then lit it. Puffs of white smoke once again perfumed the air. He shook out the match and dropped it into the ash tray. Settling back into the chair, he closed his eyes.

"Everything isn't gone," Father Murray said.

"Mary Kate is gone. Everything we had together," Liam said. "Everything I was. You don't know. I let the fucking monster loose. I'm not—I'm not human anymore. You should have let me die."

"Human beings are known to make mistakes, Liam."

"Not like this."

Father Murray smoked in silence for a time. Liam struggled with his question until he couldn't stand it anymore. "How many was it I killed?"

"When?"

"The car bomb. How many?"

The room was quiet. Liam could make out the ticking of the mantle clock in the next room.

"One," Father Murray said. "A constable. A woman who lived across the street was injured. Some children witnessed the explosion, but weren't otherwise harmed."

Liam let out the breath he'd been holding. "She saved them. Thank God."

"You can start again."

"And Father Dominic and Father Christopher? What of them?" Liam felt the top of his left ear and found a scar. It was tender to the touch. *It can't have healed already,* he thought. *Can it?*

"That… is more complicated," Father Murray said. "They're alive. Both of them. But neither will be in shape for duty for some time." He stared down at his hands, thinking. Then he took a long breath. "You're not a monster. There was no choice. You had to defend yourself. If I can see that, surely you can?"

"I don't deserve a new start."

"Deserving has nothing to do with it. I'm not talking about a holiday. What I'm suggesting, it won't be easy. It'll be very dangerous. And you're not likely to get anything in return except more danger. We won't be thanked. Ever."

"I'll think about it, Father."

Nodding, Father Murray sighed. "I should call your mother."

"I don't want to see her."

"Don't you think she'll be glad you're home?"

"I don't care."

"Why?"

"She lied to me. My whole fucking life!"

"Shhh. Calm down, Liam."

"Kept my father from me too!"

"She was only protecting you."

Liam filled his lungs as much as he could stand and gave the last all his rage. "Protecting herself, you mean! She told me so!" Something—his skin?—tore underneath the bandages and the pain intensified. Liquid oozed across his back. Squeezing his eyes shut, he gritted his teeth. He felt more than saw Father Murray get up from the chair and gently touch his arm.

"Stop this. You're only hurting yourself," Father Murray said.

Taking small breaths, Liam waited for the pain to fade back into a dull throb.

"You have every right to be angry," Father Murray said, checking the bandages and then sitting down again. "You do. But please. Try to understand something of what your mother went through."

Afraid to speak, Liam grunted in disbelief.

"There was a reason she didn't marry right away. Did she never tell you?"

Liam risked shaking his head no. He'd always assumed it was because no one had wanted her.

"She waited for your father." Father Murray blew out another smoke cloud. "There is much that passes between adults that children don't see or understand—can't see or understand."

The room blurred, and Liam shifted in an attempt to make his back stop hurting. Father Murray put down his pipe and left the room. When he returned, he held out a glass of water and two pills. "There's no need for you to suffer."

Liam accepted the pills and the water. Then he wiped his eyes clear with his sleeve. Movement wasn't easy. He had to be cautious. Father Murray settled into the overstuffed chair and retrieved his pipe.

"Tell me something," Father Murray asked. "About the bomb. Why would you want to kill a constable?"

"Don't want to talk about it, Father."

Father Murray nodded and then allowed the conversation to die.

Liam took a careful breath. "Do you—do you remember what you said when you caught me giving Andy Burns a hiding?"

Father Murray shook his head.

"You said I hadn't the right," Liam said. "I told you Andy deserved it. He called my mother a whore. Called me a filthy taig, and said all taigs should die. So, I gave him a kicking. You said, 'Vengeance is mine, sayeth the Lord.' I remember that." The drugs had started to take effect. He knew it because the throbbing in his back had eased, and he felt slow-witted. He supposed it was the painkillers talking more than anything else, but he couldn't stop himself. "Hated you at the time, but it stuck. I've been thinking about those words. After what happened. After the bomb. And I decided. You were right all along. It didn't matter if you'd only said it because you thought I was a demon to be steered away from doing wrong. Revenge is no business for anyone."

Liam listened to the beat of his heart and willed it to slow while Father Murray said nothing at all.

"'The light that shines the brightest also casts the longest shadow.'" Father Murray's voice was quiet. "When you think about it, it makes a certain amount of sense."

"Tell me what to do. I don't know anything anymore."

"When I joined the Order," Father Murray said. "I saw myself as a protector of the weak. We killed so that humanity might live. A terrible thing, but sometimes it's required. We've both seen it, you and I. The thing is, once you've accepted that role there are certain lines you cannot cross no matter what happens. The Church forgot that. And I did too."

"What lines, Father?"

"Hate. Revenge. Self-righteousness. No self-proclaimed guardian can afford them. Unfortunately, each one is a very human emotion. You can't live the life of a soldier or constable and not feel those things. To not feel them is impossible. But to act upon them is to assume the role of executioner. Assassin. That way is the path to atrocity, and atrocity is the end of everything."

"I wish there were someone else to do this. Someone better. Anyone."

"And I can't help feeling the same," Father Murray said. "But because of the terrible mistakes we've made, you and I, neither of us is likely to forget about the line between guardian and executioner ever at all. And I think that's required if we're to do what needs done."

The drugs were making Liam's eyelids too heavy to lift. He didn't want to think anymore.

"Get some sleep," Father Murray said. "We can discuss this later."

Chapter 25

Londonderry/Derry, County Londonderry, Northern Ireland
September 1977

It was nine in the morning when Kathleen Kelly started in on the pan she'd left to soak from the night before. The soapy water was warm on her hands in the chilly flat. A distorted patch of light glowed yellow on the grey-speckled linoleum. Moira's tinny transistor radio was playing Paul McCartney and Wings, and Kathleen watched disrupted dust particles waltz to "Mull of Kintyre" in the sunbeam. *1-2-3. 2-2-3. 3-2-3.* She let herself sing along and sway to the strumming guitar. *1-2-3. 2-2-3. 3-2-3.* The children were in school, and Patrick was at work. The flat was her own. The children didn't know she listened to their music during the day. Nor did Patrick. It was her little secret, her little indulgence. Rock music reminded her of the days when she would sneak out with her sister Sheila to hear Elvis Presley played on the radio—the days when she first met Bran, who would later change her life.

Not for the better, her mother would have said.

Complicated as her situation was, Kathleen couldn't bring herself to regret the choices she'd made, much as she'd tried. *I'm not a good person,* she thought. *Mary, Mother of God, forgive me. I've tried so hard to be, but I suppose I will always be that sinful girl.* She thought back to the last time she'd seen Bran and sighed. Patrick deserved more. He had rescued her from her parents, after all. He had made her honest—at least in her mother's eyes, but she didn't love him, not as much as she should. Patrick knew it, she was certain, and if he lost control of his temper, it was her fault, wasn't it? Because she didn't love him enough. Because she actually loved someone else.

This is my penance. At least Patrick is a good father to the children.

Don't lie to yourself, she thought. *He hurt Liam. Maybe not the others. But he did hurt Liam.* And that was her fault too, wasn't it? She'd pretended it wasn't happening instead of confronting Patrick, instead of stopping him. Although, the boy wasn't the only one to suffer, God knew. *Never in front of the children.* She was proud of that one thing. The children didn't know. Still, Liam bore the worst of it. And she'd pretended. It was safer for everyone, she'd thought then. Hide the bruises. Pack Liam off to his Grandmother until Patrick sobered up or cooled off. That was the answer. It was safer.

She pulled the plug on the sink, let the dirty water drain out and stared at the grit revealed in the bottom. She didn't know why she was thinking of these things now. The past was the past. Liam was grown and no longer living at home. She could keep pretending that everything was normal—except it wasn't.

She stared at the damp grit and tried not to think of the last time she'd spoken to her son, the last time she'd known he was safe.

Her whole life had been about acting out pretense after pretense. *The outright lies.* She glanced up at the little radio with Moira's name scrawled on it in her best red nail varnish and indulged in a sad smile. *Well, maybe not my whole life.* She loved her children—all of them—with a fierceness that sometimes frightened her.

The girls were too small to get into much trouble. Although, she had to admit that Moira sometimes disturbed her with stories of seeing things that weren't there. Her drawings of the Wee People had been the result of many a long chat with the nuns at the school. Although, truth be told none of the pictures depicted anyone terribly wee. Then there was little Patrick. Every day he seemed more and more sullen, and the older he got the less he listened to her. Sixteen-year-old Eileen, on the other hand, was an ideal child. However, Kathleen couldn't help wondering how much of her behavior was due to lessons she'd learned while watching her older brother. *Don't cause trouble. Don't draw attention to yourself. Stay hidden.*

Each of her children made her worry in their own way, but the one that concerned her the most of late was Liam, and there was no one that she could go to for help. *You know the RUC are right. He went and volunteered,* she thought. *He did it because of her. Mary Kate. The Gallaghers are all political. Every one. They find him—he'll go back to prison for good.* From the day Mary Kate had died, her Liam had not been the same. And now he'd shut her out. He had his reasons, to be sure. She understood. She should have told him about Bran, but she'd foolishly hoped that he wouldn't ever have to know. She'd so wanted some wee bit of normalcy for him—even if it was only a façade. Wasn't being a fatherless boy burden enough?

Imagining the worst, how Liam might be dead or in jail, had worried her sick, but Father Murray had called. He'd said Liam was safe and that she would be hearing from him or seeing him soon. When she did she resolved to apologize for all the times she'd failed him. *Why did he punish himself so? Why couldn't he stay out of trouble?* She knew the answer. Liam was still bearing the brunt of it all. That was it. Same as before. Well, it had to stop. She would make it stop.

Sins of the father.

Or is it the mother?

Someone knocked on the door. She wiped her hands on a towel and went to answer it, but by the time she got there whomever it was had gone, leaving behind a white envelope. She scanned the hallway and then picked it up. The weight of the paper told her there was a card inside. She closed the door and sat on the sofa to read it.

Meet me on the corner. Tonight at eight o'clock.

There was no signature, only the letter B.

Something about it didn't feel right. To begin with, Bran had never left her a note before. For a long time she'd wondered if he could write. The Fair Folk didn't go in much for written history as everyone knew. Nonetheless, Bran's Latin was better than hers, and he could recite long passages of Irish poetry and literature, past and present. The handwriting wasn't how she imagined it would be. The thin script was barely legible for all the swirls and embellishments. She didn't know what she expected from him, but it wasn't that. The card disturbed her. For a moment she considered that perhaps someone had meant it for another door, but the idea that it might actually be for Mrs. Foyle or Mrs. McKenna was ridiculous.

Kathleen sighed. Of course it was from Bran. Who else would send such a cryptic message? Besides hadn't she warned him to be more discrete? Bran had been seen—by Mrs. Foyle of all people, and once again Kathleen found herself the subject of disapproving stares. She didn't need him hovering over her as if she were helpless. She was a grown woman. She could take care of herself. It wasn't long before Patrick heard the gossip. He hadn't reacted well, and it'd taken much effort to convince him that she was not having an affair. Of course, it didn't help that her assertion was only a half-truth. Bran wasn't a mortal man, was he? And was it technically an affair if she wasn't sleeping with him?

I am not a good woman, she thought. *Pretense.*

She burned both card and envelope in case Patrick might find them. Then she returned to her housework, considering what excuse she would give to get away that night.

"I'm to my mother's now," Kathleen said, looking over her shoulder. It was close enough to the truth. Father Murray had called to inform her that Liam was hidden away safe at her mother's, injured but recovering. The plan was to visit Liam after the quick chat with Bran—and it would be a quick chat. She'd see to that.

Patrick grunted. "I'll be calling her to see you're not lying, woman."

"You do that," she said, attempting to keep the contempt from her tone and failing. She could always blame an army checkpoint if she were late. It was good that her mother didn't care much for Patrick. Of course, Kathleen wasn't sure her mother cared much for anyone.

In any case, Patrick had eaten his dinner already and was watching the television while drinking his beer. He'd be content for a few hours at the least. She slipped out the door and down the stairs, taking care to be especially quiet about it. To her relief, Mrs. Foyle didn't so much as stir on the other side of her door.

By the time Kathleen had gotten outside it was misting. She opened her umbrella and then pulled the collar of her coat tighter about her neck. She walked to the corner and waited, hoping she'd guessed the right one. She'd been there for a quarter of an hour when a man in a black coat walked directly to her. He was wearing a dark flat cap, and the taps on his shoes scraped the pavement. A chill went through her at the sight of him. She avoided eye contact, hoping he'd pass without noticing her.

"Are you Kathleen Kelly?" His accent was English.

Taken by surprise, she turned and stared. "I'm expecting someone."

He took her arm. "I'm sure you are."

"What? Let go!"

A car pulled up. She caught a glimpse of three men. The one sitting in the front passenger side had a large hump on his back that caused him to fit strangely in the seat. The rear passenger door opened, and she was shoved inside. A blanket was thrown over her. She screamed as she was forced to the floor and then something hard pressed against her skull.

"Shut up. Now. Or I'll kill you. Understand?" The question was accompanied by a brutal shove. The second voice didn't belong to the Englishman. It was Irish, she was certain of it.

Too frightened to speak, she nodded.

"Good. Don't move, Catholic bitch."

The car sped away. Her heart drummed in her ears, and her mouth was dry. The wool blanket smelled of gasoline and oil.

It was stored in the trunk, she thought. A sharp pebble on the plastic floor mat pressed uncomfortably into her knee while her mind raced through possibilities. Someone turned on the radio and Kenny Rogers lamented his wife, Lucille, through the speakers. The men in the car were silent, apparently content in listening to the music. *They're professional, or they've done this before.* Her first thought was that they were paramilitaries—Protestant UFF or UVF of course, but she couldn't think of anything she'd done that might have drawn such attention. She wasn't political.

Liam is in the 'Ra, she thought, and her heart froze. *What if they want to know where he is? What if this was in retaliation for something Liam has done?* She shut her eyes against the idea. *No.* Her Liam wouldn't have done anything to warrant this. She was sure of it. The note had been signed "B." So, whoever had taken her knew Bran's name. *Maybe.* The more she thought about it, the more confused she became. She finally came to the conclusion that she didn't know anything and couldn't until someone explained. She would have to wait. Chasing her fears in endless circles didn't help.

In a short time the tension became too much. She started shivering and couldn't hold still no matter how frightened she was. The pain in her knee grew unbearable. She took a chance and shifted. Pain exploded in the top of her head as one of the men hit her with something hard. *The butt of the gun.*

"I said, don't move."

Tears slipped down her face, and she resisted the urge to rub the rising bump. She focused on the ridges of the plastic car mat under her palms instead. She was terrified and couldn't help cursing herself for having warned Bran off. *I can take care of myself,* she thought. *What was I thinking?* She concentrated on breathing and slowing her pounding heart. *Calm down. You haven't done anything wrong. Wait. Find out what they want. Maybe they'll see reason.*

The car slowed and a hand shoved her farther down until she was a tight ball with her forehead resting on the warm bump in the center of the car's floor. Wrapping her hands over the back of her head for protection, she prayed. *Hail Mary, Mother of God, forgive us our trespasses—*

The car stopped.

"Not a sound now."

She heard a squeak of a window being rolled down and the temperature in the car dropped at once. A dog barked.

This is a checkpoint, she thought. *They'll notice me. They always shine a light in the back, don't they?*

Suddenly, the air tingled. There wasn't any other way of describing it. It was saturated with energy like lightning waiting to be discharged in a storm. She could almost smell the ozone in spite of being under the blanket.

"Hello, Officer." It was the man who'd met her on the corner.

The Englishman. The hope of being discovered dimmed.

British or not, they're soldiers. They're trained to look for this kind of thing. Aren't they?

"Evening, sir. License, please. Where are you headed this evening and why?"

"I'm visiting a cousin. Owns an estate outside of town."

She listened to footsteps trace a path around the car, and her heart jumped. *Please, God. Let them notice something.* A dog started barking, and the guard stopped.

"There isn't anything back there worth looking at. It's cold and damp, and you'd rather go back to your tea." The words came from the front seat in a loud whisper. It wasn't the Englishman. It was the man with the hunchback, she was sure of it.

The electrical charge in the air became so heavy that she couldn't breathe. One of the men in the back seat coughed.

Mary, Mother of God, please let him notice. Let him do something.

"Nothing back here," the guard said. The dog continued to bark and snarl. Kathleen heard a thump as something slammed into the side of the car.

Outside, someone shouted, "Get that dog away from there!"

"Very good. Everything is in order, sir. Have a good evening."

"Thank you."

The window squeaked again, and the driver gunned the engine. She felt all the blood in her body drain down into her hands and feet. The shivering grew worse. Tears traced cooling paths down her face as disappointment set in. It wasn't long before the car stopped again, and she was dragged out of the back with the blanket still over her head. The moment she thought to throw the blanket off and run, a hand clamped onto her arm, and she was guided into a building. The floors were concrete and their footsteps echoed until she was pushed again into a room. The blanket wasn't removed until she was pushed and fell onto what felt like an old sofa. It stank of mildew.

Blinking in the light, she saw her captors clearly for the first time and panicked. Three of the men were dressed in military surplus clothes. None wore masks. One of the smaller men stared right at her, but his eyes were unfocused as if he were in some sort of trance. *Drugs?* There was something wrong with the big one. Whether it was the hunched back or something else, she couldn't decide, but he didn't move like a normal person. He twitched as if he were ready to take flight, his head moving in short jerks like a bird's. She didn't like him at all. His gaze made her feel like a rabbit in a field being targeted by a human-sized owl.

"We've questions," Hunchback said. "And you've got the answers. Don't you?" The tingling returned to the air. "Don't you?"

She found herself nodding in answer because that was what he wanted from her. He smiled, and his charcoal eyes burned with such intensity that she had to look away.

It was then she noticed the Englishman's flat cap was a deep crimson edging on brown, the color of drying blood, and his teeth were filed to sharp points.

"Hello, Kathleen," the Redcap said. "I believe introductions are in order. You may call me Henry. Henry, son of Bran."

Chapter 26

Londonderry/Derry, County Londonderry, Northern Ireland
September 1977

Liam woke to someone shaking him. It was late. He knew it by the hushed ticking of the nightstand clock and the darkened window.

"You must get up." It was Father Murray, and he was speaking in a frightened whisper.

Is a punishment squad on the way? Blinking, Liam found himself tangled in the plastic tubes. In his rush to get free, he pulled something he shouldn't have and sharp pain shot up his left arm. "Get these fucking things off me. I can't move."

"Stop your thrashing. I'll be right there." Father Murray shut the door and turned on the light. "Calm yourself."

"Calm? Is it you they've come for, Father?"

"You're safe. I didn't wake you for that." Father Murray took Liam's left arm and gently attacked the bandages. Withdrawing the needle from the vein inside Liam's left elbow, Father Murray placed a cotton ball on the tiny wound and bent the arm to hold it in place while he cut fresh tape. "That's going to bruise."

He did everything with an expertise surprising in a priest. It made Liam wonder how Father Murray had acquired the skill, as well as who'd stuck the IV in his arm to begin with. He'd assumed it'd been the doctor he met in the cave but was beginning to think otherwise.

"Then what's wrong?" Liam applied pressure on the cotton ball while Father Murray wrapped surgical tape around it. *If it was Father Murray that did all this, where did he get all the equipment? Who else knows where I am?*

"How do you feel?"

"Tired. Bit hungry but otherwise fine." He tested his back by stretching his shoulders. "The pain is gone."

Father Murray raised his eyebrows and then lifted the back collar of the

T-shirt Liam was sleeping in to have a look. He tugged at a bandage there. "That's interesting."

"What is?"

"It appears the burns have healed already. Your father said that might happen." Father Murray's face squeezed into a concerned frown, then he seemed to come to a decision. "I'll take the bandages off. Then put some clothes on while I pack."

"Where are we going? What's happening?" Liam pulled the T-shirt over his head.

Father Murray stripped the hospital tape securing the bandages with practiced motions. "Your mother has gone missing."

"What? What happened?"

"She left the flat to come here and somewhere in between there and here she vanished." Father Murray finished, throwing the stained gauze in the trash. "You're done."

She was on her way here. Liam blinked and stuck an arm in the fresh shirt. His heart was drumming out a forced march. "No one saw her?"

"I'm afraid not."

"Where are we going?"

"We're to meet your father. Then we'll look for her. Together." He left the room.

Liam tugged on the blue jeans, long sleeved shirt and sweater—all were a bit too big for him. The work boots, however, were exactly the right size. Before snapping up the anorak draped on the chair, he put a hand to the back of his head and found that not only were the burns on his scalp healed but most of his hair had grown back. He decided not to waste time wondering about it until the crisis was over. Then he'd have questions. *A lot of them.* He threw open the door and stepped into the hallway only to bump into his Gran. She was wearing a white housecoat, and her gray hair was gathered in a long braid that hung over one shoulder. An apron was tied over her housecoat—the white one with the blue flowers embroidered on it. She looked right at him with her ever-present scowl and then glanced away. The expression on her face—outside the usual distaste—was unreadable.

She spoke to the wall, not to him. "Was making cocoa. Your fath—Patrick called. Father Murray said—" She stopped herself. "I suppose this means you won't be staying?"

"No, I won't."

Nodding, her jaw twitched and for a moment the tight line that was her mouth softened.

"Ma is in trouble." He was babbling a bit. He wasn't entirely sure why. She affected him like that. Always had. He shrugged on the coat.

His Gran blinked. "You were almost dead yesterday. Now, you're on your feet as if nothing happened."

He waited for whatever it was she would say next. He didn't expect it'd be grandmotherly. To his experience, it never was. His heart was beating fast, slamming against his breastbone hard enough for her to hear.

"You're one of Them, aren't you?" she asked in a whisper. "I knew it. Saw it in you from the start."

Saw it in you—

No. Liam clamped down on a bolt of anxiety.

"Even as a babe your eyes were never right. Red, they were. Like fire. I saw it. Send that boy to Church, I said. See he gets baptized. I was wrong."

"I must go, Gran."

"You never had a soul to save. You and Him both."

Clutching his rising anger in one fist, Liam moved to push past her, but she grabbed his arm, and it brought him up short. She was stronger than she appeared. There was iron in his Gran. *Steel.* No other element sprang to mind when he thought of her.

"She was a wayward child, our Kathleen. My William wanted to send her off. To the nuns. To the Laundry." She tugged at the sleeve of his shirt. "I wouldn't stand for it. That place. As much as a death sentence, that. For what? You? Still, she wouldn't give you up." She scrunched up her face in disgust. He moved to jerk away, but she clutched tighter. "No more than I would give her up. It's the way of it." She clamped down upon his arm with both hands, and it hurt. "You find her."

Father Murray walked into the hallway carrying a large duffel bag over one shoulder, and stopped. It was obvious to Liam that his Gran wasn't aware the priest was behind her. She didn't move. Liam couldn't remember a time when she'd so much as touched him, but there she was, staring up into his face with fierce eyes and tears shining on her pale cheeks. She was a specter in the half-light coming from the next room.

"Find my daughter before it's too late. She's your mother. If there's anything human in you, you'll find her. Do that and—" She swallowed, shutting her eyes with a shudder. "I will accept you as my grandson."

He wanted to tell her to sod off, but the lump in his throat prevented it. She seemed to be waiting for something from him. Her eyes were almost pleading—as close to it as he'd ever witnessed in his entire existence. Her grip on his arm tightened, and her neat fingernails were digging into his skin. Father Murray mouthed, *Go on.*

Liam gave her a nod and that was it. She finally released him.

"Go," she said. "Bring her home. Alive."

"We should leave," Father Murray said. "It's been too long as it is."

Liam followed Father Murray out of the house to an ecumenical black 1970 Volkswagen Beetle held together with leprous patches of body repair putty. Liam paused before getting in. "I don't fucking understand her."

"Who?" Father Murray asked, opening the driver's side door.

Liam looked back at the house. "Gran." He climbed into the passenger seat. The Beetle's engine snarled and then let out its distinctive purr. It rolled backward as Father Murray shifted into gear and let up on the clutch. Liam winced as the transmission gears ground together before catching and driving the car forward.

"She loves her family," Father Murray said. "What's to understand?"

"Are you fucking joking?" Liam asked. "All she's ever done is make Ma's life a misery. She never once used my name. Referred to me as 'that creature' ever since I can remember. My own Gran. Hated me from the day I was born. And now she'll claim me?"

Father Murray sighed. "She's attempting to tell you something the only way she knows how."

"And what's that?"

Turning, Father Murray's face was a mix of emotions. "She doesn't understand who you are or even what you are. You terrify her. But she loves you."

Liam blinked. "That's not what it sounded like."

"Nonetheless, it is what she was trying to say."

They drove in silence through the sleeping city. Liam couldn't make out where they were headed. He tried to relax anyway. Based upon Father Murray's circuitous route, there was time before he'd have to be ready to do anything. He shut his eyes and leaned back. When they pulled up in front of St. Brendan's he understood that Father Murray had gone the long way around to avoid a checkpoint.

The engine stopped purring and coughed once before quieting.

"Why are we here?" Liam asked.

"It's one of the places I can contact your father," Father Murray said. He climbed out of the VW Beetle and headed for the churchyard.

My real father, Liam thought. "Why is it you can reach him but I can't?"

"I've only seen him myself three or four times counting the day before. And he didn't permit me to contact him until recently. Even then, he doesn't always show himself."

"You don't know for certain if you can contact him?" Liam ran to catch up. "Why are we wasting the time? Why are we not looking for my Ma?"

Father Murray produced a white envelope from his coat pocket. "This is why."

Liam opened the envelope and slid the note card free. The handwriting was so ornate that he could barely make out the words. His stomach did a sick lurch. He'd seen the like once before. Among the destruction that had once been the home he'd shared with Mary Kate. His skin prickled, and he shuddered.

Meet at the stone circle, it read. *The one that Roman Catholic whore led you to. Raven's Hill. Bring Bran and his bastard. Tonight. Before dawn.*

"What the hell is this about?" Liam asked.

Father Murray pushed the iron gate. The hinges screamed displeasure as if angry for being awakened at such an hour. "This was also inside." He turned and placed a small disc in Liam's palm.

Tilting it toward the light, Liam recognized it at once. *First, Mary Kate. Now, Ma.* "It's that coin. The one I found the night Mary Kate died."

"It isn't the same," Father Murray said. "It's another just like it. The note is from the Redcap. The creature you told me you saw the day you were arrested. The one that almost beat your head in."

"You're telling me a bogey man is responsible for Mary Kate's death?" Liam went through the gate after Father Murray. "Was Loyalists. The fucking RUC. I saw them." *The fourth trail had led to nothing. As if the man had vanished.*

"That may be so," Father Murray said. "But the Redcap was there as well. That coin proves it."

"How?"

"There's not much time to explain," Father Murray said, stopping under a huge oak tree at the back of the churchyard. "But it was what I needed to confirm that day. When I left you. Before the—before you were hurt. I told your father about the coin that day. It's why he was able to find you as soon as he did. You'd have died."

"So, that thing I saw all those years ago. It was real? I'm not mad?"

"You're real. Your father is real. Fallen angels are real. Why not your father's sworn enemy?"

"He hates my father, but he came for Mary Kate and me and now Ma?"

"I'm afraid so."

"All that time I thought I was going off my nut. There was a real danger, and no one thought to fucking tell me about it?"

"We were protecting you."

"Protecting? Why is it whenever someone lies to me they say it's for my own good? Mary Kate died, Father. Because of me. How is that protection?" The tingling in his arms was getting worse.

"I didn't think it was my place. I made a mistake—"

"Another mistake? Father, any more of your mistakes, and I'm not likely to fucking survive it."

"Again, I'm sorry. But there'll be no more hiding the truth. I said so before, and I'm serious." Father Murray looked at his watch and then up at the night sky. "Well, I suppose we should get this over with."

"What is it you have to do?" Liam felt suddenly uneasy.

"Call his name. Your mother says that anywhere with a connection to the Other Side will work. A churchyard is easiest to find." Father Murray closed his eyes and took a deep breath. "Bran? Are you here?"

Liam searched for a sign. He looked up at the sky and then the trees. *Anything.* Nothing happened. No sound. No movement. "Father—"

"We need you. Your son needs you," Father Murray said. "Kathleen Kelly is in danger."

A wind gust swirled through the graveyard, sprinkling them with moisture the leaves had collected earlier in the night. Liam pulled his borrowed anorak tighter as the hairs on the back of his neck stood on end. He didn't like this at all. He felt a shimmer in the air before he heard an echoing whisper in the wind.

"My Kathleen."

Swallowing, Liam shifted so that his back was to the big tree.

"She's gone," Father Murray said. "It appears the Redcap took her."

"You're certain of this, priest?" Bran's voice came from behind the big Celtic cross at the center of the churchyard.

"I am. He sent a message," Father Murray said.

Liam caught the scent of old forest, blood and campfire before Bran appeared from behind the granite cross. He was dressed for a battle—a silver torc at his neck and a leather breastplate over a linen shirt and baggy trousers. He held a spear and carried a sword in a leather scabbard. A round wooden shield was strapped to his back. His clothes were dirty, torn and bloodstained. His eyes glowed red in the darkness. There was something about him that spoke of ancient power. Danger.

Bran's eyes flashed red, and Liam understood he was staring back. "You've decided to live, have you?"

Before Liam could come up with a retort Father Murray interrupted, motioning for Liam to hand over the envelope. "I discovered this note on my car an hour ago. I didn't find it until after Patrick called to say she was missing. He's called the RUC as well."

Bran scowled at the sound of Patrick's name.

"The envelope contained one of those coins," Father Murray said. "In case there was doubt, I assume. I thought you said the Redcap was in prison and would remain there?"

"I was deceived. And that was the least of the Queen's betrayals." Bran set the spear into the ground with an angry thump and then accepted the

note from Father Murray. "Cross it! The creature is mad. His timing is—"
Then suddenly, his expression changed from defeated to calculating. "Of
course. That was the plan all along, was it not?" He took in a deep breath
and then released it. "Right. There is something I must see to first. I will
meet you both at the Raven's Hill, priest. Do not enter the circle. Either of
you. Not until I'm there. Understood?"

Father Murray nodded.

"What is this about?" Liam asked.

"The short of it is—you and your mother have been caught up in a war
that is not of your making."

"Damn you, I had a family!" Liam took a step forward with a clenched
fist.

Father Murray put a restraining hand on his arm.

"Until recently, I thought I'd handled the problem," Bran said. "I thought
you and yours were safe. By the time I understood otherwise it was too late.
Your wife was— I'm so sorry."

"Because of you. And now that thing has Ma. Because of you. Why
couldn't you be arsed to marry her proper in the first place? Or was it because of me? Was it because you had no need of the responsibility?"

"You've no understanding of the matter at all." Angry, Bran freed the spear
from the ground. He paused and the rage faded. "But then how could you?
We'll discuss it. Later. After this is done. You, your mother and I."

"Aye. We fucking will," Liam said. "I promise you."

"Come on, Liam," Father Murray said.

"I'll meet you at the road. At the bottom of Raven's Hill," Bran said. He
glanced over his shoulder, and his eyes flashed once before he vanished
behind the big stone cross.

"Liam, we should go. It's a drive." Father Murray tugged on his arm.

Liam followed him out of the graveyard, slamming the gate. He got to
the car and threw himself inside the Beetle.

Silent, Father Murray turned the key. He waited to speak until they were
out of the car park. "Are you all right?"

"Me? I'm fucking grand." Liam stared out at the empty road and tried to
get control of the roaring in the back of his head. He knew this wasn't the
time or place. His mother was more important, and he was determined
to not let himself banjax everything by throwing a childish fit for being
treated like a wean.

"We can't go into this divided."

Liam slammed a fist into the dashboard. "Don't you think I know
that!"

Father Murray swallowed. He seemed to be running through a list of things to say, and Liam wondered which Uni Psychology textbook had anything to say about out-of-control Fey.

Stop it, he thought. He reached into his pocket, brought out his lighter and ran a finger over the tricolor painted on it. He took a deep breath. "Was just wondering what Mary Kate would have thought about all this."

"And?"

Liam gripped the square of steel tight in the palm of his hand. "I think she'd tell me I was being an arse."

"It's quite a lot to process."

Liam nodded.

"That said, I've some bad news."

"Aye?"

"We can't avoid all the checkpoints on the way out of Derry."

Liam felt a grim smile spread over his face. "And so I thought. When the BAs stop us what are they going to find in your wee gym bag, Father?"

Father Murray's mouth twitched. "A pistol, a rifle, ammunition and several knives."

Liam whistled. "An impressive arsenal for a pacifist."

"You know, I never told you I was a pacifist."

"How did you come by all this?"

"Sacred dispensation." Father Murray shrugged.

"I thought you quit."

"I did," Father Murray said. "Can I help that no one bothered to ask me to return my weapons?"

"And you thought we'd need all this tonight?"

Father Murray looked away. "I'm familiar with the Fallen, but I've never dealt with the Fey before—at least not to my knowledge. The Redcap doesn't appear to be the sort that can be reasoned with, and I understand steel can be useful. I thought it best to be prepared," he said. "I assume you know how to fire a gun?"

"Aye, I do," Liam said. "But I was a fucking wheelman, Father. Not the bloody infantry. And while I'm a fair shot I'm certainly no sniper."

"Were you any good at it? The driving?"

"According to Oran," Liam said, "I was the best the 'Ra had ever seen."

"Right." Father Murray slowed the car and steered to the side of the street. "I don't know the first thing about running Army checkpoints."

"Clearly. We should give this serious consideration, Father."

"All right. Do you have a better idea?"

There was no time for preparation. Volkswagen Beetles, while common, tended to stand out a bit more than a Ford four-door. He didn't know the car, and there wasn't time to get acquainted. Although he could certainly drive it, he wasn't certain he could trust it—given the state of the clutch. He didn't know the last time Father Murray had had the thing looked at by a mechanic, or even if the mechanic was good at his job. Once they were through, there were other factors to consider. What were the road conditions like outside of Derry? Not good, more than likely. The shortest way out of town would be Rossville Street to William Street to Creggan Road and straight out to Groarty Road. How would the BAs respond? How many helicopters would they have access to? How good were the Derry Peelers? There wasn't much out there. Not many places to hide and certainly not much room to evade both the Peelers and the BAs. Could he afford to be chased all the way up to the Raven's Hill? They needed to get where they were going quickly, but they also needed to do it quietly.

Too risky. Too many factors over which he had no control.

Liam remembered the times when he'd walked through the Shankill after dumping stolen cars and came to a decision. "Give me your wee bag. Before we get to the checkpoint I'll get out of the car and walk. You drive up. Talk to the nice murdering bastards. When you're done I'll meet you on the other side."

"You'll be caught. And if you're caught with guns you'll never see the outside world again."

"They won't notice me if I don't want them to, Father. I've done it before. Can't explain why it works, but it does."

"I don't like it."

"If you think this car can handle the road as well as a RS1600 and hold together in spite of being driven through a wooden barrier, and if you're willing to do for a few BAs as we run through, and if you think we can do it without you getting hit with a stray bullet... well, I'm willing to reconsider your proposition."

Father Murray slumped.

"It's better this way. If I do get stopped, you can still make the meeting. Tell my father—" The words felt strange on his lips, but it didn't feel right using his name. "—what happened. We can sort it out later. Anyway, we've established it's not me that fuck wants. It's him."

Father Murray nodded.

"If you get into trouble, I'll be there to see you through. Surprise is a guerrilla fighter's best asset. The Green Book says so." Liam winked, trying to show more confidence than he felt.

"I thought you weren't infantry."

"Aye, well, maybe so. But I did go through the training just the same, Father. So, I'm not totally useless."

Turning back onto the road with a sigh, Father Murray retraced the meandering path westward—back past Gran's, avoiding Rossville Street and William Street and looping over to Creggan Road. Liam put the lighter back into his pocket with a trembling hand. Truth was, Liam had had a few close calls in the Shankill, but he was certain the risks were more acceptable than they would be running the checkpoint. Much as he'd been willing to die before, the idea of going back to prison was worse. *Far worse.* Father Murray was right. They would put him away for good. With his luck, he'd be sent to Long Kesh. Of course, the Brits had rebuilt and renamed it after the riots of 1976, but the Maze was still the Kesh, and the Kesh was one place he never wanted to see again—certainly not as a sentenced prisoner.

Father Murray stopped the car at the corner before turning onto Creggan Road. "You're sure about this?"

"No. But there's no other option," Liam said, opening the Beetle's door.

"Wait." Father Murray held up his right hand and muttered a blessing, finishing it off by making a cross in the air. "God be with you."

"Thanks, Father. Same to you." Liam climbed out of the car and Father Murray handed over the black gym bag. It was heavy in Liam's hands. He unzipped it and grabbed one of the pistols—a Browning semi-automatic—and loaded a clip into it. There was no holster for it. So, after he checked it and flipped the safety, he stuck it in the pocket of the anorak. Shouldering the bag, he slammed the door and watched the Beetle turn left onto Creggan Road. He reached inside his shirt and pulled out the St. Sebastian medal and the crucifix. He kissed it for luck with his heart thudding in his ears. Taking a deep breath, he was overwhelmed with a bad feeling. There was a foul stench in the night air that he'd sensed before, but couldn't place where. Shifting the straps digging into his shoulder, he started his walk down Creggan Road at a brisk pace. The stink grew stronger as he approached the barricade, and it gave him a shiver. He glanced at his wrist watch, turned so that he could see it on the inside of his left wrist. It was a trick he'd picked up from Oran, to prevent the light from reflecting off the face.

Three o'clock in the morning.

He heard someone cry out, and he looked over at the barricade. Some poor wee drunken shite had been pulled over and was being given the go-over by a couple of bored BAs. *Fucking bastards.* Liam shoved down an urge to give them a seeing to. *No time for this.* His Ma was in danger. He would save her, even if he hadn't been able to save Mary Kate. The Redcap would not win. Liam would arrive in time and nothing and no one was going to stand in his way. *Not this time.*

Father Murray stopped the Beetle in front of the wooden barricade. The Beetle's engine idled while two BAs made their way to Father Murray. The third soldier stayed where he was with his gun pointed at the prone drunk's head. Liam sniffed the air and shuddered. Something about the situation wasn't right. *Something about the soldiers.* Two of them—the ones approaching the Beetle—were wearing large packs on their backs. The stench grew more powerful the closer he got until his nose was filled with decay and death. The familiar tingling started in Liam's chest, and shot down both arms.

Enemy. Danger. Kill them.

No, Liam thought back. *Not yet.* He wouldn't trust the monster. *Couldn't.* If it came to killing, he'd find another way. *Any other way but you.* There'd be no lines crossed this night—not by him.

His mouth was dry as he headed down the street at a brisk walk, praying himself into the background. *Nothing here, mate. Nothing worth noting.* The two BAs reached Father Murray's Beetle. One stationed himself at the driver's window and tapped the glass while the other directed his flashlight beam inside the Beetle through the passenger side windows, illuminating the floor and then the back seats. Father Murray rolled down his window and spoke to the big BA. Nodding, Father Murray handed over his driver's license. The big BA glanced at it and then motioned for Father Murray to get out of the car.

Fucking hell, Liam thought. *We're not done for yet. A quick search. Then it's through.*

He watched as Father Murray was thrown against a brick wall by the big BA. The second, shorter blond BA patted Father Murray down, pausing over the small of his back. It was obvious he'd found something. The big BA shoved Father Murray and then yanked the coat off him.

He was wearing some sort of sheath for a long knife at the small of his back.

The damned fool didn't give me all the fucking weapons, Liam thought with an internal groan. *We're fucked.* Liam put a hand inside the anorak's pocket and wrapped his right hand around the pistol's grip. The BAs were shouting.

The monster raged in the back of Liam's head to the point of distraction, and the hairs on the backs of both arms stood on end. *Drop the gun,* the monster snarled. *Rip them apart. Drop it. Do it. NOW.*

Liam shoved his hand deeper into his coat pockets and gripped the gun tighter in response. *Fuck you. No!*

It seemed the BAs still hadn't noticed him. Time slowed. The BAs roughly forced Father Murray to the ground. The shorter blond BA started in on Father Murray while the big BA looked on. Liam pointed his Browning at the big BA and pulled the trigger. The shock of the discharge went through both arms up to Liam's shoulders. The big BA went down at once.

What kind of ammunition does Father Murray pack for this fucking thing?

The smell of the spent round filled his nose, temporarily blocking out the rotting stink. For an instant, Liam's gaze locked onto the black lumpy splash painting the bricks. The dead BA twitched. Liam heard gunfire to his right as one of the soldiers recovered from the surprise. Liam turned to acquire his second target—the blond BA kicking Father Murray—and blinked.

He was gone.

"Looking for me?"

Liam whirled and was instantly punched in the face.

Chapter 27

Londonderry/Derry, County Londonderry, Northern Ireland
September 1977

"You still with me, Father?" Liam asked in a whisper. Either he hadn't recovered from the car bomb as thoroughly as thought or the blond soldier who'd jumped him was more powerful and faster than your average BA had any right to be. Liam had hit the ground before he had time to register what had happened. He'd been given a proper hiding before they'd tossed him into the back of the van. He could feel it. Only the drive had already lasted long enough that the pain had subsided into a dull ache. He could think clearly again. Blinking, he saw that someone had scratched "KAT" in big letters a few inches from his face.

He would've bet money the van wasn't a government-owned vehicle. "Father?" he asked, taking a risk by speaking a little louder.

"Yes. I'm here." Father Murray's whisper was unsteady.

"That's good. I think." Liam stared at the wall of the van and debated flipping onto his back so he wouldn't have to see it.

"Are you hurt?"

"A wee bruise here and there, Father. Nothing to worry about." He gazed at the letters carved into the van's paint and swallowed. *Well, not yet, anyway.*

Something was wrong. The BAs weren't acting... well, normal, and that disturbed him. To begin with, the blond BA had gone to the trouble of slipping on a glove and then gunning down both the third BA and the drunk with Father Murray's Browning. Then the blond bastard had dropped the pistol on the pavement. It was meant to be a fucking frame-up, of course. Although the gun was registered to Father Murray, Liam would be the one facing the interrogation at Castlereagh once the fingerprints were lifted. In addition, the Church's assassins would be on his neck as well because Liam had no doubt he'd be set up for Father Murray's death too when it came to it—provided he survived whatever the blond BA had in mind. On the other hand, Liam doubted his survival was all that important a factor. Nonetheless, the whole thing seemed a wee bit elaborate for something that could be resolved with a few lies. It wasn't as if the Peelers were that thorough with an IRA man handy to blame.

As if that weren't unusual enough, the corpse of the big BA Liam had topped had been arranged on the van's only bench seat in the front. That made no sense at all. Why the front? Why not dump it in the back of the van where it'd be less likely to be noticed? Better yet, why not leave the body behind? What was one more corpse in the frame-up?

Fucking false checkpoint, Liam thought. *Dammit! Why did this have to happen now of all times? Late. I'll be too fucking late again.*

Frustrated and panicked, he struggled with an urge to kick the side of the van in, but the bad feeling and the rotting stench coming off the corpse in the front seat was strong enough to stop him. His gaze traveled back to what had been scratched into the van's wall, while a cold knot solidified in his belly.

He knew what "KAT" stood for. Every Catholic in Northern Ireland did. It meant "Kill All Taigs." Combine the acronym with the fact that no one had bothered with blindfolds or bags and that was bad. *Very bad.* It meant the BA wasn't worried about being identified. It meant that someone had decided to get drunk and kidnap them a pair of taigs for some fun—fun that was intended to, no doubt, end in blood and screaming.

Well, then, Liam thought, his fury heating enough to melt the fear in the pit of his stomach. *The fucking arsehole has grabbed the wrong fucking taigs, now hasn't he?* Liam started tugging at the sleeve of his anorak, pushing it between himself and the steel cuffs. *We'll fucking see who'll be screaming soon enough.*

"Don't worry, Father," he said, forgetting to whisper in his rage. "I'll fucking get us out of this."

Something hard thumped Liam on the head and rolled away.

"Shut it, you!"

Liam tensed up against the sharp pain until it faded into the background with the rest.

When the van took a turn to the left he allowed gravity to help him onto his back. His body protested, but he could now see Father Murray as well as the rest of the van's interior. It was unfinished—the floor nothing but a piece of stained and splintered plywood. A vehicle used regularly for construction.

Or murder, by the gagging stink.

Should've dropped the gun. Should've let me go, the monster fumed in his head. *If you had, we wouldn't be here.*

Shut your fucking gob. If I have it my way, you'll never see the fucking light of day again. It's a monster, you are.

You need me, it thought back. *You'll always need me.*

Fuck you. I'd kill you if I could.

The monster laughed.

The cuffs dug deep into Liam's wrists and back with every bump in the road, and his hands were going numb. His arms were at a bad angle. He shifted to ease them into a better position. Then, bracing one work boot against the reinforcing bar riveted in the van's wall for leverage, he sat up. He awkwardly maneuvered himself onto his knees. There were no windows in the back of the van, but now he could see out the wind-screen. It was too dark to make out details—even for him. However, he got the impression that they were headed west. *Out of Derry.*

He started when he saw the dead BA turn his head to gaze out the passenger window.

The big bastard is still alive? Liam was certain he'd shot him in the middle of the back, not the leg or the arm. *He should've bled out by now.* The fuck didn't even appear uncomfortable, let alone injured. *Maybe he was wearing body armor, and I didn't notice?* Liam remembered the lumpy stain on the brick wall. *It can't be.*

Disconcerted, he faced Father Murray and attempted a reassuring smile. The BAs had been less hard on him, handling him as if they'd been reluctant to touch a priest. Still, Father Murray looked rumpled and terrified.

It wasn't fair, but Liam couldn't stop thinking, *Not used to being on this side of the operation, are you?*

He heard Father Murray gasp. When Liam looked for the source of his reaction it became apparent that Father Murray had spotted the three scratchy letters at last. *Ah, well. Best you know what the stakes are, I suppose.*

Liam returned to stuffing his sleeve under the steel cuff on his right wrist. He was less capable with his left hand, but he'd need the strength in his right if he were to do anything useful.

The van skidded to a stop, and Liam lost his balance, sliding across the floor and smashing his head into the steel bracket at the bottom of the bench seat. He squeezed watering eyes shut against the short burst of pain. The doors at the front of the van opened and closed with a thump that sent a shudder through the whole vehicle. Two sets of boots crunched on gravel outside. Liam was almost ready. He'd gotten half of his sleeve into position and as a result, the feeling was coming back into his right hand. A minute more and it'd be done. He only needed a part of the monster—not all of it. *Enough to break the cuffs. Get a gun off one of the BAs. That's all. One wee chance.* The doors at the rear of the van opened. The blond soldier grabbed

Liam by the ankle and dragged him out. Liam was then lifted to his feet by the coat, undoing his work with the sleeve in the process.

"Fucking hell!"

The big BA hit him in the jaw, and Liam landed on the gravel at the edge of the road. With his hands cuffed he couldn't catch himself, and his right shoulder, face and knee took the brunt of the fall. He lay on the ground, tasting dirt mixed with blood and feeling like he'd been hit with a wrecking ball.

Fuck! Bastard really knows how to punch. Even if he does smell like a week-old corpse.

Stepping closer, the big BA swung his leg back. Liam winced, curling into himself in anticipation of yet another beating. With his hands cuffed there wasn't anything he could do to protect his head. The pain in his jaw temporarily drowned out anything his shoulder and knee had to contribute. It was bad enough that two kicks had landed in his stomach before his nerve endings registered more input.

"Get up, you worthless piece of shit. Get up, so I can knock you flat again. Let's see what you've really got." The big BA's accent sounded English with an edge of something Liam didn't recognize. "No? Do you like pain? Are you queer for it?"

Liam spat blood. "Fuck you!" The roaring in his skull vaporized all rational thought, all concern for where he was and why, but the steel cuffs prevented the beast from reaching the surface. It clawed for freedom at the inside of his skull regardless.

"There's a response oozing with wit. Aren't you the clever one? Bet you were top of the class, queer boy." The big BA laughed.

Liam leapt to his feet. He snarled, and it wasn't the monster that made the sound. Shocked at the strength of his response, he sensed something wasn't right but couldn't stop himself from reacting. He charged headfirst at the big BA, the rage and shame so huge that it burned his skin and poured out of his eyes. The big BA stepped to the left, and Liam ran headfirst into the side of the van. Again, he fell, all but his sense of hearing consumed with blinding agony and the raving of the monster.

"Stop playing with him, Zeriphel," the blond BA said.

"He shot me. It fucking hurt."

"Later. There's no time."

"Don't tell me what to do, half-breed."

"Then you can explain to Aziziel why we're late."

The second BA let out an impatient sigh, and Liam's head cleared as suddenly as if someone had flipped a switch.

Jesus! What was that? Did that bastard hypnotize me? The realization was much worse than fighting with the monster. At least then he knew his actions for his own. He could direct the monster to some degree—even shut it down. An overwhelming sense of powerlessness mixed with shame and fear turned his stomach. Shoving aside the burst of confusing feelings for the moment, he probed his teeth with his tongue and took a quick inventory of his injuries. One of his molars was loose.

Zeriphel? What kind of a fucking name was that? Connections began to form that he didn't like at all.

"Bring him."

As Liam was yanked up from the ground the freezing cuffs bit deeper into his skin, and he swallowed another curse. When his eyes stopped watering he saw they were at the side of the road next to a farmer's field. In the moonlight, he could make out a rough path tracing a curving line up a hill crowned with trees.

Father Murray was pulled from the van. "It's the Raven's Hill," he said with surprise.

"That's right, priest," the big BA said. His face changed in the dim light of a half-moon. As Liam watched, the BA's skin grew darker until it became a charred black. His eyes flashed red. "We've a nice party planned. A family reunion. Everyone's waiting. Up the hill. Now."

Staggering up the incline, Liam looked to Father Murray who mouthed the word "Fallen." It confirmed his suspicion.

You and your new-found morals, the monster said. *Should've listened. They're not human. Could you not smell it? Should've let me kill them.*

Liam shivered. He wanted to believe it was only the cold. Scanning the darkness for some sign of his father, he struggled against despair and waited for a chance—*any chance*—and vowed to be ready for it when it came. The hill was steep and the path, rocky. What with the two beatings and the exhaustion, he had to concentrate to keep his feet under him. After the second fall, Zeriphel grabbed him by the back of his coat, dragged him a few feet and dropped him. Liam landed on his hands and knees.

Zeriphel seized him by the hair and pulled. "Get up!"

Liam didn't know how he managed it, but he got to his feet once again and staggered the remaining distance to the top of the hill. Impatient, Zeriphel shoved him forward. Liam made a drunken path through the trees. He was brought up short once they'd reached a clearing edged with short white monoliths. Taking in his new surroundings, he instantly recognized the white-bearded man in the British paratrooper uniform and blood-red beret standing in the center of the stone circle. Looking beyond the Redcap, Liam spotted his mother. She was sitting on the ground, bound and gagged at the far edge of the circle. She'd been crying but seemed otherwise unharmed.

Taking a step toward her, he was stopped by Zeriphel's vise-like grip.

"No!" It was Bran.

On the other side of the circle Liam counted four more Fallen dressed as BAs. Two of them were restraining Bran. At least, Liam assumed that was what they were. Like Zeriphel, their faces were burned black and all stank of an abandoned slaughterhouse. The monster frenzied in his skull at the sight of them. Liam's stomach dropped somewhere near his ankles.

Why the fuck did Bran come here alone? What was he thinking? Liam kept his expression blank. He didn't want to give the Redcap anything else to be happy about.

Pacing a circle, the Redcap said, "How nice of you to accept my invitation, dog." He spit on the ground. "Ready for more?"

"What the fuck is it you want from me?" Liam asked.

The Redcap punched him in the already battered stomach three times in rapid succession. Liam collapsed to his knees, the breath driven out of him.

"You speak when I say you can," the Redcap said.

"Fuck you," Liam said, gasping.

The Redcap kicked him, the toe of his steel-capped boot landing in Liam's bruised stomach. Zeriphel released Liam's arm, and he fell face-first on the grass. *Jesus, that fucking hurts.*

"You really should be more respectful," the Redcap said.

Liam shuddered and coughed, fighting to get enough air. He could hear his mother screaming from behind her gag. Landing another kick, the Redcap's boot connected with Liam's ribs, and he felt something snap just before another explosion of pain. He bit back a scream. *Fucking hell!*

"For Christ's sake, leave him alone," Father Murray said.

"Wait your turn, priest," the Redcap said. "An alliance between the Roman Catholic Church and the Fey? That idea alone deserves special punishment. As for you, little brother..." He moved closer, and Liam flinched. "It's time to answer a few questions you no doubt have, William. I think we'll start with an introduction." He laid a hand on his chest. "I, am Henry Sanders."

Liam coughed and the answering pain reminded him to be very careful. *Sanders?*

"I see you recognize the surname. You don't know me, but I very much know you. My friends have been watching you." He leaned down. "Let's start our chat with names. You've heard the legend surrounding names and the ah... Fair Folk?" The Redcap— *No, Henry*—asked, spitting out the last two words with disgust. "It would seem there's some truth in it."

Liam wrapped a protective arm around his ribs and straightened. He remained on his knees, anticipating another kick if he moved any farther.

What the fuck is he on about?

"I understand you speak Irish," Henry said. "Foul language, if you can call it that. It's entirely made up, you see. Still, that's not pertinent to the current discussion."

"For fuck's sake," Liam said, "just kill me and get it over with."

When Henry finally stopped kicking he smoothed his hair. "Do not interrupt. You'll ruin the pace of the narrative."

Liam couldn't find oxygen for ten heartbeats, and each time he coughed his ribs ground together, sending a flash of white hot pain through his body.

"Now, where was I?" Henry paused. "Ah, yes. Irish. Do you know the Irish word for 'name,' William?"

Spitting to clear his mouth, Liam wanted to tell him to sod off but didn't think he could stand another beating.

"Answer me," Henry said.

One of the Fallen BAs bent down and pushed at Liam's ribs. Blinding agony blasted him. "Jesus! Oh, fuck!"

"Not the answer I'm looking for," Henry said. "Do try a little harder." He swung back his leg.

"It fucking depends on what kind of name you want!"

"The word for 'name.' Only that."

"*Ainm!* It's fucking *ainm!*"

"Very good," Henry said, lowering his foot. "Now you're playing the game. Next, give me the word for 'soul.'"

Liam swallowed. "*Anam.*"

"'*Ainm*' and '*anam*.' They sound very much alike. Don't they?" Henry asked. "Yes, they do. In Irish, of course. English is far more complex. We aren't as… simple. Do you see where this is going, William? The relation between 'soul' and 'name'?"

Liam was getting really fucking tired of the lecture.

"Interesting thing. They say it only works if you're given the name by the person who owns it. But that isn't entirely true." Henry stooped closer. "It seems that it also works if you're given the name by the person who created it. In this case a parent. A… mother."

"What?" The word fell out of Liam's mouth before he could catch it.

"At this point a spot of history is in order, I'm afraid," Henry said. "Let's go back to—"

"History?" Bran asked. "A falsehood, you mean. Invented to control you, madman."

Henry paused while the Fallen punched the urge for further commentary out of Bran. When they stopped Henry flashed his sharp teeth in a hate-filled grimace offered in the place of a patient smile. "Let's go back to 1555. The heretic Mary the First was on the throne. May she rot in Hell. Three hundred Protestants were burned at the stake during her three-year reign. My father was among the first. At least, I thought he was my father. Only I wasn't right was I?"

Liam could hear his mother crying.

"That's a lie!" Bran gasped and fought his captors.

"No one cares, dog," Zeriphel said. His eyes flashed red, and Liam felt a shimmer of power in the air. "Belief, fear and hatred are what move this world. Nothing else."

"My mother was executed because of her association with that man." Pointing at Bran, Henry's eyes burned with the conviction of a crazed fanatic. "They said she was in league with the devil. Because of him. He raped her and left her to deal with the consequences—the rumors. Just as he did your dear mother, William. Have you figured it out yet? We're brothers, you and I? How does that make you feel?"

Liam heard his mother sob.

"I have never crossed to England," Bran said, turning to her. "Even if I had I'd never do such a thing. You must believe me."

"So sincere. So earnest," Henry said. "But you've heard it all before, haven't you, William?" He turned to Zeriphel. "Unlock one wrist. Leave the other."

Liam's right arm was wrenched upward, taking the left with it. He cried out as the shoulder joint nearly popped out of its socket. His right wrist was freed and then released. Panting, he rubbed the prickling chill out of his arm.

"Stand, William Ronan Kelly," Henry said.

Power shivered in the air, and before Liam knew it he'd scrambled to his feet.

"Good. So very good," Henry said. The calm tone didn't match his eyes, sanity clearly having left the area some time ago.

Liam looked to Zeriphel and understood who was actually in charge. *Henry is wrong. The Fallen don't need names to manipulate. Only a weakness. And no matter what Henry thinks, he isn't immune to that. None of us fucking are.*

"We've both suffered at the hands of our father, you know. A father who will admit no wrong. He left you exposed to dangers just as he abandoned me."

Sanders, Liam thought with a shudder. *The Kesh. The guard's name was Philip Sanders. Was there a connection?*

Henry reached for Liam's left wrist and produced a handcuff key. "He isn't the only one who betrayed you. There is also the priest. He kept so much from you. He was sent to kill you, you know." He placed the key inside the lock. "William Ronan Kelly, you've a great deal to be angry about when you think about it. Let's start with Mary Kate, shall we?"

Another wave of oppressive energy tingled in the air, making Liam gasp. Underneath it all burned the rage. He breathed in the electric current with care and allowed it to settle into his aching chest. It prickled down both of his arms and legs. *Another fucking Sanders.*

"The priest wanted your wife to die," Henry said. "He practically led those men to her. Do you know why?"

At the mention of Mary Kate the monster became unhinged, and roars for release filled Liam's skull to bursting. He fought the tide of rage but it was as useless as fighting a storm.

"Because his Church didn't want her to bear you any children—children classified as demons."

"What?" Now it was Bran who was incensed.

"It isn't how it was at all," Father Murray said. "I married them. I told the bishop that Liam was different." He continued with his explanation, but the words faded into the background.

The Redcap is the fourth man, the monster thought. *Smell.*

Sniffing, Liam caught the stench of old blood and nodded.

"They enjoyed their work, William. They bragged. Talked about how sweet she was. How she screamed for more. Three men."

Four, Liam thought, revulsion and rage rising in the back of his throat. *There were four. Not three. It was you. And you'll pay with the rest.*

"How she liked it."

You like it. I can feel it.

No!

Another Sanders. How?

"Each took their turn at your wife. Can you imagine what that was like? You can, can't you? Who better than you?"

"Don't." Ice-cold terror pinned Liam and he had to force the word over a numb tongue. The handcuff popped off his left wrist. The tingling under his skin instantly became unbearable. He doubled over. Wrath would warp his bones and burn his skin. There was no stopping it.

"He could've gotten you out, you know," Henry said. "Our father. He visited the prison, didn't he?"

The wolfhound. An image from the Kesh drifted to the surface amongst the chaos roiling of his mind. A wolfhound in no man's land—the area between the fences—had not been possible. Some part of him had known it then even though he hadn't given it much thought.

"Ahhhh, yes," Henry said. "He could have prevented it."

"What is he saying?" Bran asked.

Liam dropped to his knees. *Not this. Jesus, Mary and Joseph, please. Not this.*

"Yes." Henry leaned close and whispered, "I know. Because I sent him to you. Philip Sanders was a descendant. And he told me everything before ·he died. Everything. Should I tell them?"

"No!" *Shut him up. NOW! Kill him before it's too late.* Liam tasted dirt before he realized he was down. Scents and sensation flooded in as the monster took charge. Bones rippled beneath his skin—even the broken ones. The world was agony, shame and rage, and nothing else.

"Take your revenge, William Ronan Kelly," Henry said. "I compel you."

Yes. Kill them all, the monster howled. *Everyone. Kill.*

In the chaos he heard singing. The tune was distant but powerful—beautiful and profane. The air grew thick. Sounds became muffled as if trapped inside a bubble. The humiliating lack of self-control made Liam feel sick and disgusted. *Mortified.* By the time the monster got to its feet—*paws*—Henry and the Fallen had retreated outside the stone circle, leaving Bran, Father Murray and his mother inside. The monster charged at Henry, slamming into what felt like a solid wall.

Henry clicked his tongue in contempt. "Púcas. Not very bright, I'm afraid."

The monster leapt up to lunge at Henry a second time and once more met with that invisible wall. Dazed, Liam was able to wrest some control from the monster.

"You're trapped inside, you cretin. And there you will remain until I'm done with you," Henry said. "Kill them. You can't refuse. You can't even resist. I possess your full name as spoken by your mother. William Ronan Kelly. I hereby invoke it."

The monster whirled, panting. Its whole body trembled with Liam's efforts to resist.

You don't have all of me, Liam shouted at Henry from the back of the monster's brain. *Ma didn't tell you everything.* The thought was like a beam of sunlight in the darkness. *I am William Ronan Monroe Kelly. It is a small difference, but I'm still my own.* Nonetheless, Liam wasn't sure how long he could defy the order.

The others had grouped together for safety. Father Murray held out the crucifix of his rosary, terrified. In his other hand he had an open bottle of what Liam thought might be holy water. The cork was in one corner of his mouth. The monster thought he looked ridiculous. Bran—*father*—had positioned himself in front of Liam's mother as if to shield her. His hands were trapped together in steel cuffs but raised in defense.

"Won't." *He doesn't have my soul. Think. There has to be a way out,* Liam thought. *Something he hasn't planned for.*

"I said kill them! I invoke your name!"

The monster roared and for a moment Liam was blind, but he could taste salty warm blood.

Liam thought, *I will not do this.*

I can. And I will, the monster thought back. *You don't deserve to live. You're weak. Nothing. Threaten me, will you? I'll bury you so far, so deep in the dark you'll fade into memory. Then I'll see to them. I'll do for them all. And I'll be forever free of you.*

Liam was shoved under the surface of a midnight bog and rapidly sank in its cold depths. Frantic, he battled against it but couldn't find purchase. Worse, the more he struggled the more he sank. *I'm the stronger one.* Down and down. Deeper. *Die.* The monster's voice followed him, pushing him farther. *I stopped Sanders. Not you.* Liam choked. *You're weak. Didn't even fight. You would've let him*—Liam was smothered with shame—*do it again. You don't deserve to live.* The increasing weight of blackness squeezed the will from him. *You're nothing.* An incongruent sense of peace crept in. If he let go, the humiliation would fade with him. *Die.* He drifted, welcoming the numbness now. He didn't want to remember anymore. And with nothing to anchor him, he began to lose all sense of time.

A whisper penetrated the dark. "Liam."

He floated, listening.

"Liam, please. It's me." It was a woman's voice. A beam of light appeared. It was dim and weak. He flung out a hand toward it and felt an almost imperceptible warmth. Her words pulled him upward until he could see through the monster's eyes once more. She was speaking, but he didn't know her. She looked frightened, and her face was streaked with tears.

"This isn't you," she said.

The monster paused.

"Kathleen, get behind me!" It was the tall one. The one he'd bitten.

The sire, the monster thought.

She didn't move. "Please, Liam."

Staring at the woman, Liam's gaze traveled the length of her body in an attempt to understand who or what she was. She was wearing a brown coat and a blue dress underneath. Torn stockings. Shoes.

The image of a woman's empty shoe resting on pavement emerged from deep memory.

Never again. The words echoed with power within his skull. *I am William Ronan Monroe Kelly. And I will not do this. I will not cross that line. I can stop you. I've done it before.*

The monster's skin crawled and shifted. It raged against the change, the sensation making him nauseous. Liam blinked, swaying on his feet. When he was sure of himself he whirled and sprinted to the edge of the circle and again was met with that invisible wall. He picked himself up and shook his head to clear it. *There's a way out. Think.*

The woman was screaming. All was chaos. It was difficult to form coherent ideas beyond the compulsion to rip and tear.

Out. Must get out. Break the circle. He ran again, throwing his shoulder against it, and smacked into one of the stones. The impact registered but not the pain—the impact and a subtle wobble.

The stone.

Liam wrapped his arms around the limestone block and put all his fury into forcing it from the ground. When it didn't budge he backed up and charged it again. The stone moved several inches. Ignoring what seemed a million hurts and the monster's protests, he flung himself at it a third time with everything he had. Something in his shoulder snapped, and he screamed in frustration and agony.

The stone block toppled, dredging up dark chunks of damp earth with it.

A shadow leapt over him and was gone. A war-cry shouted in Irish echoed through the trees and was answered by the clatter of drawn swords. There were other shouts, fighting. He lay half-in and half-out of the circle, unable to move. Agony equal to what he'd felt in the cave tore through him, leaving him empty as it passed—vacant but for the dull and heavy throbbing in his shoulder. Still the beast in his brain frenzied. Liam grew more and more tired of fighting it. He yearned for that sense of peace. He was going to black out, he knew. Nothing mattered anymore.

A cool hand smoothed the hair from his face and that woman's voice called him again. "What have you done to yourself? Stay with me. Please."

Hands shoved a rectangle of steel into his palm. Cold burned his skin and then the pain and confusion became bearable. The monster's roars receded. Liam looked into his hand. *The lighter.* For a moment he wondered who would've thought to do such a thing, but the clash of battle took his attention to the outside of the circle.

It seemed Bran hadn't shown up alone after all—or at least not without a plan. A large group of men armed with bronze-tipped spears and swords had charged from the woods, ambushing the Fallen. As Liam watched, Zeriphel leapt an impossible fifteen feet into the air. Ragged black wings sprang from the hump on his back and spread wide. Then a bronze spear arched up, striking him with such force that it not only went right through him, it drove him into a tree and impaled him there. He screeched and squirmed like a pinned insect. The sight of Zeriphel clawing his way up the shaft was horrific, and Liam turned away. He spied Bran in the midst of the fray, wielding a sword two-handed in spite of the cuffs that bound his wrists together. Sceolán was at his side and both had backed the blond BA against another tree.

That's when Liam spotted Henry.

"Behind you!" Liam stood up and was smashed with agonizing pain as the bones in his shoulder ground together when someone pushed past. His efforts to remain upright cost him, and his vision blurred. He felt more than saw Father Murray next to him.

"Mrs. Kelly! Don't!"

Blinking, Liam saw his mother run at Henry and then shove him. Off balance, Henry missed his target and sunk his blade deep into a tree instead. Yanking the sword free, Henry turned on his attacker. Liam looked on in horror as his mother raised her hands and winced.

"No! Ma!"

Suddenly, Sceolán was at her side. He struck Henry square in the chest with his blade and twisted. Then Bran's sword cut deep into Henry's neck, striking off the Redcap's head. Sceolán kicked, and the body dropped in a fountain of arterial gore.

A triumphant whoop echoed through the clearing. Liam saw the remaining Fallen were being driven back.

Bran tapped Sceolán's shoulder in thanks, and Sceolán nodded in return before rejoining the battle. Liam slumped against one of the stones. Outside the circle, his mother reached out to Bran. Bran gave the top of her head a quick kiss, and she backed away from him but she was smiling. He gestured in the direction of an abandoned bronze short sword lying on the ground. She disagreed with whatever he'd suggested. He seemed to insist, and she gave in with a reluctant sigh. He went back to his battle, and she returned to the stone circle, carrying the sword. She stood straighter and was more alert.

Liam didn't understand why she'd risked herself for a man who'd abandoned her.

"Lie down," Father Murray said. "You're hurt."

Allowing Father Murray to ease him into a sitting position, Liam focused on staying conscious while the battle wound down around them. The tension in his stomach didn't ease until his mother entered the circle. She dropped the sword as if it were a snake and knelt beside him.

She reached out but stopped herself short of touching him. "Is it bad?"

"No." If he were honest, he would've said he didn't know. The pain in his shoulder was almost bearable, provided he didn't move, but now a crush of complex feelings lodged in his throat—anger, guilt, shame, confusion, even relief. He couldn't look her in the eye. She kept a wary distance as if he were an injured animal that might bite.

He had to admit, it was a reasonable fear.

Father Murray hefted the short sword, gave it a test swing and then took up a protective stance next to the toppled stone. He held a small rock to his eye with his other hand and peered through the hole in the center.

He's only a priest. He can't hold them off alone. Liam decided to take a place next to Father Murray, but his body protested with hundreds of sharp pains. He gritted his teeth and did it anyway. Anything was better than the expectant silence.

"I said, lie still," Father Murray said, looking over his shoulder.

Just then one of the Fallen—a big one with red hair and scorched auburn wings burst through the trees and charged Father Murray, knocking him over. Again, Liam was slammed with a decaying stench. The fallen angel lifted its pistol and aimed right at him. The gun's barrel loomed huge. His mother threw her body over his, pressing him flat in an attempt to shield him.

"No, Ma! Don't!"

Father Murray grabbed the fallen angel's jaw from behind and yanked back while whispering into its ear. The creature's eyes went wide, and the gun went off in the same instant Father Murray's blade cut across the fallen angel's throat.

The bullet passed close. Liam felt it. "Ma, no! Please!"

She shivered and sat up. "Are you all right?"

Father Murray asked, "Are either of you hit?"

"I'm fine," she said. "Liam?"

"Please, Ma. Never do that again."

"Here." Father Murray handed off the fallen angel's pistol.

Liam pocketed the lighter and accepted the gun. He'd have checked the chamber, but he didn't think he could do it one-handed. Since he wasn't sure he could use it he supposed it didn't matter.

Bending over the fallen angel's body, Father Murray felt for a pulse. Then he wiped the bronze blade clean on the grass. With that done, he reached into his coat pocket and produced a clear vial. He placed a finger over the open vial and tipped it. Using the contents of the bottle, he sketched the sign of the cross on the red Fallen's forehead and whispered in Latin. The liquid hissed as it coated the corpse's skin, and the smell of rot grew worse before it dissipated.

The whole process reminded Liam of the first night he'd met Father

Dominic and Father Christopher. Uncomfortable, he tightened his grip on the pistol with his left hand and sat, watching for danger while Father Murray finished his blessing. Fey warriors moved through the darkness, gathering the dead, helping the wounded. Two of the Fey hacked at the body of the blond Fallen, and while Liam looked on they set the butchered remains on fire. When Father Murray noticed what they were doing he left the circle and prevented them from repeating the process. Instead, he made the rounds with his little vial while Sceolán and a few of the others watched with mixed expressions of relief and wariness.

Liam remained quiet, staring at the woods while uneasy questions circled his brain. How much of Henry's threats had his parents heard?

His father approached, and his mother went to him, catching him in a tight hug. It was strange seeing the two of them together. Watching, Liam thought of the photograph she'd given him long ago, and it suddenly occurred to Liam that he'd never seen her genuinely happy in his whole life.

"Are you all right?" his father asked.

She nodded. "A little shaken, but fine. Our Liam injured himself."

His father knelt down and concern pulled at his face. "How bad is it?"

"Feels like I broke my shoulder. I'll live," Liam said and winced when he forgot himself and shrugged. "But I won't much like it for a while."

It was then he noticed the claw marks on Bran's chest as well as the mauled and bloodied right arm. Liam swallowed back his shock. "Sorry."

"Don't worry yourself," his father said. "If you hadn't broken through the circle I couldn't have given the signal to those waiting on the Other Side." He looked tired and sick and his arms hung limp as if he couldn't lift them. "Sceolán, get this crossed steel off me. My arms are numb."

Sceolán entered the circle holding a set of keys by the leather fob as if they were on fire.

"Let me," Father Murray said, putting out a hand.

Sceolán hesitated but dropped them into Father Murray's palm after Bran nodded approval. Father Murray sorted through them until he found the right one and unlocked the cuffs.

"We should go," Sceolán said. "It's almost dawn."

"I can't," Bran said. "Not yet. Give me a bit. Finish what needs doing. Then get the others together and prepare to leave."

Sceolán nodded and left the circle, shouting orders at the other Fey as he went.

Father Murray cleared his throat. "I should see if there is anything else I can do to help." And with that, he made himself scarce as well.

Only Liam and his parents remained. A cold wind pushed against the trees.

The uncomfortable silence swelled until Liam thought it might explode. He couldn't bring himself to look at either of them. *How much do they know?* Everything had come so close. *You like it. I can feel it.*

He shuddered.

Bran said, "We've a great deal to talk about."

"Aye," Liam said, feeling his bruised jaw tighten. "We do."

Bran gazed at the stones on the opposite side of the circle as if they could provide a solution. "Unfortunately, I don't think this is the time."

"For fuck's sake. You'll put me off? Again?"

"Liam," his mother said. "Please. Have some patience."

"Patience? I've been patient, Ma. My whole life, I waited. I almost died of the fucking waiting!"

His father said, "Your mother was only trying to protect you."

"Did you never think that if I'd known anything at all I might have been able to protect myself?" Liam asked. "Was your enemy murdered my family. If you'd bothered to warn me of it—"

"Don't you take that tone, young man," his mother said.

"He has a point," his father said. "The worst of it is that he doesn't understand the smallest part of what he is. There's power in him. Not only from me. From you as well. And he has to learn how to control it before it kills him."

"Power from me?" she asked.

His father gave his mother a small smile and a shake of the head. "Yes. You."

She harrumphed.

"I agree. You've the right to know, son," his father said. "Tomorrow. The next day. A month from now. Whenever you're ready. Call for me. No restrictions. Anywhere you're alone. I'll come to you. I'll answer your questions."

Liam nodded.

"And when that's done you should consider training for the Fianna," his father said. "We could use you."

"Thanks, but no," Liam said. "I'm done with the soldiering."

His father blinked. "You can't be serious."

"I am."

"You've become a pacifist?" Father Murray asked.

"Wouldn't say that," Liam said. "But I'm standing down for now."

"I don't understand," his father said with a frown.

"It's hard to explain," Liam said. "But… I can't trust myself."

"You're a púca," his father said. "You are what you are. There will always be the wild in you. A darkness that won't be controlled. It's what we are, but it isn't all of what we are. From what I've witnessed, it would be no different were you mortal."

Liam shook his head and looked away, thinking of the bottom of Raven's Hill—of running into the side of the van. "There's something not right in me. Something broken." *Shameful.* "And until it's made right I can't go back to the soldiering. I don't even know if what's wrong can be made right."

His father sighed. "I'll trust you know what you're doing. But if there comes a day when you think you're ready—"

"I'll let you know."

"If you need anything—anything at all—you know how to reach me." His father reached down and gave his good shoulder a squeeze. "Danu be with you, son." Then he turned. "My brave Kathleen. There's never been anyone else. And there'll never be another. I'll be back for you."

"Ah, sure you will," she said.

Liam looked away as they kissed. It was a private moment between his parents and not for him to see. When it was finished he watched his father limp into the trees. Bran turned once, waved goodbye and then vanished.

"Well," Father Murray said, facing the east. "Looks like we've a long walk. Think you can make it?"

Epilogue

Londonderry/Derry, County Londonderry, Northern Ireland
October 1977

Liam decided that if he'd had any sense at all he would've delayed his visit to St. Brendan's churchyard. Mist hung in the air thick enough to soak his hair in spite of the wool hat. A gusty wind thrashed the trees sheltering the rows of tombstones and sent a deep ache into his healing collarbone. His right arm was strapped in a sling to prevent him from using it, but he was already sick of dealing with the thing. Father Murray insisted he wear it for a few days and rest the shoulder because, as it turned out, he'd messed himself up pretty badly.

Liam resisted the urge to scan the street for Peelers and focused on Mary Kate's grave, daisies from a flower shop down the road in one hand and a bottle of whiskey in the other. He didn't know what to do or say. He'd been too long in coming.

Father Murray cleared his throat. "It was a lovely funeral."

"I should've been there," Liam said.

"Even if you could've been without being arrested you weren't in any shape for it. She would've understood."

Because it was what was expected, Liam bent and awkwardly placed the flowers on the grave using his wounded arm. Next, he set the bottle on top of the headstone. "I made a mess of things," he said, reaching into a coat pocket and bringing out two short glasses. He set them next to the bottle one-handed and then poured the whiskey.

"She made mistakes too, no doubt. Every relationship has two sides." Father Murray accepted a glass.

"She wanted to return after she graduated. She loved Derry."

Nodding, Father Murray sipped his whiskey. An appreciative look flashed over his features.

Liam downed the glass and then poured another while the whiskey caught fire in his throat and warmed the back of his nose. It was a good vintage, filled with the taste of oak and sunlight—a fairy vintage, if he knew what he was about. His father had left it with his Gran, knowing that was where he and Father Murray were hiding. No note. No explanation—just the bottle. Liam knew it for an apology. "I miss Mary Kate. I always will. I loved her more than anyone in my life. But I can't remember the sound of her laugh anymore, and it feels like a betrayal."

"It's been a while. That's to be expected."

"This doesn't seem right."

"Life moves forward, Liam."

Liam didn't respond other than to take another drink. The whiskey finished heating his throat and stomach and began to work on his joints. The tension in his shoulders dissipated, and he took in a deep breath. It had taken a few days, but his broken collarbone was mending. It still felt badly bruised. However, every breath was no longer a trial. Over that time, he'd had several long talks with his mother. She'd apologized—for keeping his real father from him and above all, for not protecting him from Patrick. Liam was still reeling. As Father Murray would say, it was a lot to process.

"This was a bad idea. The Peelers will have found your wee pistol by now, Father. They'll be hunting for me soon, if they haven't started already. Gran is sure to give me up."

"You should take it easy on her," Father Murray said. "In a way, she saved your life. All of our lives, if you think upon it."

"What do you mean?"

"Was her gave you that name. Monroe. Your mother pretended to be a widow. You both carried that surname until she married your stepfather and discarded the lie."

"And I was left with it."

"Aye, well. You were a child. You needed the lie, flimsy as it was."

Liam bit back any further arguments. His gaze drifted out to the street. "This will be one of the places they're sure to look. We should go."

"You need to grieve. But if you're not ready, you're not ready. No one is going to force you."

"None of it matters. Mary Kate is gone. And that's that."

Father Murray shook his head. "You can't move forward until you've stopped looking behind."

"And how is that possible when so much reminds me of her?"

"There will come a time when it won't hurt as much to think of her."

They both started at the sound of a car driving up the street.

"Maybe we should go," Father Murray said.

Liam waited until Father Murray had walked to the gate, then placed his hand on the marble stone. He whispered to her in Irish, "Goodbye, Mary

Kate. You have your forgiveness. I can only hope I can have the same. I am sorry. For everything. I did my best. I wish it'd been enough." Feeling better, he left the short glasses turned upside down on her tombstone and headed out of the churchyard.

Father Murray pushed open the gate. It squealed as it always did. Liam wondered if anyone would notice if he oiled it sometime in the night. It would make future visits less noticeable.

"Have you given my proposition any thought?" Father Murray asked.

Taking a drink straight from the bottle, Liam swallowed before answering. "Well, Father, I can't fight the Fianna's war—not now. Not yet." He thought again of the bottom of Raven's Hill and wondered if it was his vulnerability to the Fallen, his oath or the fear that prevented him from joining. "I'm wanted by both the 'Ra and the Peelers. Working with you is the only alternative. Where else am I to go? America?"

"Is that a yes?"

"I'm willing to give it a try," Liam said. "It's not as if you'll get the Fey to negotiate with the Church on your own. The killing has to stop. Anyway, if it doesn't work out, I can always look up another ex-holy assassin and ask him if he has an opening for an assistant."

Father Murray looked away and smiled.

Lord, there goes Martin Luther King
Notice how the door closes when the chimes of freedom ring
I hear what you're saying, I hear what he's saying
Is what was true now no longer so?

Hey - I hear what you're saying
Hey - I hear what he's saying
If you're after getting the honey - hey
Then you don't go killing all the bees

What the people are saying
And we know every road - go, go
What the people are saying
There ain't no berries on the trees

Let the summertime sun
Fall on the apple - fall on the apple

Lord, there goes a Buick forty-nine
Black sheep of the angels riding, riding down the line
We think there is a soul, we don't know
That soul is hard to find

Hey - down along the road
Hey - down along the road
If you're after getting the honey
Then you don't go killing all the bees

—from *Johnny Appleseed* by Joe Strummer & The Mescaleros

Acknowledgments

This book wouldn't exist were it not for the many amazing people who generously donated their time, energy, knowledge, love and support along the way: Dane Caruthers, the world's most fabulous husband, friend, lover, life-saver, timely pizza fairy and first reader; Joe Monti, the best agent ever; Jeremy Lassen for taking a chance on a new writer and a controversial topic; Brian Magaoidh for his gentle wisdom and insight as well as vast patience with a well-meaning outsider, for the book recommendations and for mailing all those books and articles I'd never have found on my own; Charles de Lint, Holly Black, Charles Vess, Jim Minz, Sharon Shinn, Elizabeth Moon, Jeff VanderMeer, Bruce Sterling, Chris Brown, Linda and Michael Moorcock, Mark Finn, Howard Waldrop, Jessica Reisman, Carrie Richerson, Melissa Tyler, Mandy Lancaster, Walton "Bud" Simons, Neal Barrett, Jr., William Browning-Spencer and Caroline Spector—all of whom contributed wisdom, inspiration, support and encouragement; Troy Hunt, Sondra Sondregger, Jack McCauley and my Dad for their auto mechanics and rally racing know-how; the generous folks at Harris Hill Road Racetrack—Eric Beverding, Bo Rivers and Cory Rueth—for the racing lessons; Joe Strummer, Rory Gallagher, Stiff Little Fingers and the Undertones for the music; Lucinda Tait for permission to use lyrics from "Hate and War" and "Johnny Appleseed"; Charles de Lint, Dan Nugent and Thad Engling music experts; Steve and Melinda Coleman, Rollin MacRae, the Austin Gaelic League, the Philo-Celtic Society and Kathleen Douglas for sharing their knowledge of Ireland, Irish culture and the Irish language; SlugTribe, Wyred Sisters, Cryptopolis, Turkey City and Tryptophan for being great writer training grounds; Rachel Raun, beta reader and best friend; BookPeople, the best bookstore on the planet—shout out to Brian, Topher, Sarah and the rest of the gang; Mom and Dad and siblings Cathy, Celina and Fred for being there.

Also, if you'd like to learn more about the history of Northern Ireland

and the Troubles, I highly recommend Tim Pat Coogan's books (*Ireland in the Twentieth Century, The IRA, 1916: The Easter Rising*), *Those Are Real Bullets* by Peter Pringle and Philip Jacobson, *Derry Memories* by Philip Cunningham, *War as a Way of Life* by John Conroy, *This Troubled Land* by Patrick Michael Rucker, *Ten Men Dead* by David Beresford, *Cage Eleven* by Gerry Adams, *The Price of My Soul* by Bernadette Devlin, *Mister, Are You a Priest?* by Edward Daly, *Ballymurphy and the Irish War* by Ciarán de Baróid, *Derry: The Troubled Years* by Eamon Melaugh and *No Go: A Photographic Record of Free Derry* by Barney McMonagle. In addition, the University of Ulster maintains a wonderful archival website at http://cain.ulst.ac.uk/index.html.

Night Shade Books Is an Independent Publisher of Quality SF, Fantasy and Horror

ISBN: 978-1-59780-199-7, Trade Paperback; $14.99

This is the story of a place that never was: the kingdom of Prester John, the utopia described by an anonymous, twelfth-century document which captured the imagination of the medieval world and drove hundreds of lost souls to seek out its secrets, inspiring explorers, missionaries, and kings for centuries.

Brother Hiob of Luzerne, on missionary work in the Himalayan wilderness on the eve of the eighteenth century, discovers a village guarding a miraculous tree whose branches sprout books instead of fruit. These strange books chronicle the history of the kingdom of Prester John, and Hiob becomes obsessed with the tales they tell. *The Habitation of the Blessed* recounts the fragmented narratives found within these living volumes, revealing the life of a priest named John, and his rise to power. Hugo and World Fantasy award nominee Catherynne M. Valente reimagines the legends of Prester John in this stunning tour de force.

Stina Leicht was born in St. Louis, Missouri, where she attended Catholic school, climbed trees, learned to skate, fought pirates and rescued her sister's dolls from terrible fates. Her father, being a practical-minded person, didn't wish his children to believe in anything that wasn't real. Unfortunately for him, her mother soon hired an Irish babysitter with a gift for storytelling and then armed her with a thick volume of fairy tales. Thus, Stina's future as a practical-minded person was forever doomed. Currently, she lives in central Texas with her husband, their shared library and a cat named Sebastian. She's famous for singing too loud to punk music in her car, reading too much, taking photographs almost no one has seen, making art out of wooden cigar boxes and baking homemade apple pie from scratch. In the course of her research, she has driven really fast in rally races, taken Irish language lessons and studied Northern Irish politics. Thanks to the Irish language lessons, she spends entirely too much time searching for the computer key combination which consistently produces a fada. She still fights pirates but has traded her trusty wooden stick for a rapier and dagger. Of course, pirate ships being somewhat rare in central Texas, she makes do with a friend's backyard—which is fine since she gets stabbed quite a lot and would only end up tossed into the sea anyway.